The Best AMERICAN SHORT STORIES 1988

GUEST EDITORS OF

The Best American Short Stories

1978 Ted Solotaroff
1979 Joyce Carol Oates
1980 Stanley Elkin
1981 Hortense Calisher
1982 John Gardner
1983 Anne Tyler
1984 John Updike
1985 Gail Godwin
1986 Raymond Carver
1987 Ann Beattie
1988 Mark Helprin

The Best AMERICAN SHORT STORIES 1988

Selected from
U.S. and Canadian Magazines
by MARK HELPRIN
with SHANNON RAVENEL

With an Introduction by Mark Helprin

HOUGHTON MIFFLIN COMPANY BOSTON 1988

Shannon Ravenel is grateful to Kathryn Conrad, who gave valuable consultation on science fiction and science fantasy.

ISSN 0067-6233
ISBN 0-395-44257-5
ISBN 0-395-44256-7 (pbk.)

Printed in the United States of America

Q 10 9 8 7 6 5 4 3 2 1

Contents

Publisher's Note

The *Best American Short Stories* series was started in 1915 under the editorship of Edward J. O'Brien. Its title reflects the optimism of a time when people assumed that an objective "best" could be identified, even in fields not measured in physical terms.

Martha Foley took over as editor of the series in 1942. With her husband, Whit Burnett, she had edited *Story* magazine since 1931, and in later years she taught creative writing at Columbia School of Journalism. When Miss Foley died in 1977, at the age of eighty, she was at work on what would have been her thirty-seventh volume of *The Best American Short Stories.*

Beginning with the 1978 edition, Houghton Mifflin introduced a new editorial arrangement for the anthology. Inviting a different writer or critic to edit each new annual volume would provide a variety of viewpoints to enliven the series and broaden its scope. *Best American Short Stories* has thus become a series of informed but differing opinions that gains credibility from its very diversity.

Also beginning with the 1978 volume, the guest editors have worked with the series editor, Shannon Ravenel, who during each calendar year reads as many qualifying short stories as she can get hold of, makes a preliminary selection of 120 stories for the guest editor's consideration, and compiles the "100 Other Distinguished Short Stories of the Year," a listing that has always been an important feature of these volumes.

In the eleven years that have passed since then, there has

been growing interest in the short story, and the form itself has grown. The range of approaches and techniques and stances it attracts is ever broader. And so is its audience. In response to this anthology's increasingly enthusiastic readership, last year's volume introduced a new feature. Each of the authors of the twenty stories selected by the guest editor is invited to describe briefly how his or her story came to be written. The contributors have accepted what is clearly a challenging assignment, and their short essays appear at the back of the volume in the "Contributors' Notes" section.

The stories chosen for this year's anthology were originally published in magazines issued between January 1987 and January 1988. The qualifications for selection are: (1) original publication in nationally distributed American or Canadian periodicals; (2) publication in English by writers who are American or Canadian; and (3) publication *as* short stories (novel excerpts are not knowingly considered by the editors). A list of the magazines consulted by Ms. Ravenel appears at the back of this volume. Other publications wishing to make sure that their contributors are considered for the series should include Ms. Ravenel on their subscription list (P.O. Box 3176, University City, Missouri 63130).

Introduction: The Canon Under Siege

NOT TOO LONG after the Second World War, I was a student in a day school in the Hudson Valley, a virtual paradise on an estate of about fifty acres overlooking the river at a point that many of its painters have memorialized in some of the best paintings America has ever seen. There I was, in this verdant place, not even ten years old, learning my lessons, returning each night to my family. From May through September we would sit outside every evening on a brick terrace under an enormous magnolia and have tea until darkness closed in. What a wealth of hours I spent with my father, talking about every subject known to man, and how easily I spent it, considering what I know now and what I would do, if I could, to bypass the laws of nature just to have a minute with him.

On the playing fields of this school we learned nearly every team sport in existence, courtesy of a short ex-Marine whom we called Coach, a good man, perhaps not too bright, but a superb athlete who never understood that when we addressed him we had secretly in mind something with four wheels and a highly shellacked door that closed with a deep click. Perhaps because he had been a Marine (we could without fear of retribution say to his face, "You are marine") he had an exquisite array of creative punishments. Most of these involved agonizing calisthenics or wearing underwear on your head or running at high speed on all fours up and down the halls of the school. But if you went beyond the pale, you were in real trouble, for then you had either to "run the gauntlet" or "stay the circle." The first of these tortures involved running down a corridor formed by a double line of boys, every one of whom had a license to hit or kick you as hard as he could. The second required of you that you stay within a small chalk circle as the entire group of athletes, one at a time, dashed into it and delivered a blow, and then dashed out beyond retaliation.

We played lacrosse and ice hockey with hardly any protection, so cuts and bruises were not unknown to us: the terror of the punishment lay not so much in the pain as in the expressions of one's classmates as they attacked. Though friends only tapped you, and people you didn't know well were mainly indifferent, enemies, it seemed, would try to kill you. Anyway, the gauntlet and the circle were rare events — until a new boy came to us from a DP camp in Eastern Europe. His English was poor, he had been put back two or three grades, and he was a bully. Gauntlet and circle became his almost daily lot. He had been lucky to join us after an evolution of sorts, in which at least half the boys would only tap the victim, because we realized that we were getting bigger and could actually do some harm, and because it seemed dishonorable to strike someone who was forbidden to strike back.

At that time my father returned from England with a book by Lord Russell of Liverpool subtitled *A Short History of Nazi War Crimes*. Books in English on the holocaust were slow in coming. This was one of the first. It was possible to imagine that the DP child had undergone all the tortures documented in the book, but, then again, since he had been only two or three years of age when the war ended, perhaps he had not. However, upon further inquiry we were told that, yes, he had been born in a camp, and, yes, his parents had been taken from him, after which he had spent most of his life behind barbed wire.

Inevitably the time came for the next punishment of the DP child (his name was almost impossible to pronounce). I refused. That in itself was dangerous, but though I was just a boy, my resolution had been steeled in the pages of Lord Russell's book. A friend of mine with a reputation for cowardice immediately joined me. He was physically weak, not much of a fighter, not much of a runner, and therefore he had little chance of escape. Such is the value of reputation. Faced with this blatant rebellion, the coach ordered the two of us into the circle. We refused. Then he lost his temper, Marine style. Though he was really a fine man and would never have hurt us, we weren't sure of that at the time, and all I remember is running through dense woods that went past in a rapid blur. After speeding through abundant obstructions, I ended up under a log that spanned a brook, breathing like someone with emphysema and staring at a stream of silver water pouring from the fissures in some mossy black rocks.

I hardly slept that night, planning my escape into the forest should the coach try to kill me, but the next day nothing happened. The coach seemed to have forgotten the rebellion, and the DP child continued to bully everyone. He even bullied my brave friend. Nothing had changed. The DP child, however, soon left, for he had too much sorrow to live among happy children, and the gauntlet and the circle seemed to go with him.

Though not expecting it, I grew up. Since the days on the athletic field surrounded by apple blossoms and beech trees, I myself have seen something of war, death, and camps. I have my own children now. I try to do the right thing. Not long after the events described I began to develop a deep love for what is unfortunately called literature, a terrible name that sounds affected and pretentious. If you didn't know the word you might guess that it was a surgical technique or an ancient technical term for part of a thatched roof, not the one word for language that can be as beautiful and hypnotic as song, for a vast summing up, in precious few words, of all that is truly important. It includes snowstorms and sunlit forests preserved in their fullness and depth by a miraculous series of codes that are of such great effect that they can often be more intense and consequential than the things they describe. It represents the extraordinary courage of a sole human voice confronting death, preserving life beyond its term, standing alone, speaking for as long as the code is conserved, even to others who have not yet been born. Is it not astounding that one can love so deeply characters who are composites, portraits, or born of the thin air, especially when one has never seen or touched them, and they exist only in an imprint of curiously bent lines?

To make a more concise argument, one lives for a very short time, and life is incomparably precious. To live has much less to do with the senses or with ambition than with the asking of questions that never have been surely answered. To ask and then to answer these questions as far as one can, one needs above all a priceless and taxing involvement with truth and beauty. These are uncommonly plentiful in music and painting, in nature itself, in the sciences, in history, and in one's life as it unfolds — if one labors and dares to see them. But nowhere do they run together with such complexity and power as in the gracefully written word. It is not, as so many people mistake it, an element of manners, a cultural obligation, a diversion, or a means of opening the conversation at dinner parties. I have devoted my life to it not because I thought it would be a good way to earn money or because I thought it might be pleasant and interesting, but, rather, because I love it — and I love it not only because it is so pleasingly beautiful, but because it is so deeply consequential.

And now, like the DP child staying the circle, it is under siege, not just from one quarter, but from many. But only temporarily, for its lasting power is well known. It has come under siege before, in ways that make the present seem quite serene: in the Middle Ages, under totalitarian oppression, and by neglect. It suffers casualties continuously. For every Emily Dickinson and Herman Melville rescued from oblivion, how many dozen others remain unknown? And eventually, though literature itself continues, everyone is forgotten after his time. But just as life is certainly worth defending even though it must end in death, so this art and craft, fleeting in detail but everlasting nonetheless, is worth a great deal of effort to preserve from afflictions and assaults that, though they are ugly, are sure to be burnt off the landscape by any one of an infinite number of rising suns.

The role of maneuver and force in war and nature is approximated in universities by that of opinion. Instead of divisions of soldiers on the march, or storms impacting upon a beach, academia has the struggle of opinions. Though the truth in opinion can be supported, even in the most objective departments of the sciences it is seldom self-evident enough not to require for its acceptance an organized coercion manifested in various collective or social mechanisms. To be certified in academia, you must learn how to change your ideas under pressure. Unfortunately, this often leaves a desire for revenge. Though many cannot bear to suffocate in factories of intellectualism, and choose instead the exhilarating anarchy of nature, commerce, or even the army (all in all a lot freer), others choose to become permanent inhabitants of one or another splendid academic asylum.

The generation now beginning to dominate departments within the university has been subject to unusual pressures that have not found relief. They had a war with which to contend, but because most of them did not actually experience it they never were allowed a catharsis. Indeed, the war was the kind of war that did not allow a catharsis even to those who did experience it. And lost wars are never over. In addition, this generation accepted some shameless flattery about itself, and set out to remake the world. A newspaper article recently questioned the fate of the Chinese Red Guards. Where are they? In remote communes? Hidden in the warrens of Shanghai? Tending goats on the Mongolian border? Who knows? Our own wrathful idealists have never really changed their address. They are right where they started, in the universities, and a few of them, absent the test of experience on the outside, seem to have lost some of their marbles.

Their operations of late in many a department of literature have been to muscle aside the aging and increasingly isolated traditionalists — most of whom probably did not join English faculties with the expectation of or preparation for Leninist political combat — for the purpose of redefining literature and warring against the canon of familiar works rather than gently modifying it as has been the practice literally for ages. The irony of their assault against what they would have us believe is a literary bastille is that no canon actually exists. Until recently no comprehensive definition of literary excellence has been in force, and works have found their way to and from reading lists rather freely and without constraint. In the guise of tearing down a bastille, the revisionists are actually raising their own, for they have a definite and particular notion of what makes literary excellence, and theirs is not a temperament to allow anarchy but rather to accomplish purges.

Lest the reader think this is imagined, consider that in a *New York Times* article, from which the title of this essay was adapted, Joseph Berger reports that "a rising group . . . contends that the idea of an enduring pantheon of writers and their works is an elitist one largely defined by white men," and that this school has "now begun to question the very idea of literary quality and has made for the teaching of writers principally for historical and sociological importance."

The measure of historical and sociological importance has led many professors, according to David Brooks, writing in the *Wall Street Journal,* to de-emphasize what they call " 'the phalluscentric canon,' in favor of books by women, preferably black women." That is why Christopher Clausen of Pennsylvania State University is willing to bet that "*The Color Purple* is taught in more English courses today than all of Shakespeare's plays combined." Brooks quotes a Wesleyan University professor who maintains that traditional reading lists exist "to conceal the real workings of society from those most hurt by it," and that this is adjunct to "a much broader social strategy" of the "professional-managerial class."

Not surprisingly, people who view literature as a tool of oppression (or, at best, a weapon against it) rather than as an impartial phenomenon that addresses essential questions beyond and apart from politics, are obsessed with structure and control. Like good urban guerrillas, they go for the "heart of the beast." Of course, they are not really interested in literature at all. Departments, institutes, journals, associations, salaries, and petty powers are their real interests and targets. They strive most of all for positions of authority — and they are succeeding, as in comic opera, a coup in a banana republic, or the internecine strife of a mental institution. This despite the fact that literature is one of the most vital and anarchic forces the world knows, and attempting to make it an ideological slave is impossible in the long run.

But they try. At Stanford the campus has been riven by a

movement to jettison "traditional" works and replace them with those by "women, minorities, and people of color." The standard proposed is by no means unusual, and is predicated upon the assumption that a book can be judged by the race, sex, or ethnicity of its author. This presupposes that a black woman, for example, is unable to find anything of lasting value in Shakespeare, because he was a white man (or, as they say at Stanford, a "white male," since a man is a male and a woman is a woman), though it does not necessarily presuppose, of course, that a "white male" cannot find anything of value in the work of a black woman. Anyway, since Shakespeare was a white male, does it not make perfect sense that his place on a reading list should be given to a black woman? The Stanford militants express this view because, they assert, black women are a minority *in California,* and a minority's claim is always more deserving than that of the majority. Even if one crosses one's eyes and accepts this argument, some quick arithmetic will show that since one third of Californians are nonwhite, and one half of the whites are female, then white males — Shakespeares — make up only one third of the population, whereas "women, minorities, and people of color" make up two thirds. That's right, you will be told, the minority is the majority, which vastly strengthens its claim. Bye-bye, Shakespeare, white male.

What is the salient characteristic of Galileo? That he perceived the workings of celestial mechanics and stood his ground (up to a point)? No. He was a white male. What about Dante? Was it his vision of the world, his inimitable poetry? No. He too was a white male. And what about the Bible, that book in the drawers of chipboard tables in motels? *White males.*

Even if the world were nothing more than a struggle between classes, might the revisionist scholars be willing to concede the existence, somewhere, somehow, of universal and eternal truths that may be apprehended and conveyed without reference to race, sex, and economics? They will not, and they cannot, anymore than a machine can tell you what it feels like to have a soul.

Perhaps because they themselves cannot comprehend the standards of the "canon," much less meet them, they have decided upon new criteria, which derive from a totalitarian political bent, and are some of the many unsolicited gifts of Marxism's inability to limit its mania for explanation. The formula is something like "numbers of oppressed group times extent of oppression equals merit." Mind you, the operational definitions of these terms are not decided disinterestedly, since the people who credit the formula are capable neither of disinterestedness nor of allowing that it exists. Their equation is convenient in pandering for support, and it snaketails quite nicely into a certain historical moment, as it is predicated on the belief that questions are best answered not by investigation but by decree.

Not only do they absurdly attempt to define merit by counting heads, but the cadres of politicized aesthetes seem to have forgotten entirely the roles of necessity and coercion (though they speak of them all the time) within the classes that they profess to champion. In their thinking, canned spaghetti would be superior to, let us say, a butterflied, marinated, charcoal-broiled leg of lamb, because the former is more familiar to "the masses." In proceeding to this conclusion *a posteriori,* they have exhibited no curiosity about what most people might choose were the choice open. In fact, the oppressed to whom they have assigned the role of arbiter of tastes and for whom they have done away with the notion of detachment are much better attuned to the objective than are they. A Vietnamese boat person with a cardboard suitcase and a pot full of fish heads is just as capable of objectivity as an English peer with a bridle leather attaché case and a bone china plate of caviar-stuffed prawns. Boat person and peer will choose and reject similarly, for the qualities of merit lie in the objects themselves rather than in the circumstances of those who perceive them. Bridle leather wears better, smells better, and feels better than cardboard (at least as a suitcase). The meat of a prawn tastes better than eyes, cartilage, and gills. And so on and so forth. Perhaps the revisionist cadres in the academic fun house, singing the praises of cardboard suitcases and fish heads, would be surprised if the people to whom they pander turn on them for the crime of romanticizing their disabilities and misfortunes, which is nothing more, really, than offering them a boot and a heel. Why teach Shakespeare to the children of poor non-English-speaking immigrants who are not even accustomed to the Roman alphabet? Can they have anything in common with him? In fact, the revisionists themselves, obsessed with shallow categorizations of the human soul, are probably the only people who share nothing in common with Shakespeare. What a shame that, having failed to take over the world, they should march on English departments.

To make literature the servant of politics has been the familiar task of Stalinism, fascism, Nazism, or the kind of third-world adaptation resulting in children's texts that read, "If three imperialists are riding down the street and you kill two, how many are left to be killed by other oppressed children struggling for their inalienable rights?" The totalitarian impulse to interpret absolutely every facet of life as part of a grand struggle for power always runs together with comic pettiness and stupidity. Perhaps one should expect this in certain quarters, but that this spore can thrive in an open society is disturbing and disheartening. Though it, too, will burn away in the sunshine, it is a blow nonetheless.

One of the best things about writing and writers is the affinity of the profession and its adherents to anarchy and individualism. Unlike human behavior in a political context, the imagination is speculative. Though much may flow from it that needs regulation lest it assault the structure of everyday life, artistic expression itself need never be subject to bureaucratic control. Though angered and saddened by licentiousness, one must still look with favor upon the tendency of Anglo-American jurisprudence to allow virtually no restraint upon the printed word. Literary anarchy is good because a good writer addresses questions over which no human authority can ever hold sway, and therefore he must be able to resist the organizational impulse that gives rise to ministries of culture, writers' unions, academies, and cliques.

But the schools, the cliques, and their supportive apparatus appear to be riding a wave. The social impulse, no matter how lamentable in this field, is just as potent within it as it is in other areas: an order of battle can be formidable in itself, apart from its elements. Other factors as well have contributed to the success of the collective impulse. An economy far richer and more specialized than ever before in history has made possible the existence of unprecedented numbers of professional writers. That in turn has led to writing schools tucked in odd corners of the universities. Nothing is wrong with writing programs except their central premise. It is simply not possible to teach someone to write. You may offer a refuge for a time, but why not just give out vouchers for a good hotel in Venice? To teach writing in classes and seminars makes as much sense as trying to teach someone to be an adventurer. The drive must come from within, and the territory of operations must be uncharted: there is no teaching this.

Though writing schools are largely innocent of harmful effect, they may be part of the reason for the malignant presence of schools of writing. A school befits many things — painting, music, fish — better than it does literature. At best it may exemplify a grand coincidence of motives and sensibilities. At worst it is a kind of fraternal order or academy, the purpose of which is to close out the unconnected, dominate the discipline, and grease the founders and caretakers. My advice to a writer about to become part of a school is to join the League of Women Voters. Writers should stand alone like oaks rather than wired together in bales like sprigs of hay.

No better illumination of the pitfalls of the collective impulse exists than the school of the minimalists. What they do is as bad as what they believe in. They appear to start from the premise that the world has unjustly offended their innate virtue and forced them to become trenchant impassive observers of its universal offensiveness. They have little to do except document the pathos and idiocy of those unintelligent enough not to have been offended, or chronicle the lives of the offended and enlightened, who seem to live mainly in diners and trailers. They have taken their stylistic cue from the haiku, and they worship spare strokes. Their novels are novellas, their novellas vignettes, and their short stories laboratory experiments in subliminal perception (I refer not to length but depth). Though the intent of minimalism may be to convey a great deal on the lightest possible frame, one has to have some bulk for the publishers. Ten thousand words are ten thousand words, but, as if to camouflage the swelling, the minimalists gut the content. This is an unconscious error comparable to that of the man who wanted to travel light and packed a peanut in a steamer trunk. Though minimalist "classics" usually are fairly brief (even if not brief enough), they lend themselves to the short form not because they are poignant but because they are anaerobic. If one of these lightless artifacts, completely without oxygen, were stretched into a novel, reading it would be like driving from Miami to San Francisco while holding your breath.

In their approach, adherents of minimalism are almost uniformly oblique, which is not surprising, since the uncomprehending often crave inscrutability as a shield behind which nothing can be something. Beyond that, we have in their inscrutability a clue that theirs is more a social than a literary movement. Subcultures develop, want, and need dialects as part of their identity, their defense, and their mechanism for sustaining an elite (those who best master the intricacies of the dialect). The dialect of the minimalists is their affectation of inscrutability and exhaustion. It is also their mask. Mice who tour lion country need masks and other tricks to have a safe trip. Besides, their unwillingness to deal with life other than obliquely is not subtlety, as they would have you think, but cowardice. And they aren't even oblique as much as they are simply sarcastic and snotty. I wonder if, in other civilizations, priestly castes and philosophers are elevated and revered because they are snotty.

Minimalists appear to be people who have not been forced to struggle, and who have not dared upon some struggle to which they have not been forced. Thus, they have contempt for their own lives of mild discomfort — and who can blame them? They live in a strange, motionless, protected world. In the world to which they are deaf, you can always be overwhelmed; thieves and murderers can strike in the night; you can find yourself, head shaved clean, in a prison camp; the people you love die, and you don't take it lightly or think it is ironic; you are not sure of the next meal, of the absence of terror, or of safety, comfort, or abundance, for you have learned that these things, far from being the state to which an unabused universe automatically reverts, are merely illusions waiting to be shattered by suffering and mortality. And because of this, or at least in conjunction with it, visions are intense, things are important, love is deep, life overflows. But they observe everything of great moment as if from a distance, as if it were in miniature, or under glass, as if when you pricked them, they would not bleed. Whence comes their sang-froid, their gluttonous pursuit of irony, their unlikely detachment in regard to love and death? (Yeats's epitaph is remarkable precisely because it is an admonition he did not honor.) Perhaps these qualities arise not in the great truth they have pretended to discover (that life is now ugly and uninteresting) but rather in the fact that they don't put themselves at risk, they don't (to paraphrase Joyce) fail, fall, or feel. What are they doing with characters that chafe a million square miles of ass-leather on diner banquettes and vinyl-covered kitchen chairs? It is really quite simple. They are sitting out all the dances.

Not only do they abstain, they have made a virtual industry out of ridicule. And what do they ridicule? Effort, perfection, devotion, fidelity, honor, belief, love, bravery, et al. Please allow the following digression. In 1976 I arrived at Magdalen College, Oxford, as a rather old postgraduate student under Hugh Trevor-Roper, intending, among other things, to train on the Isis for four years and row in the 1980 Olympics. But it rained all the time and I got very depressed living on a turkey farm where I witnessed a terrible murder, and then nearly being hit by a suicide falling from the clock tower outside All Souls library, and then witnessing two steeplejacks plunge from an enormously high cooling structure as I rode past on the train to London. It was always cloudy, the rowing master detested me and dressed like an undertaker, and I discovered a miraculous English cookie that has chocolate chips and fruit and yet is so crisp that eating it is like cracking nuts. I often found myself in the boat house, pretending to wait out a cold rain, excerpting a cookie or two from the week's supply that I attempted to carry home nearly every day. Then I would have another two. Then the entire package, then another package, and another, and, quite apart from putting on weight, the river there is so crooked and narrow and filled with swans and covered with bridges upon which stand hoodlums who pour beer on your head as you row underneath that I didn't do as much rowing as I planned, and never would have gotten to the 1980 Olympics even had the Russians not invaded Afghanistan. But I do not, now that I have failed and am over the hill, mock young oarsmen who can propel their light boats as I never could. I do not refuse to credit their will and devotion, nor reason that because I was not able to keep my vows, realize my intent, and follow my ideals, that vows, plans, and ideals are contemptible. The minimalists do, however, and it has become the fashion. In addition, they have etched into the surface of literary life a number of other strange conventions that are no less mysterious than they are distorted.

Their characters always seem to have a health problem (in addition to the nicotine addiction and alcoholism that are de rigueur) that is far more disgusting than perilous. How so many people can be sitting in so many diners, trailers, and pickup trucks with so many ingrown toenails, varicose veins, corns, bunions, boils, warts, skin infections, impetigo, itches, scars, blackheads, and scabs is the secret of the Sphinx. This school of writers does not require literary critics as much as dermatologists. Someday they will discover tropical medicine:

> The kitchen table in my trailer is covered with coffee stains. Across 203, the lights of the diner sign blink on and off. Marlene goes, you get jealous when I have coffee with people who have malaria. I go, no I don't. She goes, the Pork Tapeworm, Taeniarhynchus solium, is covered with a tough cuticle. She takes a drag on her cigarette and inspects her varicose veins, and then she goes, now why is that? I go, I don't know, why do some women have teased hair? She goes, you never talk to me. I go, right, let's talk. Let's talk about Cestoda Platyhelminthes and nematodes. Marlene gets like this, ever since I had the affair with the waitress in Butlersville, the one with the tapeworm that drove my pickup the wrong way on I-80.

The landscape of American literature is now littered with similar paragraphs, not because they reflect a compelling reality but because they reflect a particular vision that has been institutionalized. The conventions that flow from this absurd vision are nearly ubiquitous. Of the stories read for the purpose of gathering the twenty herein, more than a third dealt with divorce, separation, or extramarital affairs. Alcohol appeared in more than half, cigarettes and coffee in more than a third, brand names in about a third, and that satanic square that I can hardly bear to mention, television, in more than half. Only one story in six managed to avoid altogether these useless touchstones of American fiction. Whereas the appearance of these elements need not have any bearing on the quality of a story, still, it is tiring to travel in a land where the trees and mountains have been entirely replaced by vinyl-covered kitchen chairs.

Why are so many minimalist stories about despicable people in filthy unkempt garden apartments filled with ugly bric-a-brac, where everyone smokes, drinks, stays up all night, and is addicted to coffee? Why are the characters almost uniformly pudgy, stiff, and out of shape, even if they are in their twenties? Why do they watch so much television? Why do they have so many headaches? Why are they impotent, frigid, promiscuous, or all three combined? Why are their lives intertwined inextricably with brand names? Why are almost all of them divorced, never married, or, if married, remembering, having, or about to have an affair? Why is their hair dirty? Why don't they work at a profession or a trade? What are they doing in university towns in their middle age? Why do they seem to exist as if there were no landscape, or as if they were living in tunnels under ground? Is that why they are never sunburned? Why are they never in love (their extramarital affairs have less to do with love than with exploration and injury), or involved in something that scares the death out of them? Why do they behave as if they are going to live forever and every moment will be a curse, rather than as if they are going to live for only a very short time and every moment will be a blessing? This is probably not a reflection of the world that most people know — a world of real danger, real tragedy, real beauty, and real love. It may of course have something to do with who writes the stories and who now reads them. Though I feel that I have intruded upon a closed system, I do not hesitate to report on it, because my anxiety over the possible consequences to my livelihood (no matter, judging from my mail, most of my readers are in Trondheim and Antwerp) is dwarfed by my wonder at what I have seen. In the tunnels of contemporary American literature, the moles are singing. They are singing in unison, they are singing to each other, and they are singing of the darkness. Far be it from me to criticize some who are my colleagues. That would be dangerous. And it would be impolitic. But, then again, literature is not politics. Or is it?

Like writers, publishers have always dreamed of making a great deal of money, but even in recent memory the industry has been predicated on the provision of lasting and excellent works. That is no more. The field is in total disarray. Half the conversations in New York seem to start with sentences like this: "Have you heard? Rhonda Goldblatt has moved from Jocular House to Anthropoid and Slern, where she will chair the acquisitions committee. Her husband, Brooks Deerfield, was shaken, but will remain in his position as director of conceptual rights at Kangaroo Books." In the frenzy to coordinate various spinoffs, the T-shirts, the Japanese cassette rights, the pickle jars, the satellite tours, and all the rest, it sometimes is hard to find an editor with a manuscript and a pencil. Although many of the old guard are left, struggling against the tide, perhaps it is best to hold out for praise Rachel MacKenzie, of *The New Yorker,* who is gone. In the many hours that we spent, in the late sixties, editing manuscripts and galleys at an old wooden table, she concentrated fiercely upon the language and content of the work at hand. We could have been in a bubble spinning in space. Nothing else mattered, not circulation, not advertising, not readers' opinions, not being au courant, not winning awards, not reputation, not status, nothing — except the piece that was being edited. She treated me, a young boy, with the same courtesy she showed her authors who were known throughout the world. When we would break for lunch and go to the Algonquin she would introduce me to these people, always amused that I had never heard of them, and delighted that we both had in mind neither them, nor the poached salmon on our plates, nor anything else, but only the story that was waiting for us on the table in her office. Throughout all that time, she was dying, and she knew it, but she kept her humor, she focused her strength where she wanted it to shine, and her courage and honor were inviolable. When one was with her one felt properly connected with a worthy past.

The industry has slowly been undermined because not

enough Rachel MacKenzies have survived. Publishers put out astonishing junk with the excuse that the public wants it, and the public receives the junk with the excuse that it is what the publishers provide. Everyone is afraid to miss the boat, to say no, to do without, to have less, to prefer not to. Standards have been ratcheted downward as fast as a truck that has lost its brakes on a mountain road, for the compelling reason that if you hold to the standards of a less hysterical age you simply disappear. More and more people have learned to adapt, and the defiant ones who say, to hell with it, if I disappear, I'll disappear, find themselves as voiceless as the dead. The heroes of old who remain have had to accomplish maneuvers of incredible subtlety and flexibility, and have had to compromise in ways that make most of them seem strangely melancholy. It is all exactly like Thomas Mann's great story "Disorder and Early Sorrow," in which a world in the process of coming apart sweeps before it even the best people, even courage, even innocence.

No remedy exists for the sometimes phenomenal corruption in the world of publishing other than for the powerful forces that drive it to dissipate as they spiral like empires into air so thin that eventually it will not sustain them. Meanwhile, the disequilibrium does not favor the tranquility and concentration necessary for sustaining a real literature divorced from secondary considerations. This does not require hostility to commerce or to the magnificent orderly disorder of these energetic times. Ferment in history, the operations of the marketplace, necessity, risk, turmoil, all are necessary and good, but there must be islands of refuge, pools of water that are still and deep, though withdrawing into little cliques of the self-proclaimed pure isn't much help, since weather is made in the open sky, where the wind is. The poets of Cambridge, Massachusetts, for example, at least as they were some time ago, had very little going for them except the feeling that they were all Van Goghs over whom worshipful tears would be shed in a hundred years or so. All you had to do was tell these people that you actually published a book with a real publisher and they would disintegrate before your eyes, collapsing under the paradox of their hatred of you as a devil and their worship of you as a god. The only honorable course is to deal in the mainstream, and if you feel that the mainstream has been corrupted beyond salvation, the only honorable thing is to go bravely to oblivion. Oblivion is not such a bad place, and you are headed there anyway.

Reputation is a sword that cuts two ways. On the one hand, it can serve as a tool for choosing well and surely: at its best it is nothing more than advanced intelligence, or past experience directing one's steps in the present. On the other hand, it can be constructed by artificial means and be totally misleading: at worst it is a fraudulent bully that acts to force perception against its better judgment.

Partly to avoid the evils of reputation and partly for other reasons, the stories in this volume have been judged blindly. Shannon Ravenel graciously blacked out the names of the authors, and my wife went even further and blacked out the names of the publications. Of course we could not have obliterated characteristic graphics, styles, and voices, but I must confess that the voices were not familiar to me and that therefore no one was afforded advantage or suffered disadvantage. The other reasons are that I did not wish to favor anyone I knew or to handicap anyone I dislike, for the stories are more important than their authors (at least in this context), and they are certainly more important than my view of or relations with the authors.

After choosing the stories, I learned the names of the authors. I was surprised, delighted, and a little taken aback to discover that I had chosen stories by some people whom I do not like personally, by one who wrote one of the stupidest reviews I have ever read (of my first book, no less), and by some whose work I find very hard to bear. And yet I chose their stories. Being only human, I probably would have been unable to filter out my feelings about them had I known that they were passing before me for judgment. But their stories were among the best, and I merely did what Rachel MacKenzie would have had me do: concentrate on the work itself. In the end, only the works will remain, alone, and they should stand alone at the beginning, too.

Lately the proportion of recognizable names to those that are relatively unknown has been getting rather rich, meaning about seventy-five percent or more, the "more" being an allowance for people who are fading either in or out. This year, in judging the stories blindly, I have, it seems, unwittingly reversed the proportions, as it appears that about a quarter of the selections are by those who have been represented prior to this at three times their present rate. This inversion turns more than numbers on their heads. In judging this way, one will forgo dozens of favors from the class of writer who, expecting business as usual, now may feel excluded. People in general are not aware of the horse trading and back scratching among writers. There is, however, an incredible traffic in favors, and accounts are kept as if in ledgers. Should you be skeptical, all you need do is track the mutual admiration societies that leave indelible marks in book reviews and jacket quotations, sawing lazily back and forth from one writer to another. You might find it more difficult to keep abreast with the prize juries, the committees that apportion grants, and the incestuous relationship that not a few writers have with journalists whom they cultivate in the manner of politicians. If one is willing to play the game and follow the rules, one will, with luck, advance slowly in the eyes of those whose judgments conform to an illusory consensus or capitulate to sharp campaigns.

The faithful players of this game will deny that they are following any lead but their own disinterested inclinations. "Stimson Vonk is one of the foremost writers of his generation, a brilliant genius who works in red hot prose," you will hear from Vinic Totmule. Of Mr. Totmule, Mr. Vonk will affirm, "Vinic Totmule is the best novelist in the English language today," and who is to say that they are not simply expressing opinions conceived in the breast of fairness? But, then, who is to question the motives of Senator Burmahog when he says, "I gave the boy a job as director of contract procurement not because he is my nephew, but because even at nineteen he's one of the most talented people I know," or the accuracy of William Marcy Tweed's accounting of the budget for building a courthouse, in 1869, that included $41,190.95 for "Brooms, etc."? (When the building was completed it had cost twice as much as the United States had paid for Alaska.)

Voters pay for every gram of political patronage while they

wait in long lines at the post office, punch holes through the roofs of their cars as they take Mauna Loa–sized potholes, or need help from an alingual clerk in a drug trance. Readers pay for literary patronage in a narrowing of the landscape of literature, in the presentation of long-dead corpses as living bodies, and in the degradation of numerous criteria to accommodate the facts of ambition and public relations.

Though literature must by its very nature be judged subjectively, when its adjunct operations make it a collective endeavor should it not submit to standards of fairness common in other collective endeavors? You should know who has written the book you are about to buy, but not the book you are about to review. If book editors gave their reviewers galleys without any indication of the author or the publishing house, much would change. If prize and grant committees, short story anthologizers, and book clubs were to operate in the same fashion, the expectations of the American reader would be transformed. With some fortification against personal prejudices, vendettas, preconceived notions, and other human weaknesses that interfere with judgment, fatuous schools might be unseated from their dominance, fashions would, perhaps, be less powerful and less destructive, and much talent that is alienated by the current scene, or frozen out of it either by decree or neglect, would have an opportunity to rise.

These methods will not take root. Far from it. Nor would they be a panacea if they did. They are offered only as a symbol of what would be required to hold the line against the petty politicization of literature, against the dissolution of American publishing, against the strange deeds of lunatics who plot to commandeer English departments, against the fixes that some publishers put in with friends in the media, against literary cliques, and against anthologies of short stories packed with the work of the editors' cronies.

On the other hand, one can be confident that in the end the social operations and social products that attend to literature, no matter what powers favor them now, will simply fall away with time. For in the end only the spark that passes from a writer's work to the soul of an individual reader will matter: not reputation, not recognition, not reward, not even the judgment of history, which itself is passing and ephemeral. In the end the only validation for literature is something ineffable that can be neither captured, nor contained, nor manipulated, nor exploited. You must write for this thing itself every time you sit down to write. Since you will disappear and it will remain, it is more than worthy of your attention. Here, then, are some stories that I chose with that in mind. Some are moving, some are powerful in other ways, some are very funny, but nearly all have a quality that, you can be assured, arises from the work itself and not from any secondary notions or tainted obligations.

They range widely, and are the products of vastly differing sensibilities. An old woman in Florida looks all the way back to childhood, and although on the way to it she finds mainly regret, when she arrives she finds what she has loved all her life. In a story indebted to Harry Crews, a brave, half-mad weightlifting writing teacher gives a plausible definition of his craft. A retired executive reverses the course of his life and dies with honor in ten minutes of unexpected terror. An entomologist's record book summons the past like a group of haunting photographs. There is a story about a French pyromaniac, though that hardly does it justice; a classical New York story; a cold and brilliant imagining of the death of Chekhov; a beautifully written sad story with many of the same qualities as a Stieglitz portrait; the wonderfully lyrical and yet surprisingly spare account of the love affair — from the woman's point of view — of two American missionaries in India; and a slick and funny prep school story. In one charming story, a Chinese-American schoolgirl practices her own idiosyncratic Catholicism. You will race through the story of a child whose kidnappers have decided to kill him; you will be excited by the possibility of revenge in an expertly limned Indian reservation; and you will watch with anger and respect the travails of a child who is abandoned by his mother, in Boston, and who must take care not only of himself but of his younger brother. One story re-creates with chilling veracity the nightmarish aspects of divorce. We have a young sailor in San Diego who gets his girlfriend pregnant, and a group of magnificent Thai busboys in an insane restaurant in New Jersey, in the story that everyone who has ever worked in that kind of job has longed to write and can seldom carry off.

An intriguing mystery that you will never be able to solve is set in New Hampshire. A story set in San Francisco in the late sixties beautifully catches the mood of the time and place. And, finally, you will encounter a Vietnam veteran, in cold country north of Boston, in a story that I like the best of all because the writer's very power as a writer has lifted him beyond himself, and taken him above his story, to a striking truth.

Although in anthologies the custom often is to introduce in some depth the selections that follow, most of the time the stories are used rather disingenuously merely to flesh out the editors' essays. I thought the best course would be just to write the essay and then let the stories stand on their own. I have tried to choose them fairly.

MARK HELPRIN

The Best
AMERICAN SHORT STORIES 1988

MARY ANN TAYLOR-HALL

Banana Boats

FROM THE PARIS REVIEW

THE OLD DAYS, the Chicago days, rooms full of the smell of chicken paprikash, coffee, roasting pork, simmering prunes and apricots. Dark rooms full of dark furniture, of horsehair, claw feet, doilies, crucifixes with palm fronds stuck behind them. Of trunks and chests that women opened — Ma Kish, Aunt Jewel, Mrs. Starcheski from next door — and took things out of, their heads laid to one side: lace dickies wrapped in tissue, tea towels, starched and ironed, with crocheted edging, tiny vases of pink crystal, stroked, offered. *Here. For your hope chest.*

Dark crowded rooms, three slept in one bed. Everyone so poor, and yet there was always something to give, always something on the stove. Enough to feed anyone who came, even if it was just soup made with tomatoes and onions and dandelion greens from the park, or tripe, sliced very thin, fried with eggs. Always money for a handful of cigarettes, always music, Dvořák, Irving Berlin, Sigmund Romberg — *Come, come, I love you only, come, hero mine.* Carl the tenor, Joey the baritone, Frank the bass. Rosa could sing, in those days. She was the alto, she knew the harmonies. They all knew them. The old gang. Now her voice was a four-noted reed — thin from not much use, and also age. She tried it testingly, had to clear her throat and start again. *Lay your head upon my pillow.* She liked the sad songs with the beautiful melodies, the songs about knowing it was over. Marty Robbins, her favorite, dead now, she couldn't believe it.

Rosa watched her hands coming up out of the soapsuds. Her mother's hands came to her: down in the washtub, fishing through the water for the next shirt to scrub on the board. Thick palms, broad nails — strong hands, made for work, like her own, stretching to get around all the strings of the mop. Smelling of onions or bleach, when she lifted Rosa's face to give her a kiss. Rosa would lay her head in her mother's lap, and the big fingers would comb through her hair, checking for nits.

Father Novatny, tall, with long eyes like a saint's, grey-blue — he wanted to leave the Church to marry Rosa's mother! But she wouldn't let him. It was supposed to be a secret, but Genevieve knew somehow, because she was the oldest, and she told Agnes and Emma, and Agnes told Rosa, too young to hear things like that, Emma said — Agnes got a slap for telling. When the news came out that Father Novatny had asked to be transferred to another diocese, Rosa and Agnes ran and sat down on the steps of the church, hugging each other and crying, waiting for him to come with tears in his eyes to say goodbye to them. "Such beautiful girls," they thought he'd say. "Goodbye, take care of her for me." They kept themselves in tears for an hour, out there in the cold, but Father Novatny never showed up.

Rosa rinsed each dish and put it in the rack. Two plates, two forks, a pot. Two mugs, cheap white glass from the dime store, but they held the heat. Things got simpler and simpler, a bowl of cornflakes for breakfast, a little sandwich for lunch, then *Days of Our Lives*.

Only today, they didn't watch.

Buried alive, Gilbert had said, at the end of lunch, standing by the chair, rattling his keys in his pocket as if he wasn't sure what he would do next. The next time she saw him he was headed out the door in his Bermuda shorts and no shirt. "Where are you going, in this heat?" "To *work,* Rosa."

He used to call her his ball and chain, just kidding, a long time ago.

When she was twelve, thirteen, she would go with her mother sometimes to measure the rich Bohemian women out in Cicero for corsets. She would watch her mother working over their stout figures with her thin, flashing tape measure, gossiping with them in the old language, laughing with them in her dark way that made Rosa think she was saying something that wasn't too nice, holding the heel of her hand under her breast. She would call out the measurements for Rosa to write down in the book. Then they would all have coffee and kolache in the parlor.

Rosa's brothers and sisters in Chicago, the few still alive, could carry on a conversation in Bohemian yet, swearing and insulting each other's big behinds. She forgot, no one to talk it with here, what little she ever knew. It seemed that what stayed were the dirty words and the words to a few songs. *Ty to musíš platiti.* The one about the bad boy Pepichek stamping on the cabbages of Anninka and she says, "You, you must pay for this!" A merry tune, like a polka, for such words.

She went into the bedroom, creased the down pillows once, lengthwise, with a slap of her forearm, so that they would sit in a perfect roll along the headboard. *Lay your head upon my pillow. Hold your warm and tender body close to mine.* She smoothed the counterpane toward the head of the bed, banging all the wrinkles up under the pillows.

Her brain felt like that. Smooth.

Gil was still out there, edging and edging, to teach her a lesson, his bare chest dripping with sweat. An old man now. He looked like a baby boy, just learning to walk, teetering along, chin down, dragging the edger, his little behind poked out.

Ninety-eight degrees out there. Let him.

Sometimes she felt she lived in a deep, smooth-sided place now. Something like a well. Way up above her, people yak yak yakking. Gil telling his stories, trying to get attention. Not from her. She didn't listen anymore. She'd heard enough stories from him already.

She turned and looked out the window again. *I see London I see France.* Gil, lying on his back now in the grass, his thin legs sticking out the wide holes in his Bermuda shorts — she could see all the way to his white BVDs, a little shine up there in the dark. He made a V with the edger, which lay the other way, across the driveway. It came to her then that he might be dead, a new idea. It sent her flying back down the hall and out the front door. She was kneeling beside him, her hand on his wet, closed face.

It looked closed forever. She heard a thin sound — a little

high hum she was making up in her head. She saw her life, her life alone, a thin white sheet on the line, blowing and bellying out and snapping in the wind.

But when she saw his eyelids flutter, heard his little fake moan, the sheet stopped flapping, hung still. She thought, coldly, "Oh, this one knows how to flutter his eyelids, he knows how to moan." Pretending to be dying, she'd given him the idea by telling him to kill himself. Ninety-eight degrees and he's out edging the driveway, not even wearing his baseball cap. "It *needs doing,* Rosa." Giving a lecture. The little foot in the white sneaker stepping down on the edger, to show it always did everything right. "Stay out here then, kill yourself, if it makes you happy."

It made him happy. Pretending to be at death's door. He loved death's door. He knew how to get there, and get back.

What if she just turned around and left him there to give his brain a sunbath until he felt like coming in? *Just turned around and left him there.* She saw herself for a second backing the car down the driveway, right over the edger. At first she couldn't see why not. But then the idea made a flutter in her chest, like a bird with sharp wings trapped behind her ribs. Where would she go? She was staying. Let *him* go, if that's what he wanted.

Anyway, he didn't look too good, maybe he really did pass out, a little heat stroke maybe.

She stooped behind him and got him lifted into a sitting position, laid his arm around her shoulder and pulled him to his feet, her arms slipping up his wet back. She wasn't calling anyone for help — a big occasion, an audience, just what he wanted. She dragged him across the grass, the heat around her legs like thick water. One foot, then the other, up the three concrete steps and the last hard one, over the lintel into the air conditioning. He sagged against her across the rug, moaning. *Putting on, always putting on,* she thought, and then, *Bastard.* Heart attacks, fainting spells. All her life she was waiting for the next time his eyes rolled back in his head. The trouble was, back at the beginning, it was nothing to joke about, a lot of doctors from Johns Hopkins agreed. You never knew when he was going to keel over. But his heart had healed itself a long time ago, the way they said it would, if he lived long enough, only by then, he was used to the excitement. He couldn't break the habit. She got him to the couch, lowered him, put pillows under his feet. The whole side of her was wet with his sweat. He opened his blue eyes, pretending he didn't know where he was. They had a sliding icy look.

"You passed out from the heat," she told him. He closed his eyes again, to show he wasn't pleased with what she said. What she was supposed to say was, "Oh Gilbert, you were right, this yard's too much for us now."

She hurried to the kitchen for a basin of water, brought it back, knelt and sponged him off. Let him hire somebody to take care of the yard. He had plenty of money. Enough to buy a condominium was enough to hire somebody to take care of the yard. He lay there like a corpse in his folded brown skin. Maybe he really did faint, he could have gone that far. Maybe he'd just as soon die as stay here, buried alive. She got him a glass of water, raised his head. "Cold," he said, in a cranky voice. She wiped the water that had trickled down onto his chest, ran into the bedroom to get a quilt, came back and covered him, then straightened herself and looked at him, his brown hand laid out on his chest in a dainty way — wrist up, fingers spread. When she'd gone out before to try to make him come in he'd said, "You want to stay in this house but you have no *idea* what's involved." No *ah*dyuh, that was how he pronounced it, his Southern accent, mouth full of mush. "Out in that heat," she told him now. "Anyone would pass out." He closed his eyes. Pretty soon he was snoring.

The clock went off on the marble-topped chest. It had the same tune as Big Ben. She didn't know how to make it stop chiming. She pulled out the chest and unplugged it, so it wouldn't disturb Gilbert. Let it be 2:25 forever, it was okay with her. But she felt guilty, the kids had given it to them for their Golden, a couple of months back. It was made the same year she and Gilbert got married, Tom told her — one of the first electrics. Don't remind me, kiddo, she said. I'm one of the first electrics myself. When it stopped buzzing and clicking around, the silence came down in the house. The hum of the refrigerator was the only thing. Except the mocker in the oak tree, and Gilbert snoring quietly.

She'd been trying all day to remember the name of the President of the United States.

> Hey Joe!
> Dere dey go!
> Fifty—*Fifty what? Buses?*
> Fifty *something* in a row,
> No, Mo,
> Dem is trucks —
> Some wit cows and some wit ducks!

Wagons? Her brother Frank had taught her that, rest in peace. They would laugh till they cried. Fifty buses, was it? She couldn't remember.

Slipping. She was slipping.

She went down the alphabet, hoping a letter would jog her memory of the President's name. A, B, C. C was Carter, she remembered Jimmy Carter and his nice wife strolling down the street, hand in hand.

"Your mother's first response to everything is *no,*" he told the kids. Ball and chain. It hadn't always been *no*. Back at the beginning for a long time it was yes, yes, yes, dumb her, like a song. From the heart. Lunchtime, sitting there eating his cookie, sharp little chews, jaw popping. Then, "I'm buying. You can come if you want to. I'm not going to let you bury me alive, Rosa."

She put a chicken in the pot, for soup. That would be good for him, with carrots and parsley and noodles. She started a load of laundry, looking out across the backyard. They'd planted those live oaks, the tallest in the neighborhood now, when they moved in. Stephen was a baby here, out in the yard in his little green bathing suit, pulling up zinnias, putting them in milk bottles. A sweet baby — tears would come to his eyes if you sang him a sad song. *On a mountain stands a lady, who she is I do not know.* That was one of them. *All she wants is gold and silver, all she wants is a fine young man.*

All these years — half her life. She could take care of the yard herself, rake the leaves, weed the beds. She liked to do it. In the evenings, when it was cool.

She went into the bathroom and got her savings book out from under the stack of single sheets. Over $20,000 in there now, from the rent money on the garage apartment. Just in case. She'd started putting it away that time when he cheated on her. She had her social security, too. She didn't think he could sell the house without her consent — *her* name was on the deed, too, she knew that much.

All it was was boredom, not even boredom, just wanting something new to talk about, some new way to get attention, something important to do — sort through things, make lists, follow her around saying, Rosa, we *must* do this and Rosa, we *must* do that.

She wanted nothing, to be quiet, smooth. No wrinkles for words to hide in, *bastard, dirty two-timer,* she didn't want those words anymore. Or the other ones that always came rushing in afterwards, guilty conscience — *loving father, good times, the bad with the good, you've made your bed.* She was sick of her own words, they tired her out. *Such are the vicissitudes.* "Such are the vicissitudes of life." She said that one out loud. That was what Tom used to say in high school, to be funny. She liked to say it, liked the sound of the words, the way they brought trouble down to size, made fun of it.

She remembered only the old days, not the name of the President. What would happen to her if Gilbert left? She didn't think he would do it. *He won't,* she told herself. *He can't.* She wasn't sure whether he could or not. "Go then," she'd told him. He gave her a fast look, and then started nodding, in a sarcastic way. "As usual, you don't have the *faintest* notion what you're talking about. I couldn't buy a condominium without selling this place."

This place, he said, as if he hated it.

She was pretty sure her name was on the deed.

He didn't wake up. She kept tiptoeing in to check on him, hoping he would stir, but he slept on, on his back, as the room got darker, his mouth fallen open. Finally, Rosa changed into her nightgown, ate some soup and watched a program on whales. How they sang to each other from afar. The lonely songs seemed to come from their bellies, from their big hearts.

When the program was over, she went in and laid her hand

against Gil's forehead. It was only a little warm. He breathed in and out peacefully. She covered him to the chin, turned out all the lights.

She crawled up onto the high mattress and looked at her short bowed legs, brown against the sheet where her waltz-length nightgown ended. "Ride 'em, cowboy!" That's what the boys in Chicago yelled at her, that summer after third grade, when she finally got nits and had to have her head shaved. A wool stocking cap, all summer. The bad boys would chase her, trying to pull it off. She learned to run fast. "Ride 'em, cowboy," they yelled after her. Once Teddy Starcheski caught her. He said he wouldn't pull her cap off if she would give him a kiss. She made out she would, but when he leaned toward her, she kicked him hard in the shin and ran like crazy up the sidewalk to her house, shrieking all the way.

When Gilbert was better, when he was in a good mood, he would make up a story about what happened this afternoon, for the neighbors, or his poker club. He would tell it in his little flirty voice, how she came out and threw him over her shoulder and dumped him on the sofa. She tried to think it was funny, what had happened. *Such are the vicissitudes.* She thought how she would listen to him telling his story, how she would roll her eyes up at the ceiling and say, so everyone would think she was kidding, "I should have left him right where he fell. He had it coming."

"You'll keep me buried alive until I die," he had said this morning. Coming to her with his brochures and booklets. Pool and patio. Bridge club, Spanish lessons. "And what would *I* do?" she asked. "Stay in my five rooms and rot?" She wasn't the right one for him. Maybe once she was, but no more, not for a long time, face it. He needed somebody more like himself. Yes, and don't worry, he'd *gotten* somebody more like himself, too. Two-timer — she'd found out, never mind how, but that was over now, and now it was something else, sell the house they'd lived in thirty-five years, all paid for, and move to a condominium so he could play bridge all day with the rich Presbyterian widows — here they come with their one-dish casseroles and their nice cotton dresses.

He'll kill me yet, that man, she said to herself.

But Dr. Jordan wanted to know, later, on the telephone, if she was trying to kill *him.* When she called him, after she woke up in the middle of the night and found Gilbert on the bathroom floor. "Are you trying to kill him, Rosa?" Dr. Jordan asked. "Why didn't you call me the first time he passed out?"

She heard her voice, like a runaway horse with the cart still hitched on, explaining and explaining.

"From now on, when he faints, call me," Dr. Jordan interrupted her crossly. "He's eighty-two years old, you know."

He sent an ambulance. Two men carried Gilbert out of the house on a stretcher. Something about this rang a bell, as though on a stretcher was where Gilbert was always supposed to be. They didn't have the light flashing, too bad — if Gilbert had his way, there'd be a siren and a crowd of neighbors standing around in their bathrobes, with worried expressions on their faces telling each other, "It's Gil Cannon. Something's happened to Gil."

She followed behind the ambulance in her car, around the lake, fast, praying not to hit something.

By the time she got to his room, they had him hooked up to a machine. He was a small man, a little Ike — that's who everyone always used to say he looked like. He let out some weak, gurgling moans. "Out in the hot sun all afternoon, edging the driveway," she explained to Dr. Jordan and the nurses. "Sweat pouring off of him. It didn't even need it." The nurses looked at her, then away. Maybe she had already said that, maybe she was talking too loud. Or maybe *they* were mad at her, too. "I think he had a little heat stroke." She stood at the foot of the bed, not knowing what to do, while the nurses bustled around. Then, out of the blue, the banana boat came into her mind. *Tampa to Rio.* She hadn't thought about it in years. A hiccup of laughter rose in her chest. She bit her cheeks, looked down at Gilbert, in that white hospital gown, his dry lip caught on his eye tooth, his eyes rolled back, just slits of white showing under the lids. That only made it worse. A little corpse. She had to turn away, had to squeeze her eyes shut and pretend to be choking, because Dr. Jordan and the nurses already thought she was crazy.

"I want you to go on home, Rosa," Dr. Jordan said. He put

his hand on her shoulder. "We'll run some tests tomorrow to be sure, but I don't think there's anything much wrong with him, besides being dehydrated." *So give him a drink of water,* she thought, but she said, "I want to stay for a while." To make up for everything.

"Suit yourself," he said, smiling his thin smile, patting her shoulder, trying to be nice.

She sat in the chair in the dark corner, out of everybody's way. Just nerves. She wiped her eyes now, in private. She remembered how she and her friend Josephine used to bite their cheeks to keep from laughing in church. How they would kneel, their red faces hidden in their hands, how they would weep and sometimes wet their pants, their shoulders helplessly shaking as the priest waved the censer.

She and Josie, strolling down the street arm in arm, harmonizing. *We'll build a sweet little nest/Somewhere out in the West.* What was west of Chicago? Don't ask *them.* All they knew was which boys liked them. Counting them off on their fingers, like beads on the rosary. Putting flowers behind their ears and waltzing together. Josie's mother had beautiful black hair down to her knees when she took the pins out to brush it. No grey at all, until she was sixty. Ma Kish. She made them dobosh torte, ten thin layers, with whipped cream filling in between. "Eat, or you'll never fill out."

Dancing the Varsouviana down through the dark rooms of the Kishes' railroad flat, Ma Kish rolling out the wild chords on the old upright.

On laundry day, she and Josie would dress up in the dusty organdy curtains, and pretend they were princesses, or brides. The smell of soap and steam in the little flat, and they would be back in Ma Kish's dark bedroom, arranging the ruffled edging of the peach-colored curtains around their heads and shoulders, helping themselves to the rouge, looking at themselves in the big mirror with the gilt frame around it, hardly believing their eyes.

One of the nurses — the one with the suntan and green eyes — came in again and gave Gilbert a shot, then quickly arranged him again with the covers over him. His eyelids fluttered and he said something Rosa couldn't make out; then he was asleep again. The nurse looked at him, head to one side. "What a little doll," she said. She looked at Rosa as if to tell her she ought to appreciate him more, take better care of him.

She wished she could shake him awake, make him sit up and tell the nurse how he came down with the yellow fever after the banana boat got to Brazil, since she was so interested. Tell her how the natives carried him out of the jungle in a hammock on poles, and he screamed and screamed, out of his head. Rosa remembered his clear, serious blue eyes when he told her to explain why he put his hand over his chest like that sometimes, how near to death he had come that time, and so young. Holding her hand: *the fever scarred my heart, Rosa.* She wondered what this pretty young nurse would do with someone who held her hand and told her that, with such a sad look. What *Rosa* had done, of course, was marry him.

She was twenty-four by then, not so bad these days, but old, an old maid already, in those times, bringing presents to Josie's two little boys, Chuckie and Dennis. Rosa went into an empty church one evening after work and prayed God to send her someone to take care of. Two weeks later, God sent Gilbert, with his scarred heart and thin overcoat. Sent him to the Aragon Ballroom, sent him across the polished floor to ask her to dance, Wayne King playing "Always," the sweet clarinet sliding its narrow notes into the smoky air. She had on her new crimson dress, long-waisted. "Your name should be Rose, in that dress," he said, his voice not like any voice from around Chicago. "It's Rosa," she told him, feeling shy, because of the nice way he put his hand on her waist. He told her she was a wonderful dancer. She knew she was a wonderful dancer, but she was twenty-four, a supervisor at the telephone company, making good money, even in the Depression, because she had worked there by then for ten years. She lied about her age to get that job, the only lie she ever told.

He held her just the way a new man should, respectful of her, lightly sliding his hand — smooth and dry, not sweaty, like some — over hers; she felt, in his arms, that she could leave all the steps to him. She hardly knew she was dancing. Something was going to happen, something was happening. She relaxed, her brow finally resting against the sweet clean side of his neck. Her dreams would come true, she should relax.

A Southerner, so courteous, new in town. "Where are you from?" "From far away." A *true gentleman,* her sister Emma said. It was a cold, snowy winter. He'd found a job as a shoe salesman and he was grateful to have it, he told her. He'd lost everything in the Florida Bust. *Lost everything.* When he said that, she saw orange groves and automobiles and big white houses falling sadly through the sky. "May I see you home?" he asked, but she went home on the streetcar, with her girlfriends from the telephone company, Vi and Veronica. "May ah see you-all home?" they teased her, in their rough, jokey imitations of a Southern accent. On Monday, when she got off work, he was waiting for her under the arch, hunched against the wind with newspapers stuffed in his vest, holding a rose.

He gave her the rose. He gave her what she'd imagined — she was waltzing into seventh heaven in the arms of a blue-eyed stranger from the South, where they had plantations and moss in the trees. "You have the eyes of a banished princess," he told her. This was news to her. She'd never heard of *banished.* "Or a princess locked in a tower." It was the first time she ever reminded anybody except herself and Josie of any kind of princess.

Florida boy. *Mout' fulla mush,* her brothers said when they met him. They didn't want him around, they didn't trust him, they didn't want him for her. Her brothers were the ones who sniffed around and found out he was divorced. He forgot to tell her that. But it was too late by then, she'd gotten used to her dream coming true, she couldn't give it up, she'd never find another one like him. So she forgave him, even though it meant she had to leave the Church and her beloved statues of the Virgin and St. Theresa and St. Catherine and Christ himself, dying on the cross, his beautiful white shoulders lifted, his arms stretched out with their long muscles and blue veins. She had prayed to God, and Gil was what God sent, so she figured it was all right with Him. His scarred heart reminded her a little of Christ's sacred wounded heart. And the way his head sometimes fell to one side, like Christ's in His crown of thorns.

Her mother didn't speak much English. When Rosa took Gilbert home and showed them all her wedding ring, her mother held her hands over her heart, then crossed herself and wept. Rosa remembered her mother's square, foreign figure, and the mahogany veneer credenza behind her, where the candles burned in their red cups before the picture of the Virgin. The wedding ring on her mother's finger flashed in the candlelight when she crossed herself. *You should talk,* Rosa had thought. Posing at Uncle Rudy's in Michigan, in the doorway of the barn, looking into the distance with dreamy eyes, arms full of flowers. Forty-five years old, seven children, was too late for dreamy looks. Those hands like big white turnips hanging in the folds of her long silk skirt when she got married again finally to a man fifteen years younger than her that she brought in for Emma, and Emma wouldn't look at. *You should cross yourself for your own husband, where is he tonight?* she had thought meanly when her mother cried about Gilbert.

Rosa was falling asleep in the green hospital chair. She got up to go home. She thought maybe she should lean over and kiss Gilbert, but in the end she just walked out the door and down the empty hall, feeling light, as though she'd forgotten her purse, but there it was on her arm.

Nearly dawn when she got out to the deserted parking lot. She drove slowly, following the exit signs, and ended up at the door to the emergency room. She went back around, paying attention, but then she was at the emergency door again. Around and around, following the signs, doing what they said. She didn't get panicky, she wasn't surprised when she would come out once more at the side of the hospital. She just started through the turns again, a little faster. She couldn't see what she was doing wrong. She couldn't see what else to do. Finally, a young man in a uniform came out of the building and waved her down.

"I'm trying to get out," she told him, her heart pounding. "I don't know what I'm doing wrong."

He thought she was drunk, she knew. She held onto the steering wheel. He bent to look in the window at her, then shifted his weight and said, "Just go up to the end of the lane there, and turn left, ma'am."

"Thank you. I'm" — she knocked her knuckles against her forehead — "confused. My husband's in the hospital." She was talking too loud. She could tell by the way his eyes blinked and got polite.

He went through it again. Even so, she overshot the turn and bucked the car getting it into reverse. What he must think.

Going around and around like that. She was confused, she knew it. *Poor Rosa.* She had heard Gil tell the kids on the telephone, "Your mother's gotten so forgetful. She doesn't seem to take in what's said. She says the same thing over and over. I'm worried about her." She might be confused but she knew what *that* meant — poor Gilbert, stuck for life, worry about *him.* Maybe they ought to — "Are you trying to kill him?" That's what Dr. Jordan said.

At home she lay awake watching the darkness come away from the wall, the chairs. The mirror had light in it.

When she was five or six, she stole a ride on a bread wagon — they all did it, in her neighborhood. But that time, the wagon didn't stop at Mr. Vronka's store, where it usually did. It kept right on moving, turning corners, until she gave up hope. She hung on for dear life as it carried her away from her neighborhood. She didn't dare jump off. When it finally stopped, she was in a part of town she'd never seen. She stood on the curb crying while the breadman yelled at her. She didn't understand that she was lost and could be taken back where she came from. She thought just the opposite — that where she came from was lost, the way you might lose a ball or a doll, forever. The breadman took her to the police station. Her knees shook, she thought they would lock her in jail for stealing the ride, but they took her home. At home, they hadn't missed her yet.

But that night, her mother let her sleep in the bed with her. She wound up the silver music box, the one that Rosa's father had brought from the Old Country when he came to marry Rosa's mother. She sat down on the edge of the bed with the music box in her lap, smoothing Rosa's hair while it played the old song. When it ran down, her mother wound it up again, and sat listening to it with her, over and over, singing the words a little, until Rosa fell asleep.

The fever scarred my heart, Rosa.

She and Gil got married. How long after that, five years? Nancy just an infant, Tommy maybe two. And Gilbert there at the dinner table tinkling his spoon against the side of his coffee cup and saying, "The craziest thing happened today."

The pretty bungalow off Ogden Avenue, the nice backyard. The kitchen they had painted yellow, with the breakfast set from Carl and Shirley. *A sweet little nest.*

She would bundle the children up and put them both in the buggy and take them to meet the streetcar when Gil came home. When the children were in bed, she and Gil would smoke a cigarette and dance to the music on the radio. Sometimes they would sit at the table till all hours, drinking coffee, while Gil told her stories. How Guy Lombardo came into the furniture department of Marshall Field, where Gil was working by then, to buy a studio couch, and complimented Gil for being such a knowledgeable salesman. Or how Gil had told somebody off, in no uncertain terms.

His soft Southern voice, his handsome face with its boyish features, his white teeth and quick blue eyes. He was different from the people around her, her rough, sturdy brothers — playful, light on his feet, full of nonsense. He could talk to anybody, he had graduated college. He knew how to express himself, he used beautiful English. She was trying to improve her grammar, to say "this" instead of "dis." To improve her manners, her way of eating. He took her to Florida to meet his family. They were all thin, and lived in houses with big cool rooms and screened porches, and the women all wore light-colored plaid dresses. They sat under the trees and fanned themselves and drank iced tea with slices of orange in it. They sat mending, smiling at their needles while Gil talked to them. "Well, I swan," they would say, cooing like a bunch of pigeons.

His life was wonderful to her, full of adventures and strange doings. "The craziest thing happened today," he said, this time, and so she sat right down and opened out a newspaper on the table and started paring apples.

This time it was about walking down Michigan Avenue during his lunch hour and hearing someone calling, "Gil! Gil Cannon!" He turned around and *who* should come running up to him but his old skipper from the banana boat! He threw his arms around

Gil and said — she remembered the exact words to this day — "What in tarnation are you doing in *this* burg?" So they went and had a cup of coffee together and then, *out of the blue,* the skipper had invited him to join his crew, as second mate.

And offered him three times what he was earning at Marshall Field!

Dumb her, she sat there, still nodding, the smile still pasted across her face, an apple in her hand, half pared, as he told her, in a chipper voice, that the skipper's boat was leaving Tampa, destination Rio, at the end of that very month of November.

He took a drink of coffee, in a pleased way, and put the cup back down. Then, for a minute he said nothing, as though he had just caught on to the meaning of what he was saying, needed a little time to put a new light in his eyes. "I've thought it over, Rosa. I don't see how in the world I can turn down an offer like that. Do you?"

She looked at the apple parings, trying to think if there was any answer she could give to that question. Finally she got up her courage and asked, "What about your heart?"

"My job will be mostly paperwork." Then he added, to put her in her place, "Skipper knows about my heart condition better than anyone, of course. When I had malaria, he couldn't have worried about me more if I'd been his own son." He looked down at his cup and went on, in a nice humble voice, "In fact, he told me this afternoon that he had always thought of me as the son he never had." He put his hand down on the table the way he did, admiring his fingernails, it looked like. "We'll have a lot more money to live on than we have now. It's just that I'll only be here between trips." She got up, without a plan. How long it took to get from Tampa to Brazil and back again was something she didn't know. She went to the sink, turned on the hot water. "About every five or six months, I suppose," he said, in back of her. "For a couple of weeks. Then I'll have to turn right around and do it all again." He wasn't even trying to sound sad. He sounded excited. Like they should both be excited, for the wonderful new life he was going to have. She felt her face breaking into pieces, just like a plate. She stood running hot water over her hands, holding her shoulders rigid so that they wouldn't shake, thinking of her life with him that he didn't want.

Oh, she won. Her big victory, it wasn't that hard. She forgot how.

No, she remembered. Down on her knees, that's how. She had thought that any minute he would turn, button his coat, and walk out the door. "The chance," he was saying, "the chance of a lifetime. I've got to take it." *No* was all she thought, *no* all through her, making her that heavy, that she fell on her knees, *no* and *no* and *no* coming out of her, big ugly sobs, tears running down her face, down her dress, *Don't leave, don't go, what would I do, two small babies, don't,* and his face bent toward her then, scared, his blue eyes wide open. Gathering her up into his arms. She won, oh yes. "Don't, Rosa," he pleaded, his own eyes full of tears. "Don't. That's enough. I'm not going. Forgive me, dear." Later he said, "I'll call Skipper at his hotel, first thing tomorrow, and tell him it's out of the question. It was just such a surprise — it swept me off my feet."

"Although," he said, shaking his head, his eyes narrowed as though they were looking across the sea to Brazil, "although that job would have been the making of me."

"You won't be sorry," she promised him.

He never mentioned the banana boat again after that night. She had loved him for that, for not holding it against her, all he might have done if she hadn't held him back.

Then, five years later, Gilbert had three heart attacks in a row. They moved back to his hometown in Florida, on the doctor's advice. They stayed the first few months with his brother Branham and Branham's wife, Virginia, until Gilbert found work and got on his feet.

She and Virginia, knitting socks for the prisoners of war out of khaki yarn from the Red Cross, making meat loaves, walking Ton, the English bull that Rosa taught to sing the scale. Folding sheets together at the clothesline. "When Gilbert had malaria in Brazil," Rosa mentioned.

"What?"

"When he was on the banana boat."

Virginia came ducking through the laundry, laughing. "Rosa!

The banana boat!" she said in her Southern, amazed voice. She must have seen the look on Rosa's face; anyway, she stopped laughing. "Oh my dear," she said, putting her arms around her, and then stepped back, as if she'd thought it over and made a decision, and snapped down the words the way she snapped down her discards in gin rummy: "Gilbert was never on any banana boat." She thought about it and then added, "He never had malaria, either." She started walking Rosa to the house, holding her hand. "Something was wrong with his heart when he was a child," she explained. "They thought they were going to lose him, don't you know. He had to spend a lot of time in bed, poor little fellow, and so he read a lot. I think that's why he's always had such an active imagination. I've never held it against him, myself." Rosa didn't tell Virginia about the night she had begged him to stay, down on her knees. She wondered if Virginia would have held *that* against him.

The curtains in the bedroom blew out now in the little dawn breeze. She thought, "They'll be blowing out like that on the day I die. I'll be right here, in this bed."

First he told her that he'd gotten malaria in a jungle in Brazil, and she married him. Then he said he was leaving her and going back there, and she begged him on her knees not to go. And later, when she found out it was all a lie, a terrible lie — what had she done then?

She'd told Virginia she was going to take a little nap and climbed the stairs to the hot second story, where they slept. She'd gotten the bottle of scotch out of the bureau drawer, taken two aspirins and washed them down with a slug from the bottle, and then lain down across the bed, on her back, with her hands behind her head. She'd felt nothing, only the hot sun through the yellow shade and the grey thick pain that rose up into her head and throbbed there. The heat and the liquor together made her sick. She threw up, at last, then washed her face and hands and brushed her teeth, never looking in the mirror. She went back downstairs, took the electric fan onto the back porch and ironed clothes all afternoon, headache or no headache, every last handkerchief and pillowcase, folded each one, thumped the iron back down on it to crease it into a neat square. *Least said soonest mended,* she told herself. When Gilbert came home from work that night, she asked him if they could go to the movies after dinner, and they did.

She let him off easy.

Years later, the doctors at Johns Hopkins discovered that Gilbert had been born with a hole in his heart. Even then, when they walked out of the doctor's office together, she didn't bring up the malaria, the banana boat. A closed subject.

And then came the time when he started having to run over to Lakeland two or three times a week to talk to his accountant, John Soto. Back at dinnertime, whistling.

The mockingbird was sitting in the golden rain tree, pulling every trick out of his bag. She thought she might as well get up. The light came over the wet grass. The red flowers on the hibiscus bushes opened here and there where the sun touched them.

She'd never heard of Florida until she was twenty-four.

She sat in the little cane chair, pulling on her pantyhose. Her thick shadow rippled on the pale blue rug. Everything in this house was light — rattan, antiques from Gilbert's people, rockers of pine and oak, spindle beds, silver and glass that caught the light. A dream come true. No, just a dream sometimes, when she woke up, at first. A strange house. Light, not dark. Light, not heavy. Everything here was light, blowing away, words flew around her head, they were nothing, gnats. She didn't listen anymore. Her own mind had blown away, too. Going around and around the parking lot like that. It was a shame.

They'd had good times, sometimes, anyway. The bad with the good. *Three wonderful children,* where were they? Not here. They had flitted through these rooms on their way to their strange lives — Tom, divorced, in an old log cabin in Montana, with an outhouse and only a wood stove for heat; Nancy, also divorced, no children, by herself on a houseboat on the Ohio River that any tramp could break into and rape her; Stephen, unmarried yet, at thirty-four, down in West Palm Beach, running three times a week to that little church where he led the singing, no piano allowed. Stephen came to visit once a month, to talk to her about Jesus. "Don't you want eternal life, Mom?" "No," she told him. "I wouldn't want the trouble. I just want to rest." "That's what eternal life *is,* Mom, rest and joy." Stephen didn't know when to shut up anymore. "Rest in the bosom of Abraham." Who taught him that kind of talk? She could imagine heaven with Mary in it, all the saints, Christ with his halo and stigmata, music from a big organ and a thousand voices singing out over the golden altar. But that was gone, and Stephen's heaven, with no piano, wasn't for her. "I just want to rest in the ground, Stephen. I just want to forget about it."

She couldn't imagine anything heavier than having to be Rosa, Rosa, Rosa, through all eternity.

None of her children had found true love. Once she had said this to Tom, tears in her eyes, and he laughed and said, "*God,* you're full of sentimental drivel, Mom."

She put on her dark blue pants, her nice dark blue and crimson T-shirt. She slipped her dendrite from Brazil around her neck on its silver chain. She hated her arms, covered with dark hair, her short bowed legs and crooked toes from wearing shoes that were too small when she was a kid. Now she was old, with the same crooked toes from sixty, seventy years ago. They'd still be crooked when she was dead. A crooked-toed skeleton. Unless she was cremated. That's what Gil wanted. He wanted his ashes to be scattered over the Gulf of Mexico. Her lids drooped over her brown eyes. The eyes of a princess locked in a tower, ha.

She leaned into the mirror, smoothed on her lipstick with her little finger the way she had done ever since she was a young girl, a 1920s girl. She'd had her life, it stretched back. "Face it, Nancy, your mother's an old woman," she had said on the telephone the other day. "Nobody lasts forever, kid." Gilbert would go first, though. Not this time, but another.

Faraway places with strange-sounding names. She remembered his face, so intelligent, so happy, as he bent to the road map, marking the roads they would take to get to Devil's Lake, in Michigan, in her brother-in-law John Bonnelli's car that they borrowed. Later, with the kids hanging over his shoulder, he was always sitting at the dining room table, a map spread out in the lamplight, tracing with his little finger the road they were going to take to get somewhere, Grand Canyon, Niagara Falls, telling them what they'd see along the way and where they were going to stop.

He should have had a clean life on the high seas.

She should have had a nice husband who didn't lie all the time. And who didn't cheat on her.

A little boy in bed, reading adventure books. Why didn't he *go* then? When he grew up? He could have gotten a job on a boat, couldn't he? Maybe, because of his heart, they wouldn't hire him, or maybe he didn't think he was strong enough. So he lived an adventurous life in his mind, made up stories, and turned into a talker. A blowhard, a liar.

Or maybe he was too lazy. Maybe all he ever really wanted was to talk about it, not do it.

"Well, I'm staying here," she had told him yesterday. "That's final." Which was when he went out to edge the lawn.

A nice cup of coffee and a roll was what she wanted for breakfast. A good fresh sweet roll, like what they ate in Chicago when she was a kid, from her Aunt Jewel's bakery, with prunes and flakes of coconut and nice slivered almonds on top.

She couldn't figure out. What would have happened if she'd been another kind of woman, able to say, with no anger, no fear, "You're right. The chance of a lifetime, go and make three times as much as at Marshall Field, and when you come back we'll paint the town. But let's just get it fixed up so those checks come through, honey." Where would he have gone, no skipper, no banana boat? Would she have called his bluff, would he have stayed, made a big production out of deciding to stay? Or walked out the door forever?

If he'd walked out the door, she wouldn't have seen him again, she was pretty sure. And then what would have happened to her?

She was standing now in front of the open refrigerator, with no idea why, the jar of instant coffee in her hand. She got out the milk and closed the door, put some cornflakes in a bowl.

They'd seen the world, anyway. They'd been to Majorca, Spain, Portugal, Mexico, England, Hawaii — she couldn't remember. To Brazil. He couldn't get enough of Brazil. She'd lost track of how many times they went there.

Once, in Brazil, they took a tram up a mountain to see that famous statue of Christ. On the way down, the power went out and all the passengers had to get off and walk back to the station in the dark. Rosa fell into an open manhole and hurt herself, and had to walk, Gilbert and a Brazilian man who didn't speak English half carrying her, all the rest of the way down the mountain into the station. Finally she had fainted from the pain. She'd thought she was dying. It turned out she'd cracked two ribs. They took her to the hospital, and then from the hospital to the hotel in an ambulance. Gilbert was wonderful that time, staying close beside her, bringing her her meals in bed, going to get the prescriptions filled. She'd gotten up as soon as she could walk without fainting, and gone with him everywhere again, her chest tightly bandaged. She felt glad that he was so proud of her. "This gal *here,*" he told the children, when they got back home, "is the bravest mortal God ever made."

She was brave about some things.

Her faraway place had always been a man. He spent his childhood reading books about adventure; she spent hers wrapped up in organdy curtains, making up something that would happen. She couldn't remember what, exactly. Some big romance. To be waltzed away from herself, or into herself, in the arms of a man. In the arms of the man of her dreams. That was what they all wanted, the girls, when she was young.

All she wanted anymore was just what she had, and to keep it.

She couldn't remember the names of all the places they'd been. He came back and showed his slides to the Kiwanis Club, told about his trips to anyone who happened to drop by. *The bluest water I have ever seen, the finest fish I ever put in my mouth, bar none.* The excited voice, wanting nothing but to go on and on, and be listened to, with respect. He said what he had to say, to get attention. That they'd been invited to a party for Sophia Loren, when they'd really only overheard somebody talking about it in the bar. "Oh?" she would say, rolling her eyes at whoever else was in the room, to warn them. "*I* don't remember that." Only now she didn't even remember the things that really happened, so nobody took her warning.

Her blood had heaviness in it. It sank into silence. The more he talked, the further she sank down into the thing like a well, alone down there, wanting less and less. Words were only the blizzard that flew around her head. She paid more attention to the mockingbird.

Stupid woman, Gil had said once, in a loud voice, right out on the street. Once, when he was mad at her. She wasn't stupid, except about men. She earned her living from when she was fourteen until she was six months gone with Tommy and before she went to work, eleven, twelve, she was already taking care of a house and the two little boys. She had the best handwriting in school. Once, when the regular girl was absent, the nuns asked her to play the piano for the children to march into their classes in the morning. And she'd never had a lesson, just picked it up, by ear.

From outside the door of his room, she saw him sitting up, spooning oatmeal into his mouth. He was smiling his twinkling, devilish Ike grin at the nurse, a short, older woman, like herself. The nurse smiled at her, going out of the room, and whispered, "He's much better."

When he caught sight of Rosa, he pressed his lips together and held out his hand — they should celebrate, he was still alive.

"You look pretty good, for an old man," she said to him in a jolly voice.

His face shaded over with a sharp, displeased look. He'd had a close call, she shouldn't forget.

"Did you get some sleep?"

"For a few hours. They woke me up to do some tests." He picked up his glass of orange juice. "Dr. Jordan's not completely satisfied with my condition."

"Oh."

He looked down into his glass, swirling the orange juice like it was a scotch on the rocks. He was waiting for her, he wanted her to show how worried she was. She felt tired, tired. Fooling with this crazy man all her life. She put her face down into the overnight case she had packed, started taking out his new pajamas, his clean underwear. She felt suddenly clammy, sick. She sat down in the chair in the corner, pressed her cold fingers into her eyes. Begging him like that, down on her knees, not to leave her.

"Rosa, are you all right?" She was scaring *him* now. She couldn't help it. She couldn't think about it.

"Rosa?" His voice was full of fright. Real fright, not made up. He cared about her. He wanted to take care of her, he *had* taken care of her, all these years, but she couldn't think about it. She felt sick, sick, for her life. She pressed her cold fingers up against the bony ridges where her forehead began, trying to remember herself in the old days, before she started turning into this other one, this dull, heavy, confused one. A nice young woman in a crimson dress, wanting romance, love, marriage, children, what they all wanted, back then. *I'll be loving you, always. With a love that's true, always.*

What had she meant, what had any of them meant? They hadn't known — something wonderful, that was all. Something real, of their own.

Down on her knees, to keep what she had, to keep what she had from walking out the door on her, those big sobs coming out of her. Maybe that was part of what the songs had taught her, that pain. The blues. Heartbreak. But later, ironing those clothes all afternoon, that wasn't the blues, there was no song about the sick heavy headache, about waiting for him to come home from work so that she could begin to pretend not to know what she knew. She'd pretended all these years.

Fear and fear and fear making a liar out of *her,* too. There would never be an end to it now. It was too late to untangle her life from his. Like trying to untangle the roots of two plants growing a long time in the same pot. In five years they'd both be dead. No use.

But it wasn't that. *Never too late,* she heard the stern words — even now, at the end, it was fear. Even now, not to lose.

But what if he made her leave her house? What then? What then?

It wouldn't happen. She wasn't going to leave, and he wouldn't leave without her. She knew it. She'd seen that little look of fear he sucked back into his eyes when she said, "Go then."

He wouldn't have left that other time, either, but she hadn't known it, then. Too dumb. He had no place to go. He'd just wanted the *idea* of it, poor man: that something like that could happen to some poor so-and-so walking through the Loop in the icy wind, on his lonely lunch hour from selling furniture, and then home to the little bungalow off Ogden. He just got started and didn't know when to stop. And her, down on her knees saying, "Don't go! Don't leave us!" What a chump. Guy Lombardo had never come into the furniture department, either.

She took her hands away from her eyes, rubbed them together, hard. "You're pale!" he cried. "I'm going to ring for the nurse."

"No, I'm okay now. I just got woozy for a minute."

He looked at her still. He didn't know what to do, he put his hand on her forehead. Her head ached, but the wave of nausea had passed. She took a deep breath; she got a tissue and dried her face. "Hey," she said, "that's a cute outfit, mister. Hubba hubba. Let's see what it looks like from the back."

He told everybody all day long, "Rosa has simply worried herself *sick*."

"Look," she said. "I brought the paper for you. And a deck of cards." There was nothing wrong with him. She wasn't going to act sympathetic.

"Hot diggity dog," he said, rubbing his hands together.

People dropped in through the day. He was in a bright, joking mood. The center of attention. He forgot about the doctor not being satisfied with his condition. He turned *not* being at death's door into a way to get attention. In between visits, they played gin rummy. He got mad at her for forgetting what she'd discarded. "Thank you very much," he'd say, picking up the queen of spades. "I just *took* the jack."

"Oh so what. I'll still win."

Dr. Jordan came in in the afternoon and said he could go home the next morning. Gilbert turned to her, pretending to be overjoyed instead of disappointed. "Rosa," he said, for Dr. Jordan's benefit, "I want you to be here at eight-thirty sharp. Really and truly," he told Dr. Jordan, "I don't know when in my life I've been so anxious to be home."

"You know what?" he asked, later. She shook her head, staring at the bedrail. She couldn't look at him. "Even that damned old yard will look pretty good to me."

She nodded. "I'll get everything ready for you," she said, from a little distance, feeling formal.

There were many other cars leaving the parking lot that night; she only had to follow the leader.

She wished she hadn't begged that time, but it was over now. It was like wishing she had been a different person.

She didn't have any pictures of herself as a child, but later on, after work sometimes, she would pose in the photo booth at the dime store, in her shingled haircut with the fingerwaves set in, or her plaid wool dress with the fancy white collar. Nobody took her picture, so she took her own, smiling in her new velvet beret at some imaginary sweetheart. A thin girl with big sad brown eyes. Not meant to live alone. Gilbert had found these little snapshots, the size of postage stamps, and pasted them all on one page of the photograph album he started when they got married. At the bottom of the page he wrote, *Ten Good Reasons for Coming to Chicago.*

She'd gotten what she prayed for. They'd had their long life together, three wonderful children. They'd had good times together, sometimes. He'd cheated on her, but he came back and begged her to forgive him. She took him back.

But she never forgave him. Couldn't forgive and couldn't let go, either. Took him back, but kept up her savings account, just in case.

He wouldn't leave. They'd be together for the rest of their lives. In the empty house, she made herself a stiff bourbon and water and drank it at the kitchen sink, then poured herself another little jigger, so she would sleep this time, and took it into the bedroom. She sat back against the pillows, sipping it. Maybe it could be funny now, though it hadn't been funny at the time. A banana boat. You really had to laugh. Poor lying Gilbert, poor dumb scared Rosa, so long ago. Now they were old and still together, hooray, one with no mind, the other crazy.

Such are the vicissitudes, she thought, but in her chest was something tight, like a fist, a tight, angry sorrow for her life, almost done with now.

What if she hadn't cried that time? What if she hadn't begged? What if he'd left? What kind of life would she have had? She'd never even tried to imagine it. Not an easy one, maybe a sad one. No trips, no college for the kids, maybe not even enough to eat. Back to work at the telephone company. No father for them, no husband for her. No little Stephen coming along to make her glad as her hair turned grey.

But they would have survived, she guessed, the three of them, Tom and Nancy and her, Rosa Dubina. She hadn't even considered it. "No," was all she had considered.

"It all seems like a dream," she'd say, walking through the strange streets of Brazil. But she'd gotten something out of it, too. They had seen those falls down there, they'd gone down that river, and one night, that time she cracked her ribs, she'd heard piano music playing over a loudspeaker from the movie house across from the hotel. A simple little song, but it halted and turned in a sweet, surprising way. The record played over and over, she didn't get tired of it. It was late. Gilbert, after a long day of staying by her bed, had gone down to the hotel bar. "I think I'll see if I can scare up somebody to shoot the breeze with," he'd said. She sat by herself, the wide bandage wound tightly around her rib cage. In the dark, at the open window, one floor above the square, she had sat watching the people who lived in the town strolling by. Sometimes a voice would float up to her. A woman with brown hair in a braid around her head came along the street with some loaves of bread in a basket; *That could be me,* she'd thought, suddenly, and maybe because she was so weak, or so full of painkillers, the life of that woman filled her up: she walked through the crowd with long strides, her flowered skirt swinging against her legs. She went in a door. Rosa imagined her putting the bread down on a table, turning and striking a match to light the stove.

Rosa had sat at that window for a long time, her hands on the wide sill, enjoying herself. The bells of the old church rang out eleven times, but still small children ran around. A man with a little white pony was giving rides around the square. He had a red scarf tied around his neck, and the pony had one, too, to match. Rosa still remembered one little girl, four or five years old, in a yellow dress and bright blue tights. As the man lifted her down from the pony, he swung her around and around; her little blue legs flew out, she screamed a high, excited scream.

Rosa had sat there at the window until she heard Gilbert's key in the lock. Then she pulled the curtains together and lay down on the bed with her eyes closed. She didn't want to hear what had happened in the bar. She didn't want to tell him about the little girl — it would just turn into one of his stories. She lay beside him with her eyes closed, listening to the song playing over and over. She lay still and breathed in and out.

Ten, fifteen years ago, that was. The little girl would be a young woman by now.

The bourbon had made Rosa lightheaded. Her body seemed to float up a little way from her bones, to turn as the room was turning, in sliding circles. She switched off the lamp and laid her head back carefully on the pillow. No breath in this room now but her own. She stared for a minute into the empty sliding darkness, then closed her eyes against it. Something still turned like a slow ferris wheel behind her eyes. It made her feel sick. To take her mind off it, she remembered — just in her head, not out loud — that sweet melody from the movie house. The white pony. The little girl in blue stockings, swinging out, swinging out, screaming for joy.

RICK BASS

Cats and Students, Bubbles and Abysses

FROM CAROLINA QUARTERLY

I GOT A ROOMMATE, he's tall and skinny, when we get in arguments he says "I went to Millsaps," uses the word like what he thinks a battering ram sounds like. He's a real jerk, I could break both his arms just like that! if I wanted to, I've got a degree in English Literature from Jackson State, I was the only white on campus, I can't use "I went to Jackson State" like a battering ram, but I can break both his arms. I got a doctorate, it took me three more years. I teach out at the junior college — Freshman Comp, Heroes and Heroines of Southern Literature, Contemporary Southern Lit, Contemporary Northern Lit, that sort of crap. Piss-Ant studied geology, "pre-oil" he calls it facetiously, makes quite a ton of money, I swear I could tear an arm off his thin frail body and beat him over the head with it, I'm 5′6″ tall, eighteen inches shorter than he but I'm thirty pounds heavier, an even 195, I played for the Tiges three years and can dead lift 700 pounds and run a marathon in under three hours six minutes.

I swear one of these days I'm gonna kill him, he may have gone to Millsaps (" 'Saps," he calls it, there, you hate him too) but he doesn't know how to use a Kleenex. Instead he just goes around making these enormously tall wet sniffles, if you could hear just one of them you would first shiver and then you too would want to kill him. If they catch me and bring me to court I suppose I can always bring that up in the trial, I must go out and buy a tape recorder first thing tomorrow but first the cat needs feeding, he's a violent little sunuvabitch.

I will tell you about the cat after I tell you what I did in Arkansas.

Back when I was a hot-shot cruising timber for Weyerhaeuser I had seven hillbillies and a nigger working under me, I told them where to cut the big trees, diameter breast height and all that mess, I had lots of money then but I quit that job. I got tired of seeing all those trees falling. I'm poor now but at least I got the hell out of the tree-killing business. Perhaps I could do him in in his bed, while he slept. I could cut his throat with a razor, make it look like he had an accident shaving.

His name is W.C. He's the only thing I like about Jackson, Mississippi. He's a bad-ass: he only eats live pigeons. You know how cats can be finicky. I have to trap them for him under the interstate, off Fortification. The first time I was driving through Jackson I saw that street sign and about fell out of the car, I thought they had a street called Fornification. Everything has been sort of downhill since.

Nights, when I'm not lifting, I'm working on a fourth degree, in Computer Science, out at the junior college, all my colleagues know this and think I'm thinking about leaving for a better-paying job in a state not Southern in nationality. This worries them, I can tell, especially Slater. They don't want me to leave, we generally have a pretty well-knit little group of us that drinks and parties and carries on and badmouths the students together, none of the rest of the faculty lifts but despite this I am still a pretty well-liked guy, they think just because I keep a road map of Montana rolled up in my bottom desk drawer that that is where I want to go next.

Used to be people would only invite me over to their house when they were moving, to help them lift the refrigerator and the piano, you know, but would forget when it was time for the delicate stuff like waxing the cabinets or something, they'd invite damn near everybody except me. A person less sensitive than I might have been insulted, and left, moved away from the South. Not I. They just needed telling. In the noble West, where I used to live before I reached puberty, it was manly and virtuous not to tell people about yourself, but to let them find out.

It made it better that way. But not in Mississippi. In the South, you were supposed to tell them. They held it against you if you didn't, because it meant you were trying to hide something from them, trying to deprive them of something more precious to them than food (which is plenty precious enough, the South has lots of pretty girls yes but there's a lot of awful fat ones too, oh well). I found out it was a mistake to deprive them of anything they could gossip about. Which is what you were doing if you didn't tell them about yourself. I mean everything: good, bad, or indifferent. Tell all, do, do.

So.

Look here, I said when I had this figured out, figured out why they weren't inviting me to wax but instead only to move furniture. I am college educated. I have a degree from Jackson State. (I tried to say this like a battering ram.) Look here, I told them, I am a writer, almost.

They liked that. They started inviting me to wax cabinets, and other smart things. I was pleased. I had friends. I did not leave the South as others might have.

I did not tell you about that writing thing.

W.C. wouldn't like Montana. He'd freeze his ass off. But I don't tell them that: it is fun to think they think I'm thinking about leaving, and to tell me with knowing, understanding looks to "hang in there" whenever we part company. They all think they know what I am going through, they think I hate the South like they do. It's not much but then not many places are. I know lots of people who have gotten brave and left, gone to Texas, California, South Dakota, and places like that. Many people are leaving the South.

The reason I room with a Piss-Ant is because he helps me pay for the rent. The reason I don't room with Slater is because he yells in his sleep — lashes out at the world, very loudly, curses and even wakes the neighbors sometimes. Shit! Shit! Damn! That kind of thing.

If you were wondering but were too shy to ask, then no, I've not had W.C. castrated, he's mean enough as it is, besides, I want to make sure there's as many of him around as possible. If all cats were like W.C. they wouldn't have a bad name, not at all. I keep a set of barbells up at my desk, and when students are reading or taking a test I sometimes do light pumping sets of Scott curls over the podium to keep my arms flushed. The wood creaks as I do this, a few of them look up occasionally and with interest but not many, they're mostly candy-asses and pansies, and are waiting for the scholarships to come through so they can go to Millsaps. W.C. would not like most of them.

Except for Robby. Robby is sort of my protégé. Even though I haven't ever done anything, he calls me his mentor. That's his only flaw, his only weakness: calling an unpublished writer his mentor, when any professor in the whole frotting world would have him on, but that's the kind of writer he is, or will be. He knows what he likes, and doesn't give a rat's ass about what anybody else thinks, he's a winner in every way but that one.

Robby is not waiting for a scholarship to come through so he can go to Millsaps.

He sometimes comes over on weekends, drinks beer with me and Slater, we talk about girls, watch TV, cook a lot, we eat quite well. Slater used to be a poet, he's nothing now, and he sort of looks on Robby and me with awe because we aren't nothing yet, we haven't given up yet, awed at me because I'm thirty-one and haven't given up yet, and at Robby because he's young and has potential.

Most people stop wanting to be a writer around the age of sixteen.

We expect Robby is stuck with the curse for life.

He, Robby, hasn't really written anything yet, not any stories or anything like that, but he can write the hell out of a sentence. He writes some of the best I've ever read, it's just that they aren't ever about anything. It's like he gets tired easily. Sometimes it makes Slater's and my stomach hurt, we want so badly for him to write a whole story.

If he ever gets untracked and is able to write a whole story or a book even, say six or seven *thousand* sentences about the same thing, then the big boys up in New York are going to go nuts about him. Where did this gem come from? they will ask.

Jackson, Mississippi, Slater and I will tell them. We taught him. Would you like any more just like him? we will ask, kind of snottily, as if they grow on trees down here.

Slater teaches poetry, jazz appreciation, and an occasional humanities workshop. He smokes marijuana, even in the daytime, and has a beard.

Slater, too, hates Millsaps.

This is how we discovered Robby: we saw him walking down the hall one day with a copy of Henry James under his arm.

No one under thirty reads Henry James for no good reason. Not unless they are interested in being a writer. Slater and I tailed him at a distance out to the parking lot, took down his license plate, and went back to the registrar's office with it. Found out where he lived, and went to visit him that night. Wore sports shirts, and tennis shoes, and took a six-pack of beer and W.C.

On his dresser, in his bedroom, Piss-Ant has this picture taken of him when he was a freshman in college, maybe the best he's ever looked. He's at some tight-ass social function, there are tablecloths on the tables and lots of people and the wine glasses are still empty and turned upside down on the tables, and Piss-Ant is sitting down in this picture, wearing an ascot and a shit-faced grin, looking somehow and for once very good in this picture, sitting down so no one can tell what a freak he is, and next to him is this absolutely dynamite woman, a real woman and not a girl. She's maybe twenty-five or twenty-seven to his nineteen, and she's wearing a sequiny dress with breasts spilling out all over the place, and her hair is sand blond, white almost, and there's lots of it; her hoop earrings are silver and glittering, Piss-Ant is grinning, he's so drunk his eyes are crossed, and he's got his arm around this piece of heaven, she's grinning too, laughing even, you can see her teeth even, she's laughing so much . . .

She's got to be his mother, his sister, a cousin, a whore, something . . . She can't just be his date for that night. He's too much of a Piss-Ant.

I didn't tell you this but when he talks he sounds like the recording of a deep-voiced Iranian talking through a long hollow cardboard tube played at 17 rpm instead of 33. Like he's about to run out of batteries at any time. Like what everything he has to say is just between you and him, something he's found out through his own incredible knowledge but is going to let you in on it too. He can say "I'm going to go to the bathroom" and make it sound like he expects everyone to stop what they are doing and record the event in some sort of black notebook or diary. Slater and I sure do hate that picture.

I guess the most weight I've ever lifted is the back end of Slater's car. Robby and Slater and I took it up to Oxford to look at Faulkner's old house out in the country one Sunday. We got sort of lost and got sort of stuck in the mud. We had a couple dozen watermelons and a keg of beer in the back, it was a hot Mississippi summer, we were going to have a picnic, and the jack sank down in the mud and got lost, but I lifted the back end up anyway, as if all that beer and watermelon wasn't in the back seat at all, and Slater and Robby tossed sticks and rocks under the tires and then I let it back down and we got inside, muddy as hell, and drove out of it, went on our way, off to picnic.

We'd bought the watermelons six for a dollar in Neshoba County. We love a good deal. We got drunk and never did find Faulkner's old house, but it didn't matter. We had a great time and drove back down the Natchez Trace going about 20 mph and came creeping in around dawn and I came in still drunk and pissed in the cup Piss-Ant keeps by the side of his bed to keep his false teeth in, and then pretended to try to flush them by turning the lamp on and off, like I thought it was the toilet. "Chrnorh," Piss-Ant said in the hollow Yankee toilet-tub voice, which is how he says "oh, no," when he found out. Slater and Robby and I laughed hard and long about it, 'til we were in cramps, at lunch the next day.

I don't know if I told you this or not, Piss-Ant wears false teeth, he's twenty-seven but he's been wearing them ever since he was twenty-four, which is how old he was when I knocked them all out.

Another time we tried to get Robby a girlfriend. Slater's divorced twice, with three kids and alimony payments, can't afford women anymore, and I scare them, this is fine with me, piss on them anyway if they don't like the way I shout and yell and rage and roar when I lift weights, what do I care if they don't like this, who needs them anyway? I'm not going to give up my lifting for anyone, besides my back is as hairy as an animal's, like a pelt, they don't like that either, but so what, I piss on them all from a considerable height, but Robby, he is different, he is young, he's good looking too, he needs one, only he thinks they'd take up all his time, time he needs to be spending writing, you can see this great gulp slide up in his throat when he sees one is getting serious about him, you can see his eyes widen. He is forever getting up and leaving the room early at parties, and afterwards all the single girls ask about him, and Slater and I will go drive by his apartment after the party, drive by slowly, and almost no matter what time it is, we will see his second-story light on, and know he is in there at his desk writing some more of those damn fine sentences, with maybe a half-empty bottle of wine on his desk, that's all he drinks, white wine, at age twenty he's already become something of an alcoholic, that's why we were trying to find him a girlfriend, same thing only not as rough on the body, but we weren't having a lot of luck.

So we went home and fed W.C. a pigeon and got a six-pack out of the refrigerator and then after we had cleaned the feathers up we sat down in the den and thought about it. Piss-Ant was not in; he'd gone home to Gulfport for the weekend, and visiting his mother or some damn thing. It was after midnight. Slater is dangerous after midnight.

We thought and drank beer for about an hour. I had to get another six-pack out. It was like a genius was in my living room when Slater mentioned Maribeth Hutchings.

Maribeth Hutchings had been in one of my Contemporary Lit classes about five years ago. She was a little older than Robby, but that wasn't important. What was important was this: Maribeth had an uncle who was a writer. A real writer. He'd written three books, one of them had won an award even, and then he'd moved to Montana to write.

Another desperate Southerner, done escaped at his first chance.

Maribeth didn't write, but no matter: we could tell Robby she did. We'd never talked about it but we knew Robby well enough to know this: that if he did by some slip of self-discipline allow himself to become interested in a girl, she would have to be a writer herself, or at least be related to one.

It took us about three days to track this writer's niece down; when we found her, she was an accountant for an oil company.

She still entertained no thoughts of writing. She liked numbers. She was pleased by money and the camaraderie of office life. We saw the diploma in her office. Noticed, regrettably, that she had finally ended up going to Millsaps. But Slater and I looked at each other. These things can be overcome, Slater's eyes said. I nodded. She was about twenty-six years old. She was beautiful. She was making about $70,000 a year. We sat down and told her our plan. We had even brought a picture of Robby, and a Big Chief tablet with some of his better sentences typed out on it, numbered one through ten, like commandments.

She glanced impatiently at the list, then asked us to leave.

I do not think she liked number six, the one about the dry leaf that blows hollow and forlorn down the empty canyon. We left.

So Robby remained hornate. No nooky for him, not 'til he becomes an accomplished writer: that's his unspoken vow, we can tell. He's friendly enough around us, he snatches up our b.s. about writers and writing like a man starved for the Secret, and he is all nose-to-the-grindstone and give-'em-hell damn-the-torpedoes when he sets about trying to write some more of his good sentences, but sometimes Slater and I have seen him alone on campus, walking, carrying his writing notebook in his arms, looking down at his feet as he walks, and he'll not know we're watching him, won't be aware anyone is watching him. He'll have this unGodly fierce scowl on his face — we're sure he doesn't realize it, he's not a mean student — and we'll know what he's thinking about, and we'll know how his stomach is turning around inside and how he just wants to slam his books down on the sidewalk and thrust his arms up in the air and roar at the heavens 'til the clouds shatter and fall submissively in broken tinkling jigsaw pieces to the ground.

Like I said, Slater does it every night, in his sleep.

It's like there's this shell over him, this confining, restricting, elastic-like bubble; it's like he's got to write his way out of it.

Robby backs up, writes a sentence, writes two good sentences, hurls himself at the bubble, but the sentences aren't good enough, he bounces back, maybe lands on his butt. He gets up, dusts himself off, picks up his books, writes another sentence, hurls himself, bounces back, falls again . . .

It's frustrating as hell, I'll tell you; at Robby's age, and with his talent and potential, it's pure hell.

Most of us get used to the bubble finally, just ignore it, and quit bouncing against it, cease to hurl ourselves recklessly against the thing, and settle for moving around cautiously within its limits as best we can.

Only at night, asleep, or sometimes when we have been drinking too much, do we ever dream about how clean and crisp the air tastes on the outside of that bubble, and how for many years we labored to taste that air; only in our dreams do we ever reach for it now: asleep, or drunk.

But Robby's still young: he's imagining that he's suffocating. He thinks he's got to get into that air outside the bubble or die. He thinks it's like a curse.

He's right, in a way, but the curse of it is this: it's not death that will come if he is unable to break out of the bubble, but something worse. He will continue to live.

Usually I get pretty sick of grading papers in my Freshman Comp class. I usually don't even do it; I just throw them away, and tell the students I'm still looking at them, really pondering over them, and will probably have to return them in the mail next semester or something. I've got about a dozen bushels of them wadded up in the attic, I bring them down and use them to start the fires in the fireplace with each winter, good God they are awful, I sometimes read a page or two as I unrumple them and feed them to the fire; they make my stomach cramp and my breath come fast and shallow, Piss-Ant says I am irresponsible and maybe I am, but let me tell you these papers are awful. Having Robby write here amongst the students at the j.c. is like turning a cave man loose in the Stone Age with a real steel sword, can you imagine the luxurious piggishness it would afford him, the only one in a world still made of stones? Robby is a steel sword among stones. Invincible.

To the extent that a sword will take you. The editors up north aren't yet impressed with Robby, and Slater and I can't really blame them, for it's stories people like to read, not just sentences, but one of these days he is coming out of that bubble, he will come slashing his way out of it like a claw-raking demon, like an ax-wielding barbarian, and then people will know about him and he will become one of Them. Robby Starkley, writer. Not author, but writer.

If he can hang tough. He's only twenty.

We try to steer him away from stories of Anne Tyler, who won the Anne Flexner Creative Writing Prize at Duke and graduated when she was nineteen, who had published two novels by the time she was twenty-four. Of John Irving, who spent three years polishing his first novel at the Writers' Workshop in Iowa before finally having it published at the advanced age of twenty-five.

John Gardner spent fifteen years flinging himself against the bubble before he got out. He's dead now, of course, died three Septembers ago, it killed him, getting out did, but at least he did get out.

But still, we wish he'd get a girlfriend, a really beautiful one, elegant even, something to buffer the sting a little in case he doesn't make it, or at least a pal to bum around with his own age, instead of running around with two old ex-writers all the time. It's like he's sacrificing the present: it's like he's gambling everything on the future, and if he misses, he'll suddenly look up and be thirty-five or forty and there won't be a thing behind him: nothing but an empty, gaping abyss. He'll fall back into it.

Bubbles, abysses . . . I think about these things a lot, worry about Robby a little every day. God how I want him to make it.

In the summers, Slater and W.C. and I often drive down to the coast for a day, and lie out on towels on the beach in the sand under the sun smelling of coconut and wear sunglasses and drink cold beer with sand grains stuck on the wetness of the cans and sit up sometimes with one elbow propped and watch the girls, and listen to the cries of seagulls and the sound of the waves and the big fancy radios and generally do nothing all day. W.C. chases hermit crabs, hides in the sea oats, and watches people, and it's really all right.

Slater lashes out at the world in his dreams, at night, and in the day, alone in an empty room with mirrors, I lift heavy weights again and again until my eyes swim in black pools of pain and gold flashes streak through my arms and shoulders.

And Robby writes.

In my own dreams at night, and rehearsing in front of the mirror, this is sometimes what I feel like telling Piss-Ant when I see him come driving up in the piss-ant little MG with the top down and a pretty girl in the seat. Do not think I could not have studied pre-oil myself, you little bastard, do not think either Slater or myself could not have studied it and gotten a job in it and done damn good, because we could have, you brown-nosing candy-assing death-loving piss-anting bubble-bound little coward.

We try to keep Robby away from Piss-Ant as much as possible.

E. S. GOLDMAN

Way to the Dump

FROM THE ATLANTIC

ZUERNER WAS BREAKING AWAY from the Boston meeting to come to the Cape, but surely not because of a casual invitation extended in a passing encounter with Elligott a year ago. The two men disliked each other for no particular reason, the most incurable kind of aversion; Elligott's invitation emerged for want of something better to say; neither he nor Zuerner had expected it to be taken up. Even so, Zuerner had telephoned and asked if it would be convenient if he came by.

Was the merger on again? Did they want his stock?

"Stay for lunch," Elligott had said, impulsively, and immediately regretted this sign of weakness. He never managed to get the tone right with Zuerner. He hadn't even had the presence of mind to say, "Let me look at the calendar." Not even "Let me see if Daisy can make it for lunch."

Elligott moved the slider and stepped out onto his terrace. Unlike early settlers' houses, placed with buffers between themselves and the wind, his house had been a summer shack before the alterations and had been built right there on the low bluff above the beach. Its prospect was across the steaming bay toward an awesome pink dawn. On the way out the tide had trapped his skiff in shore grass; returning, it mirrored the forested dune. Some day! Some scene! Elligott felt the exhilaration of a discoverer. He wondered what he'd have to pay to commission this view from the fellow who did the Indian marsh paintings in Derek's gallery. It would be worth a thousand dollars. First a strong week in the market, and now a day like this!

He shrugged comfortably in his new Bean sweater; it was just the thing for this chill Sunday morning in October. October — so soon. Quarter to six. Dowling would be open in . . . now fourteen minutes.

Nobody was on the water. Nobody was anywhere. Not a bird. The only sound came from a ratcheting cricket, augmented in Elligott's hearing aid. Fat with good luck, the cricket tensed toward cover, but the man's foot was too quick. Elligott felt a small startle at the confrontation, not enough to call fear — afraid of a cricket? — but it would have read on an instrument. Perhaps a blood admonition not to kill easily. He kicked the squash over the edge into the sand, leaving a stain and a twitching leg on the mortar joint. In an impulse of compassion or guilt he stepped out the twitch.

He stood for another moment at the terrace edge, bothered slightly that the new sun-room, in the nature of all new things, had estranged the house from its environment. It had happened before, and he knew now that in a few years the rugosa, creeper, poison ivy, catbrier, fox grape, beach plum, and innumerable unidentifiable wind- and bird-brought weeds fleeing upward from the salt would blur the margins of the foundation into the land, and the shingles would darken. The house would then come fully into its destiny. It was an extraordinary house.

He thought of a small boat going by and somebody looking up and saying to himself, That's Elligott, a noticeable man. You would trust your widow to Elligott. Perhaps not your wife; look at the bush of hair for a man his age and the athletic way he carries his weight. The house is suitable to the commanding view, what you would expect of a man like Elligott.

The hydrangea that he had cleverly placed below the terrace, so that its enormous plates of bloom could be seen from above, was at its fullest. The branch he had layered stood erect in full leaf, surely rooted. He had never imagined that gardening could be so pleasurable, and that he had such a hand for it. Farther below, in the narrow courses veining the grassy marsh, blue crabs fed; they were mostly big this time of year, no chicks; big as mitts, swimming to the rotten-meat bag and taking alarm too late to escape the sneaking net.

Wait till Zuerner began to net crabs down there for his lunch.

That would get to him, all right. That would open his face! That would balance all accounts.

The irritation at his forced retirement which Elligott frequently waked with before they came to the Cape had been diminishing all year, and this morning it gave way completely to the anticipation of how boggling it would be to Zuerner to see, on this best of all possible days, how well he and Daisy lived.

Gone were the clubs and restaurants, the church and duty boards, where men who knew he had been pushed aside observed him. He had made known that resigning to become a consultant was his idea, but McGlynn, Andrewes, Draveau, Thompson, Zuerner — all of them and their wives — had known that his résumé circulated. He felt himself become transparent. To distance himself from his telephone he had the building agent's girl record that she was Mr. Elligott's office, and if you waited for the tone you could leave a message of any length. After an interval Elligott called back insurance agents he had never before heard of; the *Wall Street Journal* offered a trial subscription; business papers wanted ads for Consultant Service Indexes; somebody wanted his cousin Lewis Elligott.

And one day Daisy had said, "Why don't we fix up the cottage and see what living on the Cape would be like?"

A steadying wife — what a blessing.

From that came days like this. Today he wouldn't mind comparing lives with Andrewes, Zuerner, with McGlynn himself — any of them. Most of all Zuerner.

An odd feeling of emptiness seeped into him. He felt as he had after eagling the fifth at the Heights Club, a mixture of triumph and loss. He had been playing alone; nobody was there to see the two iron drop, nobody to take the burden of telling from him. The not quite convincing story was one he could slip into a conversation but couldn't *tell.* Zuerner was the man to sign your card. Zuerner's authority would authenticate Elligott's life to McGlynn, Andrewes, all of them at Elligott Barge & Dredge.

He decided to take the wagon. It hadn't been turned over all week; it would do the old girl good to have hot oil in her cylinders and valves. He punched the garage-door button and got in while the door complained to the top and the control panel nattered at him to put on his galoshes, comb his hair, brush his teeth, stop squinting. At The Pharmacy the *Times* would be shuffled by six. Dowling's wouldn't be busy yet; he would be able to open the paper on the counter. Be back before Daisy was even up.

The driveway crackled through the allowed disorder of scratch pines and pin oaks, bayberry and blueberry bushes, rising from the rust of pine needles. He regretted mildly that for thirty years he had let the native growth have its way when for a few dollars he could have set seedlings of better breeds that by now would have been huge, towering, elegant. You could truck in hand-split shakes for the roof and Andersen windows with instant Colonial mullions and eighteen-dollar-a-square-foot tiles, but only God could make a tree. Only time marketed tall white pines. And rhododendrons like Pauley's.

He bobbed along the stony humpbacked lane kept up by the Association — PRIVATE 15 MPH PLEASE OBSERVE — and onto the state blacktop that forked at WAY TO THE DUMP, taking him toward town by the back road past Pauley's rhododendrons.

Development had not yet made progress here. The small properties were held by owners who frugally fought mortgages every percent of the way and counted on thirty bags of December scallops to help with the fuel bills. The houses had no views. The families used to grow cranberries in adjacent bogs. Cut off by barrier roads, the bogs were reduced to wetland unbuildable by law and some years away from the sort of new owners who could see the interesting tax consequences of a gift to the Conservation Fund.

But here ancestors and young marrieds had seen thickened hedges prefigured in a few sticks. He slowed while he envied the maturities. Cedars spiked in a grove of pines; lilacs that, come spring, would bear trusses above a man's reach; Pauley's rhododendrons.

Elligott knew Pauley the way he knew half a dozen building tradesmen around town; he had assumed the driver to be the man whose name was on the truck. He had called Pauley once and asked if he would work up a price on a new shower.

I'll stop next week and look at it. You near Haseley?

Elligott explained how one could easily find his place from Haseley's. He never heard from Pauley again. Par for the trades. Meanwhile, out of courtesy, Elligott waited three weeks, lost all that time before calling another plumber.

In June the rhododendrons between the road and Pauley's house had been amazing, a jungle. Maybe the bogland accounted for it. Purples, whites, reds, creams shot with yellow, ink and blood spatters. Like a park. Fifty or sixty plants must be in there, some of them giraffe-high, twenty or forty thousand dollars' worth if you had to truck them at that size and set them, and all from a few sticks. Imagining the plumber's rhododendrons transported to border his own driveway, Elligott regretted and went on.

Not a soul on the road. Not a car. Not a fisherman. Not a mass-bound Catholic.

He swung into the business-center block and parked at The Pharmacy. The business had been sold recently by heirs of the original owner, four brothers, each more famous than the next for surliness. No one had ever been said good morning to by one of these men. Downcast or elevated, each was on his way to transact troubling business; taking inventory; looking for dropped quarters, spider webs. They had sold out to a chain whose owners — some said from Worcester, some said Quincy — could distance themselves from light-bulb specials, jewelry deals, ad tabloids, senior-citizen discounts, and generic-drug propaganda. The first act of the new owners after the opening Days of Bargains was to add a dime to the price of the Sunday *Times*.

As a businessman, Elligott conceded that combination was the order of the day and that somebody had to make up the premium paid for the Going Concern — but not necessarily Paul D. Elligott. He would have taken his trade elsewhere except that The Pharmacy still employed at its cash counter a pleasant man named Len who had overheard his name and very nearly remembered it. It was worth a dimc to have Len say, "It's Mr. Elliott. Good morning, Mr. Elliott."

"How are you today, Len?"

"Gonna make it. Will that be it? One seventy-five out of two bills. Have a nice day, Mr. Elliott."

Twice Elligott had spelled his name in full for the *Times* reservation list, but Len's memory scan rejected such an improbable reading. Elligott forgave him. Had he thought about it at the time, Elligott would have written "Len" in the space on the Board of Trade questionnaire that asked for reasons he liked to shop in town: Good selections. Good prices. Good parking. Convenience. Other . . . "Len."

Nevertheless, Elligott's acknowledging smile was of measured width. He recognized in himself a tendency to overcordiality. One of the images of Zuerner that dripped in him like a malfunctioning gland was the recollection of the day Zuerner had come aboard and had been introduced around by McGlynn. Elligott had gone out to him, welcomed him warmly, braced his arm, and gotten back — what would you call it: reserve? civility? The face made interesting by the scarred cheek had barely ticked.

"I look forward to working with you, Elligott."

He might have been talking to a bookkeeper instead of the vice president for corporate relations.

Zuerner's disfigurement conveyed the idea that something extraordinary had formed him and implied that the distinction was not only external.

Since that meeting Elligott had become increasingly aware of a recompensing phenomenon that in time brought forward men who had certain kinds of injury, handicap, unhandsomeness, names — asymmetries that when they were young had kept them down. Elligott had occasionally pointed out to people whom he suspected of thinking he lacked independent weight that the advantage of being the namesake of the founder, even in a collateral line, might get you in at first, but in the long run it was hardship. Elligott sensed he would have difficulty being taken seriously compared with a man like Zuerner, with a mark on his cheek and a bearing rehearsed to imply that he knew how to make up his mind.

In most matters whatever decision was taken, even a decision to do nothing, worked out all right if firmly asserted. Zuerner's function was to make one decision seem better than another and to identify himself in this circular way as the cause of what he was in truth an effect. McGlynn had been taken in, but not Elligott.

He thought himself wiser than Zuerner by virtue of having understood him and the power cards he played. His way of holding back to conceal his limits. His strategic unwillingness to speak early in meetings. Never answering a question if it could be turned back on the asker.

"You've given it thought. What is *your* feeling?"

"Come on, Walter," Elligott had once said, "stop the crap. Just answer the question. I'm not asking you to invest in it."

He had been certain Zuerner would retreat from such a frank challenge. But Zuerner had maintained a steady silence that made Elligott seem petulant even to himself. Involuntarily, his face repeated its recollection of Zuerner's at their first meeting, the moment watched by McGlynn, when Zuerner gained ascendancy.

At other times, when he reflected with the candor he was pleased to note in himself, Elligott conceded that the ascendancy also derived from a magical emanation from the man. He remembered from his days at Colgate an upperclassman who had the same mysterious ascendancy. For no particular reason this Clybairne occasionally appeared in Elligott's thoughts, and Elligott felt himself back down, as he had with Zuerner.

In consideration of his move to the Cape, where he could live the personality he chose, he resolved to contain himself so that nobody would ever again observe his limits in the sincerity of his smile, and have ascendancy over him.

Pleased by the exchange with Len, and enjoying the additional insight that he had risen a notch toward the status of old-timer, now that the heirs were gone, Elligott carried his newspaper the few steps to Dowling's.

As usual, others were there before him. He never managed to be the coffee shop's first customer. Even when he arrived at the opening minute and the door was unlocked for him, locals were already there, having coffee; these were insiders, friends of Dowling's who came through the kitchen door or grew in the chairs, fungus.

Two of these insiders were at a table. He recognized them and assumed they recognized him, although they were not acquaintances, not even the order of acquaintance he would have crossed a room in a distant city to greet as compatriots; at most he might in, say, Milan have widened his eyes more generously and nodded less curtly. They returned his signal in a way that indicated they might not know him even in Nairobi.

Nobody was sitting at the counter, but someone had cluttered what Elligott thought of as his regular place, at the kitchen end, with a half-finished cup of milky coffee and a cigarette burning in an ashtray. They would belong to a waitress. He disliked having to choose a stool in unfamiliar territory. He felt exposed, diminished in well-being. He was happy, however, to see that the doughnut tray had arrived from the bakery and he would not have to eat one of Dowling's double-sweet bran muffins. Brewed coffee dripped into the Silex. On the stool he arranged the *Times* in the order he would get to it: sports, business, front news, the rest.

Small tremors of alienation continued to assail him. He was still not entirely used to having breakfast in a coffee shop. Men of his rank had breakfast at home. Unless they were traveling, or early meetings required them, they never entered restaurants, let alone coffee shops, before lunch. It seemed illicit, a step over the threshold to hell, a date with Sistie Evans. It took some getting used to that among carpenters, telephone repairers, real estate agents, and insurance men were authentic businessmen, retired like himself. They, too, had discovered late in life the pleasure of coffee and a bakery doughnut that was neither staling nor slippery, not one of those mouse-skinned packaged doughnuts.

Where was the waitress?

With the Gabberts last night the subject of best-remembered meals had come up, which led to choices of what you would order if you were on Death Row. When his turn came, he said coffee and fresh cinnamon doughnuts.

They wouldn't accept a frivolous answer. He withdrew it. He asked Daisy to refresh him on what had been served that night at the governor's, still believing in the doughnuts and knowing in his soul that he mentioned dinner at the governor's only to tell the Gabberts he had been to such an event. Daisy did not remember the frogs' legs as all that remarkable.

A profile appeared in the window of the kitchen door, like a character on TV. A new blonde pushed in, not the dark girl with a dancer's tendony legs whom Elligott had expected.

While she hesitated, considering whether her first duty was to her coffee and burning cigarette or to the customer, he read her marked-down face and slightly funhouse-mirror figure, the fullnesses to be made marvelously compact throughout her life by tights, belts, bras, girdles, pantyhose, and the shiny, sanctifying nurse's uniform Dowling provided for his staff. She would smell like an hour in a motel.

"Coffee?"

"Black. Is there a cinnamon doughnut left?"

She assembled the order, remembering at the last moment what Dowling had told her about picking up pastry with a waxed square. She filled the cup two-thirds full, placed the spoon with the bowl toward him. The tag read *Linda,* in Mrs. Dowling's childish cursive. The blonde reached for two cream cups and showed a tunnel between her breasts. Sexuality is whatever implies more. Elligott drifted forward to fall within her odor, but couldn't find it. Without drawing back from the counter she tilted her head to him, intimately; the gesture may have been something she picked up from her mother.

"Will that be all?"

Their eyes met precisely. She was no longer furniture of the establishment; she had come forward and was isolated with him.

"For now."

She closed her order book, stuffed it in the apron pocket, and walked away, around the end of the counter to take up again her cigarette and milky coffee. He felt that he had opened a conversation and had been rejected. When they picked up again, he would not be so subtle. He could ask her where she came from, what she did before, what schedule she worked.

He scanned the newspaper with an inattention that would have enraged the editor. He found nothing about why the Steelers hadn't scored with all that first-half possession he had caught a mention of on the ten-o'clock news, only junk that came in before the paper went to bed: the weather and highlights from the first few series of downs, and nothing on Colgate other than the losing score. Unimportant golf and tennis this week. Horses. He didn't know anybody who paid attention to horses beyond the Derby-to-Belmont sequence in the spring, and the steeple-chase, on account of Rolling Rock and Dick Mellon. Hockey was Catholic, a real Massachusetts sport for you. Basketball was black. Nobody he knew followed those sports until the playoffs. From yesterday's paper he already knew what his stocks had done. He scanned the section all the way back to the engineering jobs and didn't see anything about Interways making a new offer for Elligott Barge. He could see her in the back-counter mirror, poking at the falling-apart bundle of her hair.

He shifted the paper and looked around column one into the tunnel of her armpit. The girl was seamed with tunnels. Her raised arms drew her back erect, giving an inviting thrust to her figure. He mused that women could come off while looking you in the eye and combing their hair, while talking about flowers, money, baked potatoes, anything, just squeezing; the hidden agenda of mothers who told their little girls to keep their legs crossed. He willed the girl onto his wavelength: right guard not that many years ago at Colgate. A girl with a figure like hers wouldn't mind a little mature fattening. He watched for a sign, an eye flicker, that she was heating with him, but she finished with her hair and slumped into her mass. She seemed to have no spine. She subsided into wasted time, dribbling smoke.

He folded with a motion that caught her eye. He raised a hand to bring her to him to fill his cup, to try again to fall within her odor of cheap powder or sweat, it made no difference, and to tell her that all he wanted was an hour of the thousands she had to give carelessly away. Why should he have to look for a new way to say God's first truth? In the Beginning was no more or less than this moment. It wasn't as though he had nothing to bring to the transaction; he would give more than he asked — more want, more skill, more risk. Elligott, husband, father, grandfather, retired vice president of corporate relations, elder, member of duty boards. More risk.

He thought of her going back to the kitchen and asking Dowling what kind of creeps he had for customers. Linda and Dowling talking about him and laughing while they challenged each other in the narrow aisle in front of the work table. He couldn't find her odor. He imagined it from Sistie Evans forty-one years ago.

"I'll take a check."

She put it in front of him and wished him a nice day. He nodded briefly, as Zuerner would have. He put the paper together again, left her a quarter more than the usual change from the dollar so that she would remember him. Who was he? What did he do?

Walking out, he saw that the plumber Pauley had joined the two at the table. That reminded him to go home again by WAY TO THE DUMP. The girl ceased to exist for him.

Car key poised at the lock, he was suddenly disoriented. *How did I get here? Where am I going? Am I stopping, or about to start? Everything is too quiet for the amount of light.* As if it were an hour ago, people weren't coming and going to get the day moving. The purity of the air and the stillness were like the moment before a tornado; everyone had taken shelter. But, of course, it was Sunday, the hours were displaced. He started up and drove out of the lot.

Having grown up in the city, where nature was the lawn, the hedge, and the golf course, he had been slow to accept the grosser performances of nature, the turning seasons and rotation of flowers. Now he saw the texture of light, predicted weather from sunsets and fuzzy moons, identified the velvet red on the roadside as poison ivy, and leaves speckled like worm-infested apples as shrub cherries. He supposed he should have gone into the landscape-gardening business early.

Like two daring girls back just in time from an all-night party, an apricot maple and a maple more golden stood in the respectable green row that shaded the Pilgrim School. He rolled the window down far enough to get a better look at them, and then at the Betty Prior roses, the ones with a pale splash, piled along the fences. A great rose, out early and still holding; next spring he would put in a couple.

At Pauley's he slowed as he had when coming to town. He was driving so slowly that he might as well stop a moment and really look at the rhododendrons. He pulled onto the shoulder, dropped the keys on the floor, as was his habit, and went over.

Every finger of leaf had the thick look of health; none were browned or curled in distress. Buds were packed so tightly that they seemed ready to explode before wintering. But they would hold until spring, when great holiday bursts would show on the big broad-leafed plants, and the crisp varieties with small clustered leaves would light up like Christmas trees. No rain had fallen since early July — where did they get their well-being? Pauley seemed unlikely to water stock this fat.

Elligott bent to the ground and scratched with a forefinger. Sandy black stuff, hard and dry as his own dirt. Did the old bog leach up here to wet the roots? Elligott didn't have a bog, but he had a hose, and the town water bill didn't amount to much. He looked for the angle of the sun and saw that it got in there a few hours every day, over the oaks, beyond where the wagon was stopped. His plantings at the Association got that much sun.

He noticed young plants a foot or two high scattered through the hedge. Probably grown from cuttings to replace the older stock. Maybe layered off the big stock. He felt for a branch that might loop into the ground and come up as a new plant. He found no connections, and decided the young plants must be cuttings.

Bent and reaching, Elligott now had an idea whose enormity tightened his chest. He pivoted to look both ways along the road. Carefully he opened the hedge to see the house. The shades were down.

Pauley owed him something for the time he had wasted waiting for the shower. Elligott grasped a plant by the throat and felt it break free of the top crust so easily that he reached for another and slung it under his arm. He looked again both ways on the road and quickly crossed.

Unlocking the tailgate delicately, to avoid a loud click, he laid the plants on the carpet. He was going around to the driver's door at the accelerated pace of someone not wanting to look pushy but nevertheless determined to get to the head of the line when he sensed an action at the house — a door or window opening — and somebody hollered, "What the hell are you doing there?"

Pauley's son.

He jumped into the seat while the voice pursued him; he dragged the door closed, found the key ring on the floor, stabbed at the ignition. The lock rejected the upside down key. He fumbled it home, jerk-started and stalled, and rammed his foot on the pedal to clear the flooded carburetor, thinking *Calm! Calm! Breathe!*, terrified that he had done himself in. He fought the key, and the engine caught at the moment frost sprang on the window lip, and he was struck on the side of the neck by what he experienced as hard-thrown gravel. He ducked and fell away from the blow and straightened again to control the careening wagon. *Get away from here fast!*

In seconds he was over a low rise and curve that distanced him from Pauley's place. He realized he was locked at mach 2, rigid arms and legs shoving him hard against the seat back. He relaxed a turn and took in air. As the tension eased from his shoulder and back, he became aware that his neck ached.

He put his hand to it and it came away wet. Blood. Blood thin as water defined the creases and whorls of his palm. He was not prepared for blood. So much.

He wiped his hand on his new sweater and felt the wound with his fingertips. It felt like no more than an open boil, but the amount of blood scared him. He rolled his head to feel if the injury went deep. It seemed to stop at the surface. A spread of light shot? Had the man been lunatic enough to shoot because someone was poking in his bushes? What if the target had been some poor bastard with bad kidneys?

Christ, look at the blood! He eased the speed and held the wheel with his bloody hand while he reached around with the other for a handkerchief, but he hadn't put one in his pocket that morning. With his knees he held the wagon in line, though falling toward the berm, unbuttoned his sweater, and ripped open his shirt to get enough cloth to plaster against the wound. He hunched his neck to cramp the cloth tight. His mind set changed from *Get away!* to *Where to?* and he couldn't deal with the options.

Home was four minutes away, the hospital emergency branch was twelve by the shortcut back past Pauley's, but he couldn't even think of going back that way. The other road around the rotary was long, very long, and he was so very bloody, his neck cramped awkwardly against his shoulder. He tried to remember the name of the doctor, and what kind of doctor he was, who had a shingle at the lane going off after the next right — or should he try for a paramedic on rescue-squad duty at the firehouse? He would have to do so much explaining. Had the wagon been identified? Just an old Chevy wagon. Who would believe it was his? His head felt enlarged, packed with engine noise and a mossy texture that resisted intelligence. It was only partly from the blow: his mind blurred in a crisis; he was not at his best at such times, he knew it, and there had never been a time quite like this.

The corner came at him faster than he could steady himself for it. The wagon waited for direction until the last instant before lunging over-steered toward the doctor, the Association, and home almost out of habit — his hands grabbing for control of the slippery wheel. The wagon bolted across the eroded center line; the tires washboarded, skidded, and sprayed berm. His neck jarred loose from the bandage. He got back in lane while blood poured down from the shoulder and sleeve of his sweater as if pumped.

As if pumped! It was more than he could get his mind around. He had just gotten up and gone for a cup of coffee and a doughnut, and his blood was slopping out down his arm into his lap. He stuffed the wad of makeshift bandage back in place and pressed hard against the wound; this is what you were supposed to do to an artery wound — press hard, and not too long, or you would black out. An *artery?* He refused the word, absorbed it into the moss of his head.

Dr. Albert F. Bernhardt's sign came out of the brush like a cue card to remind him that Daisy, joking, had said a psychiatrist lived there, if they ever needed one. He raced past the psychiatrist who wouldn't know anything about blood, about *arteries,* not as much as an Eagle Scout, in a wagon full of blood and stolen plants, and Zuerner on the way. A scrim of weakness fell. He wanted to let his eyes close. He sobbed to suppress the perception that he could be dying and didn't know what to do about Zuerner's coming just in time to find out that he stole plants in the neighborhood.

A small gray car, the first traffic on the road that morning, closed toward him, and he roused to the thought of something better than sleep: obliteration. A smashup jumbling and concealing everything, everything wiped out, blood explained in bashed rolling metal and fire.

The small car came on as innocent of danger and terror as he himself had been a short while ago. Catholics going to church. It would be easy, fast, over.

At the moment, the only moment he had, he was incapable of aiming. He felt a blurt of nobility as the small gray car went by. Did they see the blood? Did they think he held his head this way because he was sleepy? Did they know he held their lives in his hand for a moment and was merciful? He was a merciful man with no possession in the world but mercy, toward strangers, and nobody was there to sign his card.

The wagon was at the fork where the Association road came in. Barely driven, it was taking him home to tell Daisy to protect him from Zuerner. Daisy would clean up everything and think of a plausible story. He found the least strength necessary to guide onto the sudden rough and sounding surface.

He couldn't bother to steer around potholes. He went down the crown of the dirt road, jouncing and pounding the shocks, slack hand on the wheel like a dozing passenger. At the turnoff to his own driveway he knew he wasn't going to get to Daisy. He was gone, he didn't have time to tell Daisy what she had to do. He was going to pass out. In a gravel-scattering skid he entered his own long, curving drive at forty, forty-five, fifty, toward the open garage door that waited to swallow him against the far wall and create a mystery (heart attack? pedal stuck?), his name intact.

Elligott now had his last great idea of the morning.

Alongside the garage the land sloped to the cove through an insubstantial hedge of nursery plants — forsythia, hydrangea, cinquefoil, and the like — and, lower down, wild honeysuckle, briar, and saplings that had volunteered to try again where the city people had cleared. At the foot the returning tide infiltrated the bordering marsh grass.

The possibility came to him almost too late to act on. With nothing measurable to spare he veered past the corner of the garage and over the sunk railroad tie that defined the hedge line, trashed the honeysuckle, flailed through a berserk car wash of saplings, briar, rugosas, grapevines, forcing all the momentum he could into the wagon to scar through the soft wetland and on into the cove where the thrust ended almost gently, like a boat with a sail dropped or an engine cut.

The wagon tilted on a rock and stopped.

He would have to stay in motion to keep from blacking out. He pulled the latch; his weight pushed the door open and he slumped with it clumsily into a tide that took him at the knee. By noon it would be chest high. He steadied on the door. Everything was quiet after the last tearing minutes. *Forget the plants. Can't lift the door. Not unusual to carry plants in the wagon. Water will make a slop back there, mix everything up. Keep moving.*

He staggered around the drowning wagon, slipping on bottom rocks greasy with eelgrass. He glanced up at his house. Through sagging eyelids he saw that it was handsome in the early sun. He started to take his hand from the bloody bundle at his neck so he could look at his watch and verify the time, but he knew at once that the gesture was too foolish to complete. If only Daisy would appear, they could wave goodbye to each other.

Crouched, balancing with his free arm like a remembered sepia picture of a farmer scattering grain, he lurched against the heavy purpose of the tide, toward no vision of a further life or of beings natural or supernatural intended to be called up by ten thousand Sunday-morning mumblings. That and all love, error, and regret; all papers on his desk, all letters, all unkempt plantings, all things unsaid to Daisy and Margie and the grandchildren and the judge in the traffic court: gone, irretrievable. His last mercy dispensed. His last desire a girl in a doughnut shop. His last act theft. Only honor was now left to him.

His new sweater sucked up a weight of water. He swayed and stumbled over the unstable bottom. His eyes closed to a minimum blur of light and form. His head hung forward. The hand that held the blood-wet cloth failed to his side. He dragged one more step, and another, and another toward the obscure channel hidden in the grass over there where an hour ago he had imagined sneaking the net under big blue crabs so that Zuerner would sign his card. Elligott, a man whose name had decided his work and chosen his wife; and she had brought him to this place where a stranger with a gun decided when he was to die.

Or was it Zuerner, who would follow him everywhere, who had decided? Caving to his knees, fainting, falling toward drowning, his impression (the vapor of exhaustion could no longer be called something as coherent as thought) — his impression was that to die this worthily was an act of transcendent honor; beyond the comprehension of a man like Zuerner. And yet, the vapor formed, faded; what is Zuerner to me that I give him my life?

BRIAN KITELEY

Still Life with Insects

FROM FICTION

96. Sifted out of wheat taken from corners and behind liners of empty boxcars. New Prague, Minnesota. July 22, 1951.

For a moment Robin Hood Flour sacks stacked high on a flatcar caught the setting sun. The notch created by the sack I ordered taken down to be checked for seed beetle infestation was a perfect fit for the flattened sun. I had the railroad yard employees move the whole load to a boxcar because of the threat of rain. This was not my job, but I saved them some trouble. They were grateful I pointed out the precaution, despite working so late, despite the cloudless skies. The old foreman believed my forecast without a wink. I stayed in the yard in the dark after they left, checking under rocks and around the cars. A pale aurora borealis swirled over the telephone wires and grain elevators to the north. My FDA agent startled me where I'd made my find. "I heard you were still out here ordering the boys around," he said, as we sat down on the lip of the boxcar door. He was the reason I came down to New Prague — a spot inspection of a shipment of our wheat. "I don't mind you doing my job," he said. "But I thought I'd make sure you weren't poaching on my territory. And look what I find." He held up my killing bottle, laughing. We shared the same peculiar hobby. We were planning a collecting trip to the Mississippi marshes near Winona the next day, if the weather held dry. "What you got? Don't tell me. Even in this light I can tell — *Cicindela lepida.* The Dainty Tiger Beetle. I see a few up on Superior and Huron, but you know they're rare for these parts — chiefly eastern shore beetles. What's this poor devil doing so far from home?" I asked him how he could tell what it was in the dark. "Elementary — the sparkling green prothorax, the hoary white underbelly, the fantail feelers, those distinctive checkered markings. You got to have good eyes to collect these buggers — buggers!" He rumbled like a small tractor. "Good ears, too. I overheard you talking to yourself about your catch. You ought to be a bit more secretive, man. You never know who's lurking about these yards." We sat in silence for a while as I packed my gear. The air was still and noisy. The tracks parallel to us reflected a faroff light, from a streetlamp maybe, but not an approaching locomotive; the light did not waver. I mentioned the new FDA regulations and my agent sighed. "If you ask me, we were getting more nutritious flour when all those beetle parts were ground into it. You and I know how much protein there is in a good-sized grasshopper." I said I had those regulations to thank for my new position in the company — chief of extermination research. Finally my half education, an unfinished Ph.D. in entomology that I had had to abandon during the Depression, was no longer a hindrance. "But think of your poor wife up there in Canader," my FDA agent said. "Selling a house. Packing up two kids. Moving to a new country. You're a cruel man." The new job also meant a transfer from Calgary to Minneapolis. It's a cruel company, I said. They told me to butter you up, but in good conscience I couldn't. "Good conscience," he roared, slapping me on the back. When shall we meet tomorrow? I asked.

158. Sifted from Ontario Soft Winter Wheat — under boxcar. Tuscaloosa, Alabama. April 2, 1954.

A luxury after thirteen towns in a week: two nights in the same place. Another buyer here tomorrow, Monday. Today: church, rest, the relatively easy naval supply base chief petty officer. "Shore am glad you-all could come out here on the sabbath. Which religious leaning you have, sirs?" The traveling salesman from Robin Hood I hooked up with in New Orleans said, "Poker." "I've never played cards myself," the chief petty officer said, and from that point on never spoke a word directly to the salesman.

I lay down on the track and the supply officer towered overhead. The earth smelled of rust, the salesman of tobacco juice, which he spit dangerously near me. The chief petty officer tended to shift from one foot to another, rustling the heavy fabric of his trousers that must have been devilish in this Alabama heat. My salesman stood completely still. He claimed the best way to keep his clients' attention was by gesture, constant movement of the hands and shoulders and head. But apparently his natural state was stillness. His preferred posture was this calm, oblique slouch. He was not on duty now. The naval supply base was an easy customer, fat money, and besides had already filled a year's order. I was the one on duty. I stared under the boxcar. The chief petty officer was worried some grain had escaped through holes in the floor, which made no difference to me. I was looking for a stray bag of flour with green mold, marked 0–19A. In Minneapolis it had been decided I would not tell anyone what I was really looking for (the tainted flour had been discovered by accident and the company didn't want to alarm any customers). I would simply say I was there to recommend proper hygiene procedures for storage and transport of flour. The tedious search for the 0–18 and 0–19 series, throughout Alabama, Mississippi, and Georgia, had to be relieved along the way by my own search. Here, for the Striped Blister Beetle. But the salesman and supply officer had no idea what I was doing.

"Shore is hot for April," the salesman said. Voice tight from being mimicked, the chief petty officer asked me, "Do you suspect the loading dock mayn't be another spot?" "Who the hell knows what this old coot's up to." My salesman winked at me when he said this. Standing, I handed him the blister beetle so I could rummage through my bag. "What the hell," he said, but made a fist around the beetle anyway. He asked about the killing bottle, which I was opening. I explained its use, then told the salesman he might want to wash his hands. These beetles secrete a chemical, cantharidin, which blisters most human skin. "I am sorry," the supply officer said. "Water main repair this morning.

The whole base been turned off. But the bay's only half a mile over yonder." I asked to see bag 0–19A, if it hadn't been opened. The chief petty officer, escorting me toward a building the size of an airplane hangar, asked if this blister beetle was one of the causes of "all our problems." For a moment I felt a surge of guilt, deceiving this open-faced man about a possibly dangerous contamination of his supplies. But my salesman shouted, "Hey wait a minute," staring into his palm. "What about your hands? Why don't you get blisters?" Over my shoulder, I said: I seem to be immune.

> *273. From a field along the St. Lawrence. Humid early morning, low dew point. Soaked all three nets before "beaters" pointed out a net-saving strategy. Pte. Claire, Quebec. August 6, 1963.*

He stood off in the distance for over an hour as I swept slowly through the marsh. His friends, who were throwing rocks in the river and frogs on boulders, ran up to him occasionally and kneeled in front of him like supplicants or tried to whip him with weeping willow branches, but he ignored them and faced me with his hands cupped over his eyes for the sun. I waved, but he always shifted slightly in his spot, pretending to examine the willow trailers that hung around him. Later, I noticed his friends creeping along the river bank at my back, apparently about to surprise me. Seeing this made him bold. He struck out across the marsh toward me. The first few steps he sank up to his ankles in the muck, but he quickly learned the gentle tread necessary for walking on such soft earth. When he arrived he said nothing. He thrust his hands in his pockets and followed one yard behind me, stooping whenever I did, but stepping back whenever I showed him the insides of the net. But when he saw my growing frustration with the dew, he put a finger on my extra nets that I carried under one arm. He took the longer one, unscrewed the neck, and began to beat the grass in front of me with the wooden pole. He pointed to a spot just above the grass level that he meant me to sweep. I was looking for a dew-drinking beetle that was happiest in this weather — after a day of thundershowers. I applauded the boy's ingenuity, but I played it close to the chest, like he did. Because of his short pants I decided he was French. He was no more than ten years old. Soon his friends arrived and were instructed with amazingly few words to find long sticks and imitate him. I followed behind a fan of half a dozen silent children beating a field for me. I never found the beetle, but when a pregnant Ichneumon Fly emerged from my net, singing her tiny song, I gathered the boys around me. They huddled like football players. I asked them if they spoke English. The first one nodded, but he had not yet spoken a word to me. I explained how these insects plant their eggs in other insects' young. The larvae that emerge eat whatever living tissue they encounter. I said this particular mother, if she can't find a suitable host, will have to eject her eggs before they begin devouring her. The boy translated. His friends did not understand. He illustrated the idea with one hand spread flat and made a brat-brat-brat sound, like a machine gun. His friends laughed, slapping each other on the back, and imitated his divebombing plane. When an ocean-going ship passed near the shore, they dispersed. But the one boy remained, staring at his muddy shoes. The red and white hull of the big boat, as a backdrop through the trees, dwarfed him for a moment. Finally he just looked up at the sky and walked away.

> *315. Reared from white grub-like larvae in burrows in soft rotting logs. Larvae collected in November and held in poly bag in unheated garage over winter. Larvae pupated in early April following year and adult* Trichiotinus *emerged on dates shown on locality label. Roxboro, Quebec. May 5, 1967.*

Now that I'm retired I view time in larger blocks, but the days seem shorter. After a church deacons' meeting today — on a Monday morning! — I drove to my supply store in Mount Royal for the two chemicals which as ingredients in a new recipe for poison prevent the gumming of wings. Then I stopped by the Expo site to watch construction and check for any recently upturned earth — many finds. Then I crossed the river to Lac St. Louis swamp and before I knew it the sun was setting. When my wife saw the mud caked up to the hips of my pants she burst into tears. The transition, from my working to not working, is more difficult for her; she expects me to be home all day, or when I am I'm always in her way. The *Trichiotinus* in the garage amazed me — must write old Beetle Brow in Toronto to tell him of my small discovery. He used to think the stages were of stop and go growth, then sudden transformation. I can prove my point. Most of the cellular reorganization occurs in the first week of pupation. I am able with this new freedom to spend hours in utter concentration. In the swamp today I stumbled over a paper wasps' nest, but by standing still for several minutes I avoided a bad case of stings. I am practically immune, anyway. One landed upon my raised hand on the flesh between thumb and forefinger. The husky abdomen twitched back and forth. He was a handsome creature: black fringed by yellow that banded the solid brown body. Unlike cricket hunters or mud daubers, he appeared solid enough to withstand a strong wind. He stood as still as I was the instant before inserting his stinger. The filament of fiber, in certain of these insects strong and flexible enough to penetrate oak, seemed to corkscrew into my skin, then slipped out. I don't know why. He left no poison and when he flew off all the rest did, too, and I resumed my business.

1039. Sifting dense mats of short grass along a ditch in woodland dried pond. Squares of grass mats cut out with small saw and torn apart as sifted. Material damp. Pond and ditch had water within last two months. Destin, Florida. February, 1982.

Drought in this balmy climate sears the earth, as if a swarm of hover jets from the Air Force base across the bay had hung over every square inch of ground. Because the soil is saturated with water so much of the year it desiccates quickly. Normally resistant to the worst natural and manmade disasters, insect life is devastated. I find termite nests in chaos, ants eating each other. But my beetles happened to live in a rare patch of wet earth. Cutting into their thriving community made me think of Canada before the dustbowl in the thirties. Now the sun will bake them into hysteria, like all the rest of us. Two feet below them is the spongy water table. We are less than a mile from the Gulf of Mexico. My fourteen-year-old granddaughter, seated on a hillock above me, asked why they don't just dig down to the water, if it's there. They don't know it's there, I said, thinking about my own grandparents who settled on a floodplain by the Green River in Ontario because of its fertile soil. After five years of flooding they abandoned the land and the only two-story house in the district. "But what about those beetles that tell time?" my granddaughter asked. That's instinct, I said, not knowledge. Humans think, insects act on patterned impulses. But I remembered my father, who at forty insisted the only way to cure his bursitis was to sleep on the soft clay banks of the Green River. One night he was swept downriver by a flash flood. He claimed he awoke the next morning seven miles from where he'd started, dry, beached on an almost identical bank. "But how does that beetle know what time it is?" my granddaughter persisted. I tried to concentrate on the question. It doesn't know, I said. We don't know. It may be a mystery. "But when you told me the story before, you knew," she said. Well I forgot. You tell me. Her face wrinkled. She stood up and smoothed out her dress and came down to my side. She took my hand and started to lead me home. "You said it had nothing to do with the darkness," she said. "Your friend thought it was the darkness, but another friend said it was the way ferns folded up at night. Now do you remember?" I remembered my mother on the side porch, hitting an Indian on the head with the bristle end of a broom, saying, "Get away. No fire water, get away." "Grampa, " the little girl said. "Pay attention!"

RICHARD BAUSCH

Police Dreams

FROM THE ATLANTIC

ABOUT A MONTH before Jean left him, Casey dreamed he was sitting in the old Maverick with her and the two boys, Rodney and Michael. The boys were in the back, and they were being loud, and yet Casey felt alone with his wife; it was a friendly feeling, having her there next to him in the old car, the car they had dated in. It seemed quite normal that they should all be sitting in this car, which they had sold two years before Michael, their seven-year-old, was born. They were on a dream street, all angles and doorways; it was quite dark, quite late. The street shimmered with rain. A light was blinking nearby, at an intersection, making a haze through which someone or something moved. Things shifted, and all the warm feeling was gone; Casey tried to press the gas pedal and couldn't, and it seemed quite logical that he couldn't. Men were opening the doors of the car. They came in on both sides. It was clear that they were going to start killing; they were just going to go ahead and kill everyone.

He woke from this dream shaking, and lay there in the dark imagining noises in the house, intruders. Finally he made himself get up and go check things out, look in all the closets downstairs, make sure all the doors and windows were secure. For a cold minute he crouched by the living room window and peered out at the moon on the lawn. The whole thing was absurd: he had had an awful dream, and it was making him see and hear things. He went into the kitchen, poured himself a glass of milk, drank it down, and then took a couple of gulps of water. In the boys' room he made sure their blankets were over them; he kissed each of them on the cheek and placed his hand for a moment (big and warm, he liked to think) across each boy's shoulder blades. Then he went back into the bedroom and lay down and looked at the clock radio beyond the curving shadow of Jean's shoulder. It was 5:45 A.M., and here he was, the father of two boys, a daddy, and he wished his own father were in the house. He closed his eyes but knew he wouldn't sleep. What he wanted to do was reach over and kiss Jean awake, but she had gone to bed with a bad anxiety attack, and she always got up depressed afterward. She had something to work out; she needed his understanding. So he lay there and watched the light come, and after a while Jean stirred, reached over, and turned the clock radio off before the music came on. She sat up, looked at the room as if to decide who it belonged to, and got out of bed. "Casey," she said.

"I'm up," he told her.

"Don't just say 'I'm up.' "

"I *am* up," Casey said. "I've been up since five forty-five."

"Well, good. Get *up*, up."

He had to wake the boys and get them dressed and ready for school, while Jean put on her makeup and got breakfast. Everybody had to be out the door by eight o'clock. Casey was still feeling the chill of what he had dreamed, and he put his hands up to his mouth and warmed them with his breath. His stomach ached a little; he thought he might be coming down with the flu.

"Guess what I just dreamed," he said. "A truly awful thing. I mean a thing so scary —"

"I don't want to hear it, Casey."

"We were all in the old Maverick," he said.

"Please. I said no — now I mean *no,* goddamn it."

"Somebody was going to destroy us. Our family."

"I'm not listening, Casey."

"All right," he said. Then he tried a smile. "How about a kiss?"

She bent down and touched his forehead with her lips.

"That's a reception-line kiss," he said. "That's the kiss you save for when they're about to close the coffin lid on me."

"God," she said, "you are positively the most morbid human being in this world."

"I was just teasing," he said.

"What about your dream that somebody was destroying us all. Were you teasing about that, too?" She was bringing out of the closet what she would wear that day. Each morning she would lay it all out on the bed before she put anything on, and then she would stand gazing at it for a moment, as if at an image of herself.

"You're still lying there," she said.

"I'll get up."

"Do."

"Are you all right?" he said.

"Casey, do you have any idea how many times a day you ask that question? Get the boys up or I will not be all right."

He went into the boys' room and nudged and tickled and kissed them awake. Their names were spelled out in wooden letters across the headboards of their beds, except that Rodney, the younger of the two, had some time ago pulled the R down from his headboard. Because of this, Casey and Michael called him Odney. "Wake up, Odney," Casey murmured, kissing the boy's ear. "Odney, Odney, Odney." Rodney looked at him and then closed his eyes. So he stepped across the cluttered space between the two beds to Michael, who also opened his eyes and closed them.

"I saw you," Casey said.

"It's a dream," Michael said.

Casey sat down on the edge of the bed and put his hand on the boy's chest. "Another day, another school day."

"I don't want to," Michael said. "Can't we stay home today?"

"Come on. Rise and shine."

Rodney pretended to snore.

"Odney's snoring," Michael said.

Casey looked over at Rodney, who at five years old still had the plump, rounded features of a baby, and for a small, blind moment he was on the verge of tears. "Time to get up," he said, and his voice left him.

"Let's stop Odney's snoring," Michael said.

Casey carried him over to Rodney's bed, and they wrestled

with Rodney, who tried to burrow under his blanket. "Odney," Casey said. "Where's Odney? Where did he go?"

Rodney called for his mother, laughing, and so his father let him squirm out of the bed and run, and pretended to chase him. Jean was in the kitchen, setting out bowls and boxes of cereal. "Casey," she said, "we don't have time for this." She sang it at him as she picked Rodney up and hugged him and carried him back to his room. "Now, get ready to go, Rodney, or Mommy won't be your protector when Daddy and Michael want to tease you."

"Blackmail," Casey said, delighted, following her into the kitchen. "A clear case of blackmail."

"Casey, really," she said.

He put his arms around her. She stood quite still and let him kiss her on the side of the face. "I'll get them going," he said. "Okay?"

"Yes," she said. "Okay."

He let go of her and she turned away, seemed already to have forgotten him. He had a sense of having badly misread her. "Jean?" he said.

"Oh, Casey, will you *please* get busy."

He went in and got the boys going. He was a little short with them both. His voice had just enough irritation for them to notice and grow quiet. They got themselves dressed, and he brushed Rodney's hair and straightened his collar while Michael made the beds. Then they all walked into the kitchen and sat at their places without speaking. Jean had poured cereal and milk and made toast. She sat eating her cereal and reading the back of the cereal box.

"All ready," Casey said.

She nodded at him. "I called Dana and told her I'd probably be late."

"You're not going to be late."

"I don't want to have to worry about it. They're putting that tarry stuff down on the roads today, remember? I'm going to miss it. I'm going to go around the long way."

"Okay. But it's not us making you late."

"I didn't say it was, Casey."

"I don't want toast," Rodney said.

"Eat your toast," Jean said.

"I don't like it."

"Last week you loved toast."

"Nu-*uh.*"

"Eat the toast, Rodney, or I'll spank you."

Michael said, "Really, Mom. He doesn't like toast."

"Eat the toast," Casey said. "Both of you. And Michael, you mind your own business."

Then they were all quiet. Outside, an already gray sky seemed to grow darker. The light above the kitchen table looked meager; it might even have flickered, and for a bad minute Casey felt as if the whole morning were something presented to him in the helplessness of sleep.

He used to think that one day he would look back on these years as the happiest time, frantic as things were: he and Jean would wonder how they got through it; Michael and Rodney, grown up, with children of their own, might listen to the stories and laugh. How each day of the week began with a rush to get everyone out the door on time. How even with two incomes they never had enough money. How time and the space to put things were so precious and how each weekend was like a sort of collapse, spent sleeping or watching too much television. And how when they *had* a little time to relax, they felt in some ways just as frantic about that, since it would so soon be gone. Jean was working full time as a dental assistant, cleaning people's teeth and telling them what they already knew — that failure to brush and floss meant gum disease; it amazed her that so many people seemed to think that no real effort or care was needed. The whole world looked lazy, negligent, to her. And then she would come home to all the things she lacked energy for. Casey, who spent his day in the offices of the Point Royal Ballet Company, worrying about grants, donations, ticket sales, and promotions, would do the cooking. It was what relaxed him. Even on those days when he had to work into the evening hours — nights when the company was performing or when he was involved with a special promotion — he liked to cook something when he got home. When Michael was a baby, Jean would sometimes get a baby sitter for him and take the train into town on the night of a performance. Casey would meet her at the station, which was only a block away from the hall. They would have dinner together, and then they would go to the ballet.

Once, after a performance, as they were leaving the hall, Jean turned to him and said, "You know something? You know where we are? We're where they all end up — you know, the lovers in the movies. When everything works out and they get together at the end — they're headed to where we are now."

"The ballet?" he said.

"No, no, no, no, no. Married. And having babies. That. Trying to keep everything together and make ends meet, and going to the ballet and having a baby sitter. Get it? This is where they all want to go in those movies."

He took in a deep breath of air. "We're at happily ever after, is what you're saying."

She laughed. "Casey, if only everyone was as happy as you are. I think I was complaining."

"We're smack dab in the middle of happily ever after," Casey said, and she laughed again. They walked on, satisfied. There was snow in the street, and she put her arm in his, tucked her chin under her scarf.

"Dear, good old Casey," she said. "We don't have to go to work in the morning, and we have a little baby at home, and we're going to go there now and make love. What more could anyone ask for?"

A moment later Casey said, "Happy?"

She stopped. "Don't ask me that all the time. Can't you tell if I'm happy or not?"

"I like to hear you say you are," Casey said, "that's all."

"Well, I *are.* Now walk." She pulled him, laughing, along the slippery sidewalk.

Sometimes, now that she's gone, he thinks of that night and wonders what could have been going on in her mind. He wonders how she remembers that night, if she thinks about it at all. It's hard to believe the marriage is over, because nothing has been settled or established; something got under his wife's skin, something changed for her, and she had to get off on her own to figure it all out.

He had other dreams before she left, and their similarity to the first one seemed almost occult to him. In one, he and Jean and the boys were walking along a quiet, tree-shaded road; the shade grew darker, and they came to another intersection. Somehow they had entered a congested city street. Tenements marched up a hill to the same misty nimbus of light. Casey recognized it, and the shift took place: a disturbance, the sudden pathology of the city — gunshots, shouts. A shadow figure arrived in a rusted-out truck and offered them a ride. The engine raced, and Casey tried to shield his family with his body — only the engine was at his back, and then a voice whispered, "Which of you wants it first?"

"A horrible dream," he said to Jean. "It keeps coming at me in different guises."

"We can't both be losing our minds," Jean said. She couldn't sleep nights. She would gladly take his nightmares if she could just sleep.

On the morning of the day she left, he woke to find her sitting at her dressing table, staring at herself. "Honey?" he said.

"Go back to sleep," she said. "It's early."

He watched her for a moment. She wasn't doing anything. She simply stared, as if she had seen something in the mirror. "Jean," he said, and she looked at him exactly the same way she had been looking at the mirror. He said, "Why don't we go to the performance tonight?"

"I'll be too tired by then," she said. Then she looked down and muttered, "I'm too tired right now."

She had awakened the boys; they were playing in their room. Their play grew louder, and then they were fighting. Michael screamed; Rodney had hit him over the head with a toy fire engine. It was a metal toy, and Michael sat bleeding in the middle of the bedroom floor. Both boys were crying as Casey made Michael stand and located the cut in his scalp. Jean had come with napkins and the hydrogen peroxide. She was very pale, all the color gone from her lips. "I'll do it," she said, when Casey tried to help. "Get Rodney out of here."

He took Rodney by the hand and walked him into the living room. Rodney still held the toy fire engine and was still crying.

Casey bent down and took the toy, and then moved to the sofa and sat down so that his son was facing him, standing between his knees. "Rodney," he said, "listen to me, son." The boy sniffled, and tears ran down his face. "Do you know you could have really hurt him, you could really have hurt your brother?"

"Well, he wouldn't leave me alone."

The fact that the child was unrepentant, even after having looked at his brother's blood, made Casey a little sick to his stomach. "That makes no difference," he said.

Jean came through from the hallway, carrying a bloody napkin. "Is it bad?" he said to her as she went into the kitchen. When she came back, she had a roll of paper towels. "He threw up, for Christ's sake. No, it's not bad. It's just a nick. But there's a lot of blood." She reached down and yanked Rodney away from his father. "Do you know what you did, young man? Do you? Do you?" She shook him. "Well, do you?"

"Hey," Casey said, "take it easy, honey."

"*Agh,*" she said, letting go of Rodney. "I can't stand it anymore."

Casey followed her into the bedroom, where she sat at the dressing table and began to brush her hair furiously.

"Jean," he said, "I wish we could talk."

"Oh, Jesus, Casey." She started to cry. "It's not even eight o'clock and we've already had this. It's too early for everything. I get to work and I'm exhausted. I don't even think I can stand it." She put the brush down and looked at herself, crying. "Look at me, would you? I look like death." He put his hands on her shoulders, and then Rodney was in the doorway.

"Mommy," Rodney whined.

Jean closed her eyes and shrieked, "Get out of here!"

Casey took the boy into his room. Michael was sitting on his bed, holding a napkin to his head. A little pool of sickness was on the floor at his feet. Casey got paper towels and cleaned it up. Michael looked at him with an expression of pain, of injured dignity. Rodney sat next to Michael and folded his small hands in his lap. Both boys were quiet, and Casey wondered if he could teach them something in this moment. But all he could think to say was, "No more fighting."

*

Dana is the wife of the dentist Jean has worked for since before she met Casey. The two women became friends while Dana was the dentist's receptionist. The dentist and his wife live in a large house on twenty acres not far from the city. They have an indoor pool and tennis courts, fireplaces in the bedrooms. They have plenty of space for Jean, who moved in on a Friday afternoon almost a month ago. That day she just packed a suitcase; she was going to spend a weekend at Dana's, to rest. It was going to be just a little relaxation, a little time away. Just the two days. But then, Sunday afternoon, she phoned to say she would be staying on through the week.

"You're kidding me," Casey said.

And she began to cry.

"Jean," he said, "for God's sake."

"I'm sorry," she said, crying. "I just need some time."

"Time," he said. "Jean. *Jean.*"

She breathed once, and when she spoke again he heard resolution in her voice, a definiteness that made his heart hurt. "I'll be over to pick up a few things tomorrow afternoon."

"Look," he said, "what is this? What about us? What about the boys?"

"I don't think you should let them see me tomorrow. This is hard enough for them."

"*What* is, Jean?"

She said nothing. He thought she might have hung up.

"Jean," he said. "Good Christ. Jean."

"Please don't do this," she said.

Casey shouted into the phone. "You're saying that to *me!*"

"I'm sorry," she said, and hung up.

He dialed Dana's number, and Dana answered.

"I want to speak to Jean, please."

"I'm sorry, Casey — she doesn't want to talk now."

"Would you —" he began.

"I'll ask her. I'm sorry, Casey."

"Ask her please to come to the phone."

He heard a shuffling sound, and he knew Dana was holding her hand over the receiver. He heard another shuffling, and Dana spoke to him. "I hate to be in the middle of this, Casey, but she doesn't want to talk now."

"Will you please ask her what I did."

"I can't do that. Really. Please, now."

"Just tell her I want — goddamn it — I want to know what I did."

He heard yet another shuffling sound, only this time Casey could hear Dana's voice, sisterly and exasperated and pleading.

"Dana," he said.

Silence.

"Dana."

And Dana's voice came back, very distraught, almost frightened. "Casey, I've never hung up on anyone in my life. I have a real fear of ever doing anything like that to anyone, but if you curse at me again, I will. I'll hang up on you. Jean isn't going to talk to anyone on the phone tonight. Really, she's not, and I don't see why I have to take the blame for it."

"Dana," he said, "I'm sorry. Tell her I'll be here tomorrow — with her children. Tell her that."

"I'll tell her."

"Goodbye, Dana." He put the receiver down. The boys' room was quiet, and he wondered how much they had heard, and — if they had heard enough — how much they had understood. He had dinner to make, but he'd done it before, so it offered no difficulty except that he prepared it knowing that his wife was having some sort of nervous breakdown and was unreachable in a way that made him angry as much as it frightened him. The boys didn't eat the fish he fried, or the potatoes he baked. They had been sneaking cookies all day while he watched football. He couldn't eat either, and so he didn't scold them for their lack of appetite and only reprimanded them mildly for their pilferage. Shortly after the dinner dishes were done, Michael began to cry. He said he had seen something on TV that made him sad, but he had been watching *Dukes of Hazzard* reruns.

"My little tenderhearted man," Casey said, putting his arms around the boy.

"Is Mommy at Dana's?" Rodney asked.

"Mommy had to go do something," Casey said.

He put them to bed. He wondered, as he tucked them in, if he should tell them now that their mother wouldn't be there in the morning. It seemed too much to tell a child before sleep. He stood in their doorway, imagining the shadow he made with the light behind him in the hall, and told them good night. Then he went into the living room and sat staring at the shifting figures on the television screen. Apparently, *The Dukes of Hazzard* was over; he could tell by the music that this was a serious show. A man with a gun chased another man with a gun. It was hard to tell which one was the hero, and Casey began to concentrate. Both men proved to be gangsters, and Jean, who used to say that sometimes she put TV on only for the voices, the company at night, had just told him that she was not coming home. He turned the gangsters off in midchase and stood for a moment, breathing fast. The boys were whispering and talking in the other room.

"Go to sleep in there," he said, keeping his voice steady. "Don't make me have to come in there." He listened. In a little while, he knew, they would begin it all again; they would keep it up until they got sleepy. He turned the television back on, so that they wouldn't have to worry that he might hear them, and then he lay back on the sofa, miserable, certain that he would be awake all night. But sometime toward the middle of the late movie he fell asleep and had another dream. It was, really, the same dream. He was with Jean and the kids in a building, and they were looking for a way out. One of the boys opened a door on empty space, and Casey, turning, understood that this place was hundreds of feet above the street. The wind blew at the opening like the wind at the open hatch of an airliner, and someone was approaching from behind them. He woke up sweating, disoriented, and saw that the TV was off. With a tremendous settling into him of relief, he thought that Jean had changed her mind and come home, had turned the TV off and left him there to sleep. But the bedroom was empty. "Jean?" he said into the dark. "Honey?" No one was there. He turned the light on.

"Daddy, you fell asleep watching television," Michael said from his room.

"Oh," Casey said. "Thanks, son. Can't you sleep?"

"Yeah."

"Well — good night, then."
"Night."

So Jean is gone. Casey keeps the house and the boys. He's told them their mother is away because these things happen; he's told them she needs a little time to herself. He hears Jean's explanations to him in everything he says, and he can't think of anything else to say. It's as if they are all waiting for her to get better, as if this trouble were something physiological, an illness that deprives them of her as she used to be. Casey talks to her on the phone now and then, and it's always oddly as if they have never known anything funny or embarrassing about each other, and yet are both now funny and embarrassed. They talk about the boys; they laugh too quickly and stumble over normal exchanges, like *Hello* and *How are you?* and *What have you been up to?* Jean has been working longer hours, making overtime from Dana's husband. Since Dana's husband's office is right downstairs, she can go for days without leaving the house if she wants to. She's feeling rested now. The overtime keeps her from thinking too much. Two or three times a week she goes over to the boys' school and spends some time with them; she's been a room mother since Michael started there, two years ago, and she still does her part whenever there's something for her to do. She tells Casey over the phone that Rodney's teacher seems to have no inkling that anything has changed at home.

Casey says, "What *has* changed at home, Jean?"

"Don't be ridiculous," she says.

The boys seem in fact to be taking everything in stride, although Casey sees a reticence about them now; he knows they're keeping their feelings mostly to themselves. Once in a while Rodney asks, quite shyly, when Mommy's coming home. Michael shushes him. Michael is being very grown up and understanding. He acts as if he's five years older than he is. At night he reads to Rodney from his Choose Your Own Adventure books. Casey sits in the living room and hears this. And when he has to work late, has to leave them with a baby sitter, he imagines the baby sitter hearing it, and feels soothed somehow — almost, somehow, consoled, as if simply to imagine such a scene is to bathe in its warmth: a slightly older boy reading to his brother, the two of them propped on the older brother's bed.

This is what he imagines tonight, the night of the last performance of *Swan Lake,* as he stands in the balcony and watches the hall fill up. The hall is sold out. Casey gazes at the crowd and the thought runs through his mind that all these people are carrying their own scenes, things that have nothing to do with ballet, or polite chatter, or finding a numbered seat. The fact that they all move as quietly and cordially to their places as they do seems miraculous to him. They are all in one situation or another, he thinks, and at that instant he catches sight of Jean; she's standing in the center aisle below him. Dana is with her. Jean is up on her toes, looking across to the other side of the hall, where Casey usually sits. She turns slowly, scanning the crowd. Casey imagines that he knows what her situation is. The crowd surges around her. And now Dana, also looking for him, finds him, touches Jean's shoulder, and actually points at him. He feels strangely inanimate, and he steps back a little, looks away from them. But this is too obviously a snub, and he knows it, and a moment later he steps forward again to see that Dana is alone down there, that Jean is already lost somewhere else in the crowd. Dana is gesturing for him to remain where he is. The orchestra members begin taking their places in the orchestra pit and tuning up; there's a smattering of applause. Casey finds a seat near the railing and sits with his hands folded in his lap, waiting. When this section of the balcony begins to fill up, he rises, looks for Dana again, and can't find her. Someone edges past him along the railing, so he moves to the side aisle, against the wall; he sees Jean come in, and watches her come around to where he is.

"I was hoping you'd be here tonight," she says, smiling. She touches his forearm and then leans up and gives him a dry little kiss on the mouth. "I wanted to see you."

"You can see me anytime," he says. He can't help the contentiousness in his voice.

"Casey," she says, "I know this is just the worst time. It's just that — well, Dana and I were coming to the performance, you know, and I started thinking how unfair I've been to you, and, and it just doesn't seem right."

Casey stands there looking at her.

"Can we talk a little," she says, "outside?"

He follows her up to the exit and out along the corridor to a little alcove leading to the restrooms; she finds a red velvet armchair, which she sits in, and then she pats her knees as if she expected him to settle into her lap. But she's only smoothing her skirt over her knees, stalling. Casey pulls another chair over and then stands behind it, feeling a dizzy, unfamiliar sense of suffocation. He thinks of swallowing air, pulls his tie loose, and breathes.

"Well," she says.

"The performance is going to start any minute," he says.

"I know," she says. "Casey —" She clears her throat, holding the backs of her fingers over her lips. It is a completely uncharacteristic gesture, and he wonders if she might have picked it up from Dana. "Well," she says, "I think we have to come to some sort of agreement about Michael and Rodney. I mean, seeing them in school" — she sits back, not looking at him — "you know, and talking on the phone and stuff — I mean, that's no good. I mean, none of this is any good. Dana and I have been talking about this quite a lot, Casey. And, you know, just because you and I aren't together anymore — that's no reason the kids should have to go without their mother."

"Jean," he says, "what — what —" He sits down. He wants to take her hand.

She says, "I think I ought to have them a while. A week or two. Dana and I have discussed it, and she's amenable to the idea. She has plenty of room and everything, and pretty soon I'll be — I'll be getting a place." She moves the tip of one finger along the soft surface of the chair arm, and seems to have to fight off tears.

He reaches over and takes her hand. "Honey," he says.

She pulls her hand away, quite gently, but with the firmness of someone for whom this affection is embarrassing. "Did you hear me, Casey? I'm getting a place of my own. We have to decide about the kids."

Casey stares at her, watches as she opens her purse and takes out a handkerchief to wipe her eyes; it comes to him very gradually that the orchestra has begun to play. She seems to notice it too now. She puts the handkerchief back in her purse and snaps it shut, and then seems to gather herself.

"Jean," he says, "for God's sweet sake."

"Oh, come on," she says, her eyes swimming, "you knew this was coming. How could you not know this was coming?"

"I don't believe this," he says. "You come here to tell me this. At my goddamn job." His voice has risen almost to a shout.

"Casey," she says.

"Okay," he says, rising. "I know you." It makes no sense. He tries to find something to say to her; he wants to say it all out in an orderly way that will show her. But he stammers. "You're not having a nervous breakdown," he hears himself tell her, and then he repeats it, almost as if he were trying to reassure her. "This is really it, then," he goes on. "You're not coming back."

She stands. It's as if she's not sure he's serious. She steps away from him and gives him a regretful look.

"Jean, we didn't even have an argument," he says. "I mean, what is this about?"

"Casey, I was so unhappy all the time. Don't you remember anything? Don't you see how it was? And I thought it was because I wasn't a good mother. I didn't even like the sound of their voices. But it was just unhappiness. I see them at school now and I love it. It's not a chore now. I work like a dog all day and I'm not tired. Don't you see? I feel good all the time now, and I don't even mind as much when I'm tired or worried."

"Then —" he begins. He can't say anything. He's left with the weight of himself, standing there before her.

"Try to understand, Casey. It was ruining me for everyone in that house. But it's okay now. I'm out of it and it's okay. I'm not dying anymore in those rooms and everything on my nerves and you around every corner —" She stops.

"You know what you sound like?" he says. "You sound ridiculous, that's what you sound like." And the ineptness of what he has just said, the stupid, helpless rage of it, produces in him a tottering moment of wanting to put his hands around her neck. The idea comes to him so clearly that his throat constricts and a fan of heat opens across the back of his head. He holds on to the chairback and seems to hear her say that she'll be in touch, through a lawyer if that will make it easier, about arrangements concerning the children. He knows it's not cruelty that brought her here to tell him a thing like this, it's cowardice.

"I wish I knew of some other way," she tells him, and then turns and walks along the corridor to the stairs and down. He imagines the look she'll give Dana when she gets to her seat; she'll be someone relieved of a situation, glad something's over with.

Back in the balcony, in the dark, he watches the figures leap and stutter and whirl on the stage, and when the performance ends, he watches the hall empty out. The musicians pack their music and instruments; the stage crew dismantles the set. When he finally rises, it's past midnight. Everyone's gone.

He makes his way home and, arriving, doesn't remember driving there. The baby sitter, a high school girl from up the street, is asleep on the sofa in the living room. He's much later than he said he would be. She hasn't heard him come in, and so he has to try to wake her without frightening her. He has this thought clear in his mind as he watches his hand roughly grasp her shoulder and hears himself say, loudly, "Get up!"

The girl opens her eyes and looks blankly at him, and then she screams. He would never have believed this of himself. She is sitting up now, still not quite awake, her hands flying up to her face. "I didn't mean to scare you," he says, but it's obvious that he did mean to scare her, and while she struggles to get her shoes on, her hands shaking, he counts out the money to pay her. He gives her an extra five dollars, and she thanks him for it in a tone that lets him know it mitigates nothing. When he moves to the door with her, she tells him she'll walk home; it's only up the block. Her every movement expresses her fear of him now. She lets herself out, and Casey stands in his doorway under the porch light and calls after her that he is so very sorry and he hopes she'll forgive him. She goes quickly along the street and is out of sight.

Casey stands there and looks at the place where she disappeared. Perhaps a minute goes by. Then he closes the door and walks back through the house, to the boys' room. Rodney is in

Michael's bed with Michael, the two of them sprawled there, arms and legs tangled, blankets knotted and wrapped, the sheet pulled from a corner of the mattress. It's as if this has all been dropped from a great, windy height. Casey kisses his sons, and then gets into Rodney's bed. He looks over at the shadowy figures across from him. The lights are still on in the hall and in the living room. He thinks of turning them off, and then dreams that he does, that he walks through the rooms, locking windows and closing doors. In this dream, he can't quite see, he can't open his eyes wide enough. He hears sounds. An intruder is in the house. Many intruders. He's in the darkest corner, and he can hear them moving toward him. He turns, still trying to get his eyes wide enough to let light in, only now something has changed: he knows he's dreaming. It comes to him with a rush of power that he's dreaming and can do anything now, anything he wants to. He luxuriates in this as he tries to hold on to it, feels how precarious it must be. He takes a step, and it is as quiet as the sound after death. He knows he can begin now, so he begins. He glides through the house, tracks the intruders down. He is relentless. He destroys them, one by one. He wins. He establishes order.

GISH JEN

The Water-Faucet Vision

FROM NIMROD

To PROTECT MY SISTER Mona and me from the pains — or, as they pronounced it, the "pins" — of life, my parents did their fighting in Shanghai dialect, which we didn't understand; and when my father one day pitched a brass vase through the kitchen window, my mother told us he had done it by accident.

"By accident?" said Mona.

My mother chopped the foot off a mushroom.

"By accident?" said Mona. "By *accident?*"

Later I tried to explain to her that she shouldn't have persisted like that, but it was hopeless.

"What's the matter with throwing things?" She shrugged. "He was *mad.*"

That was the difference between Mona and me: fighting was just fighting to her. If she worried about anything, it was only that she might turn out too short to become a ballerina, in which case she was going to be a piano player.

I, on the other hand, was going to be a martyr. I was in fifth grade then, and the hyperimaginative sort — the kind of girl who grows morbid in Catholic school, who longs to be chopped or frozen to death but then has nightmares about it from which she wakes up screaming and clutching a stuffed bear. It was not a bear that I clutched, though, but a string of three malachite beads that I had found in the marsh by the old aqueduct one day. Apparently once part of a necklace, they were each wonderfully striated and swirled, and slightly humped toward the center, like a jellyfish; so that if I squeezed one, it would slip smoothly away, with a grace that altogether enthralled and — on those dream-harrowed nights — soothed me, soothed me as nothing had before or has since. Not that I've lacked occasion for soothing: though it's been four months since my mother died, there are still nights when sleep stands away from me, stiff as a well-paid sentry. But that is another story. Back then I had my malachite beads, and if I worried them long and patiently enough, I was sure to start feeling better, more awake, even a little special — imagining, as I liked to, that my nightmares were communications from the Almighty Himself, preparation for my painful destiny. Discussing them with Patty Creamer, who had also promised her life to God, I called them "almost visions"; and Patty, her mouth wadded with the three or four sticks of Doublemint she always seemed to have going at once, said, "I bet you'll be doin' miracleth by seventh grade."

Miracles. Today Patty laughs to think she ever spent good time stewing on such matters, her attention having long turned to rugs, and artwork, and antique Japanese bureaus — things she believes in.

"A good bureau's more than just a bureau," she explained last time we had lunch. "It's a hedge against life. I tell you: if there's one thing I believe, it's that cheap stuff's just money out the window. Nice stuff, on the other hand — now that you can always cash out, if life gets rough. *That* you can count on."

In fifth grade, though, she counted on different things.

"You'll be doing miracles too," I told her, but she shook her shaggy head and looked doleful.

"Na' me," she chomped. "Buzzit's okay. The kin' things I like, prayers work okay on."

"Like?"

"Like you 'member that dreth I liked?"

She meant the yellow one, with the crisscross straps.

"Well gueth what."

"Your mom got it for you."

She smiled. "And I only jutht prayed for it for a week," she said.

As for myself, though, I definitely wanted to be able to perform a wonder or two. Miracle-working! It was the carrot of carrots: it kept me doing my homework, taking the sacraments;

it kept me mournfully on key in music hour, while my classmates hiccuped and squealed their carefree hearts away. Yet I couldn't have said what I wanted such powers *for,* exactly. That is, I thought of them the way one might think of, say, an ornamental sword — as a kind of collectible, which also happened to be a means of defense.

But then Patty's father walked out on her mother, and for the first time, there was a miracle I wanted to do. I wanted it so much I could see it: Mr. Creamer made into a spitball; Mr. Creamer shot through a straw into the sky; Mr. Creamer unrolled and replumped, plop back on Patty's doorstep. I would've cleaned out his mind and given him a shave en route. I would've given him a box of peanut fudge, tied up with a ribbon, to present to Patty with a kiss.

But instead all I could do was try to tell her he'd come back.

"He will not, he will not!" she sobbed. "He went on a boat to Rio Deniro. To Rio Deniro!"

I tried to offer her a stick of gum, but she wouldn't take it.

"He said he would rather look at water than at my mom's fat face. He said he would rather look at water than at me." Now she was really wailing, and holding her ribs so tightly that she almost seemed to be hurting herself — so tightly that just looking at her arms wound around her like snakes made my heart feel squeezed.

I patted her on the arm. A one-winged pigeon waddled by.

"He said I wasn't even his kid, he said I came from Uncle Johnny. He said I was garbage, just like my mom and Uncle Johnny. He said I wasn't even his kid, he said I wasn't his Patty, he said I came from Uncle Johnny!"

"From your Uncle Johnny?" I said stupidly.

"From Uncle Johnny," she cried. "From Uncle Johnny!"

"He said that?" I said. Then, wanting to go on, to say *something,* I said, "Oh Patty, don't cry."

She kept crying.

I tried again. "Oh Patty, don't cry," I said. Then I said, "Your dad was a jerk anyway.

The pigeon produced a large runny dropping.

It was a good twenty minutes before Patty was calm enough for me just to run to the girls' room to get her some toilet paper;

and by the time I came back she was sobbing again, saying "to Rio Deniro, to Rio Deniro" over and over again, as though the words had stuck in her and couldn't be gotten out. As we had missed the regular bus home and the late bus too, I had to leave her a second time to go call my mother, who was mad only until she heard what had happened. Then she came and picked us up, and bought us each a Fudgsicle.

Some days later, Patty and I started a program to work on getting her father home. It was a serious business. We said extra prayers, and lit votive candles; I tied my malachite beads to my uniform belt, fondling them as though they were a rosary, I a nun. We even took to walking about the school halls with our hands folded — a sight so ludicrous that our wheeze of a principal personally took us aside one day.

"I must tell you," she said, using her nose as a speaking tube, "that there is really no need for such peee-ity."

But we persisted, promising to marry God and praying to every saint we could think of. We gave up gum, then gum and Slim Jims both, then gum and Slim Jims and ice cream — and when even that didn't work, we started on more innovative things. The first was looking at flowers. We held our hands beside our eyes like blinders as we hurried by the violets by the flagpole, the window box full of tulips outside the nurse's office. Next it was looking at boys: Patty gave up angel-eyed Jamie Halloran and I, gymnastic Anthony Rossi. It was hard, but in the end our efforts paid off. Mr. Creamer came back a month later, and though he brought with him nothing but dysentery, he was at least too sick to have all that much to say.

Then, in the course of a fight with my father, my mother somehow fell out of their bedroom window.

Recently — thinking a mountain vacation might cheer me — I sublet my apartment to a handsome but somber newlywed couple, who turned out to be every bit as responsible as I'd hoped. They cleaned out even the eggshell chips I'd sprinkled around the base of my plants as fertilizer, leaving behind only a shiny silverplate cake server and a list of their hopes and goals for the summer. The list, tacked precariously to the back of the kitchen door, began with a fervent appeal to God to help them get their wedding thank-yous written in three weeks or less. (You could see they had originally written "two weeks" but scratched it out — no miracles being demanded here.) It went on:

> Please help us, Almighty Father in Heaven Above, to get Ann a teaching job within a half-hour drive of here in a nice neighborhood.
> Please help us, Almighty Father in Heaven Above, to get John a job doing anything where he won't strain his back and that is within a half-hour drive of here.
> Please help us, Almighty Father in Heaven Above, to get us a car.
> Please help us, A.F. in H.A., to learn French.
> Please help us, A.F. in H.A., to find seven dinner recipes that cost less than 60 cents a serving and can be made in a half-hour. And that don't have tomatoes, since You in Your Heavenly Wisdom made John allergic.
> Please help us, A.F. in H.A., to avoid books in this apartment such as You in Your Heavenly Wisdom allowed John, for Your Heavenly Reasons, to find three nights ago (June 2nd).

Et cetera. In the left-hand margin they kept score of how they had fared with their requests, and it was heartening to see that nearly all of them were marked "Yes! Praise the Lord" (sometimes shortened to PTL), with the sole exception of learning French, which was mysteriously marked "No! PTL to the Highest."

That note touched me. Strange and familiar both, it seemed like it had been written by some cousin of mine — some cousin who had stayed home to grow up, say, while I went abroad and learned what I had to, though the learning was painful. This, of course, is just a manner of speaking; in fact I did my growing up at home, like anybody else.

But the learning *was* painful: I never knew exactly how it happened that my mother went hurtling through the air that night years ago, only that the wind had been chopping at the house, and that the argument had started about the state of the roof. Someone had been up to fix it the year before, but it wasn't a roofer, it was some man my father had insisted could do just as good a job for a quarter of the price. And maybe he could have, had he not somehow managed to step through a knot in the wood under the shingles and break his uninsured ankle.

Now the shingles were coming loose again, and the attic insulation was mildewing besides, and my father was wanting to sell the house altogether, which he said my mother had wanted to buy so she could send pictures of it home to her family in China.

"The Americans have a saying," he said. "They saying, 'You have to keep up with Jones family.' I'm saying if Jones family in Shanghai, you can send any picture you want, *an-y* picture. Go take picture of those rich guys' house. You want to act like rich guys, right? Go take picture of those rich guys' house."

At that point my mother sent Mona and me to wash up, and started speaking Shanghaiese. They argued for some time in the kitchen while we listened from the top of the stairs, our faces wedged between the bumpy Spanish scrolls of the wrought iron railing. First my mother ranted, then my father, then they both ranted at once until finally there was a thump, followed by a long quiet.

"Do you think they're kissing now?" said Mona. "I bet they're kissing, like this." She pursed her lips like a fish and was about to put them to the railing when we heard my mother locking the back door. We hightailed it into bed; my parents creaked up the stairs. Everything at that point seemed fine. Once in their bedroom, though, they started up again, first softly, then louder and louder, until my mother turned on a radio to try to disguise the noise. A door slammed; they began shouting at one another; another door slammed; a shoe or something banged the wall behind Mona's bed.

"How're we supposed to *sleep?*" said Mona, sitting up.

There was another thud, more yelling in Shanghaiese, and then my mother's voice pierced the wall, in English. "So what you want I should do? Go to work like Theresa Lee?"

My father rumbled something back.

"You think you're big shot because you have job, right? You're big shot, but you never get promotion, you never get raise. All I do is spend money, right? So what do you do, you tell me. So what do you do!"

Something hit the floor so hard that our room shook.

"So kill me," screamed my mother. "You know what you are? You are failure. Failure! You are failure!"

Then there was a sudden, terrific, bursting crash — and after it, as if on a bungled cue, the serene blare of an a cappella soprano, picking her way down a scale.

By the time Mona and I knew to look out the window, a neighbor's pet beagle was already on the scene, sniffing and barking at my mother's body, his tail crazy with excitement; then he was barking at my stunned and trembling father, at the shrieking ambulance, the police, at crying Mona in her bunny-footed pajamas, and at me, barefoot in the cold grass, squeezing her shoulder with one hand and clutching my malachite beads with the other.

My mother wasn't dead, only unconscious, the paramedics figured that out right away, but there was blood everywhere, and though they were reassuring about her head wounds as they strapped her to the stretcher, commenting also on how small she was, how delicate, how light, my father kept saying, "I killed her, I killed her" as the ambulance screeched and screeched headlong, forever, to the hospital. I was afraid to touch her, and glad of the metal rail between us, even though its sturdiness made her seem even frailer than she was; I wished she was bigger, somehow, and noticed, with a pang, that the new red slippers we had given her for Mother's Day had been lost somewhere along the way. How much she seemed to be leaving behind as we careened along — still not there, still not there — Mona and Dad and the medic and I taking up the whole ambulance, all the room, so there was no room for anything else; no room even for my mother's real self, the one who should have been pinching the color back to my father's grey face, the one who should have been calming Mona's cowlick — the one who should have been bending over us, to help us to be strong, to help us get through, even as we bent over her.

Then suddenly we were there, the glowing square of the emergency room entrance opening like the gates of heaven; and immediately the talk of miracles began. Alive, a miracle. No bones broken, a miracle. A miracle that the hemlocks cushioned her fall, a miracle that they hadn't been trimmed in a year and a half. It was a miracle that all that blood, the blood that had seemed that night to be everywhere, was from one shard of glass, a single shard, can you imagine, and as for the gash in her head, the scar would be covered by hair. The next day my mother cheerfully described just how she would part it so that nothing would show at all.

"You're a lucky duck-duck," agreed Mona, helping herself, with a little *pirouette,* to the cherry atop my mother's chocolate pudding.

That wasn't enough for me, though. I was relieved, yes, but what I wanted by then was a real miracle, not for her simply to have survived, but for the whole thing never to have happened — for my mother's head never to have had to be shaved and bandaged like that, for her high, proud forehead never to have been swollen down over her eyes, for her face and neck and hands never to have been painted so many shades of blue-black, and violet, and chartreuse. I still want those things — for my parents not to have had to live with this affair like a prickle bush between them, for my father to have been able to look my mother in her swollen eyes and curse the madman, the monster that could have dared do this to the woman he loved. I wanted to be able to touch my mother without shuddering, to be able to console my father, to be able to get that crash out of my head, the sound of that soprano — so many things that I didn't know how to pray for them, that I wouldn't have known where to start even if I had the power to work miracles, right there, right then.

A week later, when my mother was home, and her head beginning to bristle with new hairs, I lost my malachite beads. I had been carrying them in a white cloth pouch that Patty had given me, and was swinging the pouch on my pinky on my way home from school, when I swung just a bit too hard, and it went sailing in a long arc through the air, whooshing like a perfectly thrown basketball through one of the holes of a nearby sewer. There was no chance of fishing it out: I looked and looked, crouching on the sticky pavement until the asphalt had crazed the skin of my hands and knees, but all I could discern was an evil-smelling musk, glassy and smug and impenetrable.

My loss didn't quite hit me until I was home, but then it produced an agony all out of proportion to my string of pretty beads. I hadn't cried at all during my mother's accident, and now I was crying all afternoon, all through dinner, and then after dinner too, crying past the point where I knew what I was crying for, wishing dimly that I had my beads to hold, wishing dimly that I could pray but refusing, refusing, I didn't know why, until I finally fell into an exhausted sleep on the couch, where my parents left me for the night — glad, no doubt, that one of the more tedious of my childhood crises seemed to be finally winding off the reel of life, onto the reel of memory. They covered me, and somehow grew a pillow under my head, and, with uncharacteristic disregard for the living room rug, left some milk and pecan sandies on the coffee table, in case I woke up hungry. Their thoughtfulness was prescient: I did wake up in the early part of the night; and it was then, amid the unfamiliar sounds and shadows of the living room, that I had what I was sure was a true vision.

Even now what I saw retains an odd clarity: the requisite strange light flooding the room, first orange, and then a bright yellow-green, then a crackling bright burst like a Roman candle going off near the piano. There was a distinct smell of coffee, and a long silence. The room seemed to be getting colder. Nothing. A creak; the light starting to wane, then waxing again, brilliant pink now. Still nothing. Then, as the pink started to go a little purple, a perfectly normal middle-aged man's voice, speaking something very like pig Latin, told me quietly not to despair, not to despair, my beads would be returned to me.

That was all. I sat a moment in the dark, then turned on the light, gobbled down the cookies — and in a happy flash understood I was so good, really, so near to being a saint that my malachite beads would come back through the town water system. All I had to do was turn on all the faucets in the house, which I did, one by one, stealing quietly into the bathroom and kitchen and basement. The old spigot by the washing machine was too gunked up to be coaxed very far open, but that didn't matter. The water didn't have to be full blast, I understood that. Then I gathered together my pillow and blanket and trundled up to my bed to sleep.

By the time I woke up in the morning I knew that my beads hadn't shown up, but when I knew it for certain, I was still disappointed; and as if that weren't enough, I had to face my parents and sister, who were all abuzz with the mystery of the faucets. Not knowing what else to do, I, like a puddlebrain, told them the truth. The results were predictably painful.

"Callie had a *vision,*" Mona told everyone at the bus stop. "A vision with lights, and sinks in it!"

Sinks, visions. I got it all day, from my parents, from my classmates, even some sixth and seventh graders. Someone drew a cartoon of me with a halo over my head in one of the girls' room stalls; Anthony Rossi made gurgling noises as he walked on his hands at recess. Only Patty tried not to laugh, though even she was something less than unalloyed understanding.

"I don' think miracles are thupposed to happen in *thewers,*" she said.

Such was the end of my saintly ambitions. It wasn't the end of all holiness; the ideas of purity and goodness still tippled my brain, and over the years I came slowly to grasp of what grit true faith was made. Last night, though, when my father called to say that he couldn't go on living in our old house, that he was going to move to a smaller place, another place, maybe a condo — he didn't know how, or where — I found myself still wistful for the time religion seemed all I wanted it to be. Back then the world was a place that could be set right: one had only to direct the hand of the Almighty and say, just here, Lord, we hurt here — and here, and here, and here.

MAVIS GALLANT

Dédé

FROM THE NEW YORKER

PASCAL BROUET is fourteen now. He used to attend a lycée, but after his parents found out about the dealers in the street, outside the gates, they changed him to a private school. Here the situation is about the same, but he hasn't said so; he does not want to be removed again, this time perhaps to a boarding establishment, away from Paris, with nothing decent to eat and lights-out at ten. He would not describe himself as contriving or secretive. He tries to avoid drawing attention to the Responsibility clause in the treaty that governs peace between generations.

Like his father, the magistrate, he will offer neutrality before launching into dissent. "I'm ready to admit," he will begin, or "I don't want to take over the whole conversation . . . " Sometimes the sentence comes to nothing. Like his father, he lets his eyelids droop, tries to speak lightly and slowly. The magistrate is famous for fading out of a discussion by slow degrees. At one time he was said to be the youngest magistrate ever to fall asleep in court: he would black out when he thought he wasn't needed and snap to just as the case turned around. Apparently, he never missed a turning. He has described his own mind to Pascal: it is like a superlatively smooth car with an invisible driver in control. The driver is the magistrate's unconscious will.

To Pascal a mind is a door, ajar or shut. His grades are good, but this side of brilliant. He has a natural gift — a precise, perfectly etched memory. How will he use it? He thinks he could as easily become an actor as a lawyer. When he tells his parents so, they seem not to mind. He could turn into an actor-manager, with a private theater of his own, or the director of one of the great national theaters, commissioning new work, refurbishing the classics, settling questions at issue with a word or two.

The Brouets are tolerant parents, ready for anything. They met for the first time in May of 1968, a few yards away from a barricade of burning cars. She had a stone in her hand; when she saw him looking at her, she put it down. They walked up the Boulevard Saint-Michel together, and he told her his plan for reforming the judiciary. He was a bit older, about twenty-six. Answering his question, she said she was from Alsace. He reminded her how the poet Paul Éluard had picked up his future wife in the street, on a rainy evening. She was from Alsace, too, and starving, and in a desperate, muddled, amateurish way pretending to be a prostitute.

Well, this was not quite the same story. In 1968 the future Mme. Brouet was studying to be an analyst of handwriting, with employment to follow — so she had been promised — in the personnel section of a large department store. In the meantime, she was staying with a Protestant Reformed Church pastor and his family in Rue Fustel-de-Coulanges. She had been on her way home to dinner when she stopped to pick up the stone. She had a mother in Alsace, and a little brother, Amedée—Dédé."

"Sylvie and I have known both sides of the barricades," the magistrate likes to say, now. What he means is that they cannot be crowded into a political corner. The stone in the hand has made her a rebel, at least in his recollections. She never looks at a newspaper, because of her reputation for being against absolutely everything. So he says, but perhaps it isn't exact: she looks at the pages marked "Culture," to see what is on at the galleries. He reads three morning papers at breakfast and, if he has time, last evening's *Le Monde.* Reading, he narrows his eyes. Sometimes he looks as though everything he thinks and believes had been translated into a foreign language and, suddenly, back again.

When Pascal was about nine, his father said, "What do you suppose you will do, one day?"

They were at breakfast. Pascal's Uncle Amedée was there.

Like everyone else, Pascal called him Dédé. Pascal looked across at him and said, "I want to be a bachelor, like Dédé."

His mother moaned, "Oh, no!" and covered her face. The magistrate waited until she had recovered before speaking. She looked up, smiling, a bit embarrassed. Then he explained, slowly and carefully, that Dédé was too young to be considered a bachelor. He was a student, a youth. "A student, a student," he repeated, thinking perhaps that if he kept saying it Dédé would study hard.

Dédé had a button of a nose that looked ridiculous on someone so tall, and a mass of curly fair hair. Because of the hair, the magistrate could not take him seriously; his private name for Dédé was "Harpo."

That period of Pascal's life, nine rounding to ten, was also the autumn before an important election year. The elections were five months off, but already people argued over dinner and Sunday lunch. One Sunday in October, the table was attacked by wasps, drawn in from the garden by a dish of sliced melon — the last of the season, particularly fragrant and sweet. The French doors to the garden stood open. Sunlight entered and struck through the wine decanters and dissolved in the waxed tabletop in pale red and gold. From his place, Pascal could see the enclosed garden, the apartment blocks behind it, a golden poplar tree, and the wicker chairs where the guests, earlier, had sat with their drinks.

There were two couples: the Turbins, older than Pascal's parents, and the Chevallier-Crochets, who had not been married long. Mme. Chevallier-Crochet attended an art-history course with Pascal's mother, on Thursday afternoons. They had never been here before, and were astonished to discover a secret garden in Paris with chairs, grass, a garden rake, a tree. Just as their expression of amazement was starting to run thin and patches of silence appeared, Abelarda, newly come from Cádiz, appeared at the door and called them to lunch. She said, "It's ready," though that was not what Mme. Brouet had asked her to say; at least, not that way. The guests got up, without haste. They were probably as hungry as Pascal but didn't want it to show. Abelarda went on standing, staring at the topmost leaves of the poplar, trying to remember what she ought to have said.

A few minutes later, just as they were starting to eat their melon, wasps came thudding against the table, like pebbles thrown. The adults froze, as though someone had drawn a gun. Pascal knew that sitting still was a good way to be stung. If you waved your napkin, shouted orders, the wasps might fly away. But he was not expected to give instructions; he was here, with adults, to discover how conversation is put together, how to sound interesting without being forward, amusing without seeming familiar. At that moment, Dédé did an unprecedented and courageous thing: he picked up the platter of melon, crawling with wasps, and took it outside, as far as the foot of the tree. And came back to applause: at least, his sister clapped, and young Mme. Chevallier-Crochet cried, "Bravo! Bravo!"

Dédé smiled, but, then, he was always smiling. His sister wished he wouldn't; the smile gave his brother-in-law another reason for calling him Harpo. Sitting down, he seemed to become entwined with his chair. He was too tall ever to be comfortable. He needed larger chairs, tables that were both higher and wider, so that he would not bump his knees, or put his feet on the shoes of the lady sitting opposite.

Pascal's father just said, "So, no more melon." It was something he particularly liked, and there might be none now until next summer. If Dédé had asked his opinion instead of jumping up so impulsively, he might have said, "Just leave it," and taken a chance on getting stung.

Well; no more for anyone. The guests sat a little straighter, waiting for the next course: beef, veal, or mutton, or the possibility of duck. Pascal's mother asked him to shut the French doors. She did not expect another wasp invasion, but there might be strays. Mme. Chevallier-Crochet remarked that Pascal was tall for his age, then asked what his age was. "He is almost ten," said Mme. Brouet, looking at her son with some wonder. "I can hardly believe it. I don't understand time."

Mme. Turbin said she did not have to consult a watch to know the exact time. It must be a quarter to two now. If it was, her daughter Brigitte had just landed in Salonika. Whenever her daughter boarded a plane, Mme. Turbin accompanied her in her mind, minute by minute.

"Thessalonika," M. Turbin explained.

The Chevallier-Crochets had spent their honeymoon in Sicily. If they had it to do over again, they said, they would change their minds and go to Greece.

Mme. Brouet said they would find it very different from Sicily. Her mind was on something else entirely: Abelarda. Probably Abelarda had expected them to linger over a second helping of melon. Perhaps she was sitting in the kitchen with nothing to do, listening to a program of Spanish music on the radio. Mme. Brouet caught a wide-awake glance from her husband, interpreted it correctly, and went out to the kitchen to see.

One of the men turned to M. Brouet, wondering if he could throw some light on the election candidates: unfortunate stories were making the rounds. Pascal's father was often asked for information. He had connections in Paris, like stout ropes attached to the upper civil service and to politics. One sister was married to a cabinet minister's chief of staff. Her children were taken to school in a car with a red-white-and-blue emblem. The driver could park wherever he liked. The magistrate's grandfather had begun as a lieutenant in the cavalry and died of a heart attack the day he was appointed head of a committee to oversee war graves. His portrait, as a child on a pony, hung in the dining room. The artist was said to have copied a photograph; that was why the pony looked so stiff and the colors were wrong. The room Pascal slept in had been that child's summer bedroom; the house had once been a suburban, almost a country dwelling. Now the road outside was like a highway; even with the doors shut they could hear Sunday traffic pouring across an intersection, on the way to Boulogne and the Saint-Cloud bridge.

The magistrate replied that he did not want to take over the whole conversation but he did feel safe in saying this: Several men, none of whom he had any use for, were now standing face to face. Sometimes he felt like washing his hands of the future. (Saying this, he slid his hands together.) However, before his guests could show shock or disappointment, he added, "But one cannot remain indifferent. This is an old country, an ancient civilization." Here his voice faded out. "We owe . . . One has to . . . A certain unbreakable loyalty . . . " And he placed his hands on the table, calmly, one on each side of his plate.

At that moment Mme. Brouet returned, her cheeks and forehead pink, as if she had got too close to a hot oven. Abelarda came along next, to change the plates. She was pink in the face, too.

Pascal saw the candidates lined up like rugby teams. He was allowed to watch rugby on television. His parents did not care for soccer: the players showed off, received absurd amounts of money just for kicking a ball, and there was something the matter with their shorts. "With all that money, they could buy clothes that fit," Pascal's mother had said. Rugby players were different. They were the embodiment of action and its outcome, in an ideal form. They got muddied for love of sport. France had won the Five Nations tournament, beating even the dreaded Welsh, whose fans always set up such eerie wailing in the stands. Actually, they were trying to sing. It must have been the way the early Celts joined in song before the Roman conquest, the magistrate had told Pascal.

No one at table could have made a rugby team. They were too thin. Dédé was a broomstick. Of course, Pascal played soccer at school, in a small cement courtyard. The smaller boys, aged six, seven, tried to imitate Michel Platini, but they got everything wrong. They would throw the ball high in the air and kick at nothing, leg crossed over the chest, arms spread.

The magistrate kept an eye on the dish Abelarda was now handing around: partridges in a nest of shredded cabbage — an entire surprise. Pascal looked over at Dédé, who sat smiling to himself, for no good reason. (If Pascal had continued to follow his father's gaze he might be told gently, later, that one does not stare at food.)

There was no more conversation to be had from M. Brouet, for the moment. Helping themselves to partridge, the guests told one another stories everybody knew. All the candidates were in a declining state of health and morality. One had to be given injections of ground-up Japanese seaweed; otherwise he lost consciousness, sometimes in the midst of a sentence. Others kept going on a mixture of cocaine and vitamin C. Their private means had been acquired by investing in gay bars and foreign wars, and evicting the poor. Only the Ministry of the Interior knew the nature and extent of their undercover financial dealings. And yet some of these men had to be found better than others, if democracy was not to come to a standstill. As M. Brouet had pointed out, one cannot wash one's hands of the future.

The magistrate had begun to breathe evenly and deeply. Perhaps the sunlight beating on the panes of the shut doors made him feel drowsy.

"Etienne is never quite awake or asleep," said his wife, meaning it as a compliment.

She was proud of everyone related to her, even by marriage, and took pride in her father, who had run away from home and family to live in New Caledonia. He had shown spirit and a sense of initiative, like Dédé with the wasps. (Now that Pascal is fourteen, he has heard this often.) But pride is not the same as helpless love. The person she loved best, in that particular way, was Dédé.

Dédé had come to stay with the Brouets because his mother, Pascal's grandmother, no longer knew what to do with him. He was never loud or abrupt, never forced an opinion on anyone, but he could not be left without guidance — even though he could vote, and was old enough to do some of the things he did, such as sign his mother's name to a check. (Admittedly, only once.) This was his second visit; the first, last spring, had not sharpened his character, in spite of his brother-in-law's conversation, his sister's tender anxiety, the sense of purpose to be gained by walking his little nephew to school. Sent home to Colmar (firm handshake with the magistrate at the Gare de l'Est, tears and chocolates from his sister, presentation of an original drawing from Pascal), he had accidentally set fire to his mother's kitchen, then to his own bedclothes. Accidents, the insurance people had finally agreed, but they were not too pleased. His mother was at the present time under treatment for exhaustion, with a private nurse to whom she made expensive presents. She had about as much money sense as Harpo, the magistrate said. (Without lifting his head from his homework, Pascal could take in nearly everything uttered in the hall, on the stairs, and in two adjacent rooms.)

When they were all four at breakfast Mme. Brouet repeated

her brother's name in every second sentence: wondering if Dédé wanted more toast, if someone would please pass him the strawberry jam, if he had enough blankets on his bed, if he needed an extra key. (He was a great loser of keys.) The magistrate examined his three morning papers. He did not want to have to pass anything to Harpo. Mme. Brouet was really just speaking to herself.

That autumn, Dédé worked at a correspondence course, in preparation for a competitive civil-service examination. If he was among the first dozen, eliminating perhaps hundreds of clever young men and women, he would be eligible for a post in the nation's railway system. His work would be indoors, of course; no one expected him to be out in all weathers, trudging alongside the tracks, looking for something to repair. Great artists, leaders of honor and reputation, had got their start at a desk in a railway ofice. Pascal's mother, whenever she said this, had to pause, as she searched her mind for their names. The railway had always been a seedbed of outstanding careers, she would continue. She would then point out to Dédé that their father had been a supervisor of public works.

After breakfast Dédé wound a long scarf around his neck and walked Pascal to school. He had invented an apartment with movable walls. Everything one needed could be got within reach by pulling a few levers or pressing a button. You could spend your life in the middle of a room without having to stir. He and Pascal refined the invention; that was what they talked about, on the way to Pascal's school. Then Dédé came home and studied until lunchtime. In the afternoon he drew new designs of his idea. Perhaps he was lonely. The doctor looking after his mother had asked him not to call or write, for the moment.

Pascal's mother believed Dédé needed a woman friend, even though he was not ready to get married. Pascal heard her say, "Art and science, architecture, culture." These were the factors that could change Dédé's life, and to which he would find access through the right kind of woman. Mme. Brouet had someone in mind — Mlle. Turbin, who held a position of some responsibility in a travel agency. She was often sent abroad to rescue visitors or check their complaints. Today's lunch had been planned around her, but at the last minute she had been called to Greece, where a tourist, bitten by a dog, had received an emergency specific for rabies, and believed the Greeks were trying to kill him.

Her parents had come, nevertheless. It was a privilege to meet the magistrate and to visit a rare old house, one of the last of its kind still in private hands. Before lunch Mme. Turbin had asked to be shown around. Mme. Brouet conducted a tour for the women, taking care not to open the door to Dédé's room: there had been a fire in a wastepaper basket only a few hours before, and everything in there was charred or singed or soaked.

At lunch, breaking out of politics, M. Turbin described the treatment the tourist in Salonika had most probably received: it was the same the world over, and incurred the use of a long needle. He held out his knife, to show the approximate length.

"Stop!" cried Mme. Chevallier-Crochet. She put her napkin over her nose and mouth; all they could see was her wild eyes. Everyone stopped eating, forks suspended — all but the magistrate, who was pushing aside shreds of cabbage to get at the last of the partridge.

M. Chevallier-Crochet explained that his wife was afraid of needles. He could not account for it; he had not known her as a child. It seemed to be a singular fear, one that set her apart. Meantime, his wife closed her eyes; opened them, though not as wide as before; placed her napkin neatly across her lap; and swallowed a piece of bread.

M. Turbin said he was sorry. He had taken it for granted that any compatriot of the great Louis Pasteur must have seen a needle or two. Needles were only a means to an end.

Mme. Brouet glanced at her husband, pleading for help, but he had just put a bite of food into his mouth. He was always last to be served when there were guests, and everything got to him cold. That was probably why he ate in such a hurry. He shrugged, meaning, Change the subject.

"Pascal," she said, turning to him. At last, she thought of something to say: "Do you remember Mlle. Turbin? Charlotte Turbin?"

"Brigitte?" said Pascal.

"I'm sure you remember," she said, not listening at all. "In the travel agency, on Rue Caumartin?"

"She gave me the corrida poster," said Pascal, wondering how this had slipped her mind.

"We went to see her, you and I, the time we wanted to go to Egypt? Now do you remember?"

"We never went to Egypt."

"No. Papa couldn't get away just then, so we finally went back to Deauville, where Papa has so many cousins. So you do remember Mlle. Turbin, with the pretty auburn hair?"

"Chestnut," said the two Turbins, together.

"My sister," said Dédé, all of a sudden, indicating her with his left hand, the right clutching a wine glass. "Before she got married, my mother told me . . ." The story, whatever it was, engulfed him in laughter. "A dog tried to bite her," he managed to say.

"You can tell us about it another time," said his sister.

He continued to laugh, softly, just to himself, while Abelarda changed the plates again.

The magistrate examined his clean new plate. No immediate surprises: salad, another plate, cheese, a dessert plate. His wife had given up on Mlle. Turbin. Really, it was his turn now, her silence said.

"I may have mentioned this before," said the magistrate. "And I would not wish to keep saying the same things over and over. But I wonder if you agree that the pivot of French politics today is no longer in France."

"The Middle East," said M. Turbin, nodding his head.

"Washington," said M. Chevallier-Crochet. "Washington calls Paris every morning and says, Do this, Do that."

"The Middle East and the Soviet Union," said M. Turbin.

"There," said M. Brouet. "We are all in agreement."

Many of the magistrate's relatives and friends thought he should be closer to government, to power. But his wife wanted him to stay where he was and get his pension. After he retired, when Pascal was grown, they would visit Tibet and the north of China, and winter in Kashmir.

"You know, this morning —" said Dédé, getting on with something that was on his mind.

"Another time," said his sister. "Never mind about this morning. It is all forgotten. Etienne is speaking, now."

This morning! The guests had no idea, couldn't begin to imagine what had taken place, here, in the dining room, at this very table. Dédé had announced, overjoyed, "I've got my degree." For Dédé was taking a correspondence course that could not lead to a degree of any kind. It must have been just his way of trying to stop studying so that he could go home.

"Degree?" The magistrate folded yesterday's *Le Monde* carefully before putting it down. "What do you mean, degree?"

Pascal's mother got up to make fresh coffee. "I'm glad to hear it, Dédé," she said.

"A degree in what?" said the magistrate.

Dédé shrugged, as if no one had bothered to tell him. "It came just the other day," he said. "I've got my degree, and now I can go home."

"Is there something you could show us?"

"There was just a letter, and I lost it," said Dédé. "A real diploma costs two thousand francs. I don't know where I'd find the money."

The magistrate did not seem to disbelieve; that was because of his training. But then he said, "You began your course about a month ago?"

"I had been thinking about it for a long time," said Dédé.

"And now they have awarded you a degree. You are perfectly right — it's time you went home. You can take the train tonight. I'll call your mother."

Pascal's mother returned, carrying a large white coffeepot. "I wonder where your first job will be," she said.

Why were she and her brother so remote from things as they are? Perhaps because of their mother, the grandmother in Colmar. Once, she had taken Pascal by the chin and tried to force him to look her in the eye. She had done it to her children. Pascal knows, now, that you cannot have your chin held in a vise and undividedly meet a blue stare. Somewhere at the back of the mind is a second self with eyes tight shut. Dédé and his sister could seem to meet any glance, even the magistrate's when he was being most nearly wide awake. They seemed to be listening, but the person he thought he was talking to, trying to reach the heart of, was deaf and blind. Pascal's mother listens when she needs to know what might happen next.

All Pascal understood, for the moment, was that when Dédé had mentioned taking a degree, he was saying something he merely wished were true.

"We'll probably never see you, once you start to work," said Pascal's mother, pouring Dédé's coffee.

The magistrate looked as if such great good luck was not to be expected. Abelarda, who had gone upstairs to make the beds, screamed from the head of the staircase that Dédé's room was full of smoke.

Abelarda moved slowly around the table carrying a plum tart, purple and gold, caramelized all over its surface, and a bowl of cream. Mme. Turbin glanced at the tart and shook her head no: M. Turbin was not allowed sugar now, and she had got out of the habit of eating desserts. It seemed unfair to tempt him.

It was true, her husband said. She had even given up making sweets, on his account. He described her past achievements — her famous chocolate mousse with candied bitter orange peel, her celebrated pineapple flan.

"My semolina crown mold with apricot sauce," she said. "I must have given the recipe away a hundred times."

Mme. Chevallier-Crochet wondered if she could have a slice half the size of the wedge Abelarda had already prepared. Abelarda put down the bowl of cream and divided the wedge in half. The half piece was still too much; Abelarda said it could not be cut again without breaking into a mess of crumbs. M. Chevallier-Crochet said to his wife, "For God's sake, just take it and leave what you can't eat." Mme. Chevallier-Crochet replied that everything she said and did seemed to be wrong, she had better just sit here and say and do nothing. Abelarda, crooning encouragement, pushed onto her plate a fragment of pastry and one plum.

"No cream," she said, too late.

Mme. Brouet looked at the portrait of her husband's grandfather, then at her son, perhaps seeking a likeness. Sophie Chevallier-Crochet had seemed lively and intelligent at their history-of-art class. Mme. Brouet had never met the husband before, and was unlikely ever to lay eyes on him again. She accepted large portions of tart and cream, to set an example, in case the other two ladies had inhibited the men.

M. Turbin, after having made certain that no extra sugar had been stirred into the cream, took more cream than tart. His wife, watching him closely, sipped water over her empty plate. "It's only fruit," he said.

The magistrate helped himself to all the crumbs and fragments of burnt sugar on the dish. He rattled the spoon in the bowl of cream, scraping the sides; there was nearly none left. It was the fault of M. Chevallier-Crochet, who had gone on filling his plate, as though in a dream, until Abelarda moved the bowl away.

The guests finished drinking their coffee at half past four, and left at a quarter to five. When they had gone, Mme. Brouet lay down — not on a couch or a settee but on the living room floor. She stared at the ceiling and told Pascal to leave her alone. Abelarda, Dédé, and the magistrate were up in Dédé's room. Abelarda helped him pack. Late that night, the magistrate drove him to the Gare de l'Est.

Dédé came back to Paris about a year ago. He is said to be different now. He has a part-time job with a television polling service: every day he is given a list of telephone numbers in the Paris area and he calls them to see what people were watching the night before and which program they wish they had watched instead. His mother has bought him a one-room place overlooking Parc de Montsouris. The Brouets have never tried to get in touch with him or invited him to a meal. Dédé's Paris — unknown, foreign almost — lies at an unmapped distance from Pascal's house.

One night, not long ago, when they all three were having dinner, Pascal said, "What if Dédé just came to the door?" He meant the front door, of course, but his parents glanced at the glass doors and the lamps reflected in the dark panes, so that night was screened from sight. Pascal imagined Dédé standing outside, watching and smiling, with that great mop of hair.

He is almost as tall as Dédé, now. Perhaps his father had not really taken notice of his height — it came about so gradually — but when Pascal got up to draw a curtain across the doors that night at dinner, his father looked at him as if he were suddenly setting a value on the kind of man he might become. It was a steady look, neither hot nor cold. For a moment Pascal said to himself, He will never fall asleep again. As for his mother, she sat smiling and dreaming, still hoping for some reason to start loving Dédé once more.

ROBERT LACY

The Natural Father

FROM CRAZYHORSE

HER NAME WAS Laura Goldberg. She had thick black hair and a "bump" in her nose (as she put it), but she dressed well and she had a good figure. She worked as a typist in an abstract office in downtown San Diego, and when Butters first met her in the fall of 1958 they had both just turned nineteen.

They met through a boot camp buddy of his who had gone to high school with her up in San Francisco, where she lived before her parents were divorced. Within a week he was taking her out. Butters was still in radio school at the time and didn't have a car, but Laura did, and she began picking him up several afternoons a week in the parking lot across the highway from the Marine base.

They made love on their third date, on the couch in her mother's apartment out in El Cajon, with the late-afternoon sunlight casting shadow patterns on the walls. It was hurried and not very satisfactory, and Butters was embarrassed by his performance. He felt he ought to apologize or something.

"It's okay," Laura said. "It's okay."

After that, though, they made love nearly every time they were alone together, often in the front seat of her car parked late at night on suburban side streets, with the fog rolling up off the bay to conceal them. One night they did it on her bed in the apartment, then had to spend frantic minutes picking white bedspread nap out of his trousers before her mother got home. Another time she met him at the front door, fresh from her shower, wearing nothing but a loose kimono, and they did it right there on the living room carpet, with the sound of the running shower in the background.

Butters was from a little town in eastern Oklahoma and hadn't known many Jewish girls before. In fact, he couldn't think of any. However, Laura's being Jewish didn't matter nearly as much to him as it seemed to matter to her. She was forever making jokes about it, and she liked to point out other Jews to him whenever they came across them, in restaurants or on TV. "Members of the Tribe," she called them, or "M.O.T.s." Butters pretended to share in the humor, but he was never quite sure what he was being let in on. Where he came from, tribes meant Indians.

Still, he was amazed at some of the people she identified as Jewish. Jack Benny, for example. And Frankie Laine. Every time they watched TV together in the apartment the list got longer. One night she even tried to convince him Eddie Fisher was a Jew.

"Bull," he said. "I don't believe it."

"He is, though," she insisted. "Ask mother when she gets here."

"He's Italian or something," Butters said. "I read it somewhere. Fisher's not his real name."

"Nope. He's a genuine M.O.T."

"Uh-uh."

"He is too, Donnie. Bet you a dollar."

"Make it five."

"You don't have five."

"I can get it."

"All right, Mister Sure-of-Yourself, five then. Shake."

They shook hands.

"How about Debbie Reynolds?" he said. "What's she?"

In march Butters was graduated from radio school and promoted to private first class. Then he was transferred to the naval base down at Imperial Beach to begin high-speed radio cryptography school. Imperial Beach was twelve miles due south of San Dicgo. Thc basc sat out on a narrow point of land. At night you could see the lights of Tijuana across the way.

One night after he had been there about a month Laura picked him up, late, at the main gate, drove back up to a hamburger stand in National City, and told him she was pregnant.

Butters was astounded, of course. This was the sort of thing that happened to other people.

"How do you know?" he said.

"I've missed two periods."

"Jeez. Did you see a doctor?"

"Yes."

"What did he say?"

"He said I was pregnant."

"Yeah, but what did he *say?*"

"He said I was a big, strong, healthy girl, and I was going to have a baby sometime in October. He said I had a good pelvis."

"Is that all?"

"Yes. He gave me some pills."

"For what?"

"One for water retention and one for morning sickness."

"You been sick?"

"Not yet. He says I might be."

"Jeez."

They sat in silence for a while, not looking at each other. Finally he said, "Well, what do you think we should do?"

She spoke slowly and carefully, and he could tell she had given the matter some thought. "I think we ought to get engaged for a month," she said. "Then get married. I know where we can get a deal on a ring."

"What kind of a deal?"

"Forty percent off, two years to pay."

"Where?"

"Nathan's. Downtown."

"You already been there?"

"I go by it every day at lunch."

"They give everybody forty percent off?"

"I know the manager. He's a cousin."

On the way back to the base Laura spoke of showers, wedding announcements, honeymoons in Ensenada. She said she thought they ought to sit down with her mother that very weekend, to get that part of it out of the way. Butters, who was hoping to get back on base without further discussion, said he thought he might have guard duty.

"You had guard duty last weekend," she reminded him.

"There's a bug going around," he said. "Lots of guys are in sickbay."

"Come Sunday night," she said. "I'll cook dinner. Elvis is on *Ed Sullivan.*"

"I'll have to see," he said.

"Sunday night," she said.

Sunday was four days away, which gave him plenty of time to think. And the more he thought the more he knew he didn't want to marry Laura Goldberg. He didn't love her, for one thing, and he wasn't ready to get married anyway, even to someone he did love. He was only nineteen years old. He had his whole life in front of him. Besides, he couldn't imagine Laura back home in Oklahoma.

That Sunday evening he caught a ride into San Diego with one of the boys from the base, then took a city bus out to the apartment in El Cajon. Laura met him at the door wearing an apron, a mixing spoon in her hand.

"Hi, hon," she said. "Dinner's almost ready."

Laura's mother, Mrs. Lippman, was seated on the living room sofa smoking a cigarette. She had her shoes off and her stockinged feet up on an ottoman. Mrs. Lippman was a short, heavyset woman with springy gray hair and sharp features. She always looked tired.

"Hello, Donald," she said. "What's with Betty Furness in there? Usually I can't get her to boil water."

"Hello, Mrs. Lippman," Butters said. "How's things at the paint store?"

Mrs. Lippman managed a Sherwin-Williams store down on lower Broadway and complained constantly about the help, most of whom were Mexican-American.

"Terrible," she said. "Don't ask. The chilis are stealing me blind."

Laura had fixed beef stroganoff, a favorite of Butters's, and when it was ready they ate it off TV trays in the living room while watching Elvis — from the waist up — on *The Ed Sullivan Show.* The meal was well prepared. Laura had even made little individual salads for each of them, with chopped walnuts on top and her own special dressing. When they were through eating she put the coffee on, then she and Butters scraped and stacked the dishes in the kitchen while Mrs. Lippman watched the last of the Sullivan show alone in the living room.

"You nervous?" Laura said to him in the kitchen. "You've been awfully quiet since you got here."

"I'm all right," Butters said, scraping a plate.

"Is something *wrong?*"

"No. I'm all right, I told you."

"Well, you certainly don't act like it. You haven't smiled once the whole evening."

Butters didn't say anything. He reached for another plate.

"Look at me," Laura said.

He looked at her.

"It's going to be *okay,*" she said. "We'll just go in there and tell her. What can she say?"

"Nothing much, I guess."

"Do you want to do the talking, or do you want me to?"

"Either way. You decide."

"All right. You do it. That's more traditional anyway."

"What about the other?"

"What other?"

"You know."

"Oh. We don't mention that. Why upset her if we don't have to?"

When the coffee was ready Laura poured out three cups and she and Butters returned to the living room. The show was just ending. Ed Sullivan was on stage, thanking his guests and announcing next week's performers. Laura stood for a moment watching her mother watch the screen, then she set the coffee on her mother's tray.

"Mother," she said, "Don and I have —"

"Sh!" Mrs. Lippman said, shooing her out of her line of sight. "I want to hear this."

On screen, Ed Sullivan was saying that his guests next week would include a Spanish ventriloquist and a rising young comedian. Headlining the show, he said, would be Steve Lawrence and Eydie Gorme.

"Oh, goodie," Mrs. Lippman said. "Laura, don't let me make plans."

"All right, mother." Laura had taken the wingback chair across the room and was sitting forward in it, her cup and saucer balanced on her knees. She was wearing her pleated wool skirt and a gray sweater, damp at the armpits.

When the Sullivan show at last gave way to a commercial she said, "Mother, Don and I have something to tell you — don't we, Don?"

Butters was seated on the sofa with Mrs. Lippman, the center cushion between them. "Yeah," he said.

Mrs. Lippman looked at Laura, then at Butters. She narrowed her eyes. "What is it?" she said.

"Don?" Laura said.

Butters was studying his coffee. At the sound of his name he looked up and took a deep breath. When he opened his mouth to speak he had no idea what he was going to say, but as soon as the words were out he knew they were the right ones.

"Mrs. Lippman," he said, "your daughter is pregnant."

There was a moment of silence, then Mrs. Lippman brought her hand down, very hard, on the armrest of the sofa. The sound was explosive in the small apartment.

"I knew it!" she said. "I knew it, I knew it, I knew it!"

She looked at Laura. "How long?" she said.

Laura was looking at Butters.

"How long?"

Laura looked at her mother. "Two months," she said softly.

"Who'd you see? Jack Segal?"

"Yes. Last week."

"I knew it. He won't be able to keep his mouth shut, you know. He'll tell Phyllis. God knows who *she'll* tell. *Look at me.*"

"I didn't know what else to do," Laura said, her voice barely above a whisper.

"You've got a mother, you know."

"Oh, mother."

"Well, you've broken my heart. I want you to know that. You have absolutely broken your mother's heart. And *you,*" she said, turning on Butters, "you've really done it up brown, haven't you, hotshot? And to think, I took you into my home."

"God," Butters said, "I feel so rotten. I can't tell you how —"

"Oh, shut up," Mrs. Lippman said. "I don't care how rotten you feel. I want to know what you're going to do about it. Look at her. She's knocked up. You couldn't keep it in your pants, and now *she's* knocked up. So tell me: what are you going to do about it?"

Butters didn't say anything.

"Don?" Laura said. "Donnie? Aren't you going to tell her what we decided?"

He looked at Laura. His eyes were round with grief. "I'm sorry, hon," he said. "I really am."

Laura began to cry. Her shoulders shook, and then her whole body, causing her cup and saucer to clatter together in her lap.

"This is going to cost you money, hotshot," Mrs. Lippman said. "You know that, don't you?"

Their first thought was abortion. Mrs. Lippman knew a man there in San Diego who agreed to do it, but after examining Laura he decided it was too risky (something about "enlarged veins"). So Tijuana was suggested; somebody knew a man there. But this time Laura balked. She didn't want any Mexican quack messing around inside her. Then Mrs. Lippman got the idea of hiring a second cousin of Laura's to marry her ("just for the name, you understand"), and she went so far as to get in touch with him — he was a dental student at Stanford — but he turned her down, even at her top price of five hundred dollars. So eventually, as the days slipped away and it became more and more apparent that Laura was going to have to have the baby, they began scouting around for an inexpensive place to send her. What they found was a sort of girls' ranch for unwed mothers over in Arizona. It was Baptist-supported and the lying-in fee was only a hundred dollars a month, meals included.

"What's it like?" Butters asked when Mrs. Lippman told him about it over the phone.

"How do *I* know?" she said. "It's clean. Jack Segal says it's clean."

"Well, that's good, isn't it?" Butters said. "That it's clean?"

"Listen," Mrs. Lippman said. "Spare me your tender solicitude. I don't have time for it. What I need from you is three hundred dollars — your half."

"*Three* hundred?"

"Three hundred. She'll be there six months, counting the postpartum."

"What's that?"

"You don't even need to know. Just get me the three hundred, okay?"

That was in April. In the meantime Butters had washed out of high-speed school and had been sent back to San Diego to await assignment overseas. He was placed in a casual company, with too little to do and too much time on his hands, and it was there that he met, one afternoon in the supply room, a skinny little buck sergeant named Hawkins, who rather easily convinced him that maybe he was being had. Happened all the time, Hawkins said. Dago was that kind of town. Why, there were women there who knew a million ways to separate you from your money, and it sounded to him like Butters had fallen for one of the oldest ways of all. Then he asked Butters what his blood type was.

"O positive," Butters said. "Why?"

"Universal donor," Hawkins said. "They can't prove a thing."

The upshot was that two days later, following Hawkins's advice, Butters found himself sitting in the office of one of the two chaplains on base. This chaplain was a freckle-faced young Methodist with captain's bars on his collar and an extremely breezy manner. He tapped his front teeth with a letter opener the whole time Butters was telling his story, and when Butters was done said he thought Butters owed it to himself to ask around a bit, make some inquiries, find out what other boys Laura had been seeing.

"I mean, after all, fella," he said, "if she did it for you, why not someone else?"

And for a few days after that Butters actually considered getting in touch with the boot camp buddy who had introduced him to Laura. He knew where the boy was — up at El Toro, in the NavCad program — all he had to do was call him. In the end, though, he didn't do it. It was just too much trouble. What he did was hole up on base instead. He quit going into town and he quit taking phone calls. He developed the idea that as long as he stayed on base they couldn't touch him. And it worked for a while. He was able to pass several furtive weeks that way, sticking to a tight little universe of barracks, PX, base theater and beer garden. But then one afternoon while he and Hawkins were folding mattress covers in the supply room a runner came in and said the Catholic chaplain wanted to see him. This chaplain's office was at the far end of the grinder, half a mile away, and as he made his way up there Butters tried to occupy his mind with pleasant thoughts. He didn't bother wondering why he was being summoned, and when he entered the office and saw who was sitting there he knew he had been right not to.

"Hello, Miz Lippman," he said. "I figured it might be you."

"You quit answering your phone," she said. "So I came calling. You owe me money."

This chaplain wore tinted glasses and had a stern, no-nonsense air about him. He listened impatiently to Butters's side of the story, then he asked Butters how he, "as a Christian," viewed his responsibilities in the matter. He left little doubt how he himself viewed them.

"You *are* a Christian, aren't you, private?" he said.

"Uh, yes, sir," Butters said.

"Well, what's your obligation here then? Or don't you feel you have one?"

"I don't know, sir. I'm confused."

"Call me father. What do you mean you're 'confused'? Did you agree to pay this woman, or didn't you?"

"Yes, sir. But that was before I talked to the other chaplain."

"What's that got to do with it? Did you agree to pay her? Call me father."

"Yes, sir. Father."

"Did you have intercourse with her daughter?"

Butters blushed. "Yes, sir."

"More than once?"

"Yes, sir."

"Did her daughter get pregnant as a result?"

"Yes, sir. I guess."

"You guess?"

"I guess it was me. But it *could* have been someone else."

Mrs. Lippman bristled. "I resent that," she said. "Laura's not a tramp and you know it."

"Do you *think* it was someone else?" the chaplain said.

"She's no tramp, father," Mrs. Lippman insisted.

"Do you, private?"

"No, sir," Butters said.

"That's what I thought," the chaplain said. "Now let's get down to business."

So once again it was agreed that Butters would pay half of Laura's lying-in expense, or fifty dollars a month for six months. But this time they drew up a little contract right there in the chaplain's office, which the chaplain's secretary typed and the three of them signed, the chaplain as witness. That night, lying in bed waiting for lights out, Butters thought back over the day's events and decided things had worked out about as well as he could expect. At least he could come out of hiding now.

Just before lights out the charge-of-quarters came in and said there was a phone call for him out in the orderly room. *Jeez,* Butters thought as he got up to follow the CQ, *what now?*

The phone was on the wall just inside the orderly room door. He picked up the dangling receiver and said, "Hello?"

"Hello — Donnie?"

"Laura? Where are you?"

"Arizona. Where do you think?"

"Well. How're you doing?"

"How'm I doing?"

"Yeah. You know: how're you doing?"

"Not too good, Donnie. Not too good."

"You crying?"

"Yeah."

He thought so. "What's the matter, hon?"

"Matter? Oh, nothing. I'm just pregnant, and unmarried, and three hundred miles from home, and scared and lonely. That's all. Nothing to get upset about, right?"

"Don't cry, Laura."

"I can't help it."

"Please?"

"I'm just so miserable, Donnie. You oughta see us. There's

about thirty of us, and all we do is sit around all day in our maternity smocks *looking* at each other. Nobody hardly says a word. One of the girls is only fourteen. She sleeps with a big stuffed rabbit."

Butters felt very bad for Laura. She sounded so blue. "Aren't there any horses?" he said.

"What?"

"Horses. Aren't there any horses?"

"*Horses!* God, Donnie, you're worse than a child sometimes. What do you think this is, a dude ranch? You think we sit around a campfire at night singing 'Home on the Range'?"

Butters fingered a place on the back of his neck. "Your mother says it's pretty clean," he ventured.

"Clean?"

"That's what she said."

"When did you talk to her?"

"About that? About a month ago, I guess."

"And she said it was clean?"

"Yeah."

"What else did she say?"

"Nothing. Just that it was clean."

"I see. Well, yes, it's very clean. Spic and span. And the food's good too. We had chicken à la king tonight — my favorite."

"We had meatloaf. It tasted like cardboard."

"Poor you."

"What?"

"I said, 'Poor you.' "

"Oh."

They fell silent, and the silence began to lengthen. Through the orderly room windows Butters could see the movie letting out across the grinder. Guys were coming out stretching and lighting up cigarettes.

"Listen," Laura said finally, "I'll let you go. I can tell you don't want to talk to me anyway. I just called to tell you that I've decided to go ahead and have this stupid baby. For a while there I was thinking about killing myself, but I've changed my mind. I'm gonna go through with it, Donnie. I'm gonna do it. But my life will never ever be the same again, and I just thought you ought to know that."

Then she hung up.

Two weeks later he was on a boat bound for Okinawa.

That was in mid-May. By the time he reached Okinawa, halfway around the world, it was early June. He had made his May payment to Mrs. Lippman on the day after the meeting in the chaplain's office, and he mailed her his June payment as soon as he got off the boat. The July payment he mailed her too, but late in the month. The August payment he skipped altogether. And sure enough, not long afterwards, sometime in early September, the company clerk came looking for him one afternoon in the barracks with word that the company commander wanted to see him.

"Did he say what it was about?" Butters asked.

"No," the clerk said. "He don't confide in me much. I think you better chop chop, though."

It was the same old story. The company commander, a major with a good tan, showed him a letter from Mrs. Lippman and asked him what was going on.

Butters told him.

"She claims you owe her money," the major said. "Do you?"

"Yes, sir," Butters said. He was standing at ease in front of the major's desk, looking at the letter in the major's hands. It was on blue stationery.

"How much?"

"A hundred and fifty dollars, sir."

"Well, what do you plan to do about it?"

"Pay her, sir. I guess."

"You guess?"

"Pay her, sir."

"Do you have it?"

"No, sir."

"Where do you plan to get it?"

"I don't know, sir."

"You don't *know?* You think you might just dig it up out of the *ground,* private? Pick it off a *tree?* What do you mean you don't know?"

"I don't know, sir. I guess I'll have to think of something."

"You 'guess.' You 'don't know.' It strikes me, private, that you're just not very sure about anything — are you?"

Butters didn't say anything. A phone rang somewhere.

The major shook his head. "How old are you, son?" he said.

"Nineteen, sir. I'll be twenty next month."

"I see. Well, here's what I want you to do. There's a Navy Relief office over at Camp Hague. I want you to go over there tomorrow morning and take out a loan."

"A loan, sir?"

"A loan."

"They'd *lend* it to me?"

"That's what they're there for, private."

A loan! Now why hadn't he thought of that? Getting it turned out to be remarkably easy too. Oh, he had to answer a few embarrassing questions, and there was a final interview that had him squirming for a while, but when it was all over, in less than two hours, he had a cashier's check for the full amount in his hand, with a full year to repay it and an interest rate of only three percent. He was so elated at the sight of the check that it was all he could do to keep from dancing the woman who gave it to him around the room. Rather than risk temptation he sent the entire one-fifty off to San Diego that same day by registered mail. He considered sticking a little note in with it — something like, "Bet you thought you'd never see this, didn't you?" — but thought better of it at the last minute.

And it was funny, but in the days that followed he felt like a different person. He bounced around the company area with such energy and good humor that people hardly recognized him. One morning he was first in line for chow.

"Jeez, Butters," said the boy serving him his eggs, "what's got into you? You hardly ever even *eat* breakfast."

"Just feed the troops, lad," Butters said. "Feed the troops."

But then it was October, the month the baby was due. Throughout the spring and summer and into the early days of a rainy Okinawan autumn he had done a pretty good job of shutting it out of his mind. He had simply refused to contemplate the fact that what had happened back in February in foggy San Diego was destined, ever, to result in anything so real as a baby. But as October crept in it got harder. He found he couldn't help wondering, for example, whether it would be a boy or a girl. He hoped it was a boy. Being a boy was easier — girls had it rough. One night he found himself imagining it curled up in Laura's womb, its knees tucked up under its chin, its tiny fingers making tiny fists. And, lying there, he began trying to make out the baby's face. He wanted to know who it looked like, but, try as he might, he couldn't tell. Later that night he dreamed he was swimming underwater somewhere, deep down, and that floating in the water all around him were these large jellyfish, each of which, on closer inspection, appeared to have a baby inside. He couldn't make out these babies' faces either.

But October passed and nothing happened. At least not in his world. Nobody contacted him, by phone or mail or otherwise. Nobody got in touch. And as the days went by and still he heard nothing, slowly he began to believe that maybe it was all over with now, that what had happened was finally history and he could go about his daily business just like everyone else.

He had made friends by then with a boy named Tipton, from Kansas, and the two of them had begun spending their weekends in a tin-roofed shanty outside Chibana with a pair of sisters who worked in a Chibana bar.

One Saturday morning Butters was sitting out on the back steps of the shanty, watching one of the sisters hang laundry in the yard, when Tipton arrived from the base by taxi, bearing beer and groceries and a letter for him.

Butters took the letter and looked at it. There were several cancellations on the envelope, indicating it had been rerouted more than once. He opened it up and took out a single folded sheet of paper. It read:

Dear Don,

The baby is due any day now, they tell me. You should see me. I'm huge. You probably wouldn't even recognize me. I think the baby is a "he." It sure kicks like one anyway. It even keeps me awake some nights with its kicking and rolling around alot.

The nurses say I don't have to see it if I don't want to. They say it's entirely up to me. Sometimes I think I want to and sometimes I think

I don't. Silly me, huh? Guess I had better make up my mind pretty soon, though, and quit all this procastinating (sp?).

Don, since I know now I am never going to see you again I guess this will have to be goodbye. I'm not bitter anymore. I was for a while, I admit, but I'm not now. And I'm still glad I knew you. I just wish things could have turned out better, that's all.

Best always,
Laura

P.S. You owe me $5. (See clipping)

Butters looked inside the envelope again and saw a small folded piece of paper he had missed before. He took it out and unfolded it. It was a photograph clipped from a magazine — *Time* or *Newsweek,* it looked like — and it showed Elizabeth Taylor and Eddie Fisher during their recent wedding ceremony in Beverly Hills. They were standing before a robed man with a dark beard. Both Fisher and the robed man had small black caps perched on the back of their heads. An arrow had been drawn, in red ink, pointing to the cap on Fisher's head, and along its shaft had been printed, in big block letters, also red, the initials "M.O.T."

Butters sat looking at the clipping for a while. Then he put it and the letter back in the envelope, folded the envelope in half, and stuffed it in his back pocket.

"Your mom?" Tipton said.

"Huh?"

"The letter. Is it from your mom?"

"No. A girl I knew."

"Oh," Tipton said. "You want a beer?"

The legal papers didn't arrive until the first week in December. They were from the office of the county clerk of Maricopa County, Arizona, and they consisted of a form letter, a release document, and an enclosed envelope for which no postage was necessary.

They came on a Friday, as Butters and Tipton were preparing to leave for town.

Butters read the form letter first, sitting on his bunk in his civvies. The letter was very short, just two paragraphs. The first paragraph said that a child had been born on such-and-such a date in the public maternity ward of such-and-such a hospital in Phoenix, Arizona, and that, according to the attending physician, it was free of physical and mental defects. The second paragraph merely asked him to read and then sign the accompanying release. The child was identified, the words typed into a blank space in the middle of the first paragraph, as "Baby Boy Butters, 7 lbs, 6 oz."

When he was finished with the letter Butters set it carefully beside him on the bunk and picked up the release. It was short too, just a single legal-sized page. It asked him to understand what he was doing — waiving all rights and responsibilities in the care and upbringing of the child — and it cited the pertinent sections of Arizona law, which took up most of the rest of the page. Toward the bottom, however, there was a dotted line that caught Butters's eye. He skipped over much of the legal language, but he lingered at the dotted line. "Signature of Natural Father," it was labeled. He looked at it. That was him. He was the natural father. He turned the page over to see if there was anything on the back. There wasn't. It was blank. He turned it back over and looked at the dotted line. Tipton was standing just a few feet away from him, waiting. They had already called their taxi. It was on the way.

He looked up at Tipton. "You got a pen?" he said.

LOUISE ERDRICH

Snares

FROM HARPER'S MAGAZINE

IT BEGAN AFTER CHURCH with Margaret and her small granddaughter, Lulu, and was not to end until the long days of Lent and a hard-packed snow. There were factions on the reservation, a treaty settlement in the Agent's hands. There were Chippewa who signed their names in the year 1924, and there were Chippewa who saw the cash offered as a flimsy bait. I was one and Fleur Pillager, Lulu's mother, was another who would not lift her hand to sign. It was said that all the power to witch, harm, or cure lay in Fleur, the lone survivor of the old Pillager clan. But as much as people feared Fleur, they listened to Margaret Kashpaw. She was the ringleader of the holdouts, a fierce, one-minded widow with a vinegar tongue.

Margaret Kashpaw had knots of muscles in her arms. Her braids were thin, gray as iron, and usually tied strictly behind her back so they wouldn't swing. She was plump as a basket below and tough as roots on top. Her face was gnarled around a beautiful sharp nose. Two shell earrings caught the light and flashed whenever she turned her head. She had become increasingly religious in the years after her loss, and finally succeeded in dragging me to the Benediction Mass, where I was greeted by Father Damien, from whom I occasionally won small sums at dice.

"Grandfather Nanapush," he smiled, "at last."

"These benches are a hardship for an old man," I complained. "If you spread them with soft pine-needle cushions I'd have come before."

Father Damien stared thoughtfully at the rough pews, folded his hands inside the sleeves of his robe.

"You must think of their unyielding surfaces as helpful," he offered. "God sometimes enters the soul through the humblest parts of our anatomies, if they are sensitized to suffering."

"A god who enters through the rear door," I countered, "is no better than a thief."

Father Damien was used to me, and smiled as he walked to the altar. I adjusted my old bones, longing for some relief, trying not to rustle for fear of Margaret's jabbing elbow. The time was long. Lulu probed all my pockets with her fingers until she found a piece of hard candy. I felt no great presence in this cold place and decided, as my back end ached and my shoulders stiffened, that our original gods were better, the Chippewa characters who were not exactly perfect but at least did not require sitting on hard boards.

When Mass was over and the smell of incense was thick in all our clothes, Margaret, Lulu, and I went out into the starry cold, the snow and stubble fields, and began the long walk to our homes. It was dusk. On either side of us the heavy trees stood motionless and blue. Our footsteps squeaked against the dry snow, the only sound to hear. We spoke very little, and even Lulu ceased her singing when the moon rose to half, poised like a balanced cup. We knew the very moment someone else stepped upon the road.

We had turned a bend and the footfalls came unevenly, just out of sight. There were two men, one mixed-blood or white, from the drop of his hard boot soles, and the other one quiet, an Indian. Not long and I heard them talking close behind us. From the rough, quick tension of the Indian's language, I recognized Lazarre. And the mixed-blood must be Clarence Morrissey. The two had signed the treaty and spoke in its favor to anyone they could collar at the store. They even came to people's houses to beg and argue that this was our one chance, our good chance, that the government would withdraw the offer. But wherever Margaret was, she slapped down their words like mosquitoes and said the only thing that lasts life to life is land. Money burns like tinder, flows like water. And as for promises, the wind is steadier. It is no wonder that, because she spoke so well, Lazarre and Clarence Morrissey wished to silence her. I sensed their bad intent as they passed us, an unpleasant edge of excitement in their looks and greetings.

They went on, disappeared in the dark brush.

"Margaret," I said, "we are going to cut back." My house was close, but Margaret kept walking forward as if she hadn't heard.

I took her arm, caught the little girl close, and started to turn us, but Margaret would have none of this and called me a coward. She grabbed the girl to her. Lulu, who did not mind getting tossed between us, laughed, tucked her hand into her grandma's pocket, and never missed a step. Two years ago she had tired of being carried, got up, walked. She had the balance of a little mink. She was slippery and clever, too, which was good because when the men jumped from the darkest area of brush and grappled with us half a mile on, Lulu slipped free and scrambled into the trees.

They were occupied with Margaret and me, at any rate. We were old enough to snap in two, our limbs dry as dead branches, but we fought as though our enemies were the Nadouissouix kidnappers of our childhood. Margaret uttered a war cry that had not been heard for fifty years, and bit Lazarre's hand to the bone, giving a wound which would later prove the death of him. As for Clarence, he had all he could do to wrestle me to the ground and knock me half unconscious. When he'd accomplished that, he tied me and tossed me into a wheelbarrow, which was hidden near the road for the purpose of lugging us to the Morrissey barn.

I came to my senses trussed to a manger, sitting on a bale. Margaret was roped to another bale across from me, staring straight forward in a rage, a line of froth caught between her lips. On either side of her, shaggy cows chewed and shifted their thumping hooves. I rose and staggered, the weight of the manger on my back. I planned on Margaret biting through my ropes with her strong teeth, but then the two men entered.

I'm a talker, a fast-mouth who can't keep his thoughts straight, but lets fly with words and marvels at what he hears from his own mouth. I'm a smart one. I always was a devil for convincing women. And I wasn't too bad a shot, in other ways, at convincing men. But I had never been tied up before.

"Booshoo," I said. "Children, let us loose, your game is too rough!"

They stood between us, puffed with their secrets.

"Empty old windbag," said Clarence.

"I have a bargain for you," I said, looking for an opening. "Let us go and we won't tell Pukwan." Edgar Pukwan was the tribal police. "Boys get drunk sometimes and don't know what they're doing."

Lazarre laughed once, hard and loud. "We're not drunk," he said. "Just wanting what's coming to us, some justice, money out of it."

"Kill us," said Margaret. "We won't sign."

"Wait," I said. "My cousin Pukwan will find you boys, and have no mercy. Let us go. I'll sign and get it over with, and I'll persuade the old widow."

I signaled Margaret to keep her mouth shut. She blew air into her cheeks. Clarence looked expectantly at Lazarre, as if the show were over, but Lazarre folded his arms and was convinced of nothing.

"You lie when it suits, skinny old dog," he said, wiping at his lips as if in hunger. "It's her we want, anyway. We'll shame her so she shuts her mouth."

"Easy enough," I said, smooth, "now that you've got her tied. She's plump and good looking. Eyes like a doe! But you forget that we're together, almost man and wife."

This wasn't true at all, and Margaret's face went rigid with tumbling fury and confusion. I kept talking.

"So of course if you do what you're thinking of doing you'll have to kill me afterward, and that will make my cousin Pukwan twice as angry, since I owe him a fat payment for a gun which he lent me and I never returned. All the same," I went on — their heads were spinning — "I'll forget you bad boys ever considered such a crime, something so terrible that Father Damien would nail you on boards just like in the example on the wall in church."

"Quit jabbering." Lazarre stopped me in a deadly voice.

It was throwing pebbles in a dry lake. My words left no ripple. I saw in his eyes that he intended us great harm. I saw his greed. It was like watching an ugly design of bruises come clear for a moment and reconstructing the evil blows that made them.

I played my last card.

"Whatever you do to Margaret you are doing to the Pillager woman!" I dropped my voice. "The witch, Fleur Pillager, is her own son's wife."

Clarence was too young to be frightened, but his mouth hung in interested puzzlement. My words had a different effect on Lazarre, as a sudden light shone, a consequence he hadn't considered.

I cried out, seeing this, "Don't you know she can think about you hard enough to stop your heart?" Lazarre was still deciding. He raised his fist and swung it casually and tapped my face. It was worse not to be hit full on.

"Come near!" crooned Margaret in the old language. "Let me teach you how to die."

But she was trapped like a fox. Her earrings glinted and spun as she hissed her death song over and over, which signaled something to Lazarre, for he shook himself angrily and drew a razor from his jacket. He stropped it with fast, vicious movements while Margaret sang shriller, so full of hate that the ropes should have burned, shriveled, fallen from her body. My struggle set the manger cracking against the barn walls and further confused the cows, who bumped each other and complained. At a sign from Lazarre, Clarence sighed, rose, and smashed me. The last I saw before I blacked out, through the tiny closing pinhole of light, was Lazarre approaching Margaret with the blade.

When I woke, minutes later, it was to worse shock. For Lazarre had sliced Margaret's long braids off and was now, carefully, shaving her scalp. He started almost tenderly at the wide part, and then pulled the edge down each side of her skull. He did a clean job. He shed not one drop of her blood.

And I could not even speak to curse them. For pressing my jaw down, thick above my tongue, her braids, never cut in this life till now, were tied to silence me. Powerless, I tasted their flat, animal perfume.

It wasn't much later, or else it was forever, that we walked out into the night again. Speechless, we made our way in fierce pain down the road. I was damaged in spirit, more so than Margaret. For now she tucked her shawl over her naked head and forgot her own bad treatment. She called out in dread each foot of the way, for Lulu. But the smart, bold girl had hidden till all was clear and then run to Margaret's house. We opened the door and found her sitting by the stove in a litter of scorched matches and kindling. She had not the skill to start a fire, but she was dry-eyed. Though very cold, she was alert and then captured with wonder when Margaret slipped off her shawl.

"Where is your hair?" she asked.

I took my hand from my pocket. "Here's what's left of it. I grabbed this when they cut me loose." I was shamed by how pitiful I had been, relieved when Margaret snatched the thin gray braids from me and coiled them round her fist.

"I knew you would save them, clever man!" There was satisfaction in her voice.

I set the fire blazing. It was strange how generous this woman was to me, never blaming me or mentioning my failure. Margaret stowed her braids inside a birchbark box and merely instructed me to lay it in her grave, when that time occurred. Then she came near the stove with a broken mirror from beside her washstand and looked at her own image.

"My," she pondered, "my." She put the mirror down. "I'll take a knife to them."

And I was thinking too. I was thinking I would have to kill them.

But how does an aching and half-starved grandfather attack a young, well-fed Morrissey and a tall, sly Lazarre? Later, I rolled up in blankets in the corner by Margaret's stove, and I put my mind to this question throughout that night until, exhausted, I slept. And I thought of it first thing next morning, too, and still nothing came. It was only after we had some hot *gaulette* and walked Lulu back to her mother that an idea began to grow.

Fleur let us in, hugged Lulu into her arms, and looked at Margaret, who took off her scarf and stood bald, face burning again with smoldered fire. She told Fleur all of what happened, sparing no detail. The two women's eyes held, but Fleur said nothing. She put Lulu down, smoothed the front of her calico shirt, flipped her heavy braids over her shoulders, tapped one finger on her perfect lips. And then, calm, she went to the washstand and scraped the edge of her hunting knife keen as glass. Margaret and Lulu and I watched as Fleur cut her braids off, shaved her own head, and folded the hair into a quilled skin pouch. Then she went out, hunting, and didn't bother to wait for night to cover her tracks.

I would have to go out hunting too.

I had no gun, but anyway that was a white man's revenge. I knew how to wound with barbs of words, but had never wielded a skinning knife against a human, much less two young men. Whomever I missed would kill me, and I did not want to die by their lowly hands.

In fact, I didn't think that after Margaret's interesting kindness I wanted to leave this life at all. Her head, smooth as an egg, was ridged delicately with bone, and gleamed as if it had been buffed with a flannel cloth. Maybe it was the strangeness that attracted me. She looked forbidding, but the absence of hair also set off her eyes, so black and full of lights. She reminded me of that queen from England, of a water snake or a shrewd young bird. The earrings, which seemed part of her, mirrored her moods like water, and when they were still rounds of green lights against her throat I seemed, again, to taste her smooth, smoky braids in my mouth.

I had better things to do than fight. So I decided to accomplish revenge as quickly as possible. I was a talker who used my brains as my weapon. When I hunted, I preferred to let my game catch itself.

Snares demand clever fingers and a scheming mind, and snares had never failed me. Snares are quiet, and best of all snares are slow. I wanted to give Lazarre and Morrissey time to consider why they had to strangle. I thought hard. One- or two-foot deadfalls are required beneath a snare so that a man can't put his hand up and loosen the knot. The snares I had in mind also required something stronger than a cord, which could be broken, and finer than a rope, which even Lazarre might see and avoid. I pondered this closely, yet even so I might never have found the solution had I not gone to Mass with Margaret and grown curious about the workings of Father Damien's pride and joy, the piano in the back of the church, the instrument whose keys he breathed on, polished, then played after services, and sometimes alone. I had noticed that his hands usually stayed near the middle of the keyboard, so I took the wires from either end.

In the meantime, I was not the only one concerned with punishing Lazarre and Clarence Morrissey. Fleur was seen in town. Her thick skirts brushed the snow into clouds behind her. Though it was cold she left her head bare so everyone could see the frigid sun glare off her skull. The light reflected in the eyes of Lazarre and Clarence, who were standing at the door of the pool hall. They dropped their cue sticks in the slush and ran back to Morrissey land. Fleur walked the four streets, once in each direction, then followed.

The two men told of her visit, how she passed through the Morrissey house touching here, touching there, sprinkling powders that ignited and stank on the hot stove. How Clarence swayed on his feet, blinked hard, and chewed his fingers. How Fleur stepped up to him, drew her knife. He smiled foolishly and asked her for supper. She reached forward and trimmed off a hank of his hair. Then she stalked from the house, leaving a taste of cold wind, and then chased Lazarre to the barn.

She made a black silhouette against the light from the door. Lazarre pressed against the wood of the walls, watching, hypnotized by the sight of Fleur's head and the quiet blade. He did not defend himself when she approached, reached for him, gently and efficiently cut bits of his hair, held his hands, one at a time, and trimmed the nails. She waved the razor-edged knife before his eyes and swept a few eyelashes into a white square of flour sacking that she then carefully folded into her blouse.

For days after, Lazarre babbled and wept. Fleur was murdering him by use of bad medicine, he said. He showed his hand, the bite that Margaret had dealt him, and the dark streak from the wound, along his wrist and inching up his arm. He even used that bound hand to scratch his name from the treaty, but it did no good.

I figured that the two men were doomed at least three ways now. Margaret won the debate with her Catholic training and decided to damn her soul by taking up the ax, since no one else had destroyed her enemies. I begged her to wait for another week, all during which it snowed and thawed and snowed again. It took me that long to arrange the snare to my satisfaction, near Lazarre's shack, on a path both men took to town.

I set it out one morning before anyone stirred, and watched from an old pine twisted along the ground. I waited while the smoke rose in a silky feather from the tiny tin spout on Lazarre's roof. I had to sit half a day before Lazarre came outside, and even then it was just for wood, nowhere near the path. I had a hard time to keep my blood flowing, my stomach still. I ate a handful of dry berries Margaret had given me, and a bit of pounded meat. I doled it to myself and waited until finally Clarence showed. He walked the trail like a blind ghost and stepped straight into my noose.

It was perfect, or would have been if I had made the deadfall two inches wider, for in falling Clarence somehow managed to spread his legs and straddle the deep hole I'd cut. It had been invisible, covered with snow, and yet in one foot-pedaling instant, the certain knowledge of its construction sprang into Clarence's brain and told his legs to reach for the sides. I don't know how he did it, but there he was poised. I waited, did not show myself. The noose jerked enough to cut slightly into the fool's neck, a too-snug fit. He was spread-eagled and on tiptoe, his arms straight out. If he twitched a finger, lost the least control, even tried to yell, one foot would go, the noose constrict.

But Clarence did not move. I could see from behind my branches that he didn't even dare to change the expression on his face. His mouth stayed frozen in shock. Only his eyes shifted, darted fiercely and wildly, side to side, showing all the agitation he must not release, searching desperately for a means of escape. They focused only when I finally stepped toward him, quiet, from the pine.

We were in full view of Lazarre's house, face to face. I stood before the boy. Just a touch, a sudden kick, perhaps no more than a word, was all that it would take. But I looked into his eyes and saw the knowledge of his situation. Pity entered me. Even for Margaret's shame, I couldn't do the thing I might have done.

I turned away and left Morrissey still balanced on the ledge of snow.

What money I did have, I took to the trading store next day. I bought the best bonnet on the reservation. It was black as a coal scuttle, large, and shaped the same.

"It sets off my doe eyes," Margaret said and stared me down.

She wore it every day, and always to Mass. Not long before Lent and voices could be heard: "There goes Old Lady Coal-bucket." Nonetheless, she was proud, and softening day by day, I could tell. By the time we got our foreheads crossed with ashes, she consented to be married.

"I hear you're thinking of exchanging the vows," said Father Damien as I shook his hand on our way out the door.

"I'm having relations with Margaret already," I told him, "that's the way we do things."

This had happened to him before, so he was not even stumped as to what remedy he should use.

"Make a confession, at any rate," he said, motioning us back into the church.

So I stepped into the little box and knelt. Father Damien slid aside the shadowy door. I told him what I had been doing with Margaret and he stopped me partway through.

"No more details. Pray to Our Lady."

"There is one more thing."

"Yes?"

"Clarence Morrissey, he wears a scarf to church around his neck each week. I snared him like a rabbit."

Father Damien let the silence fill him.

"And the last thing," I went on. "I stole the wire from your piano."

The silence spilled over into my stall, and I was held in its grip until the priest spoke.

"Discord is hateful to God. You have offended his ear." Almost as an afterthought, Damien added, "And his commandment. The violence among you must cease."

"You can have the wire back," I said. I had used only one long strand. I also agreed that I would never use my snares on humans, an easy promise. Lazarre was already caught.

Just two days later, while Margaret and I stood with Lulu and her mother inside the trading store, Lazarre entered, gesturing, his eyes rolled to the skull. He stretched forth his arm and pointed along its deepest black vein and dropped his jaw wide. Then he stepped backward into a row of traps that the trader had set to show us how they worked. Fleur's eye lit, her white scarf caught the sun as she turned. All the whispers were true. Fleur had scratched Lazarre's figure into a piece of birchbark, drawn his insides, and rubbed a bit of rouge up his arm until the red stain reached his heart. There was no sound as he fell, no cry, no word, and the traps of all types that clattered down around his body jumped and met for a long time, snapping air.

RAYMOND CARVER

Errand

FROM THE NEW YORKER

Chekhov. On the evening of March 22, 1897, he went to dinner in Moscow with his friend and confidant Alexei Suvorin. This Suvorin was a very rich newspaper and book publisher, a reactionary, a self-made man whose father was a private at the battle of Borodino. Like Chekhov, he was the grandson of a serf. They had that in common: each had peasant's blood in his veins. Otherwise, politically and temperamentally, they were miles apart. Nevertheless, Suvorin was one of Chekhov's few intimates, and Chekhov enjoyed his company.

Naturally, they went to the best restaurant in the city, a former town house called the Hermitage — a place where it could take hours, half the night even, to get through a ten-course meal that would, of course, include several wines, liqueurs, and coffee. Chekhov was impeccably dressed, as always — a dark suit and waistcoat, his usual pince-nez. He looked that night very much as he looks in the photographs taken of him during this period. He was relaxed, jovial. He shook hands with the maître d', and with a glance took in the large dining room. It was brilliantly illuminated by ornate chandeliers, the tables occupied by elegantly dressed men and women. Waiters came and went ceaselessly. He had just been seated across the table from Suvorin when suddenly, without warning, blood began gushing from his mouth. Suvorin and two waiters helped him to the gentlemen's room and tried to stanch the flow of blood with ice packs. Suvorin saw him back to his own hotel and had a bed prepared for Chekhov in one of the rooms of the suite. Later, after another hemorrhage, Chekhov allowed himself to be moved to a clinic that specialized in the treatment of tuberculosis and related respiratory infections. When Suvorin visited him there, Chekhov apologized for the "scandal" at the restaurant three nights earlier but continued to insist there was nothing seriously wrong. "He laughed and jested as usual," Suvorin noted in his diary, "while spitting blood into a large vessel."

Maria Chekhov, his younger sister, visited Chekhov in the clinic during the last days of March. The weather was miserable; a sleet storm was in progress, and frozen heaps of snow lay everywhere. It was hard for her to wave down a carriage to take her to the hospital. By the time she arrived she was filled with dread and anxiety.

"Anton Pavlovich lay on his back," Maria wrote in her *Memoirs*. "He was not allowed to speak. After greeting him, I went over to the table to hide my emotions." There, among bottles of champagne, jars of caviar, bouquets of flowers from well-wishers, she saw something that terrified her: a freehand drawing, obviously done by a specialist in these matters, of Chekhov's lungs. It was the kind of sketch a doctor often makes in order to show his patient what he thinks is taking place. The lungs were outlined in blue, but the upper parts were filled in with red. "I realized they were diseased," Maria wrote.

Leo Tolstoy was another visitor. The hospital staff were awed to find themselves in the presence of the country's greatest writer. The most famous man in Russia? Of course they had to let him in to see Chekhov, even though "nonessential" visitors were forbidden. With much obsequiousness on the part of the nurses and resident doctors, the bearded, fierce-looking old man was shown into Chekhov's room. Despite his low opinion of Chekhov's abilities as a playwright (Tolstoy felt the plays were static and lacking in any moral vision. "Where do your characters take you?" he once demanded of Chekhov. "From the sofa to the junk room and back"), Tolstoy liked Chekhov's short stories. Furthermore, and quite simply, he loved the man. He told Gorky, "What a beautiful, magnificent man: modest and quiet, like a girl. He even walks like a girl. He's simply wonderful." And Tolstoy wrote in his journal (everyone kept a journal or a diary in those days), "I am glad I love . . . Chekhov."

Tolstoy removed his woollen scarf and bearskin coat, then lowered himself into a chair next to Chekhov's bed. Never mind that Chekhov was taking medication and not permitted to talk, much less carry on a conversation. He had to listen, amazedly, as the Count began to discourse on his theories of the immortality of the soul. Concerning that visit, Chekhov later wrote, "Tolstoy assumes that all of us (humans and animals alike) will live on in a principle (such as reason or love) the essence and goals of which are a mystery to us. . . . I have no use for that kind of immortality. I don't understand it, and Lev Nikolayevich was astonished I didn't."

Nevertheless, Chekhov was impressed with the solicitude shown by Tolstoy's visit. But, unlike Tolstoy, Chekhov didn't believe in an afterlife and never had. He didn't believe in anything that couldn't be apprehended by one or more of his five senses. And as far as his outlook on life and writing went, he once told someone that he lacked "a political, religious, and philosophical world view. I change it every month, so I'll have to limit myself to the description of how my heroes love, marry, give birth, die, and how they speak."

Earlier, before his t.b. was diagnosed, Chekhov had remarked, "When a peasant has consumption, he says, 'There's nothing I can do. I'll go off in the spring with the melting of the snows.' " (Chekhov himself died in the summer, during a heat wave.) But once Chekhov's own tuberculosis was discovered he continually tried to minimize the seriousness of his condition. To all appearances, it was as if he felt, right up to the end, that he might be able to throw off the disease as he would a lingering catarrh. Well into his final days, he spoke with seeming conviction of the possibility of an improvement. In fact, in a letter written shortly before his end, he went so far as to tell his sister that he was "putting on a bit of flesh" and felt much better now that he was in Badenweiler.

Badenweiler is a spa and resort city in the western area of the Black Forest, not far from Basel. The Vosges are visible from nearly anywhere in the city, and in those days the air was pure and invigorating. Russians had been going there for years to soak in the hot mineral baths and promenade on the boulevards. In June 1904, Chekhov went there to die.

Earlier that month, he'd made a difficult journey by train from Moscow to Berlin. He traveled with his wife, the actress Olga Knipper, a woman he'd met in 1898 during rehearsals for *The Seagull.* Her contemporaries describe her as an excellent actress. She was talented, pretty, and almost ten years younger than the playwright. Chekhov had been immediately attracted to her, but was slow to act on his feelings. As always, he preferred a flirtation to marriage. Finally, after a three-year courtship involving many separations, letters, and the inevitable misunderstandings, they were at last married, in a private ceremony in Moscow, on May 25, 1901. Chekhov was enormously happy. He called Olga his "pony," and sometimes "dog" or "puppy." He was also fond of addressing her as "little turkey" or simply as "my joy."

In Berlin, Chekhov consulted with a renowned specialist in pulmonary disorders, a Dr. Karl Ewald. But, according to an eyewitness, after the doctor examined Chekhov he threw up his hands and left the room without a word. Chekhov was too far gone for help: this Dr. Ewald was furious with himself for not being able to work miracles, and with Chekhov for being so ill.

A Russian journalist happened to visit the Chekhovs at their hotel and sent back this dispatch to his editor: "Chekhov's days are numbered. He seems mortally ill, is terribly thin, coughs all the time, gasps for breath at the slightest movement, and is running a high temperature." This same journalist saw the Chekhovs off at Potsdam Station when they boarded their train for Badenweiler. According to his account, "Chekhov had trouble making his way up the small staircase at the station. He had to sit down for several minutes to catch his breath." In fact, it was painful for Chekhov to move: his legs ached continually and his insides hurt. The disease had attacked his intestines and spinal cord. At this point he had less than a month to live. When Chekhov spoke of his condition now, it was, according to Olga, "with an almost reckless indifference."

Dr. Schwöhrer was one of the many Badenweiler physicians who earned a good living by treating the well-to-do who came to the spa seeking relief from various maladies. Some of his patients were ill and infirm, others simply old and hypochondriacal. But Chekhov's was a special case: he was clearly beyond help and in his last days. He was also very famous. Even Dr. Schwöhrer knew his name: he'd read some of Chekhov's stories in a German magazine. When he examined the writer early in June, he voiced his appreciation of Chekhov's art but kept his medical opinions to himself. Instead, he prescribed a diet of cocoa, oatmeal drenched in butter, and strawberry tea. This last was supposed to help Chekhov sleep at night.

On June 13, less than three weeks before he died, Chekhov wrote a letter to his mother in which he told her his health was on the mend. In it he said, "It's likely that I'll be completely cured in a week." Who knows why he said this? What could he have been thinking? He was a doctor himself, and he knew better. He was dying, it was as simple and as unavoidable as that. Nevertheless, he sat out on the balcony of his hotel room and read railway timetables. He asked for information on sailings of boats bound for Odessa from Marseilles. But he *knew*. At this stage he had to have known. Yet in one of the last letters he ever wrote he told his sister he was growing stronger by the day.

He no longer had any appetite for literary work, and hadn't for a long time. In fact, he had very nearly failed to complete *The Cherry Orchard* the year before. Writing that play was the hardest thing he'd ever done in his life. Toward the end, he was able to manage only six or seven lines a day. "I've started losing heart," he wrote Olga. "I feel I'm finished as a writer, and every sentence strikes me as worthless and of no use whatever." But he didn't stop. He finished his play in October 1903. It was the last thing he ever wrote, except for letters and a few entries in his notebook.

A little after midnight on July 2, 1904, Olga sent someone to fetch Dr. Schwöhrer. It was an emergency: Chekhov was delirious. Two young Russians on holiday happened to have the adjacent room, and Olga hurried next door to explain what was happening. One of the youths was in his bed asleep, but the other was still awake, smoking and reading. He left the hotel at a run to find Dr. Schwöhrer. "I can still hear the sound of the gravel under his shoes in the silence of that stifling July night," Olga wrote later on in her memoirs. Chekhov was hallucinating, talking about sailors, and there were snatches of something about the Japanese. "You don't put ice on an empty stomach," he said when she tried to place an ice pack on his chest.

Dr. Schwöhrer arrived and unpacked his bag, all the while keeping his gaze fastened on Chekhov, who lay gasping in the bed. The sick man's pupils were dilated and his temples glistened with sweat. Dr. Schwöhrer's face didn't register anything. He was not an emotional man, but he knew Chekhov's end was near. Still, he was a doctor, sworn to do his utmost, and Chekhov held on to life, however tenuously. Dr. Schwöhrer prepared a hypodermic and administered an injection of camphor, something that was supposed to speed up the heart. But the injection didn't help — nothing, of course, could have helped. Nevertheless, the doctor made known to Olga his intention of sending for oxygen. Suddenly, Chekhov roused himself, became lucid, and said quietly, "What's the use? Before it arrives I'll be a corpse."

Dr. Schwöhrer pulled on his big mustache and stared at Chekhov. The writer's cheeks were sunken and gray, his complexion waxen; his breath was raspy. Dr. Schwöhrer knew the time could be reckoned in minutes. Without a word, without conferring with Olga, he went over to an alcove where there was a telephone on the wall. He read the instructions for using the device. If he activated it by holding his finger on a button and turning a handle on the side of the phone, he could reach the lower regions of the hotel — the kitchen. He picked up the receiver, held it to his ear, and did as the instructions told him. When someone finally answered, Dr. Schwöhrer ordered a bottle of the hotel's best champagne. "How many glasses?" he was asked. "Three glasses!" the doctor shouted into the mouthpiece. "And hurry, do you hear?" It was one of those rare moments of inspiration that can easily enough be overlooked later on, because the action is so entirely appropriate it seems inevitable.

The champagne was brought to the door by a tired-looking young man whose blond hair was standing up. The trousers of his uniform were wrinkled, the creases gone, and in his haste he'd missed a loop while buttoning his jacket. His appearance was that of someone who'd been resting (slumped in a chair, say, dozing a little), when off in the distance the phone had clamored in the early-morning hours—great God in heaven! — and the next thing he knew he was being shaken awake by a superior and told to deliver a bottle of Moët to room 211. "And hurry, do you hear?"

The young man entered the room carrying a silver ice bucket with the champagne in it and a silver tray with three cut-crystal glasses. He found a place on the table for the bucket and glasses, all the while craning his neck, trying to see into the other room, where someone panted ferociously for breath. It was a dreadful, harrowing sound, and the young man lowered his chin into his collar and turned away as the ratchety breathing worsened. Forgetting himself, he stared out the open window toward the darkened city. Then this big imposing man with a thick mustache pressed some coins into his hand — a large tip, by the feel of it — and suddenly the young man saw the door open. He took some steps and found himself on the landing, where he opened his hand and looked at the coins in amazement.

Methodically, the way he did everything, the doctor went about the business of working the cork out of the bottle. He did it in such a way as to minimize, as much as possible, the festive explosion. He poured three glasses and, out of habit, pushed the cork back into the neck of the bottle. He then took the glasses of champagne over to the bed. Olga momentarily released her grip on Chekhov's hand — a hand, she said later, that burned her fingers. She arranged another pillow behind his head. Then she put the cool glass of champagne against Chekhov's palm and made sure his fingers closed around the stem. They exchanged looks — Chekhov, Olga, Dr. Schwöhrer. They didn't touch glasses. There was no toast. What on earth was there to drink to? To death? Chekhov summoned his remaining strength and said, "It's been so long since I've had champagne." He brought the glass to his lips and drank. In a minute or two Olga took the empty glass from his hand and set it on the nightstand. Then Chekhov turned onto his side. He closed his eyes and sighed. A minute later, his breathing stopped.

Dr. Schwöhrer picked up Chekhov's hand from the bedsheet. He held his fingers to Chekhov's wrist and drew a gold watch from his vest pocket, opening the lid of the watch as he did so. The second hand on the watch moved slowly, very slowly. He let it move around the face of the watch three times while he waited for signs of a pulse. It was three o'clock in the morning and still sultry in the room. Badenweiler was in the grip of its worst heat wave in years. All the windows in both rooms stood open, but there was no sign of a breeze. A large, black-winged moth flew through a window and banged wildly against the electric lamp. Dr. Schwöhrer let go of Chekhov's wrist. "It's over," he said. He closed the lid of his watch and returned it to his vest pocket.

At once Olga dried her eyes and set about composing herself. She thanked the doctor for coming. He asked if she wanted some medication — laudanum, perhaps, or a few drops of valerian. She shook her head. She did have one request, though: before the authorities were notified and the newspapers found out, before the time came when Chekhov was no longer in her keeping, she wanted to be alone with him for a while. Could the doctor help with this? Could he withhold, for a while anyway, news of what had just occurred?

Dr. Schwöhrer stroked his mustache with the back of a finger. Why not? After all, what difference would it make to anyone whether this matter became known now or a few hours from now? The only detail that remained was to fill out a death certificate, and this could be done at his office later on in the morning, after he'd slept a few hours. Dr. Schwöhrer nodded his agreement and prepared to leave. He murmured a few words of condolence. Olga inclined her head. "An honor," Dr. Schwörer said. He picked up his bag and left the room and, for that matter, history.

It was at this moment that the cork popped out of the champagne bottle; foam spilled down onto the table. Olga went back to Chekhov's bedside. She sat on a footstool, holding his hand, from time to time stroking his face. "There were no human voices, no everyday sounds," she wrote. "There was only beauty, peace, and the grandeur of death."

*

She stayed with Chekhov until daybreak, when thrushes began to call from the garden below. Then came the sound of tables and chairs being moved about down there. Before long, voices carried up to her. It was then a knock sounded at the door. Of course she thought it must be an official of some sort — the medical examiner, say, or someone from the police who had questions to ask and forms for her to fill out, or maybe, just maybe, it could be Dr. Schwöhrer returning with a mortician to render assistance in embalming and transporting Chekhov's remains back to Russia.

But, instead, it was the same blond young man who'd brought the champagne a few hours earlier. This time, however, his uniform trousers were neatly pressed, with stiff creases in front, and every button on his snug green jacket was fastened. He seemed quite another person. Not only was he wide awake but his plump cheeks were smooth-shaven, his hair was in place, and he appeared anxious to please. He was holding a porcelain vase with three long-stemmed yellow roses. He presented these to Olga with a smart click of his heels. She stepped back and let him into the room. He was there, he said, to collect the glasses, ice bucket, and tray, yes. But he also wanted to say that, because of the extreme heat, breakfast would be served in the garden this morning. He hoped this weather wasn't too bothersome; he apologized for it.

The woman seemed distracted. While he talked, she turned her eyes away and looked down at something in the carpet. She crossed her arms and held her elbows. Meanwhile, still holding his vase, waiting for a sign, the young man took in the details of the room. Bright sunlight flooded through the open windows. The room was tidy and seemed undisturbed, almost untouched. No garments were flung over chairs, no shoes, stockings, braces, or stays were in evidence, no open suitcases. In short, there was no clutter, nothing but the usual heavy pieces of hotel room furniture. Then, because the woman was still looking down, he looked down, too, and at once spied a cork near the toe of his shoe. The woman did not see it — she was looking somewhere else. The young man wanted to bend over and pick up the cork, but he was still holding the roses and was afraid of seeming to intrude even more by drawing any further attention to himself. Reluctantly, he left the cork where it was and raised his eyes. Everything was in order except for the uncorked, half-empty bottle of champagne that stood alongside two crystal glasses over on the little table. He cast his gaze about once more. Through an open door he saw that the third glass was in the bedroom, on the nightstand. But someone still occupied the bed! He couldn't see a face, but the figure under the covers lay perfectly motionless and quiet. He noted the figure and looked elsewhere. Then, for a reason he couldn't understand, a feeling of uneasiness took hold of him. He cleared his throat and moved his weight to the other leg. The woman still didn't look up or break her silence. The young man felt his cheeks grow warm. It occurred to him, quite without his having thought it through, that he should perhaps suggest an alternative to breakfast in the garden. He coughed, hoping to focus the woman's attention, but she didn't look at him. The distinguished foreign guests could, he said, take breakfast in their rooms this morning if they wished. The young man (his name hasn't survived, and it's likely he perished in the Great War) said he would be happy to bring up a tray. Two trays, he added, glancing uncertainly once again in the direction of the bedroom.

He fell silent and ran a finger around the inside of his collar. He didn't understand. He wasn't even sure the woman had been listening. He didn't know what else to do now; he was still holding the vase. The sweet odor of the roses filled his nostrils and inexplicably caused a pang of regret. The entire time he'd been waiting, the woman had apparently been lost in thought. It was as if all the while he'd been standing there, talking, shifting his weight, holding his flowers, she had been someplace else, somewhere far from Badenweiler. But now she came back to herself, and her face assumed another expression. She raised her eyes, looked at him, and then shook her head. She seemed to be struggling to understand what on earth this young man could be doing there in the room holding a vase with three yellow roses. Flowers? She hadn't ordered flowers.

The moment passed. She went over to her handbag and scooped up some coins. She drew out a number of banknotes as well. The young man touched his lips with his tongue; another large tip was forthcoming, but for what? What did she want him to do? He'd never before waited on such guests. He cleared his throat once more.

No breakfast, the woman said. Not yet, at any rate. Breakfast wasn't the important thing this morning. She required something else. She needed him to go out and bring back a mortician. Did he understand her? Herr Chekhov was dead, you see. *Comprenez-vous?* Young man? Anton Chekhov was dead. Now listen carefully to me, she said. She wanted him to go downstairs and ask someone at the front desk where he could go to find the most respected mortician in the city. Someone reliable, who took great pains in his work and whose manner was appropriately reserved. A mortician, in short, worthy of a great artist. Here, she said, and pressed the money on him. Tell them downstairs that I have specifically requested you to perform this duty for me. Are you listening? Do you understand what I'm saying to you?

The young man grappled to take in what she was saying. He chose not to look again in the direction of the other room. He had sensed that something was not right. He became aware of his heart beating rapidly under his jacket, and he felt perspiration break out on his forehead. He didn't know where he should turn his eyes. He wanted to put the vase down.

Please do this for me, the woman said. I'll remember you with gratitude. Tell them downstairs that I insist. Say that. But don't call any unnecessary attention to yourself or to the situation. Just say that this is necessary, that I request it — and that's all. Do you hear me? Nod if you understand. Above all, don't raise an alarm. Everything else, all the rest, the commotion — that'll come soon enough. The worst is over. Do we understand each other?

The young man's face had grown pale. He stood rigid, clasping the vase. He managed to nod his head.

After securing permission to leave the hotel he was to proceed quietly and resolutely, though without any unbecoming haste, to the mortician's. He was to behave exactly as if he were engaged on a very important errand, nothing more. He *was* engaged on an important errand, she said. And if it would help keep his movements purposeful he should imagine himself as someone moving down the busy sidewalk carrying in his arms a porcelain vase of roses that he had to deliver to an important man. (She spoke quietly, almost confidentially, as if to a relative or a friend.) He could even tell himself that the man he was going to see was expecting him, was perhaps impatient for him to arrive with his flowers. Nevertheless, the young man was not to become excited and run, or otherwise break his stride. Remember the vase he was carrying! He was to walk briskly, comporting himself at all times in as dignified a manner as possible. He should keep walking until he came to the mortician's house and stood before the door. He would then raise the brass knocker and let it fall, once, twice, three times. In a minute the mortician himself would answer.

This mortician would be in his forties, no doubt, or maybe early fifties — bald, solidly built, wearing steel-frame spectacles set very low on his nose. He would be modest, unassuming, a man who would ask only the most direct and necessary questions. An apron. Probably he would be wearing an apron. He might even be wiping his hands on a dark towel while he listened to what was being said. There'd be a faint whiff of formaldehyde on his clothes. But it was all right, and the young man shouldn't worry. He was nearly a grownup now and shouldn't be frightened or repelled by any of this. The mortician would hear him out. He was a man of restraint and bearing, this mortician, someone who could help allay people's fears in this situation, not increase them. Long ago he'd acquainted himself with death in all its various guises and forms; death held no surprises for him any longer, no hidden secrets. It was this man whose services were required this morning.

The mortician takes the vase of roses. Only once while the young man is speaking does the mortician betray the least flicker of interest, or indicate that he's heard anything out of the ordinary. But the one time the young man mentions the name of the deceased, the mortician's eyebrows rise just a little. Chekhov, you say? Just a minute, and I'll be with you.

Do you understand what I'm saying, Olga said to the young

man. Leave the glasses. Don't worry about them. Forget about crystal wine glasses and such. Leave the room as it is. Everything is ready now. We're ready. Will you go?

But at that moment the young man was thinking of the cork still resting near the toe of his shoe. To retrieve it he would have to bend over, still gripping the vase. He would do this. He leaned over. Without looking down, he reached out and closed it into his hand.

RALPH LOMBREGLIA

Inn Essence

FROM THE ATLANTIC

FOR A COUPLE of months here we had peace, relative peace, more peace anyway than you expect in the restaurant business. The occasion of this peace was the delivery of Victor, our pastry chef, to a mental hospital. He went there to recover from the breakdown he'd had in the kitchen one dark March afternoon. And even for a little while after Victor returned, things were good. He was taking his medication, his wife and kid were back from her mother's, he had a new life to think about. Once again he was in his own special zone of the kitchen, making the most glorious chocolate desserts in the tri-state area. Some people say that Victor's creations go beyond culinary experience and into the realm of sex or voodoo. They say that on a good night finishing a meal at Inn Essence with the raspberry-laced chocolate torte or the Cointreau-bathed chocolate mousse is like having your body inhabited by the pastry chef himself.

Me, I try not to eat sweets, so I wouldn't know. But the point is, our peace is now gone. Victor has lost his mind again.

And for this reason I'm driving Route 80 east across northern New Jersey at 10:45 A.M., sleepy-headed in the right-hand lane, my blinker on for the exit that takes me to the restaurant. Forty miles more and I'd be on the George Washington Bridge, all of Manhattan lying before me like an antipasto tray. Right now I'd like to lean back and coast straight into it. At nine o'clock my telephone rang twice in rapid succession. I let the machine do its job, slept another hour, and then rolled out and listened to the messages. They were both from Jimmy Constanopolous, my employer.

"Jeffrey," Jimmy said to me in the first message, "my God, what a heartache this business is. Why are you working here, Jeffrey? You're a romantic, that's why. You think the restaurant business is romantic — don't deny it. I used to think that too. But now I'm a realist. I've had twenty years, I don't think I can take one more. Jeffrey, I've reconsidered our recent conversation. Go back and finish college. Get your degree. Yes, I said I wanted to groom you, turn you into a restaurateur. And I could do that. I could teach you to buy provisions, gain the trust of a staff, talk to the bank when the bank needed to be talked to. Manny could show you the famous veal medallions, the sauces that get written up in the papers. You already do beautiful salads. You could learn to mix a drink and hide cash from the registers at night. All the things I promised. But why, Jeffrey, why? So you could make the same mistakes I made? You'd stay with me a few years, I'd learn to love you like a son, and then the inevitable would happen. You'd want your own place. Because you're too smart to work for another man your whole life. You'd come to me for help—a down payment, leverage with the liquor-license people — and I wouldn't be able to turn you down. I'd have to help you. And then your life would be destroyed, like mine.

"Jeffrey," Jimmy went on, "I'm only going to say this once. Don't ever — under any circumstances, no matter what happens — even consider, for one minute, the idea of opening a restaurant."

Jimmy hung up. And then the second message came on. "Jeffrey, I know you're there. Get over here right now. I know, you're not on until three today. I'll make it up to you. Victor just tried to kill one of the Thai students — the little one, what's his name? — with a carving knife, no less. He said they stole pastries from his walk-in. And then he disappeared. Victor, I mean. I can't find him. And now the Thai students won't come out of their house and work, and I'm short-handed already, and we don't have enough desserts, and today is — what day is it, anyway? Christ, it's Friday. I've got to get my meat man on the phone. My bread man. I've got to find Victor. Jeffrey, I won't forget the way you've helped me. I'll set you up in business someday, you'll have your own place. Just get over here and talk to the Thai people. They like you. You're their friend." And then Jimmy hung up again.

Yes, I think to myself now, I could go for a day of hooky in Nueva York. The bookstores, the theaters, the streets full of people living lives of mysterious meaning. My foot wavers between the brake and the gas. But then I think of the thousands of restaurants in Manhattan, five or six of them on every block, and I almost lose control of the car.

The day Victor got out of the mental hospital, Jimmy offered him a deal. If Victor would come back to work and make his brilliant desserts, take his tranquilizers, and behave himself, Jimmy would remodel the old carriage house in back of the restaurant, and Victor and his family could live in it free of charge. The desserts Jimmy had been buying in Victor's absence were like the shadows in Plato's cave, and this idea had a precedent, Manny the chef having occupied the carriage house rent-free in the early days of Inn Essence. Since then, true, the place had fallen into wretched disrepair, lying empty or barely keeping rain off the heads of the assorted dishwashers and busboys Jimmy was forever trying to rehabilitate. I know, because I spent my own first month in its dank and peeling rooms. But the basic construction was the solid, old-fashioned kind, with enormous potential. He would put in skylights, Jimmy told Victor, and a working fireplace, a totally new kitchen and bath, and fresh paint on everything. He emphasized the old-fashioned gentility of it — the gifted chef-in-residence on the estate, waking with his wife to birdsong each morning, strolling to work through the woods like a country squire, fishing with his son at the stream when the day's desserts were done.

Victor came back to us a different man — quiet, productive, minding his own business, taking coffee breaks alone out back, where for a week or so, while Jimmy arranged for the carpenters to come, he could be seen staring past the dumpsters at the carriage house in a kind of reverie.

By this time it was early May, and one afternoon a red Mustang pulled up to Inn Essence. At the wheel was Kampon Padasha, an electrical-engineering student from Thailand. College was out now and Kampon wanted a summer job. He came in and explained this to Ethel, our hostess, who was sitting at the bar smoking and sorting out credit-card receipts from the day before. She looked him over and nodded while he spoke. His English wasn't great. He was thin and gangly, not handsome, overly polite in that disturbing foreigner's way. He had a sad haircut and thick black-rimmed glasses. He was not of Ethel's race. She smiled and shook her head and said she was sorry. She was showing Kampon the door when Jimmy walked into the bar. He was probably on his way to find me. We have at least one good chat a day about the meaning of life, usually around that hour — about four in the afternoon, the happiest point in the daily curve of Jimmy's relationship to whiskey. But he ran into Kampon first, and snatched him away from Ethel.

In his office Jimmy poured two drinks and sat the young engineer across from him at his desk. He told Kampon of his lifelong fascination with Kampon's part of the planet. "As the years go by," Jimmy said, "I think I'm becoming more and more of an Eastern mystic myself." He swept his arm in a gesture meant to encompass the entire world. "The physical plane means less and less to me every day."

"I am good worker," Kampon said.

"Of course you are," Jimmy said. "You come from an industrious people. Not like us," he said, laughing and slapping himself in the stomach. "Lazy and fat." He leaned over his desk. "Your people will inherit the earth. We will be your servants."

Kampon was bewildered. He said nothing, but slid forward in his chair, his face hovering at the edge of Jimmy's desk as if to inhale any life-giving vapors that might emanate from the big American.

"I will teach you to wait on tables," Jimmy said. "You will make tips — a custom we have. To Insure Prompt Service. You'll see." He held out his hand and smiled. The teeth in Jimmy's smile are straight and fine and white in front, and then, going back on either side, you see generous helpings of gold.

His mouth is like another man's purse is the rough English equivalent of what Kampon thought then in his native tongue.

Jimmy led his new employee out the back door onto the stretch of asphalt where the trucks back in to make deliveries and empty the dumpsters. They strolled together around the building into the parking lot. "This is a great country," Jimmy said to Kampon, "even though our civilization is a tiny infant compared with yours."

"Very great country," Kampon said, nodding his head up and down.

"Many types of people are needed to make a world," Jimmy said. "We don't have to destroy each other."

"Not destroy!" Kampon said, shaking his head and hands with alarm. He stopped alongside his red Mustang. Inside the car were four other young men from Thailand, attending college in America. "My friends," Kampon explained, smiling and pointing to them.

Four clear-complected faces looked out at Jimmy, each one framed by a helmet of lustrous black hair. Jimmy called them out of the car to look them over. *All right,* he thought, *I see what I have to do.* After he had hired them all, Jimmy discovered that the Thai students were forbidden to hold jobs in the United States under the terms of their student visas. This in itself was not a disaster. Keeping people off the books is as common as bread in the restaurant business. But then Jimmy learned that they had no money and nowhere to live. They'd been put out of their college dormitory that very morning.

This was how Jimmy explained it to Victor: The Thai students would live in the carriage house only for the summer, three or four months, the restaurant's busiest season. And the trees and rampant vegetation around the carriage house made it a dark, unpleasant place in the summer anyway. Then, the instant they went back to school in September, a work crew would transform the place and Victor's family would dwell there in time for the fall foliage.

And this was how Victor responded to Jimmy's explanation: a chocolate ricotta pie pitched against the metal door of the walk-in cooler he uses to store his decadent desserts. We've lived with Victor for almost a month since then, his psyche collapsing darkly like a dying star, amid eruptions of tantrums, insults, and erratic pastry production. And now, attempted murder.

I pull into the long tree-lined drive that leads down to the sprawling white form of Inn Essence, nestled in a shady grove on a defunct spur of the Erie-Lackawanna line. Twenty years ago, when Jimmy opened this place, the train was still running on this stretch of track — stopping at the old rambling inn this actually once was — and the land out there on the interstate where you see all those Martian-looking mirror-faced corporate headquarters was nothing but pasture full of cowplops. Now our parking lot can hold more than two hundred cars, though only a handful are in it so far today.

I park all the way down at the end, near the woods behind the dumpsters. As soon as I set foot on the shaded path that leads to the carriage house, Bucky comes running out of it to meet me. He's the sweet little guy of the Thai group, gregarious and completely devoid of guile. Just like Victor to pick on the littlest one. Maybe I should forget about peace, I think, and just help them finish Victor off.

"Hello, Señor Buck," I say when he reaches me on the path. "I hear you had a little run-in with Mr. Cream Puff."

"I get kill almost!" he says, grabbing my arm and imploring me with his wonderful almond eyes. Then he releases my arm and steps back, and makes the motions of a big knife piercing his chest. He falls to one knee with this great blade inside him, his protruding teeth making it all the more heartbreaking. "Almost!" he cries.

"Why did he come after you, Buck?"

"I do no thing!" he says.

"Nothing?" I say. "You didn't eat any of his goodies?"

"No!"

"You didn't laugh at him? Snicker when his back was turned?"

"Snicker?"

I demonstrate a snicker for Bucky, hand over my mouth.

"No!"

"Okay, I believe you." I pat his back and help him stand up.

"Bad man!" he says with a shudder. "Very terrorful!"

"Calm down, Buck," I say. "We'll fix it up."

"Thank!" he says, and we walk together up the path.

"Bucky" is not Bucky's actual name. The waitresses named him Bucky because of his teeth. He doesn't understand that, fortunately, and he likes the name. In fact, all the Thai students are quite pleased with the nicknames they were given by the waitresses almost immediately upon their arrival; it makes them feel very American. Plus, they're much bigger flirts than even the waitresses are, and receiving any nickname at all from a woman signifies something pretty good in their book.

We go into the carriage house. It's dark inside even though the luminescent orange polyester curtains are open. What little light comes through the windows is soaked up instantly by wall paneling so depressingly cheap that the wood-grain pattern repeats exactly every eighteen inches. Rocky and Toots are sitting on the ratty sofa in the living room, decked out in the black, satin-lapeled toreador jackets that Jimmy has his waiters and busboys wear. But they have their clip-on bow ties in their breast pockets and they're showing no signs of going in to start the lunch shift. Kampy and Buzz, off until dinner anyway, are sunk cross-legged in armchairs. The house is full of bad vibrations, a humid, conspiratorial air. "Hi, dudes," I say. Nobody says anything. Kampy, my best buddy among the Thai students, stares at me with a wistful face.

"Look, guys," I say. "Here's the thing about Victor. Victor is a sick man. He has visions. He see things that aren't there. He hears voices. That's why he was in the hospital before you started working here."

"So why Mister C. take him from hospital to here?" Rocky says. "Why not stay at hospital if sick?"

"It's not that simple, Rocky. The hospital is very expensive in America, and Victor is not crazy enough to stay there all the time anyway. Plus, his desserts are famous. And he wasn't always crazy. He lost his mind while he was working here. Many years of service. Mister C. feels responsible. You understand that, don't you? Isn't that the way it would be in your country? Wouldn't a boss feel responsible for a sick worker?"

"But not responsible for Thai students," Toots says.

"Yes, responsible for you, too. He gave you this house to live in, didn't he? He likes you. That's what caused the problem. Victor is jealous. His feelings are hurt."

"What about Thai worker feelings?" Buzz says.

"Yes, what about?" Rocky says, shaking the straight black luster of his hair.

Next to him on the sofa Toots holds up an arm and grabs the flesh of it with his other hand. "What about Thai worker skin?" he says, shaking his forearm and grimacing.

So things are much worse here than I thought. And meantime, Kampy is just sitting there letting me dangle in the breeze. "Kamp," I say. "You understand, right? You appreciate this difficult situation."

"What I can say?" Kampy says. "Bloodfall happening at this place."

"No," I say, "that's not true. Nothing like that has happened and nothing is going to happen." I turn to Rocky and Toots on the sofa. "Come on, you guys. Take Bucky inside and have some lunch. And then I want you to get out there and throw some food at those customers like only you know how."

"Very bad man," they say, but grudgingly they clip on their bow ties.

"Kampy," I say, "let's take a little walk."

He gets up and follows me outside. In the sunlight he looks me up and down as if seeing me for the first time. I'm wearing my pink Converse high-tops, wiped-out blue jeans, and a T-shirt with a cartoon of some happy snow peas dancing above the slogan BE A HUMAN BEAN.

I'm the salad man here at Inn Essence.

Kampy meditates on my T-shirt for a minute, moving the words around in his mouth. Finally he shakes his head and lets it go.

I put my hand on his shoulder and lead him along the path, which is dappled by flashes of yellow light coming down through the trees. We emerge from the cool, shady grove, and then we stroll along the edge of the underbrush that covers the old railroad tracks. Grasshoppers are springing out of the dandelions like trick party favors; the air is full of spicy weed smells. It's a beautiful June. On either side of the abandoned tracks thick stands of trashy sumac trees have grown to a height of forty feet or so and then fanned out flat on top into a canopy of pointy finger-leaves. They give the back of the restaurant a jungle feeling.

I point up at the sinewy, sour-smelling trees. "Does Thailand look like this, Kamp? These kinds of trees? Little hills like that in the distance?"

Kampy looks up at the sumacs and then all around himself. He half shakes, half nods his head. "Maybe someway," he says. "Yes, little bit."

I laugh. "The sky is blue over there?"

He laughs too. "Yes, sky is blue."

We sit down on a fallen tree next to the railroad bed.

"Yes, we have railroad in Thailand," Kampy says, not waiting for me to ask. "Very similar."

"Hey, Kamp," I say. "Mister C. had another brainstorm. He thinks I should have you teach me to speak Thai. So I can become more of a citizen of the world. He was telling me the other day."

Kampy smiles. "Very hard for you. Not like English."

"But I know you're a good teacher. I've been hearing about these cooking lessons of yours."

Here Kampy laughs out loud. "Oh, ho," he says. "Mister C. say, 'Kampon, I must know true Thai way of cooking. Tell me exact way you eat in your house over there. Maybe I serve some of these things here at restaurant.' I tell him, 'American people not like Thai home-style, Mister C.' But he not listen."

"Yes, he's good at that."

"He say, 'Kampon, food is key to world culture. All people must learn to eat together.' "

"Sounds like our boss, all right."

"But is not true."

"No?"

"People are different ways in this world, Jeffrey. People have loyalness with their own way. I, Kampon, understand this. Victor scream and bang at Thai workers. Mister C. say no thing to Victor. Now Victor do violence against Bucky. You, Jeffrey, my friend, yes, but you say, 'Kampon, have forgetfulness.' No, Jeffrey. Thai workers must glue their selves in one lump."

"I agree with that, Kampy. I think you should stick together.

But look. Jimmy will get Victor to go back on his medicine, and then everything will be fine."

"No, Jeffrey. Not true. Thai people can never work here tomorrow again, unless."

"Unless what?"

"Mister C. must punish Victor." He stands up and walks away from me, out to the parking lot. "Farewell," he says, holding up his hand.

I stand up too. "Kampy, I'm going to see you in a few hours," I say. "When you come on for dinner."

"My heart flows," Kampy says, his hand on his breast. Then he cocks his head quizzically and stares at me, and suddenly he starts to laugh. "Oh, human bean," he says. "I got you. That's a funny one."

I scuffle back through the underbrush toward the restaurant, passing by the *Aqua Marie* on the way. This is Jimmy's cabin cruiser, a thirty-two-foot monster he keeps parked on its trailer in a clearing next to the dumpsters. The boat is named in honor of Jimmy's wife — the Invisible Woman, we call her. I've heard Marie Constanopolous's voice on the phone but I've never seen her; except for Manny, who's been here forever, no one at Inn Essence has ever met the woman our boss is married to. Part of Jimmy's arrangement with Marie is that she has nothing to do with the restaurant and is expected never to come here for any reason. Other aspects of Marie's conjugal life are speculated upon endlessly by the waitresses, who get what they can out of Manny and invent the rest. Marie is commonly presumed to have an unbelievable wardrobe, unlimited money to spend, and at least one handsome lover, if not a brace of handsome lovers — nice young ones in their twenties, the waitresses say, if she's got any brains. Even a nineteen-year-old wouldn't be out of the question; any woman can stand to recharge occasionally with a nineteen-year-old, the waitresses tell me.

The waitresses think that Marie Constanopolous's situation comes as close to perfection as anything women have achieved in the history of the world.

But, even more than Marie, the waitresses have to wonder about Ethel, our hostess here at Inn Essence. How has she hung on all this time? Why does she put up with Jimmy's crap? What is she getting? What lies is he telling her? What does she feel when she answers the phone and hears Jimmy's wife on the other end? What goes through poor Ethel's mind when she walks out back and sees a huge, fine cabin cruiser with the wife's name painted on it in letters two feet high?

I understand the waitresses' fascination, but I think they might as well be doing algebra with angels, or trying to see the human soul by sprinkling cornstarch on people as they die. Me, I have an old friend in California named Ricky, a psychologist. Ricky has the word on this. "Nobody understands the boy-girl stuff, Jeffrey," Ricky says. "Not even God."

I walk across the loading area to the outside door of Jimmy's office, which is actually a one-bedroom apartment in its own small wing at the back of the restaurant. This is where for three years now Jimmy has been making love to Ethel. The blinds on the office windows are shut today, but behind the closed screen door the wooden door is ajar. I rap on the aluminum frame and call through the screen. "Bwana Jim, the natives are restless. I think you may have a revolt on your hands here. Spears and arrows may start flying out of the trees any minute now."

He doesn't answer me. When I cross the threshold, I smell Ethel's strong perfume. The waitresses say she alternates between Opium and Poison. If somebody comes out with a perfume called Sex or Death, straight out, Ethel will wear it. But then, so will everybody else. The woman herself is on the sofa, with a Scotch sour in one hand and a handkerchief in the other. She's had her hair done since yesterday, tinted a light bronze this time and sprayed into stiff swirls around her head. She's wearing a white silk blouse and a baby-blue suit. Her eyes are red and she's dabbing at her nose with the hanky. The bottle of Dewar's is on the coffee table — one third gone and it's not even noontime. Between Jimmy and Ethel, they're killing a good liter of it a day.

"Trouble in Thailand?" she says, tilting her head toward the carriage house.

"Well, Victor tried to murder Bucky this morning, and they're a little upset about it, that's all."

"I know, I heard," Ethel says. She takes a long drag on her

cigarette and then sips her drink, smoke pouring out of her face over the glass. She puts her stockinged feet up on the coffee table. "They'll get over it."

"I don't think so, Ethel. This was pretty abusive, even for Victor."

"Honey, we all have to take our share of abuse, now don't we?"

"Some of us have to take more than others."

"Tell me about it," she says. "Actually, I thought it was kind of amusing, Victor running around the parking lot in those little Italian shoes, waving that big knife. We don't have enough excitement around here."

Ethel has her own waitress-given nickname. Miss Frosty, they call her.

"Jimmy around?" I say.

"No, he's out looking for the mad muffin." Her own joke makes her smile. "The king of pork loin is searching for the mad muffin."

"That's pretty good."

"It really is, isn't it? I'm pretty creative, aren't I? I don't give myself enough credit."

"Most people don't."

"Some people give themselves too much," she says.

"The Thai students want Jimmy to punish Victor," I say.

"Ha," Ethel says.

"They say Jimmy must make some show of righting this wrong. Their heritage demands it."

Ethel leans her head back and cackles at the ceiling, coughing on her drink. "I didn't think anybody could do it today," she says. "But you're doing it. You're making me laugh." She giggles in a macabre way for a half minute or so, until, with no perceptible transition, she's weeping.

"Ethel, is something wrong?"

We all have to pretend that we don't know about Ethel's life, how her husband left her on account of Jimmy and how she's been waiting two years now for Jimmy to do the right thing.

"None of your business," she says through the handkerchief. After a minute she gets herself under control, blots her eyes, and has another taste of her drink. "What exactly is it that they want Jimmy to do to Victor, by the way?"

"I don't know," I say. "A gesture. Something to restore their dignity. Make him apologize, I suppose."

"Can you imagine Victor apologizing to anybody about anything?"

"No."

"Me neither. Maybe you and Jimmy can philosophize about it when he gets back. Maybe he'll have a theory about it. He was looking for you before. He wanted to ask you about a word. It's on his desk."

I walk over to Jimmy's desk. There's a legal pad with the word "epistemology" written on it, spelled incorrectly.

Ethel says, "He wanted to know if that word meant there were some things he'd never get to the bottom of."

I think about it for a minute. "Yeah, I guess you could say that."

Nine months ago I started here busing tables. Then, after a couple of weeks, Jimmy gave me my choice of moving up to waiter or going to the kitchen. Most people would have chosen to be a waiter, for the tips. I didn't think I needed daily contact with the public, and I certainly didn't need to work under Ethel out there. But I chose the kitchen for another reason, one that surprised me as much as anyone else. After two weeks of observing the impeccable ballet of our chefs, and tasting the results, I discovered that I wanted to be able to cook like that.

So they brought me back and started me in on salads. At most restaurants this would have been like permanent exile; salad chefs are usually a notch above busboys and not going anywhere. But at Inn Essence people have respect for salad. I'm a colleague here, encouraged to be creative. And I'm in training for bigger things.

Ordinarily I show up in the kitchen in the middle of the afternoon and scrub my vegetables. I wash my lettuce, reserving the best leaves for cups and baskets, tearing the rest into pieces. Then I get out my gleaming little knife for the magical part — the radish roses, the kiwi-fruit lotus pads, the celery palm trees, the gift bows out of cantaloupe shavings, the apples peeled and carved into carnations, the whole vegetable fantasy world I've learned to do so well.

But now, early in the dinner hour, all my salad chores are done and I'm having my latest cooking lesson. I'm learning to make the famous stuffed medallions of veal, as done by the Venezuelan-born Manny Quintero, the head chef of Inn Essence. We're together at his counter, our backs to the ovens, cutting the veal and talking about the stuffing of legend.

So far I've heard nothing from Jimmy. If he's lost interest in where things stand with the Thai students, that's his lookout.

"I use butter," Manny says. "You hear? Butter. I use fresh garlic, fresh mushrooms, only fresh herbs. Some so-called chefs, they use soybean oil, garlic and mushrooms from bottles, herbs from little cans." He tosses a veal medallion on the pile and wipes his hands on his long cook's apron. "I pity the bastards."

"Me too," I say, nodding my head.

Manny's two assistant chefs are working to our left, at the range, in a flurry of smoke and steam, putting up orders for the dining room. Rocky and Toots arrive to load the plates onto their trays. They're aloof and businesslike, still full of fear and hurt pride.

"Are the citizens of America happy tonight?" I ask them. "Do they have that hungry light in their eyes? Men, are they ripping those salads apart?"

"Citizens pretty happy," Toots says.

Manny says, "When I cook, I like to think of them as people who stayed in this inn when they were young, and now, tonight, they're back for the first time in twenty years. It inspires me."

I take a step backward to look at him. "You're getting as dreamy as the guy who owns this place," I say. "And all this time I thought you were secretly driving the bus."

"I thought you were," he says.

Suddenly a high-pitched burst of Thai exclamation comes out of Rocky. He's staring at the back door of the kitchen, around the corner from Manny's ovens. Victor has just strolled in, dressed in his dazzling whites, right up to the towering puff of chef's toque. He must drive his car in this outfit. His feet are as tiny as a girl's in their little black pumps.

"What do you know," Manny calls out. "It's the mousse man. Hey, mousse man, we don't have any desserts tonight. What happened, Mister Mousse?"

Victor ignores Manny. Instead he looks at me. "Will you get a load of this," he says, pulling the big metal handle of his walk-in to open it. "Manny is training Jimmy's little pet."

He waits for me to respond but I don't give him the satisfaction. He steps into his walk-in, and the door snaps shut behind him. Rocky and Toots are simmering in the hot red light of the warming lamps, looking mean. "Waiters," I say to them, "pick up your orders and take them out to the people. Be professionals."

They do so, but their concern is justified. There's something very eerie about seeing Victor in the kitchen at this hour of the day. His routine is to start in the early morning and be long gone by the time the first blackened red snapper comes off the grill at night. I refuse to believe he's here out of guilt over leaving us without desserts.

"We have to send that boy back to the nut bin," I say to Manny.

"No, they can't help him there," Manny says, shaking his head. "They just give him the drugs and stare at him all day, make him worse than he was before. He's happy when he bakes. So I say let him bake. And when the man gets crazy, knock him down."

I look at Manny flexing his nut-brown arm. He's referring to the way he handled the episode last March. Victor comes out of his walk-in and installs himself in the L-shaped baking zone at the rear of the kitchen, where he has his long counters of work space, his own special ovens and range. He doesn't look tranquilized to me. He's removed several big aluminum trays of flaky pastry puffs from his cooler, and now he sticks them in their sides with the business end of a pastry bag, squirting them full of chocolate-cream filling. He seems to be taking unusual delight in this operation.

I hear Ethel call my name. She's standing inside the kitchen's swinging doors. "Jimmy wants to see you," she says, nodding in the direction of his office. I see her take note of Victor's presence. Then she shoulders open the right-hand door and spins away through it.

"Boss wants to see his little pet," Manny says to me, really enjoying himself, showing all of his gleaming tusks.

"Give me a break, Manny," I say.

"One break coming up," he says.

I walk out from behind the chefs' area, untying my apron on the way. I stop at the swinging doors and look through their windows. Ethel is at the waiters' station, talking to Kampy, Buzz, and Bucky. They're gesturing with their hands and she's nodding her head. Rocky and Toots appear with their empty table trays and join in this conversation. Ethel is actually listening to them, which is odd; she's not known for her sympathy, certainly not to the Thai students, whom she's tried to ignore from the day they started.

Two waitresses, Cheryl and Nadine, are sitting here in the kitchen by the uniform closet, having a cigarette. I mention what I'm seeing out there — Ethel being chummy with the Thai waiters.

"Oh, yeah, she's the good mother tonight," Cheryl says, nodding her head so that the plumes of smoke from her nostrils make waves. "She had a big fight with Jimmy, and now she's being real nice to everybody."

"They should fight all the time," Nadine adds. "It makes her almost like a person."

A smoke ring leaves Cheryl's mouth. "They do fight all the time."

Stepping out of the kitchen, I nod to Ethel and the guys. I walk into the open corridor with the restrooms and pay phones, turning to take another look at them from the quiet, carpeted dimness. Sometimes, in the middle of the dinner rush, Jimmy will stand here like this, next to the cigarette machines, watching the Thai waiters interact with the public and each other. He has an anthropologist's fascination with them as they make their way through the world; their customs and doings are deep, mysterious things to him.

His office door is all the way down at the end of the hall. I knock on it.

"Oh, it's you," he says when I walk in. "So what's going on out there? Do I still have a restaurant?" He's sitting slumped on the sofa, a heavy man in a gray tropical suit, shirt collar open, no tie, holding a Scotch-and-water in his lap.

"No man ever knows what he really has," I say.

He laughs with great Greek delight, eyes wrinkling, golden teeth flashing in the corners of his mouth. "I like you, Jeffrey," he says. "I can always count on you." He points to a chair and I sit down. "You think it's easy being the guy in charge?"

"Of course not," I say. "It's hell."

"Correct." He sips his Scotch. The liter of Dewar's is still on the coffee table, maybe one drink left in it now. "Have I ever told you about when I was in Korea?"

"You've mentioned it."

"You wouldn't even have been born yet."

"No."

"I was a sergeant, did you know that?"

"You told me."

"It was an amazing thing, Jeffrey. Koreans were all around us. Everywhere you looked you saw Korean people and Korean life."

"Well, Jimmy, you were in Korea."

"Exactly. I'm saying it was their country, but we were there. We were the strangers."

"I'm with you so far."

"But the weird thing was, Jeffrey, *we were in charge.* We were there to solve their problem. They were looking to us for *answers.* And Jeffrey?"

"Yeah?"

"We didn't even know what the question was. We didn't know the first thing about those people's lives. I was giving out orders, for Christ's sake, and I didn't even know what I was doing over there. But for the first time in my life I had incredible power. And I discovered something."

"What?"

"I loved it. I loved the power. It didn't matter at all that I was an ignorant schmuck. Having that power canceled out everything else."

"Strange. Listen, Jimmy, Victor's here. He's baking in the kitchen right now."

"Yeah, I know, I just talked to him." He parts the blinds on the window next to the sofa and looks out at the carriage house. Often he secretly observes the comings and goings of the Thai students from this window. "I learned another thing in the service," he says. "You always hear that people everywhere are basically the same, that all anybody really wants is to be loved. That's true, but they also want to make sure nobody gets any but them."

"Jimmy, I think a lot of those people in Korea just wanted not to get shot by you or have a bomb dropped on their house. They wanted to wake up the next day, and that was about it."

"Those are the accidents of history, Jeffrey. I'm talking about the big, eternal things, like the fact that all people are greedy and self-centered and they make excuses for it with ideas like 'honor' and 'saving face.' "

"You talked to Ethel about the Thai students."

He shakes his head and deeply sighs her name. "Ethel." Then he belts down the rest of his drink. "What am I going to do about Ethel?"

"She was crying in here before."

"She cries all the time," he says. "Okay, everybody wants a piece of Jimmy. All right, fine, I accept that. But Ethel's not satisfied with her piece, and she's letting it ruin her life. Let me tell you something, Jeffrey. I never promise anybody anything I can't deliver. If I can't deliver, I don't promise. It's a good rule, one you could live by if you're interested. Ethel has gotten everything she was ever promised and a lot more. If she wants to walk out, she can walk out."

"Is that what she wants to do? Walk out?"

"No, I told you. She wants to be the only puppy in the litter. Since she can't have that, she's going to find a different way to make me miserable every day. But tonight she's unbelievable. Tonight — get this — she wants me to punish Victor for running after Bucky with the knife."

"No kidding."

"Yeah, she insists on it. The dignity of her staff requires it, she says. I said forget it. I'm not punishing anybody."

"Maybe you should. If it would keep her happy."

"Jeffrey, yesterday Ethel couldn't stand the Thai people, all right? Don't argue with me, I know how to handle this. Now listen carefully, kid, you're about to learn something. Here's what I do. I call the Thai students in and — humbly, with gratitude for good service — I offer them more money. Right out of the blue, I give them a big raise."

"I'm sure they'll appreciate that."

"But I say nothing to them about Victor. Victor's name is never mentioned. I make no connection between Victor and their reward. Okay? And now, do I then turn around and punish Victor? Far from it. Pay attention, Jeffrey, I've never let anyone else in on this. *I call Victor in and I give him more money too.* In fact, I've already done it. You see what I'm saying? Money is love, Jeffrey, and now everybody has more than they had before. Presto, peace is restored to the garden. All the animals can live happily together again. But the brilliant part is that this love doesn't make judgments. It doesn't take sides. It's love that forgives. Frankly, Jeffrey, it's the love Jesus was talking about. I resolve the conflict by giving everybody more money, Victor and the Thai students equally, even though Victor did something very bad."

"He tried to kill Bucky."

"Oh, no, something much worse than that. Something to hurt me personally, his benefactor and friend."

"He did? What?"

"He called Immigration, the jerk."

"He didn't."

"Oh, yes, he did. He ratted on me about the Thai students. He admitted it to me here in this office just now. He called them from his house, and then he came back here to be on hand for the excitement. He strolled in and sat right there, puffed up with his secret betrayal. But he couldn't carry it off. He became remorseful and confessed. I let him stew in his own guilt for a minute, and then I just blew him away with his raise. You think he was confused before? Now he's really confused. But he's confused by love, which is good."

"Jimmy, what about Immigration?"

"Yeah, them. You're right, we should take some defensive action. We should hide the Thai students. Would you do that for me? Go hide the boys and then buzz me when the feds get here."

I'm up out of my chair and walking away when something occurs to me. "This idea of putting love in people's paychecks — you ever try that on Ethel?"

"Are you kidding? Ethel makes so much money here now it's ridiculous. But that doesn't work for her anymore. It's my fault, I let Ethel get keyed in to a different symbol. You know, I always wondered why mystics and saints denied the body, why priests, those poor bastards, had to be celibate. Now I think I get it. Jesus kept the company of whores, but I've never read anything in there about him messing around with them. Sex changes everything, Jeffrey, don't ask me why."

I tell Jimmy my friend Ricky's line about boy-girl business.

"A friend of yours said that?" Jimmy says. "Hey, does this guy want a job? The man who said that can come work for me anytime."

"I'll let him know," I say. "Now I better get out there and save our butts."

"Good. You do that."

I'm halfway out the door when he calls me back again.

"Hey, one second," he says. "I had a few recipe ideas I wanted to run by you. Wait till you hear these. What would you think of moussaka with — brace yourself — hot curry and a peanut sauce? Or feta-cheese pie with ginger and snow peas? And how does baklava with coconut milk and litchi nuts grab you?"

"Don't tell me," I say. "Greek-Thai cuisine."

"You got it," he says. "Inspired, right? A whole new contribution. East meets West. Two ancient cultures united. I hope Manny doesn't give me a hard time about it. You get to be my age, Jeffrey, and you start thinking about the big picture. You start asking some basic questions about your existence. 'Did his menu reflect his vision of life? Did he *have* a vision of life? Did he have anything new to offer? Did he have anything to say?' Things like that."

*

I hurry out to the head of the corridor and stand behind the cigarette machines, scanning the dinning room. Just inside the front door, next to the sign that says OUR HOSTESS WILL SEAT YOU, are two hard guys in rumpled suits. They look hungry all right, but not for anything we serve here. They're swiveling their heads on their big necks, checking the place out real good. Our hostess will seat you! For the first time in my career at Inn Essence I'd give anything to see Ethel walk around the corner — her face carved out of flesh-colored ice, her hair sprayed into a bronze battle helmet. She could make crème brûlée out of these guys. But, incredibly, in the middle of the dinner rush, she's not on duty. Just across from me Nadine is picking up a drink order at the end of the bar. I sidle up to her and point out the feds. "Head those guys off, Nadine!" I whisper. "Stall 'em. They're here to bust us for illegal aliens." She looks back and forth between me and the front door like I've just dropped down from Neptune.

"Do it, Nadine!" I cry. Then I burst through the swinging doors into the kitchen. The Thai waiters are nowhere to be seen. Neither is Victor. But then I see that all the way at the back of the kitchen, by the exit to the parking lot, the door of Victor's walk-in is just closing.

Manny, still doing the veal medallions, sees me standing there. "Here's how they look when you're done," he calls out, holding on his palm the glistening meat wrapped neatly around its stuffing.

I run up to the glass partition beneath the warming lamps. "Never mind the veal, Manny!" I bark at him. "Where are the Thai students?"

He looks around. "I don't know," he says. "They were just here."

"Manny, Victor called Immigration! They're at the front door!"

He catches this hot potato like the pro he is, dropping the veal and bolting out of his work space toward the dining room. I run the other way past him and around the corner to Victor's walk-in. I'm going to take care of Victor, I think to myself. I'm going to fix this clown. I yank open the door of his cooler and leap inside.

In doing so, I smack into Ethel and nearly knock her down.

"What the hell are you doing in here?" I snap at her. She snaps the same thing at me. Then the heavy door of the walk-in snaps shut and I can't see anything. The only light in Victor's huge cooler comes from two low-wattage bare bulbs on either side of the ceiling fan, and my eyes are accustomed to the brightness outside. It's cold, but deliciously so, compared with the swelter of the kitchen.

I'm about to tell Ethel what I'm doing in here, when my eyes adjust enough to see that all the Thai workers are standing in here with her. I throw my arms around her shoulders. "You're beautiful, Ethel!" I say. "Good going! But is it safe enough?"

She pushes me away. "Safe enough for what?" she says with great irritation.

And then I see Victor. He's sitting against the rear wall of the walk-in, legs stretched out in front of him, arms behind his back, hands and feet bound with crisp cloth napkins fresh from the linen service. His mouth is wide open as if in amazement, but that's because one of his own cream puffs has been stuffed all the way into it to gag him. His narrowed eyes are fixed on me — not with fear or rage or even supplication, not with any emotion at all, but with the unnerving vacancy of a man in shock. I look at him more closely in the thin yellow light. Squiggles of dark brown chocolate cream are all over his body — stripes of it up and down his arms and legs and outlining the pockets and buttons of his baker's uniform. He looks like a gingerbread man in reverse, brown frosting on white. Bucky is kneeling on the floor next to him, the chocolate-cream-filled pastry bag in his hands.

"Do his face now, Bucky," Ethel says. "He needs some nice eyebrows, doesn't he, boys?"

All the Thai students giggle their agreement. Bucky chortles with delight and sets to work on the brows, squeezing thick lines of chocolate onto Victor's face. Suddenly Victor comes to life and struggles violently for a moment, making scary animal noises around the cream puff in his mouth and messing up the frosting on his eyebrows.

"Baking man not want to be cookie," Bucky says, flashing all his protruding teeth. He puts some chocolate on Victor's nose, and then he sets to work decorating Victor's tall white hat. Kampy and Toots and Rocky and Buzz are all smiling and nodding their heads up and down. Then Kampy turns to me.

"Mr. C. understand Thai worker feelings," he says. "He send Miss Ethel to tell us good idea of punishment for Victor. We have such ways like this in Thailand, too. No person get hurt, and Thai workers have honor restored. Mister C. is very wise man. America is fair country."

I look at Ethel. She glares at me. I turn to the metal door of the walk-in and press my ear tightly against it. The bitter chill gives me a headache instantly, but I stay there.

"We have a report that you have employed illegal alien workers from Thailand," I hear Immigration saying, faintly through the door. "Let's go, chef. Where are they? Let's see these Thai workers."

Victor sees me listening at the door, and he starts making a fuss again in the back of the cooler, bucking and snorting some guttural sounds. But his walk-in was once the inn's meat locker, with solid walls and a heavy rubber seal around the opening; no one will ever hear him out there.

I put my ear back to the cold agony of the door. Manny's distant voice materializes, the volume fluctuating up and down. He must be following Immigration around the kitchen. "Thailand?" he says. "You must mean Venezuela! It's me you looking for? Manny Quintero from Venezuela? But I ain't no illegal, man! I got my papers twenty years now! Just 'cause I'm a foreigner one time you come after me? Let's go to my house, I show you some papers. Gonna be egg on you faces, misters."

Ethel slides a tray of Victor's cream puffs halfway out of a rack, picks one up, and raises it above her head. She throws like a girl, but her aim is good. Chocolate cream and flaky pastry splatter across Victor's face. The Thai students applaud. Then Bucky stands up and Ethel passes cream puffs out to the boys. They all get one and wait for me to get mine.

Now Jimmy comes storming into the kitchen. "Where did you get this crap?" he says. "Who said these things about me? Where is my accuser? Let him show his face. Come out wherever you're hiding, you bastard."

"It was an anonymous tip," Immigration says. "On the telephone. We don't know who it was."

"Come on, Jeffrey, take your cream puff," Ethel says.

"You don't know who it was?" Jimmy screams. "You don't know who it was? Well, I know who it was! I'll tell you who it was! It was the man in the moon! You come to my place of business with this slander, this libel, these filthy lies, trying to get my name in the papers, trying to ruin my good reputation, trying to shut down the nicest restaurant in New Jersey on the basis of a telephone prank? I could make a stink about this you wouldn't believe! I know people in Trenton! I could have your jobs! I could get you Border Patrol in the Texas scrub! For life! Get the hell out of my restaurant!"

"I don't want one," I say.

"I knew it," Ethel says. "Sensitive Jeffrey doesn't want a cream puff. That's because you are a cream puff, Jeffrey. This is a ritual, everybody has to do it. Take it."

I remove my ear from the door. "No, Ethel."

Now the Thai students are confused. Jeffrey's not taking a cream puff. They stand there looking at me, not knowing what to do.

"Fine, Jeffrey. You don't have to participate. But you don't get to stay and watch the fun, either. Just open the door and get out."

"No," I say. "I can't do that."

"Oh, you are such a wimp, Jeffrey. You are such a little teacher's pet. Never mind him," Ethel says to the Thai students. "This is the ancient American way. Mister C. knows it, I know it. You have your old customs in Thailand, we have ours here. Throw those cream puffs, boys. Jeffrey's just anti-American, aren't you, Jeffrey?"

Pressing my head against the freezing metal door must have numbed my brain, because suddenly I'm dizzy and can't even talk to Ethel anymore. I have to close my eyes for a second to collect my thoughts. I have to see if I have this straight. I'm one of eight people hiding in a dim restaurant walk-in, our breath coming out of our faces in little mingling clouds. The proprietor of the walk-in is tied up on the floor, and federal agents are outside trying to bust us, but not for tying him up. The owner's mistress is calling me names because I won't take a cream puff she's offering me, while five young men from a distant land are looking at me with questioning eyes, the sweet pastries of revenge already in their hands. They're waiting for me to confirm that whatever we're doing is indeed the way justice is done in my country.

Can I deny it?

EDITH MILTON

Entrechat

FROM THE KENYON REVIEW

I

THE STORY IS that my father was shot down over Japan in 1944, about three days after I was born, and that my mother gave me to his parents as a sort of consolation prize. We won't go into the logic of this: I mean the business of why *she* was giving *them* a consolation prize. Or why, long before you could tell whether my consoling functions were really working, she'd already found herself a rather glamorous apartment attached to the household of a very glamorous Colonel to whom she got married six months later. Work out for yourselves whatever theories you feel comfortable with regarding motives, but just take it from me, that was the story.

When you hear a story from my mother often enough it gets to be more than the truth: it solidifies. What you end up with is a palpable object too solid to ignore gracefully or to embrace without being awkward about it. So it just sits there in the middle of your life, like too much lunch. Present but not accounted for. An undigested verity.

My mother has a lot of stories of this sort, and I go into this one only to make it clear that though she married Colonel Gordon and had another kid, who I suppose is my sister, more or less, I don't consider myself a Gordon in any way: not even a relative Gordon or a step-Gordon. My grandparents were kind, simple, decent people. There are those who might have felt resentful, or at least ambivalent, about finding themselves at the age of fifty with a tiny infant suddenly underfoot. But Gramp and Gramma just thought it was too good to be true; they were always under the impression that someday my mother would come to her senses and ask for me back. All my childhood, they treated me with tremendous respect and care, like something borrowed. They did their honorable best to make sure I saw my mother every year around Christmastime, and that I wrote to thank her and the Colonel, punctually, whenever packages of toys and clothes arrived for me from their travels, usually shop-worn and sometimes damaged: my mother likes thrift shops.

Gramma also reminded me to get a birthday card each Ides of March for my semi-sister, Fairlee. It struck me as a lousy day to be born on. But I didn't mind her. I didn't exactly like her, either, but I didn't mind her.

She was seven years younger than me. During my annual, reluctant yuletide visits, my mother had fun annoying me by pointing out how good Fairlee was and how sweet she looked on the Colonel's knee, while he did his Walter Pidgeon impersonation and smoked a cigar between her golden curls. Not that I wasn't envious, but even then I thought her a bit pathetic: a pale, solemn, tiny girl with a big high forehead delicately veined in blue, so it always looked bruised. My mother stage-managed her as if she were some second-act, walk-on angel to be called on for uplift whenever things got boring. In the middle of dessert, for instance, when you'd all but forgotten that Fairlee was even there. "Oh, Fairlee, my darling, show us your *entrechat!*" my mother might call from out of the blue, maybe explaining that Fairlee'd had a ballet lesson that afternoon, but more likely leaving us to guess the connection between *entrechats* and normal life. All Mother ever drank was white wine, but she started early; I think she kept a bottle by her toothbrush for morning use, and by demitasse time she could be counted on to be well beyond human logic. She'd get red in the face by noon, and her eyes would be funny, as though they'd just declared their independence from her face. Then after her nap, she'd lose her glasses or forget something upstairs or leave her book someplace she couldn't remember. It was a desperation of boredom, I suppose. At dinner she'd pick arguments with anyone who'd talk to her. And then, blessedly, she'd remember Fairlee. It never failed. As soon as Fairlee began to regale us with her *entrechat* my mother was sound asleep.

Just for the record, we need to add two more Gordons: the sons of the Colonel and his first (dead) wife. Scott's the older one; I've never fixed him in my mind properly, and on every family occasion I have to work out once again who the dark boy with the mustache, or the balding man with the beard, must be. John is about my age. I have a fellow-feeling for him, maybe because of that. Maybe because in the command performances — the birthdays, the anniversaries, the retirement celebrations, which my mother shames people into putting on — we were the ones who'd get the bit parts and do the cleaning up. Also, he has a nice face: a bland, handsome, chocolate box sort of face that's been squashed into an expression of such unchanging politeness that after a time, after a few years, you begin to sense the effort of its self-control.

John was the only Gordon to come to my grandmother's funeral. My mother, never one to be upstaged by anyone, not even by someone in a coffin, called in sick from Santa Barbara, where she and the Colonel had retired ten, twelve years before. "I can't move, my darling," she told me over the phone, "can you manage without me?" This wasn't too surprising. What amazed me was that John came in, just before the service started, and sat in the pew next to me. It made me doubt myself. It made me wonder if I belonged to the Gordons, somehow, after all.

I was living in Waltham at the time, working at Brandeis, which is maybe a two-hour drive from Deering, New Hampshire, where Fairlee was. Not that I ever paid any attention to where Fairlee was or gave the slightest heed to living, cosmically speaking, right next door. Until that instant when John sat down in the pew beside me and suddenly there I was: feeling myself a Gordon. By adoption at the very least. And possibly by genetic fact.

He told me that no one saw Fairlee much anymore. That she'd become a recluse. That she seemed unhappy. At the time I thought that the new family feeling blossoming in my heart made me feel sudden interest in her well-being. But probably it was just the same old stepsister *Schadenfreude,* happy-to-hear-she's-getting-her-just-deserts. In any case, for whatever reason, I found myself calling her to see when we could get together.

By then Fairlee'd been married about seven years, but in what I assumed was our mutual evasion of Gordons, I'd never even met her husband. For that matter, I only heard about the wedding three months after the event when my mother happened to write me one of her rare letters: she mentioned it almost casually; Fairlee'd run off and got married, she said. Mostly what she wrote about was her own wedding present to the happy pair; she'd given them Grandmother Gordon's silver. It was a bit on the old-fashioned side for her own use. But for Fairlee it would do splendidly.

Now this was odd. Not the thing about the wedding present, which was typical, but the offhand mention of the wedding, I mean. My mother goes in for big celebrations: cathedral nuptials and Forest Lawn interments. I couldn't figure out why we were suddenly doing this Gretna Green business. What species of monster had Fairlee slunk off with for what unmentionable reasons? Had Prince Charming escaped the Little Princess after all and left her with one of the dwarves? Or was it something else?

A couple of letters later when my mother wrote that Edmond de la Tour wasn't a nice man, I came to the conclusion it was something else. Unsavory reputation. Foreigner, to boot. Owner of about ten different surnames with conveniently attached little hooks of *des, dels,* and *vons* to string them together by if you wanted to keep them as a set. Which seemed unnecessary, considering they were unpronounceable and probably phony, like his title, which the Colonel had had investigated and declared genuine, but she didn't believe it for a moment. He wasn't even French. He was something sinister no one ever heard of except in horror movies, like Romanian or Yugoslavian or some such. He was more than twenty years older than little Fairlee. His reputation wasn't entirely savory, and there were stories . . . Still, it had to be admitted that his nose was good. He was graying at the temples. He claimed to be widowed, but who knows.

I think this is when the truth dawned on me: that what my mother was describing wasn't Fairlee's husband so much as Jane

Eyre's. I was being introduced to Mr. Rochester. Or maybe Maxim de Winter in *Rebecca.* We were distinctly in the middle of Gothic fiction, at least, and of course in Gothic fiction people don't go in for big weddings, not the heroines, anyway. What they do is, they elope.

I could see this had to be another one of my mother's stories and that poor Fairlee would probably be stuck with it, half masticated, for life.

But in the long run, as it happened, though he may not have worked out too well for Fairlee, he worked out even worse for my mother. Over the next seven years I heard nothing to his credit and a great deal to his discredit: he was lazy, he was greedy, he was poor; the family mansion on the Danube had been sold, or seized by the Russians, or never existed; the family business had gone bankrupt or been imagined; the family itself was dead, or Communists, or living in debt in California. He'd probably married Fairlee for Grandmother Gordon's silver, in the first place.

I didn't try to organize these inconsistent reproaches into any kind of sense, but I wasn't really surprised that my mother was unhappy about him: it must be hell being Mr. Rochester's mother-in-law.

Also, over the last few years she'd begun to complain more and more about the young Gordons in general; her posture toward them was draped in melancholy. I was clearly the only child who'd failed to disappoint her, and that was because I wasn't worth being disappointed by. From *my* unpromising upbringing in Worcester you couldn't expect much more than a librarian.

But as for the rest of them! Scott — the great athlete-to-be — never was; John — the governor, the senator, the dare-we-say-it President — taught Latin and Greek in Winnetka. My mother and the Colonel tried to offer these squalid facts to their friends as attractively as they could. "The most highly thought-of classical instructor . . . ," they'd announce at dinner parties, " . . . the most intrepid white-waterer . . ." They blew up quotations from yearbooks and company newsletters like balloons to raise their children to the extraordinary on hot air. But Fairlee was close to impossible: how far does a good *cassoulet* and nice penmanship get you in California society these days? Her only real accomplishment in life had been to marry an aging failure with a minor title, and my mother valiantly made the best she could out of that mediocre fate by talking it into being at least an interesting catastrophe.

Meanwhile, poor Edmond de la Tour lost his romantic patina and came out of my mother's drubbings with a shiny nose. What was worst of all, more useless even than poverty, was that he'd been discovered to have a besetting and totally unforgivable flaw: his health had failed. He had diabetes, ulcers, and high blood presure: much too sordid and uninteresting by way of diseases to deserve my mother's pity. And nothing at all like what Mr. Rochester might have got.

II

I drove up to Deering on Good Friday.

Fairlee gave me quite a welcome: none of your conventional "happy to see you" stuff. This was pure desperation, the sort of thing you'd expect from a castaway marooned for a dozen years. She came rushing through the door to meet me when I was only half out of the car, pulling myself together after four miles of dirt road in mud season. I was paralyzed with wonder at the little white cottage, glowing domestically against the gray New Hampshire day; it looked like something my mother might have found for one of her rustic weekend scenarios. There were clumps of narcissus and daffodil in the meadow behind the house, and a soft curl of smoke coming out of the chimney. The whole thing spoke sweetly of wood stoves and virtue: a commercial for country living.

"How perfectly heroic of you to be here at Easter!" Fairlee exclaimed, kissing me ceremonially left and right. The years had faded her a bit, but she hadn't really changed: she was still diminutive, pastel and vulnerably regal, a little Dresden Princess made for admiring and breaking. *"Dieu merci,* it refrained from pouring during your drive up. One has been known to sink to the withers! But darling, don't struggle with your luggage. Edmondo will bring it in. He'll be quite insulted if you persist in being so independent!" We had made our way, by then, through the little hall into the front room, where a rotund chow dog luxuriantly furred in black and sunning itself by the fire was introduced as Goneril. "*Prego. Avanti!* Shall I outline the week-end drill? I have told Goneril, scout's honor, that she may have a piece of our Easter *pashka* for brunch tomorrow. And she was so pleased. Weren't you, chouchou?" Under obligation, Goneril waved her tail politely and went back to sleep. I thought that maybe Fairlee's breathless cheerfulness put a bit of a strain on her. It wasn't really the way you'd talk to a dog, or even a kid. It was old-lady talk. "Edmondo insists we have the *gigot* for Sunday dinner, but he refuses to hear of an Easter egg hunt, such a rotten sport. Didn't we use to have lovely egg hunts? *Alfresco?* Do you remember?"

At the time, though I'd hoped for indifference, I was pretty much charmed by her chatter: it was like listening to the language of an adult recalling the language of a child who is trying to speak the language of an adult. The house was charming in the same way, full of bric-a-brac from the past: African weights and antique teddy bears and Japanese textiles. She'd organized them everywhere you looked and brought the dark colonial corners alive with whimsy. In fact, we were in a world of such quaint make-believe it managed to miss the present altogether; this was a fairy tale. And Fairlee, who'd always enjoyed getting herself admired for being good and neat and pretty and on time, had spent a life in training for the fairy princess, Cordelia, sort of thing.

As far as I was concerned, she could have it. Give me a wicked stepsister any day, I told fat Goneril as I slipped her one of the scones, which had not only appeared magically, at my entrance, but had arrived in the company of strawberry jam and clotted cream. Goneril had manners. She wagged. But what she'd really have liked would have been the cream which Edmond, who ate with the dedication which most men reserve for prayer and exercise, had already reduced to utter ruin.

I didn't much go for Edmond. He did have a good nose, like my mother said, and in his heyday must have been all-around pretty good looking, but he was too soft to age well. And he was much too polite. He told me three times how wonderful it was to meet me "at last," and he held the chair for me, and opened doors. Spooky. The man apparently thought he was back in the nineteenth century, before women developed two separate legs like the rest of the human race. He resented it: the confusion, I mean, having to pull out chairs and carry bags for muscular types who clearly didn't admire him for doing it. I don't know: I suppose he was just a creature of habit in a changing universe but I didn't take to him and I thought Goneril was being pretty undiscriminating, sitting with her face on his shoe.

We spent the evening in front of the TV; Edmond fell asleep to *Miami Vice* while Fairlee read and I worked on the puzzle of the scones: I could see more or less how she'd managed to organize them into making their appearance at the precise moment I did. She must have had all the ingredients measured out, ready and waiting, to be mixed and put in to bake as soon as my car slowed down by the picket fence. The unanswerable question was why?

Later, in my quilt-covered bed under the vine-wreathed eaves I couldn't sleep. Goneril was whimpering most of the night, and I kept hearing the door bang as she was let out, and then again when she came in. Someone was up. I could hear footsteps on the ancient timbers downstairs, and through a crack in my floorboards a light shone up intermittently from the kitchen below. Toward dawn, which was when I finally dozed off, I caught an unpleasantly nostalgic smell, something halfway between an antiseptic and a garbage can, which as long as I can remember had always come into a room with my mother. Either I was into olfactory hallucinations, or someone in the house was marinating in wine.

By the time I came downstairs next morning it was almost eleven. *"Tu as bien dormi?"* Fairlee asked, kissing me continentally at the bottom of the stairs; and this time I got annoyed. What was she trying to tell me with her stuck-up French? That she'd done more traveling than me? I sniffed that familiar scent of vinous preservative at the edges of her ladylike climate of Arpège, or I thought I did. She looked pale, and her eyes were puffy; the blue veins made a livid bruise on her white forehead. But you had to hand it to her: wrapped in pale gold linen her debilities looked like the precious crackling on a figurine of country life. She managed to apply good cheer like lacquer to hide her flaws: she'd laid the coffee cake and *pashka* out on festively flowered china, and there were fresh tulips on the table. "What a simply beautiful sunshining morning we have just for you, my love," she chirped. But I don't think she was out to convince really: not trying to make you think she was happy, only that she was doing her best to pretend to be.

At noon Edmond appeared, wrapped in an ancient velour garment so stately you wouldn't dare call it a dressing gown. As soon as he'd pointed himself at the *pashka* he announced, "Americans are without ceremonies. They have no Easter traditions."

"Oh, I don't know," I said; I was trying for a bit of light breakfast chitchat. "What about the Easter Parade?"

"*Hats!*" he exclaimed. "I am not talking about hats." I was looking for a polite way of putting it to him that hats were probably a tradition as worthy of preservation as cottage cheese stuffed inside a flower pot, when he explained his position further.

"Americans have no soul," he said. "Except my beautiful wife, of course, Do you agree she is beautiful?" I obligingly agreed she was beautiful. "And clever," he added. "She is remarkably clever." I wasn't sure if he was being sarcastic or saccharine. Or why. Fairlee wasn't any help. She was picking almonds out of the *pashka* for Goneril, and she gave every appearance of having left the room: her body was still with us, but her spirit was clearly no longer attached. "She even cooks, my darling," Edmond confided to me, furthering my sense that she wasn't there. "If it were not for her barbarous name, one might be tempted to think of her as civilized!'

After that weekend, I kept in touch with her. Or vice versa, really; she kept in touch with me. She answered my two-sentence postcards with seven-page letters, and when I fled the city heat for Deering on occasional summer Sundays she met me with that invariable shipwrecked gratitude. She wouldn't ever come to see me. At first she always had an excuse: Edmond needed her, Goneril was sick, the library was having a tea. Finally when she got tired of her own inventions she told me simply she was afraid: of cities, of strangers, of leaving home. In fact, what she described was total, universal panic.

"Agoraphobia?" I asked, having just read an article about it in the Sunday *Globe*.

"Edmond says there is no such thing," she told me. "He says I am making it up."

I decided to tackle Edmond: I suppose, briefly, it occurred to me that Fairlee was being perversely feeble in going along with him, but when you're afraid of everything, I told myself, you can be forgiven for being feeble. So I took his education on myself; the next time I came up to see them I brought along the *Globe* article to make my point.

I waited till Fairlee was in the garden picking beans and tomatoes for lunch. Edmond was recumbent on his lounge chair, as usual, with Goneril's nose trailing over his knee. I began on a modest speech to prepare him to see the light; then I gave him the paper. He did take a look at the piece for a minute or two. "This is an American disease," he told me, handing it back. "Very fashionable. In Europe it is less stylish; we call it being a coward."

So that was that.

I suppose even then I realized that getting close to a Gordon, who was moreover a blood relation of my mother's, was probably a bad idea, but a maternal passion I never even knew I owned had been born in me. "I've never talked to anyone the way I talk to you," Fairlee would tell me. "You're the first real friend I feel I've ever had."

I made light of it, of course. "What else are sisters for?" I asked, but my new young feeling would stretch, and warm itself for days in the glow of her affection.

I wasn't alone. Everyone loved Fairlee. At least everyone who was under twenty or over seventy. Little boys maneuvered their bicycles into amazing turns in front of her house and then knocked on her door to be admired and given one of the chocolate chip cookies she always kept on hand. Amy, the thirteen-year-old who helped in the garden, came by with a bunch of crimson phlox she had picked, and her baby brother trailed not far behind with a dog biscuit for Goneril. As for the Barr sisters, decaying in the leaky cottage down the road, Fairlee often said they couldn't do without her, and they almost always invited us up for Sunday tea when I was there; as her sister, I got pouring privileges. "My dear, how lucky you are," Agatha told me; she was the one who'd been an ingénue in the movies and had never got over it. "It must be simply heavenly to have a sister like Fairlee."

"You've dropped your sponge cake again, you old fool," said Maude, who was older and healthier, and who made up for having almost no hair by dyeing what she did have the color of tomato juice.

In their presence, Fairlee was demonstrative; on the way home, however, she was cool. "I should take a bath. They are truly filthy women," she said. "Not to mention poisonous cooks."

"I thought you enjoyed them. Why do you go?"

"Oh how could I not!" Fairlee was shocked. "I'm everything they have. I was the one who diagnosed Agatha's pneumonia, you know, last winter. One judges from the color. It's a trick I learned in the Dordogne." And she put the straw flowers they'd made for her next to her own bed, beside Amy's vibrant phlox, where no one but Fairlee herself could see them. "Pink," she said, shuddering. "It offends every sense."

"Why not just throw them out?" I asked. "Or put them in a dark corner?" I was embarrassed by the crudeness of my own taste, which makes no judgment on the color of flowers.

"Oh how could I!" she exclaimed. As if that explained everything.

Deering is the ideal place for your nostalgic Thanksgiving. And there were corn shucks and winter squash all around the little house, which smelled of apples and cloves and roasting turkey.

Its inmates, though, weren't so delightfully seasonal, and as soon as I walked in I knew we were in trouble. Fairlee's embrace was fervent to the point of hysteria, while Edmond hardly nodded by way of greeting and kept right on reading his paper. Even Goneril lurked in a corner instead of by the fire where she belonged, and barely made it onto her four feet to wag at me. When she did, she began to wheeze and had to sit down again.

"The ladies are in what I believe is known as a tizzy," Edmond explained. "Would you care to join them?" Over his head, Fairlee was motioning me secretly into the kitchen.

"Be careful," she whispered as she stirred flour into the turkey drippings. *"Cet animal est méchant."*

"What?"

"He is in a vile, unspeakable mood. His brother refused to send him some money he's asked for."

"Money?" I asked, not having any insight into this side of their lives. They seemed to exist in the sort of comfort, the sort of fairy-tale comfort, that doesn't cost anything. "Do you need money?"

"Oh, my dear!" said Fairlee.

Later she wept. Edmond, having silently wrapped himself outside of half of a turkey and most of two bottles of wine, had fallen asleep while Fairlee and I did the dishes. "He ran over my poor little puppy," she said, and overcome, she applied a pair of sunglasses behind which to hide her outrage. She was crying so much I couldn't understand what she was saying most of the time. But she seemed to be indicating they were in desperate financial straits and that Edmond had been in debt ever since they'd been married. I did understand, quite clearly, that he'd sold all Grandmother Gordon's silver some time ago. She repeated that over and over like some confession of her own unworth and helplessness to be cleansed from her soul. He had taken her dowry and she had nothing left. She dwelled on that at length: having nothing left seemed to have considerable significance for her.

When his brother's letter arrived, Edmond was furious, got drunk, jumped in the car and backed down the driveway right over Goneril, whose rib cage was distinctly the worse for wear. "Crushed," said Fairlee, choking on tears. Nor was it the first time in his murderous life he'd done something like this, she added, having already killed Goneril's sister.

"Regan?" I said, making a wild guess.

"He ran over her too. The drunken fool. The hateful,

drunken, despicable fool." And, what was worse, what was *worst,* was that he denied everything. He had not even taken either of the dogs to the vet. "Can you see why I must stay home? Why I can never leave?" she sobbed.

And at that point, before I could ask the obvious questions that came to mind, my mother called. Taking advantage of the holiday rates, I suppose, and the two-for-one opportunity of Fairlee and me being together. I spoke to her briefly before I turned her over to Fairlee to twitter foreign phrases at.

"And what does Mummy have to say?" Edmond asked when I fled back to the living room. He was distressingly alert, but for the moment, at least, cheerful. "Mummy was no doubt witty at my expense?" he suggested. She had, in fact, made rather a point of referring to him as Noah Count, probably in the vain hope that he was listening in on the hall extension. "Mummy enjoys making phone calls to be witty at my expense. A *quid pro quo* I suppose: she pays for the phone call; I pay for the wit. She is really admirably inventive. Like her daughter. Did my darling wife tell you that she tried to run over the dog last night?"

"What?" I said.

"Or perhaps she has forgotten about it. She had, after all, been drinking for three days straight without any food and without any sleep. Remarkable stamina! It is a miracle she still survives. That any of us survives."

"*She* ran over the dog?" I asked, feebly.

"Well, someone ran over the dog. And since she was sitting in the car at the time the dog began to howl one assumes it was she. What did she tell you?" I didn't answer that, of course. But I think he figured it out for himself. "I see," he said. "She's quite mad, you know. Some years ago, she ran over the other dog, too."

"Regan?" I muttered.

He had made it onto his feet and found himself a full bottle of bourbon and a water glass, which he announced that he was going to take up to bed. He said that he quite agreed with what he knew I was thinking. As miracles went, survival was a bit of a waste.

III

I am not eager to go back to Deering soon.

Fortunately, Christmas will not be a problem. Fairlee always spends it in Santa Barbara; an entire year's worth of resolution goes into getting her out of the house and onto the plane, and she throws up at both airports: before she gets on and as soon as she gets off, round-trip. On the plane she hyperventilates, probably scaring the hell out of all those close by — except Edmond, who has brought his own bottle with him and remains unconscious from coast to coast.

You can't really blame him entirely.

Before they leave, Fairlee calls me. She sounds awful, as if she has a cold; also, her voice is tight and apprehensive.

"Why in God's name are you going?" I ask, possibly out of sympathy for her hard work at being so goddamn good, probably out of spite for making me look so goddamn bad by comparison.

She doesn't answer the question, of course. The reason she's calling, she says, is to thank me for my Christmas present: a little metal bird cage with a little toy bird in it. The bird, which is made of real feathers, looks like a real bird, and the cage is, in fact, a music box. When you wind a key at the bottom, the song of an English meadowlark pours out of a golden clockwork box. The sound is composed of purely mechanical elements, but the little caged bird moves its head and wings, as if it were really singing. I saw it in a pretty pricey antiques shop on Newbury Street, and it reminded me so instantly and intensely of Fairlee that despite the cost I decided to get it for her. She's in tears as she tells me how much she loves it. "I shall bring it with me to the Wild West," she says. "My *Zaubervogelein* to keep me safe from Barbarians." As we wish each other Merry Christmas and hang up, her gratitude and tenderness have brought tears into my own throat; I feel like a louse for having thought ill of her.

But not for long.

My mother always sends my Christmas present late, and I never send her anything at all. Every year, nevertheless, punctually two weeks after Christmas, my box arrives: filled, I've always assumed, with the rejected offerings from her other friends and relations. How else to explain the frog basket or the obscene glasses case? In a normal year, I unwrap the things and put them straight in a paper bag for the Salvation Army.

This year is not a normal year. There are five presents in my mother's package and one of them is a music box in the form of a gilded cage with a toy bird in it that flaps its wings and sings when you wind it up.

We don't talk to each other for a while. Fairlee writes me one of her long letters telling me all about Christmas with the Barbarian Saints, as she calls them, and I am briefly tempted to feel sympathy for my mother for having to spend the holidays with such a superior little snip. Anyway, I never answer. Two more letters come in January and early February; the last one is a bit hysterical. Are you ill? Are you in love? Tell me what's wrong.

By then, I've recovered a little from the speechless shock of opening my mother's Christmas box. I do as she says: I write and tell her what's wrong.

By return mail I get a volume of explanation, not that I care. It seems that Mother feel in love with the little music box on sight, that she sang its praises to Fairlee obsessively: how exquisite it was, how precious, how unique! There was something strange, something demented in her admiration: something dangerous, writes Fairlee, who, to protect me from Maternal Jealousy, has never hinted to anyone that I was the one who gave her the little bird cage. "I threw her off the mark heroically, my love. You would have been proud of me."

None of this explanation makes the slightest sense. In fact, it's so bizarre that I can't quite accept it for anything as simple as a lie: lies tend to be logical. This is more like hysteria. Hallucination. A dream dance of some sort. My mother is frequently crazy and almost always unpleasant: but jealous? of me? of Fairlee? That doesn't seem quite her style. And even if she was, why should we care?

Reading the letter, I feel I'm browsing in *The Lives of the Saints:* what this mumbo jumbo seems to be building toward is a final, inevitable martyrdom. And, yes, here we are and here it comes:

Fairlee selflessly rewraps the little bird and puts it under the Christmas tree for Mother: "Although I wept as I let it go.

"How could I do otherwise?" Fairlee writes.

I am beginning to understand that perhaps, that probably, she couldn't. That like those of saints and psychopaths, her orders may come from above. I tell myself that I shouldn't really hold it against her that her delusions are neither illuminating nor diabolic and that, unlike saints and psychopaths, she has no moral aim. We live in fallen times.

I read her voluminous letter again and then again. I can see she exists in some other world than I do: a world fraught with symbols and the perilous magic of dreams. It occurs to me that the little bird's return may be a message in cipher, signaling something I don't understand, something intense and threatening. I can imagine Fairlee putting my caged meadowlark under the tree as one might put a message in a bottle and float it out to sea. The message has reached me through a miracle.

Unfortunately I have no idea what it's telling me.

On the morning of her birthday I finally call her. Saturday, March 15. I'm still not over being annoyed at her, but I can tell myself she's fragile after all.

She sounds like hell. Every few seconds she pauses to cough, and between wheezes her voice is small and alarmingly weak. She says that she has had pneumonia for most of the three months since I saw her last, and that nothing the doctor is giving her is helping. Goneril, however, has recovered her health completely. "And that is an exchange I would happily make on any day," she tells me, as though we lived inside some ogre's dream of tricks and bargains, as though she's the savior-princess of some fairy tale. The assumption that her life has cosmic overtones irritates me. "I long to see you, *chérie,*" she says. "And today it's so beautiful here. So very beautiful."

Sure it's beautiful! It's snowing anyway. A spring nor'easter which would serve as my excuse, except that my Subaru is known to have four-wheel drive and, despite its delicacies, to be at its finest in a blizzard. I am still working out some other, more sturdy explanation of why I should stay home this weekend when Fairlee adds, croaking gently, "But *bien entendu* you must stay safe in the Big City. Driving this weekend is beyond thinking of. I forbid you to think of it."

Wheedling I can withstand, but prohibition demands defiance. I refuse her cowardly premise and set out for Deering at once; I am well on my way, driving through the drifting snow on 93 south of Manchester, by the time it comes to me that maybe I've been had.

She needs a hospital. That much is immediately clear.

Edmond is pickled, in any sense of the word, so scared out of his few wits he's trying to preserve what remains in sourness and alcohol. But when I appear he is surprisingly, poignantly relieved. Lurching ponderously around Fairlee's desk, he finds me a phone number for her doctor, Dr. Toppan, who of course reminds me, via his answering machine, that it's Saturday. In case of emergency I must apply to the hospital for the doctor on call.

I go in to speak to Fairlee again. She looks as if she inhabits another and less fleshly world. She gasps and chokes on the impure air of ours. I measure her temperature at 105, and her pallor and emaciation are dramatic. They are also somehow Victorian: people nowadays don't get themselves in such a state and often die looking healthier than this.

As Edmond passes out, with a bottle of bourbon in hand for a waking emergency, Goneril and I settle down to our Dickensian watch beside Fairlee's bed. The snow is climbing along the outside window ledge, but in the distance, on the hardtop going to Hillsborough, I can hear the comforting sound of the plows.

I tell Fairlee that I am calling the hospital, but it takes her a long time to understand what I am saying and her answer is distracted: she keeps looking into a corner of the room as if she sees something that isn't there. I tell myself that in another century I would have known what this meant: it would have meant *she is slipping away.*

Dr. Rosenberg calls back almost at once. "What's up?" she says. It turns out she's calling from home, ten minutes down the road from us in Francestown. She asks me how I feel about driving in a blizzard, and I tell her I don't know the way to the hospital anyway. So she offers that if I'll make a pot of coffee, she'll come by the house and drive us in herself.

She's younger than I'm expecting; my age more or less. She galumphs about in a pair of knee-high lace-up boots that would do a lumberjack proud. But never mind; I'm so happy to see her that she takes on a sort of preternatural glow, and I am eager to see her charmlessness as competence.

I'm scared by then. Fairlee isn't speaking anymore, and her eyes are rolling around from side to side as if they're looking for an escape route. I've tried to make contact with Edmond, but he's beyond reach. I can't blame him. The sound of Fairlee's breathing is the sound of one's own mortality under duress. And Dr. Rosenberg after one brief look decides to call an ambulance.

"Saturday night in a country blizzard, and there's been an accident in Hancock. It may take an hour," she tells me when she gets off the phone. "But I'd rather wait than get stuck in a ditch and have her die in the car." We settle down with the coffeepot. "How did she get this sick?" Dr. Rosenberg asks. "How long's she been like this?"

We decide a vaporizer might help the breathing a little. Since Edmond tends to asthma, I know there must be one around. But it isn't in any likely closet: not in the bathroom, in the hall, in the bedroom, in the spare room. Applied to for help, Edmond looks intelligent for an instant and then passes out again. I glance up in the attic; I check in the cellar. It's something to do.

"Well, never mind," Dr. Rosenberg says. But I have just remembered an old Korean campaign chest at the foot of Fairlee's bed, where she stores a few of the cast-off ball gowns that mother passes on to her at the rate of five or six a year: poor Fairlee, who never goes to a ball!

It seems worth a try, anyway.

Fairlee died of pneumonia early the following morning, a couple of hours after we got her to the hospital. My mother put on a pretty terrific funeral for her in the Deering Community

Church, I think before poor Edmond ever quite realized the entire family first came and then left again. He was paralyzed by shock — or something. And he certainly didn't notice that when my mother left she took Grandmother Gordon's silver with her. I doubt if he even knew what Grandmother Gordon's silver was.

But that's another story. And until the moment my mother arrived to lay her body to rest, the stage was Fairlee's.

We never did find the vaporizer. What was in the Korean campaign chest, among the crumpled dresses, was another, smaller chest, with a lock on it. It had been left lying open, though; I guess because the last time Fairlee found use for it, she was too weak to bother locking it up.

Inside there were pills. About a hundred bottles of pills, give or take a dozen. As far as I could tell, looking at the labels, Dr. Toppan had signed all the prescriptions. More than half of them were barbiturates: FAIRLEE DE LA TOUR; AS NEEDED FOR INSOMNIA, they said. The rest were mainly antibiotics. Maybe five, maybe six bottles were dated after Christmas and obviously intended for her present illness. They were all still full.

"Good Christ!" said Dr. Rosenberg, admiring this cache of pills to take and pills untaken, a treasure chest for suicide. There was something else in the chest: under the hoarded pills, among the rumpled silks and satins. A lumpy package wrapped in a hand-knit blanket with REGAN embroidered in one corner. I think I knew what I was going to find inside before I actually spread it out on the bottom of the bed.

"A bit heavy for regular use," suggested Dr. Rosenberg, who didn't seem to see anything odd about keeping silver in a doggy blanket, even a very heavy, very baroque service for twenty, plus innumerable extras. I recognized it at once as Grandmother Gordon's famous silver, which Fairlee, weeping at the shame she had brought on herself and her family by letting him do it, had told me again and again Edmond had sold for cash some time ago.

Had she hidden the silver out of pure malice, to make Edmond look bad? Or was she crazy? Or maybe she suffered from amnesia?

Or what?

The ambulance arrived a good bit earlier than we'd dared hope for. By the time the paramedics, covered with snow, rushed in to arrange Fairlee on the stretcher, her eyes were open again. They floated with her mind round the room.

"You'll be fine," I said. Drifting by me, her focus shifted like wreckage. She was beyond pain, I think. But she looked terrified. "I'll come with you," I told her. "Don't worry." Goneril was whining at the bottom of the bed, and Fairlee's random glance finally anchored there: on the dog, and on the mound of silver place settings, uncovered, next to the dog. For an instant she seemed to come to grips with some sort of reality: her eyes settled on the teaspoons, and grew large. "What are those?" she whispered. Even death, apparently, wasn't enough to dim her acting talent. Unless, of course, she'd forgotten that she'd ever put the stuff there. Or unless maybe she hadn't put the stuff there. She sounded genuinely confused, anyway, like someone in a dream, dreaming of waking; I was beginning to feel a bit unreal myself.

"It's nothing," I said. "Shh. I won't tell."

By this time the ambulance had roused even Edmond. He came staggering out of his lair; swaying slightly, he propped himself by the bedroom door as Fairlee was wheeled by. Her eyes, riveted on the silver, veered an instant in his direction, then floated free. To control them was an obvious effort, but she managed it, at last. I had the sense that she was forcing thirty years, all the unused resolve of a lax lifetime, into this terminal moment, fixing her look on me: willing my understanding and my witness to the unblemished perfection of her life.

In any case, her voice was extraordinarily clear. Her face fell apart, but she was quite heroic. "My God, he did it, he put it there for you to find after I'm dead!" she told me; who knows if it was the final truth or the final desperate invention. All I can tell you is the last thing I ever heard her say was: "He wanted you to think I was a liar, that I was completely mad!" To this day I have no idea if that is what I do think or only what I would like to think. John, who gave the eulogy at her funeral, said he had never known her to tell a lie, except in kindness.

It boils down to a question of simplicity. And on the whole, I prefer not to make up my mind.

WILL BLYTHE

The Taming Power of the Small

FROM EPOCH

TWO MEN AND A BOY were driving in a battered Mustang toward the Texas border, with the wind and ahead of the rain. Every now and then, heat lightning flared in the night sky, illuminating the landscape like a photograph. Miles behind them were black cumulus clouds and what they believed was their old life. The men sat in the front seat, the balding, curly haired one driving, cradling a quart of orange juice between his legs, the other one passing him french fries from a paper bag. "Boom," he said, aiming a gnarled french fry at the driver's head. Wedged over his thigh was a worn copy of the I-Ching. The boy was hidden in the trunk, wrapped in rope like a kite spool.

Baron handled the wheel with one hand, ignoring Napperstick. "What does that chink book say about a motel?" Baron said.

Napperstick just smiled, ketchup flecking his pale wispy mustache. He shook his head like a man who was tired of the same old joke.

They meandered down the moonlit highway, the center line phosphorescent, floating above the asphalt in the car's weak headlights. At last they came to a green sign with a longhorn steer and a moon rocket. Texas. For most of their hurried trip, Napperstick got excited whenever they crossed into a new state. He hadn't been many places. But this border let him down; his disappointment hung in the car like the odor of fried food and rotting upholstery. "Idaho was better than this," he said, looking up from his book.

He'd never been to Texas, but the name had already betrayed him, had promised him more than this land, which was as bleached as bone, luminescent only in its blankness. Baron looked straight ahead and said, "We're in the middle of the desert. What did you expect?"

"Something else, I guess," Napperstick said. He was ignoring the state of Texas, studying his I-Ching by the green glowing numerals of the radio dial. He'd picked up the book from a waitress he'd slept with in Las Vegas. She was a headstrong woman who used to dance at the Sands. She made everything she did seem appealing. She'd shown him how to toss the coins, the basics. She taught him to respect the book, to treat it with a dignity he granted nothing else in his life. "There are Chinese sages," she said, "who study this book for forty years and still get surprised." But he told Baron that he'd already mastered the I-Ching. He liked the system, the way it applied to everything. He liked having something help him figure out what things meant, what was supposed to be. In Baron's eyes, he acted like the book was something alive, something that sat faithfully with him on the hot car seat.

"You'll get over it," Baron said. He rolled his eyes. Napperstick was such a boy. They were both in their late twenties, but Baron looked at himself as the leader, as the voice of experience.

They drove on across the Texas flatlands, hewing to the speed limit like an old couple, pulling into drive-ins for food, buying gas at lonely self-service pumps, and stopping occasionally to empty their bladders on the shoulders of long stretches of road. As they pissed, they watched oncoming headlights looming faintly in the distance, drifting toward them across the desert night in slow motion.

"What if he needs to piss?" Napperstick asked.

"Then he'll piss," Baron said. "We're not taking the chance."

"He doesn't cry much, does he?" Napperstick said.

"It's tough with a gag."

By afternoon of the next day, they crossed into Louisiana and entered the terrible green woods of the South, where the midday roar of locusts ricocheted in the greenery with a sepulchral buzz, like voices in a pipe. They passed by kudzu-covered fields and trees.

"What the hell is that?" Napperstick asked. "Looks like something from outer space."

"Some kind of plant," Baron said. "That's obvious."

"That's one mean plant," Napperstick said. "I wouldn't take a nap around it."

They drove on, crossing from light into darkness in quick-blinding succession. Tree shadows dimmed the road and cooled the air like night. Ahead, in a gloat of sunlight stood an abandoned Sinclair station, the cheerful green brontosaurus pockmarked with bullet holes. This seemed like the kind of country a man could hide in, but Baron knew better than that. People in this kind of country knew when outsiders in strange cars came through; they noticed the cars even more than they did the flat twangy western accents. The dark green safety of hackberry and water oak and hickory was an illusion.

"I used to collect dinosaurs," Napperstick said. "I had a lot. My mother threw them down the toilet when I broke a two-by-four on my sister's head. I never forgave her for that."

"Jesus Christ, man."

"Yeah, I know. It's strange the things you get attached to."

"No, I mean your sister. What happened to her?"

"I don't know. Brain damage maybe. It could be why she married that black guy."

"Man, you almost give *me* the creeps."

"*I* do? How about that?" Napperstick grinned like a shy man given a compliment.

The light was vanishing slowly from the afternoon. Every now and then, they passed a Cadillac or a Lincoln coming from the Gulf Coast. The cars all had gauzy screens stretched across their grilles to keep the insect world from their fiery pistons. "When I'm rich, I'm going to get me one of those cars." Napperstick said.

It was midevening, summertime dusk, when they came to a brick motel with a lustrous sign, the color of moon, that pleaded VACANCY. If the motel had a name, Baron didn't notice it. They had been traveling for three days straight. It was a motel. That was enough.

A year before, Baron's wife had left him for nothing in particular — "anything is better than this," she'd said — and he began blowing back and forth across the country in his Mustang, a man tumbling in crosswinds of rage and numbness. Baron was a terrible husband but he had loved his wife with a passion that made him tattoo her face with the blue and black marks of his fists. "I'll never stop loving you," he cried, pounding her around the bedroom on the night she left, thinking *she's history, she's history,* pounding her until he was sobbing and she was spitting at him like a cat from the corner of the room. "Thank God I didn't have your baby," his wife spat. "Thank God for small favors like that."

So he had gone driving. He felt like a guest in his own life, someone wearing the wrong clothes, not knowing whether to kiss or shake hands. In the summer, he had been speeding through Nevada, lost in a fragile glory of amphetamines and desert light, able, as long as both persisted, to maintain an acceptable vision of what lay ahead. Of course, he had narrowed his vision to where the future was a matter of days, and next month loomed as blank as outer space, an emptiness he did not even want to imagine.

For a man whose future extends about as far as a windshield, automotive difficulties can mark a sea change as profound as divorce or death in the family or winning the lottery. Somewhere in the desert, between Reno and Carson City, Baron's Mustang threw a rod. A piston heated up as orange as an ingot and the motor locked. The radio was playing so loudly that Baron did not hear the engine's clattering, the sound of a steam radiator banging away in the dead of winter. He noticed the acrid smell of burning oil, though for a moment the odor was unattributable in the swelter of sagebrush and baked sand.

Then the car just quit.

Baron let the Mustang roll onto the shoulder and finished listening to a song, "Dead Flowers," by the Rolling Stones. The speed was still pumping through him, a river of energy. He kept beat with the song, tapping on the dashboard, his arms as brown as a Mexican's.

The desert spread out around him, yellow and white, the monotony broken only by a few shriveled yucca plants, sagebrush, rocks. It felt like home.

When the song was over and a commercial for an airline roared onto the air, he switched off the radio, grabbed his sunglasses and his pills, and began walking. "Fuck you," he yelled in a voice that was his and that came from nowhere. He had a rage that he was born with. A mountain range, as black as coal, cut an austere and parallel track miles to the north. He plunged on down the highway, walking with an antic speed that did not wilt in the sun. It was Napperstick who finally stopped, placid and smiling, a young man, baby-faced, with an incongruous scar slicing down his cheek.

"How about an ice cold beer?" Napperstick said, dangling a Budweiser out the window.

"All right, buddy," Baron said. As he reached for the beer, the man jerked the can inside the car. "Jesus H. Christ," Baron said. "Is that supposed to be funny?"

"I'm just fooling with you," Napperstick said, grinning. "Here you go, man." He handed Baron the beer and opened the passenger door. "That your Mustang back there?"

"I'm walking cross-country," Baron said.

"That's a good one. Serves me right."

They drove together, first to a mechanic Napperstick knew in Monroe, then to the grocery store for another six-pack, after which Napperstick decided to quit his most recent job as a day laborer on a new hospital. Baron sat drinking with the man, remembering the joy of exchanging words, stories. He didn't know a soul in the world. They spent the rest of the afternoon finishing a bottle of tequila in the mechanic's backyard, listening to the ring of a hammer and the clang of engine parts on the cement floor of the aluminum shed, watching stars nestle in the darkening blue space between the sharp peaks in the distance.

They remained at ease in their silence for a while. Then Napperstick said, "I figure you're my 'approaching emperor.' "

"What in hell are you talking about?" Baron said.

"The Ching said I had to 'advance over the plains with an approaching emperor.' I take that to mean you; you can't take these things too literally. We don't have emperors anymore. Anyway, I've got to get my butt in gear, change my life. I've been stuck here too long."

"What the fuck's the Ching?"

"The Chinese book of prophecy."

"You believe that stuff?"

"Sure. Why not? I mean, I might as well."

Toward one o'clock in the morning, the mechanic hoisted the motor back onto the block, took what was left of Baron's money — Napperstick had already made him a loan — and went to bed. "You can sit around all night if you want," the mechanic said. Through the bright haze of the tequila, Baron felt a camaraderie for the baby-faced man with the scar and the lank, blond hair. He wanted them to move, to do something before the pale, dissipating edge of daylight sapped him of his sudden ambition, his sense of infinite possibility.

"Let's go somewhere," Baron said.

"I've got nothing else to do," Napperstick said.

They got into the Mustang and barreled out of town, going north, through the desert, toward the range of mountains. Baron rolled down his window with a pair of pliers, and inhaled the aroma of sage growing out in the desert. The wind was blowing away the hair he had carefully arranged over his bald spot, but he was drunk, and it was cool and dark, so he didn't mind. He admired his own insouciance.

"This is what it's all about," Baron said.

"You said it," Napperstick said.

They kept on driving for months, hemmed in only by the Spanish language to the south, tundras to the north, and oceans on either side. There was still enough space to roam, and both of them had all the time in the world.

At the motel, Napperstick was reclining on one of the beds, leafing through the I-Ching and watching a porno movie. He kept clicking the toes of his cowboy boots together, and trailing his fingers down the knife scar that ran like a gulch down his cheek. His touch was as light and dreamy as a lover's.

"You really love that scar, don't you?" Baron said, chewing a vitamin C tablet that was as bitter as a child's aspirin. He'd read that vitamin C prevented hair loss, and he kept touching his scalp to check on his hairline.

"Love what?" Napperstick said, gazing at the screen's wan light.

"You know what," Baron said. His voice had the sharp edge of rebuke to it.

Napperstick smiled and scratched his cheek. A warm breeze blew in the window from the parking lot, heavy with the scent of gasoline. "It's Channel Blue," he grinned. "Twenty-four hours of uninterrupted sensuality."

"They don't do much for your self-image, do they?" Baron meant, anatomically.

Napperstick just smiled, as enigmatic as a woman in an advertisement.

"We have to pay for those movies," Baron added. "They're not free."

"That's all right. We're going to be rich," Napperstick said, still smiling.

"You little pissant. Turn that shit off."

Napperstick just lay there, studying his book. Baron snapped the TV off.

There hadn't been any news since the weekend, three days ago, no news, no word, no deals, no ransom. They'd taken the boy from a backyard pool in the resort of Sun Valley, high in the mountains of Idaho. It had been as simple as circling the brown-eyed boy with curly dark hair in *People* magazine. "The Wealthy at Play." The boy was going to be a heartbreaker when he grew up. Most rich people were, Baron thought. "He's ours," Baron said. "He's ours if you're up to it. I think we're entitled, and I'm the emperor." Napperstick went along because he always went along, succumbing to the prophecy and the profane eloquence of Baron's flat voice.

The boy had been sitting at the edge of his parents' pool, lazily kicking his feet back and forth in the cool blue water. He was reading a picture book, green elephants and pink giraffes, his chin perched on his hand, his eyelashes long and feminine. Baron came up behind him, his tennis shoes squeaking on the smooth cement. The boy didn't even turn around. Baron cupped the boy's mouth and whispered in his ear, "You're a sweet little gumdrop," wondering where that came from. He kept cooing sweetness into the boy's ear, carrying him, as light as balsa, back to the car where Napperstick was gunning the motor. They raced down into the flatlands on their way south. When the news came on the radio, they panicked, tying the boy up and shutting him in the trunk. Then they continued on down the highway, laughing in their daring and relief like college boys on a prank.

But that had been the last of it. There'd been no ransom delivered, and no explanation, no news. No one had shown up in Reno, no one had shown in Vegas. They'd had enough time to get it straight.

"What are we going to do?" Napperstick said, his voice as toneless as he could make it.

"I've been thinking about it," Baron said.

"Well?" Napperstick said.

"I'm still thinking."

"If it would make it easier on you, I'll shoot him."

"It's not that simple," Baron had said. But maybe it was.

That night the boy screamed out in his sleep. Baron heaved himself out of unrecallable dreams, unsure of whether the scream had been nightmare or worse, and listened intently to the room's buzzing silence. The boy cried out again, full-throated fear, and Baron went to him, kneeling against the cold porcelain of the tub where they had bound him, shaking him gently by the shoulders, rubbing his hair, whispering *Hey man, hey man* into his ears.

The boy's eyes opened wide for a moment, then closed, and he mumbled something unintelligible. "What was that?" Baron said. "What did you just say?" As if the boy were telling him important news, prophecies from beyond his waking knowledge. But the boy's body relaxed again into more comfortable sleep; he licked his lips in somnambulistic contentment and was silent. Baron pulled the blanket smooth over the boy and left him sleeping in the bathtub.

"This is getting on my nerves," Napperstick said. He was rolling a joint, using a telephone book to collect the seeds.

Baron said nothing. The smoke swirled across the room, as sweet in his memory as the scent of rain on a parking lot. He drifted off to sleep, dreaming of traveling to a new place, fresh and unencumbered.

Despite the emphatic light of midmorning, the room remained as grey and grainy as a newspaper photograph. Baron, half asleep, his face burrowed into the pillow, was listening to the maids wheeling their carts down the sidewalk. The maids' voices were husky, full of confidential laughter; to Baron, the women were speaking a foreign language with inflections of menace. One cart clattered to a stop and a maid began rapping on the door.

"Get the fuck out of here," Baron yelled. The cart rolled on down the sidewalk, to the accompaniment of a sudden, aggrieved silence.

Baron went into the bathroom, shadowy and cool, and pissed with relief. The boy was watching him, as wary as an animal. His cheeks were red, imprinted with tiny circles from the shower mat he'd slept on.

Baron closed the lid and sat down on the toilet.

"How'd you sleep last night?" he asked.

"Fine," the boy said, his voice timorous, faint.

"What'd you dream about?"

"I don't remember," the boy said, looking down at the drain.

"You were having a nightmare," Baron said.

The boy said nothing.

"Don't you remember?"

"I had a bad dream," the boy said. He looked shy and embarrassed. Baron marveled at how adaptable the boy was, how all children were as pliant as water, taking the shape of the lives they were leading, warm when it was warm, icy when it was cold.

Baron knew a little something about a boyhood in motels. "Watch TV for a couple of minutes," his father had said, twenty-two years ago, leaving their room for a beer and a pack of cigarettes and going all the way to Flagstaff, Arizona, to get them. Baron had watched TV for the next three days, drinking warm Cokes and listening to coyotes out in the Mojave, and to the blue laughter from the room next door. He'd kept the curtains shut against the desert and just sat there, watching his shows until his mother showed up, all the way from Norfolk, Virginia. *I had to leave a good time for this mess,* she said, gesturing at the boy, the cartoons, the rumpled bed. *Oh be nice to him,* his mother's boyfriend had said, settling down on the bed to watch cartoons.

That kind of thing ran in the family. Baron knew that much by now. His heart had been chipped by hard weather into a muscle as clean and as sharp as obsidian. He was proud of that, he could stand almost anything.

And yet he felt a flash of love and pity for the boy, as sudden as a bolt of electricity striking him just beneath his ribs. It wasn't the boy's fault that he'd had such an easy time of it, that he had floated through his life like it was a warm pool. That was the way his world had been. Now he knew that there was more to it than that.

"You hungry?" Baron asked the boy.

The boy nodded.

"Speak up," Baron said. "You have to speak up for what you want."

"Yes."

"Yes what?"

"Yes, I'm hungry."

"That's a good boy," Baron said. "We'll go get something to eat real soon. Get out of this place. It's getting kind of old here."

"Yes."

"Yes what?"

"It's getting kind of old here."

"There you go," Baron said. "That's my little man."

When he crossed back into the bedroom, he saw Napperstick, shirtless, wearing only blue jeans, hunched over the edge of the bed, throwing the I-Ching. He rattled the pennies together and let them fall to the carpet, as intent as a man in a casino. He was sweating. Another porno movie flickered on the screen, spattering him with a tropical light, green and orange. The sound was turned down, but Baron could still hear saxophone music and occasional moaning.

"I've got a better idea," Baron said. "We'll let the boy decide what his future's going to be."

Napperstick turned and stared. "I'm telling you, it's no joke."

"Okay," Baron said. "Let's be fair about it. It's his fate."

"It's all of ours." Napperstick sounded like a minister; the I-Ching was one of the few things he took seriously.

"Yeah, yeah. Go get the kid."

"You're serious. Great, man. That's fantastic. You'll see. It'll tell you the right thing. It always does. You just have to approach it seriously." He held up his tattered green copy as if it were a Bible. "I mean it, I don't know where I'd be without it."

Napperstick unbound the boy and brought him into the bedroom. The boy's gaze landed for a moment on the movie. "Look at him watching that movie." Napperstick laughed. "You ain't never seen any tits like that, have you?" he asked the boy. The boy shook his head.

"Can you believe that?" Napperstick said. "He said no, he'd never seen any tits like that."

Baron shook his head, bemused. He lay down on the bed, crossing his legs, looking up at the paneled ceiling.

"Okay," Napperstick said, giving the boy the three pennies. "Shake these up and throw them down. Just like you were playing Monopoly or something. Six times. Ask the I-Ching what we should do with you. Concentrate real hard. Okay? Let's do it."

The boy closed his eyes, as if in prayer, and shook the pennies in both hands, rattling them together for a long time before he let them fall to the carpet.

"*All right,*" Napperstick exclaimed. "That's a good one." The boy smiled, pleased with himself. Napperstick recorded the tosses on a sheet of motel stationery, a series of lines, some full, some broken. His brow was wrinkled, a child concentrating on a drawing, Baron thought. He was whistling, too, a slight hissing sound as he sucked the air inward between his teeth.

Baron kept watch from the bed, drumming his fingers on the

night table, smirking as he always did when confronted by someone else's idea of the inevitable.

The boy finished throwing the pennies and knelt on the floor, staring at the television. Napperstick was glancing back and forth between the stationery and the book. He let his pencil drop to the floor. "The Taming Power of the Small," he announced.

"What's the word?" Baron said.

"Dense clouds, no rain from our western region," Napperstick intoned.

"Is that the weather report?" Baron asked.

"That's the Judgment, man. Listen to this Hexagram: Wind Blowing Over Heaven. You don't fuck with the wind, I know that much. 'By it the Model Man renders his virtuous excellence worthy of admiration.' "

"So what's the verdict?" Baron asked. He was rubbing the small whorl of hairs, baby-fine, that were left at his crown.

"Hold on, listen to this one, in the fourth place. 'Owing to Confidence, bloody and terrible deeds are avoided.' That says it all. We've got to let the kid go. The Chinese didn't fuck with the winds. No way. You can't do it."

"We're not chinks," Baron said. "We're white people."

Napperstick wasn't listening. "You lucked out, little fella," he told the boy, thrusting the stationery with its pencil lines of yin and yang in the boy's face. The boy looked at the lines as if they were hieroglyphics, math problems.

"Take it," Napperstick said. "You'll want to keep this. This is your passport home."

The boy took the prophecy, holding it in front of him with both hands like a choirboy with sheet music. It was Napperstick who watched the movie now.

"What does that book say about our fucking money?" Baron asked. The whole charade had gone too far, had sickened him with scorn. He'd never seen successful people, rich people, peering into sheep guts, consulting palm readers, staking their lives on a coin toss. The only people who tried to figure out the future were people who needed more luck than they were ever going to get.

Napperstick looked up from the movie, startled, wild-eyed.

"Hey, I thought we were going to score some big bucks. I really did. I never lost hope, no matter what it seemed like. I thought we had a pretty sharp deal going."

"Don't we?" Baron asked.

"We shouldn't be thinking about money." Napperstick was beseeching him, his voice as soothing and intense as a preacher on TV. For him, the matter was settled. "Virtue. I know it sounds weird but we've got to get us some virtue. Virtue is its own reward. That's not just my opinion; that's the universe talking."

"How do I know you understand what that book says? How do I know you can make any more sense out of those squiggles than that boy there?"

"Read it, read it yourself." Napperstick held out the book to Baron. "Just read it."

"I don't need to do that," Baron said. "I can just look outside and see what the weather's like." He gestured at the curtained windows.

"The I-Ching cannot be wrong," Napperstick said.

"We'll see," Baron said. He wasn't sure what he would do.

That evening, they left the motel and drove into the countryside, the wind gusting from all directions buffeting the car, bending the pines like limbo dancers, sweet with the scent of approaching rain. The whole green world seemed in motion, flooded with eddies of air. "The winds of heaven," Baron smirked.

"Still hungry?" he asked the boy.

"Yes, I'm hungry," the boy said.

Baron smiled. They pulled into a Dairy Queen where the red umbrellas over the picnic tables had been blown inside out, a row of red canvas tulips.

"You can have anything you want," Baron told the boy.

"I'm getting some french fries," Napperstick said.

The boy ordered a hamburger and a milkshake, and sat between the two men, like a child between his parents. He ate the hamburger with slow precision, wheeling it around, taking tiny, evenly spaced bites. He was still wearing his bathing suit and terry cloth sweater.

They left the Dairy Queen and drove east, the woods swaying and creaking around them like a green ship. The boy sucked on his milkshake, holding the cup to his chest. Fifty miles down the highway, Baron swerved into the parking lot of a Holiday Inn.

"Are we stopping already?" Napperstick asked.

"We're going to get a room for the boy," Baron said.

"We'll be rewarded for this, I guarantee you."

"Aren't you going to come say goodbye?" Baron said.

They paid the clerk for a room and took the boy there, Baron leading him by the hand. He unlocked and pushed the door open. The boy stood hesitantly in the doorway, cradling his milkshake. The wind had brought out goosebumps on his legs.

"Go on in," Baron said to him. "Make yourself at home." Napperstick and Baron followed, Baron tapping the door shut behind them with his foot. Baron flipped on the TV, spinning through the channels until he came to a nature documentary. The scene was Africa, at the edge of the forest. A gold moon hung over the trees, while down on the floor of the savannah, photographed by stealth, were two chimpanzees, pounding on a log. The narrator said that they were looking for insects, but why then, Baron wondered, out there on the grasslands, all by themselves, while the other chimps were sleeping in the trees?

Baron thought of himself and Napperstick, their epic voyages of futility, crisscrossing the country, bickering like old maids, killing nothing but time.

The boy had scooted up on one of the beds, and was watching the chimps. Napperstick remained standing by the door, waiting for something to happen.

Baron went into the bathroom, slipped his Smith and Wesson from under his jacket, and clicked open its chambers. He turned the gun upside down and shook the bullets into his palm, where they gleamed golden in the room's fluorescence. He pocketed the bullets and emerged into the bedroom, spinning the Smith and Wesson's cylinder.

"Here," he said to Napperstick, handing him the pistol by the barrel. "Russian roulette. Let's see how smart those chinks are." The boy was watching them in the mirror that ran behind the TV. He just sat there, as still as stone.

"Go ahead." Baron gestured toward the boy.

"This is too cruel, man."

"You already said you'd shoot him."

"I would have, you know me."

"If this is his lucky day, you won't stop him from enjoying it. Go ahead. I'm the emperor, man. Like you said. Let's see how seriously you take that I-Ching shit."

Napperstick shook his head slowly, mournfully, twirling the cylinder himself and placing the barrel at the base of the boy's skull, just below the V of his haircut. The barrel was blue and cool, about the circumference of a flute. He held the gun there, as lightly as a finger. "Damn," he said. "Damn."

The boy flinched at the touch of the gun, and Baron held him by the shoulder, the way a man would steady a subject for a photograph. Napperstick closed his eyes and pulled the trigger.

Nothing.

"I told you," Napperstick burst out laughing. "I told you." The boy was crying, silently, still facing the TV. "This is your lucky day, little fella," Napperstick said, tousling the boy's hair.

Baron opened up the pistol and said, "Look Mom, no bullets."

"Oh my God," Napperstick howled. "I'm such a fool, I'm such a fool."

They left the boy in the motel room, sitting on the edge of the bed, watching the strange habits of animals in the wild. Baron swung the Mustang westward, back toward the clouds, the country they'd been fleeing. The wind was rattling the car, still holding out the promise of a sweet rain. The trees were still dancing.

"It really was his lucky day, after all," Napperstick said. "The I-Ching doesn't lie." The book was sitting in his lap.

"You're full of shit," Baron said, satisfied again with his knowledge of the world, his vision, his command. "That book is full of shit. I rigged the whole deal, you know that. You think *this* was his lucky day?"

"I do," Napperstick said. "I really do. He was saved by the I-Ching, no matter what you say. We're virtuous men. Our reward will come. I hope it's money."

They drove on into the night, retracing their path, whirling past hamlets they'd never remembered, past fields and dark green woods.

"Well," Baron finally said, the fire rising within him. "I'd just hate to see him have an unlucky day, if you know what I mean."

But Napperstick did not respond. He was slumped back on the seat, mouth open, his head against the window, sleeping the easy sleep of the virtuous, of the true believer.

RICHARD CURREY

Waiting for Trains

FROM THE NORTH AMERICAN REVIEW

THE SIGN ABOVE the garage doors says *HAPPY OTORING.*

Hollis wipes his big hands on a dirty rag. We stand together side by side on the concrete apron, and after a moment he says, "Took me damn near two months to get a new letter for that sign. Last time this happened."

"Last time?" I say. Making conversation.

"Niggers stole it," Hollis says. "That's what I figure."

We gaze together at the sign.

"Shoved a ladder up there and took it right down." Hollis pushes the rag into his hip pocket, looks at me. "That's one reason I need someone around here at night. Keep an eye on things."

I nod.

Hollis turns to watch the traffic go by. "Thing I'd like to know," he says, "is what's so damned fascinating about the letter M?"

"They took the same letter last time?"

Hollis looks at me, frowning. "Same damned letter. You believe that?"

Hollis is looking for someone to pump gas after dark, keep the station open until midnight. He spits on the concrete, turns his back to the traffic again. "Had to be those damned niggers," he says. "Who else'd do a thing like that?"

I stand with my hands in my pockets looking at the space where the letter should have been.

I get the job.

*

I meet her at The Pump House, a diner across the street from the station that serves breakfast around the clock. I go afternoons before the shift starts and she takes my order. I learn what tables she covers so I know where to sit, joke with her, make faces at the food. Call her Hamburger Queen. When I call her that she tells me her name is Shirl.

Shirl has fading yellow hair and eyes like the eyes of coal miners' wives sitting on shadowed porches I remember from childhood — hollowed-out, wistful — and I am eating scrambled eggs on the day she brings my second cup of coffee and sits down across from me in the red vinyl booth.

She watches me take a bite of toast. "Let's go for a ride tonight," she says.

I pepper my eggs, smiling down at them. "Sounds good," I say. "But I don't have a car. I come up on the bus."

"I've got a car," she says. "We're both off at midnight. I'll pick you up."

I sip some coffee, look at her. "You know," I tell her, "you don't know me. Not beyond this place anyway."

"I *know* you," she says. "Listen, it's an invitation, O.K.? We'll just take a cruise. I'll just give you a lift home."

She pulls into the station lot at ten minutes past midnight. I turn out lights, make sure no junkies are asleep in the restrooms. Night receipts are in the floor safe. Wash my hands over a stained deepsink in the garage, go out through the office, and the radio is on in her car: Janis Joplin on a blue ride into the night.

"You won't believe it," Shirl says as I slide in on the passenger side.

"What?"

"I need some gas."

"Should have told me before I closed out, could have pumped you some free."

She waves a hand. "No problem," she says, "we'll find some." She eases the sedan out into a thin traffic stream. "So where to?"

"You mean where do I live?"

She lights a cigarette with the dashboard lighter, smiling at me. "Well," she says, blowing smoke, "I mean I got some time, I'm not too tired. Want to go somewhere?"

I think about it. "Let's go to the ocean," I say.

"The ocean? You mean, like Seal Rock?"

I tell her I just want to fill up on a little salt air.

"Hey, I know," she says, stopping for a light. "Let's go up to the Golden Gate. You know that little pull-off right before you get on the bridge? Ever been up there this time of year? The smell of those flowers up there is just like you wouldn't believe."

"Don't forget the gas," I say.

She accelerates away from the intersection and changes lanes to pick up an all-night Phillips 66 on the right, moves the car in beside the pumps and turns the engine off. "So is that an O.K. idea?"

"The bridge?"

"Yeah. You can see the water from there." She smiles. "You can smell it, too."

"Sure," I say, "let's roll up there and smell the flowers."

A middle-aged man is at her window. He has the demolished face of an ex-boxer. She works in her purse and hands out three singles. "Regular," she says.

We ride and I begin to fade in the silence between us. She asks about me and I tell her about getting out of the Marines, about finding a job on a laundromat bulletin board.

She asks if I am back from Nam. She sounds as if she has been there herself.

She talks about waitressing, says she was originally from Tennessee. Her father was career military. Retired, she says. Works part time as a security guard.

I watch out the open window, cool burgundy air and passing cars, bougainvillea and rose arbors in amber-lit doorways.

"Hey, you O.K.?"

I turn to her and she glances away from the road to look at me.

"Sure," I tell her. "Just thinking."

"Thinking about what?"

I don't answer, and we keep each other's eyes a moment before she turns back to the road.

The car drops and turns through the dark Presidio, walkways and guardrails sliding close, and I see the double arcade of light walking out ahead, Golden Gate levitating toward Marin. She brakes, turns into the visitors' lot.

We get out and the wind picks us up, stronger than I'd expected, gusting and cold. The smell of blossoms is what she'd described, a rich vapor cascading under the wind's roar.

Shirl walks ahead and I catch up at a bend in the path: the lights of Berkeley and Oakland and San Francisco rise out of the black body of the bay and the wind is rushing at us, turning us back. The shape of the bridge rears above us. I feel like an intruder.

"This is a famous suicide jump," I shout, my voice sounding sudden.

Shirl shifts her purse from one shoulder to the other. "God," she yells. "Don't go morbid on me."

A moment passes, both of us watching off across what we know is water but cannot see, and Shirl hooks her arm through mine, pulling me back up the slope. "Seen enough?"

"Smelled the flowers?"

"Come on," she says. "Let's go. It's cold."

Shirl picks me up at the station the next night, and the next night after that, and in a week it is as if we have been meeting every night all our lives, riders crossing the night, bottle of cheap wine on the seat between us. The radio fills the silences when we drive, and the older songs remind me of the summer I was drafted, the last summer before the war. I played in a journeyman band, juke and bar circuit up and down the Eastern Shore, Jersey south to Virginia. I lived on the money, pizza for breakfast from boardwalk vendors, walking the beaches past sunburned families on vacation, beach towels fluttering and whipping like alien flags. Afternoons passed in arcades shooting pinball, finding my favorite games, the ones I could beat. I collected penny fortunes from the stand-up machines that delivered my weight on small blue cards with pre-printed destinies. *You will invest well and marry wisely. An ocean voyage will bring prosperity. A tall dark man will change your life.*

"You lost in yourself again?" Shirl glances at me, and checks the rear view. "You can really go off, you know?"

"Yeah," I say. "I know."

One night Shirl is driving in Oakland, abandoned freight yards, single lights lit over empty parking lots. Pallets stacked two stories high, broken glass and baled newspapers in mounds and at a corner in the middle of all this chain-link is what looks like an old Tudor house. Shadows of turrets and cupolas against the sky. I ask Shirl what it is.

"Train station," she says. "I don't think they use it anymore. Not for passenger trains, anyway."

I look at the silhouette. "Freight depot?"

"I guess."

"Let's go over."

"Probably locked up."

"Just check it out. Might be worth looking at. I always liked trains anyway."

When I was a boy in West Virginia my brother and I shared what we belived was a secret, a place where we crouched with the smell of ramps and bitterweed and wild gladiolus, dark glade above a watercourse, waiting for trains. We said *down at the river* like it was a natural mystery, swam under the trestle, fifteen feet wide and no more than ten feet at the deepest under the bridge where the silt had been dug out years before to plant the stanchions. When I heard about drownings I thought about that water under the bridge, shadow's fall, darker and cooler. When my brother and I swam our feet never made bottom, we actually swam, full-bodied and sided against the heart and risk of the stream.

The railroad bridge emerged and crossed, native woods cut and nailed into place when the tracks went through, carbonized from years of heat and weight. When the trains pushed out of the glen they came in a rush, whisper and explosion of locomotive muscle and roar blowing out of some older time. I treaded water, looking up and thinking there was no other way to live:

that easy speed whirling the forest, wind and potent silence in the wake.

We threw stones against the boxcars, hearing them resound hollow or full, laid pennies on the track and gathered them after a train passed over for our trading collections. I imagined how we must have looked from the passenger coaches: sunflash of two boys bobbing white against the green pane of placid creek.

Shirl listens to me talk about the water and the power in the trains, about boyhood summers in that place. After a moment she says, "So where's your brother now?"

"Dead," I say.

"Jesus," she whispers. "I'm sorry."

We are inside the station sitting on a scarred bench that can still gleam mahogany in the half-light. A janitor sweeps around us and never asks what we are doing here. "Jeep accident," I tell Shirl. "In Panama." Looking at a faded chalkboard listing departure times I see the last passenger train left for Fresno late in 1964.

"So what was he doing in Panama?"

"Army." I look at her. "There was a rule at the time. Two brothers in the Army couldn't be in combat at the same time. I went to Nam. He was supposed to be the lucky one."

"Not so lucky, I guess," Shirl murmurs, looking at the floor.

"Not so lucky," I say.

Shirl lights a cigarette, and there is another moment between us before she says she is going for a drink of water. I walk out on the platform. The rails shine blue in moonlight, trailing away from the station yard. The janitor is out here too, pushing a pile of dust and candy wrappers over the edge. Shirl's voice behind me: she says it's getting late.

"I guess the lady's right," I say to the janitor.

"Yes sir," he says with exaggerated politeness, "I believe that she is."

Shirl set a night for a dinner, our first real dinner together, and when I find the address she'd given me the door is open and I hear voices from the back of the house. I knock but no one comes so I step in, stand in the doorway, call her name. I think

I hear her answer. Then she walks through a hallway, nothing on but bra and panties, out of sight again, hurrying, and a door closes. In that light her face seemed bruised. A toilet flushes and a man comes into the hallway carrying a beer can, no pants on, only a ripped T-shirt straining over a gut, stops short when he sees me.

We stand, staring at each other, not speaking, startled.

Then he says: "Who the fuck are you?"

I start to tell him.

"Get the hell out of here," he shouts. I can smell him: drunk, hostile. He steps closer. "I could kill you and be within my rights," he says, now a heavy whisper, "walking in here like this."

I want to explain, open my mouth to speak and he throws the beer can. I step sideways and the can hits the wall behind me, beer frothing and bubbling down the wall to the floor. I think I hear Shirl crying behind a closed door.

I walk back to the bus stop in the bright afternoon and stand alone and wait, windswept.

I don't see Shirl for a week. She isn't at The Pump House, doesn't come to the station at night. On an afternoon after breakfast I ask the waitress about her.

"Shirl?" Writing out my check, pausing to think. "Lessee, you had the two eggs scrambled?"

"Yeah."

"Shirl, yeah. She quit. That's what I heard."

"Quit?"

"Yeah. Lot of family problems." She stacks my dishes and sponges the Formica surface in two sweeps. "Why?"

I count out change for the bill and put a tip on the table. "We were friends. I just missed her being around, wondered what happened."

"Seems like trouble with her husband," the waitress tells me. "That's what I heard. Guess she just needed time to sort out."

"She was married?"

The waitress smiles at me, raises her eyebrows. "I wondered if you knew."

I walk across the road to the station, thinking of the man I had seen in Shirl's house. Probably her husband. Hollis is in the bay; I hear him talking to himself underneath an old Ford pickup. I sit on the torn naugahyde sofa provided for the occasional waiting customer, watch the traffic move and try to imagine how things begin, how anything finds a first moment and drives out of that darkness into a life.

Hollis leaves about three, waving from the wrecker he always drives home.

Near closing time, at the desk counting receipts for the shift and I look up to see the boy. Late teens, hair oiled blue-black, Mediterranean, and the heavy nickel-plated pistol pointed down into my chest. He looks at my body, the area the barrel is trained on. A moment passes before he speaks.

"Just the money," he says, "and I'm out of here."

I don't move.

"Come on, *move*." His voice is hoarse.

I get up, look out the window. An early-model Mercury sits between me and the pumps, chrome and fins, a pale tan. A woman sitting inside the car has hair the same color.

"Never mind out there," the boy with the gun says. "Nobody can see us from the street." He waves the pistol at the cash register. "Just get the money."

I try to unlock the cash register and my hand shakes. I imagine the ways I might be found dead in the morning. The boy goes behind the desk and looks at the circular lid of the floor safe, pointing the pistol at it as if he is going to shoot. Then he steps back and tells me to open it.

I move behind the desk, stoop to pry up the lid and turn the combination. Pull the canister out, empty it on the floor, stand, back away.

"Just stand still."

He pushes the gun barrel through the checks and credit card slips, looks at the pile a moment before standing up, bringing the gun back to bear on my chest, just below my chest, dead center.

"See the bag?" He jerks his head to the rear. Behind him, a neatly folded grocery sack on the naugahyde sofa. I nod.

"Just empty the register into that bag."

I move around him, close enough to smell him, drugstore

cologne and tobacco, pick up the bag and clear the trays and put everything in. "That's it," I say.

"Now just hold it." He reaches down to the phone line, pulls, loose cord skitters out from under the desk. He pulls again and the phone comes down, hits the floor with the bell echoing, pulls again and the cord gives way. He steps forward and takes the sack and backs toward the door pointing the big pistol at me, walks backward watching me until he hits the Mercury. As soon as he turns to get in I step into the garage, lean against the wall, blow out a long breath.

I try to breathe evenly, feel the breaths coming and try to count them, concentrate on counting them. A car left overnight sits coolly in half-silhouette, impassive. The sea air coming through a high transom in the back wall chills my sweat.

In the office I put the phone on the desk and plug the jack back into the wall socket. The Mercury is gone and traffic drifts by in a simple ordinary way and the lit station sign turns slow circles against the night sky.

"Jesus Christ," Hollis says, staring down into the empty cash register drawer. He looks up at me. "You let the son of a bitch have everything in here. You know that?"

"Hollis," I tell him, "the guy had a gun big as my goddamn head. He could have anything he wanted."

Hollis glares at me.

One of the policemen who answered my call says, "Your boy did the right thing. Never pays to argue with a firearm."

Hollis keeps the look on me, but says to the policeman: "I can see you ain't running your own business for a living."

The policeman is the younger of the two. His partner is in the garage, throwing a flashlight beam over the brick walls. The younger one stands and arranges a sheet of paper on a clipboard. "I'll need to go through a few questions," he says.

Hollis asks me, "How much'd he get off with?"

I shrug. "Forty, maybe fifty dollars."

Hollis looks back into the cash drawer, shaking his head. "Fifty goddamn dollars."

"Mr. Hollis?" The younger cop. "Why don't you just have a seat over there so I can get this done?"

Hollis turns, sullen.

"Please," the policeman says.

Hollis goes to the naugahyde sofa and slumps. While I describe the boy, car, and gun, the older cop steps in from the garage, listens to me. "That's real good," he says. "Lotta detail."

"Real fine," the younger cop says. "This'll help."

"Hell," the older one says. "It's enough to jerk the guy inside a week. He'll do three-to-five in San Quentin for a shitty little fifty bucks."

"Nothin' shitty about that fifty dollars," Hollis calls from the sofa. "That's hard-earned money."

Both of the policemen look at Hollis.

"What about my letter, anyway?" Hollis says. "You people never did a damn thing about that either."

The older cop says, "Your letter?"

"My letter M. I reported it stolen."

"Forget it," I say.

"Right, forget it," Hollis says, lifting both hands into the air, a supplicant. "That's probably what you told the guy that robbed the place."

The younger cop has me sign the statement. "Might need you again if we get the guy," he tells me. "You'll hear from us."

"Cold day in hell," Hollis mumbles.

I splash water on my face over the deepsink in the garage and walk out of the station with Hollis talking to me. I pick up a bus across the street and ride it bright and empty up the boulevard.

I am remembering, for some reason, the coast of Vietnam in springtime, flying north of the Delta, green headlands easing away and smoking, water close enough to see flying fish break surf and glitter sun-filled into the face of the next wave, the air after a summer storm: breathless, serene, empty.

The bus makes a stop and outside on the street corner a blind black woman taps her cane and rocks, singing an *a cappella* blues. The driver looks out from his cubicle and back down the long aisle.

"Everything O.K.?" he asks me.

"Absolutely," I tell him. "Couldn't be better."

C. S. GODSHALK

Wonderland

FROM THE IOWA REVIEW

WHEN THE ROOM was like this, in the dark, with only the window letting in moonlight and the white blanket looming up pale and square, anything could be in it. Anyone. Merle could be curled up on the day bed grinding his teeth, his small knees jammed into his chest. He was. She could be rolling over on the big fold-out couch, snoring lightly, or just there. She wasn't. But in the night Paulie was never completely sure. He let this uncertainty fold over him, the dreamy possibility of his mother's presence in the room would roll up under his chin, and he would sleep.

In the morning it was just himself and Merle, but it was all right because in the morning he was energetic and there were things to do fast. Juice and cereal and Bugs Bunny vitamins and hot milk heated in the little pot on the good burner and the pot run full of water right away so he could clean it out easily when they got back. Then rinsing and stacking the dishes in the sink and smoothing out the beds. He got Merle's jacket and hat and gave him the fifty cents. He had made her fill out the form saying they needed lunch for fifty cents and not a dollar like the other kids, only a lot of the other kids had the same form.

Sometimes, when he first woke up but didn't open his eyes, knowing she'd be nowhere in the room, he would panic. He'd decide then to tell them, he'd yell to them all off the back stairs of the apartment and down the halls of Our Lady of the Snows, that she had left. "What kind of a mother is she!" they would cry. "A whore! A drunk!" And he would rush into their arms, into all their arms. But it would be Peg holding him, smiling with her cigarette and that stretched pink and silver sweater, looking nothing like anybody's mother, and a tremendous ache would fill his chest. That's when he dropped an arm off the bed and groped for his sneakers. He knew if they were there, exactly as he left them, side by side with the toes perfectly even, it would be all right and he could get up.

He poured the milk out of the pot over two bowls of Cap'n Crunch while Merle's headless form stumbled out of the bathroom. Paulie reached out with his free hand and yanked at the little boy's shirt until the large grey eyes appeared, the shirt still hitched on the nose, the face of a baby robber.

"Did you go to the bathroom? Did you DO anything?" The small boy looked up gravely, his red cheeks almost comical under Paulie's long pale chin. Despite their differences, the children shared a wide mouth and straight, almost broomlike reddish hair. "That bed damn well better be dry!" Paulie said.

After the dishes, Paulie took the plastic watering can from under the sink and watered all the plants. Then he shoved Merle's arms into a leather jacket and zipped up both their jackets, checked for the key in his breast pocket, and slammed the door. That part of the day was finished right. Outside, down the rickety back stairs, they stepped carefully over the brilliant bits of ice, beneath Nudorf's underwear lifting flat and frozen in the sunlight, mid-high to the peeling bottle of Myers's rum shooting its tremendous cap and stars off the billboard into the bright blue sky.

The house itself listed. It looked like all the other broken-down three-deckers in East Boston, except it was tilted slightly forward so that, they had discovered, a marble rolled on their bathroom floor on the second floor would continue out across the linoleum, slowly increasing speed, making a little leap over the TV wire, over the kitchen door jamb and out the back door, dropping in little crystal slaps down the twenty-seven steps, staying in the depression in the middle of each, before it fell backward off the twenty-seventh step and clanked on the trash cans.

They had told Peg about the marble. Paulie told her exactly how it would go but she just shoved him away, holding her cigarette inside the cup of her hand the way she did when she touched them. Later she came out on the back porch with her fake fur jacket over her robe and grabbed Paulie's neck and steered him back inside to the bathroom and smacked a marble in his hand. She shuffled back out to the porch and yelled "Go!" and he squatted and let the marble go, he didn't push it, he just let it roll away, and it passed her dirty pink slippers and started to bounce and she leaned over the wooden rail and watched it hop down below her until the final chink on the can and she said "Holy shit!" with that smile. She wasn't drunk then and she wasn't sober. She was in between and she was nice.

That was the week before she left. He got back from school with Merle and there was a box of cream-filled cupcakes on the dinette. On top of the box was a long envelope with Magic Marker writing. The Magic Marker was still there with its top off. She never put the tops back on and they always got dry. "Paulie," it said on the envelope, "I'm going away for a while," and he closed his eyes. "I'm going on a trip. You're almost twelve. That's no baby! Make sure Merle eats and don't take any crap. If you need me, *a real emergency,* go up to Nudorf and use this number." It was the number of the new guy from Texas. Mitch. "Uncle" Mitch. Inside the envelope were eight twenty-dollar bills and a piece of yellow paper. "Use this slow," it said on the paper. "I'll be back before it's gone, or I'll send your father." A bright set of her lips was pressed into the paper.

"Fuck her," he said in a high, choked voice. He ripped open the cupcakes and shoved them at Merle. Merle pushed a cupcake into his mouth and backed away.

"Fuck her!" Paulie said again and the little boy started to cry. Chocolate squeezed out of the sides of his mouth and onto his shirt. "Fuck her!" Paulie screamed, and Merle moaned, a slow bright circle of water surrounding his darkened pants as if the tears were too much for the eyes alone to discharge.

"You pig!" Paulie said. "You little pig!" Merle began to wail and Paulie shoved him into a chair and stared at him savagely until he was quiet. Then he went over and dumped out the twenty-dollar bills. He took one and folded it up and shoved it deep in his breast pocket and he stuffed the rest in a jar and put it way in back of the freezer part of the refrigerator. He took the envelope and tore it into bits and dropped them in the trash. "We're not calling her," he said, pulling off the small boy's shoes and socks and pants and wrapping him around with a dishtowel. "Ever."

He decided the first thing to do, despite the cash in the jar, was to get a job. He went to Foodland the next afternoon and applied for a job bagging. He was younger than the other bag boys, but he was tall and acted polite and they didn't hassle him. At first it was only for Saturday, but by the next week they told him he could come every day after school. Between Foodland and Peg's cash, he figured they could last for quite a while.

Except for the nights, which Merle screwed up, it was better than it had been. They got to school on time. The place looked good. They ate right. "If anybody asks," Paulie said to Merle repreatedly, "Old man Nudorf, Sister Cecilia, *anybody,* Peg's outa town. Say we got our aunt to cook and do stuff. Say Peg sends us postcards."

"Where?" Merle suddenly brightened.

"Where what?"

"Where are the postcards?" The child's eyes shone even more. "I want to see 'em!"

"There ARE no postcards, you little shit. Pay attention!" Merle looked at him blankly. He started to rock, as if a light breeze had entered the room. "Now," Paulie said again. "What are you going to say if someone asks — like Sister Cecilia?"

"What?"

"What are YOU going to say?" Paulie's fingers dug into the small arm. "YOU say — 'My aunt is staying with us and cooks and stuff. My mother will be BACK SOON!' "

"She will?" Merle cried in pain.

Paulie let go of his arm and sunk into the yellow chair. "Yeah," he said blackly. They had gone eleven days, though, and nobody asked. When Nudorf finally squared them off on the stairs, putting down his bag of soda bottles and drilling into them with small, colorless eyes, they both wet their lips. "Where's your mother?" the old man said, and before Paulie could jerk back he grabbed a pinch of white cheek. "Jesus, you two look nice!" Nudorf's eyebrows raised like little hats. "She must have run outa booze in there and had nothing to do but polish you up!" He bent over and heaved the bottles against his chest and pushed past. They watched his galoshes push up under the dirty coat, disappearing and reappearing like pedals, until the old man vanished around the bend of stair and sky.

Our Lady of the Snows elementary school was a huge yellow building set between the church on one side and the convent and rectory on the other. Our Lady herself stood in yellow stucco in front of the church, balancing her bare feet on a little globe. Merle waited here for Paulie each day because the second grade always got out before the seventh. He stood in front of Our Lady while the buses pulled up and hundreds of kids rushed out and around him and then he held on to the gate so as not to be pushed out of place. Eventually he'd see Paulie's purple ski hat bouncing through the crowd.

Paulie would push up his collar and they'd walk together to Foodland. Sometimes Angel Ruiz would join them. Ruiz was smaller and older than Paulie. He looked like a monkey with dark, skinny arms and a wide mouth. He was always happy looking. He'd shuffle up fast in his stupid little jacket, the small shoulders twitching back and forth, his sneakers bouncing.

Ruiz was the only one Paulie told about Peg. "No shit!" he said, smiling. "Wow, if my old lady took off I'd grow some fucking wings or something!" He reversed to a moonwalk. Ruiz could moonwalk for blocks. "But why Foodland? I mean FOODLAND!" He slapped his forehead and rocked back drunkenly. "My old lady puts you on a roof, two hours you make fifty bucks. Just have to 'look'! Just tell 'em who's going down the street. FOODLAND!" Ruiz stumbled backwards again, laughing.

"Your old lady," Paulie said, shoving Merle forward. "How long is she going to do that thing with the string? A guy whistles in the alley — down comes Rosita's string with the stuff. I mean EVERYBODY sees it. What does she need a guy on the roof for?" Paulie had sat on the roof with Ruiz once or twice. The last time it was freezing, and they sat there watching the street and fooling with the steam coming out of their mouths. Suddenly Ruiz jumped up and began a little break routine on the ledge, jiving fast, before Paulie yanked him back down on the tar. "Ruiz is crazy," he said to Merle later. "Don't hang around with him unless I'm there."

Usually Ruiz left them at Dean Street, but this time he went all the way to Foodland. He hung around inside for a while, then he slipped some gum into his jeans and did a fancy move on the electric eye mat and waved goodbye without turning back.

The day after Paulie told him about Peg, Ruiz came to the apartment. He had a big bag full of Fritos and Sprite and Spanish stuff in cans. He said he could get more if Paulie needed it. At home, Paulie knew, Ruiz ate strangely. There'd be nothing for days and then Rosita would have fifty people over and there would be meat and bananas, big cooked bananas, beans and beer and guys in beautiful tight shirts. Only now Rosita's parties were small. Ruiz suddenly had real money because of these parties. He did his first trick with two guys she had up there over Christmas. "You gotta get out of there," Paulie said when he told him. "Yeah." Ruiz smiled softly. "Next week I'm going to Miami."

After Ruiz left Foodland, Paulie put on the yellow jacket and took Merle to the receiving area in back of produce. He sat him on a box between other boxes and gave him some old comics and told him not to move. Most of the time he wouldn't. He sat there turning the pages, rubbing his feet together. The first day Paulie told the assistant manager that he had to watch Merle sometimes after school and the guy said "No way," but when he passed the small boy sitting with the comic books a few days later, he shrugged and walked away. Merle ate stuff in back of Foodland, but he was careful. Paulie told him not to take anything out of the store that wasn't in his stomach and he didn't.

Going home, they wouldn't talk for blocks. They'd walk through the alley behind the store, down and over the MTA tracks and up the small embankment toward the fading light in the west. Sometimes Paulie would pretend she was there waiting for them in the gold armchair, and the pale yellow light became part of the vast chair, her reddish hair spread out above, her wide lips smiling over the bank of clouds like something floating on a movie screen. Once the light spread out in a dappled band and he saw her suddenly in her leopard kerchief the way she was that one time she came to school. She came for the Christmas play and she stood in the hallway with her fur jacket and her hair high and puffy under the leopard kerchief. She was the only adult there and she looked somehow saved when she saw him. "Paulie! Where do I go?" He was walking in a line of boys and he just kept in line as they passed her. "Home," he spat.

"What? Whatya mean?" she cried. "You said ten o'clock!" But he kept going. "I'm EARLY!" she screamed, rushing after him and yanking him around so that the kids in back bunched up and then walked around them, staring. "Ten o'clock yesterday," he said with venom, then pushed past. At the end of the hallway he glanced back and she was still standing there in that stupid kerchief, her hands dangling dead out of the jacket. He flung the image from his mind and twisted round to look for Merle. The small, pinched face pushed all sorrow from his heart.

By the time they turned onto their street the sun had usually disappeared, but Nudorf's laundry still caught the high lemon color, waving to them like bright cardboard cutouts of himself. The top of the huge billboard bottle glinted too in the yellow air, and they knew they were home.

One time, starting up the stairs, Paulie stopped. "What's that?" he asked, and Merle slipped a small brown ball into his pocket.

"A kiwi."

"I told you NOT to take stuff out of the store!"

"I didn't take it. I was LOOKING at them and Lifson gave me one.

"They're green inside," Merle said more quietly, "like green jelly."

"Open it."

"No."

"Why not, for Christ's sake! I want to see. It'll get rotten like that other crap you stashed away."

"So what."

The boys climbed the stairs silently, the higher windows blinding them in the last iridescence. "You're saving it for her!" Paulie said suddenly. "You dumb jerk! That's what you're doing! All that stuff! The dried up Fritos, those cupcakes! You're saving them for her!" Merle pressed his baby lips together and looked away.

"Christ," Paulie said.

Inside he hung the two jackets on doorknobs and looked

around. It still surprised him to get in and find everything so quiet and neat. The lousy smell was gone, the cigarette butts pushed into food were gone, her make-up all over the place was gone. She always wore make-up and she never put any of it away. He liked her best in the morning when her eyes were plain and they didn't jump out of her face like they did later. She'd start with a tube of light brown stuff and then build on it. A few times she put this stuff on Merle after she hit him. Once on his arm where Kenny had pressed it. She was nice after times like that, sometimes for days. She tried to put the brown stuff on him one time, over a split cheek, but he shoved her off.

At night the two of them usually had cereal and then watched TV in their pajamas, which Paulie already took twice to the laundromat with their other stuff. Sometimes they had tuna because for some reason Peg had a four-year supply of tuna in the kitchen, or like this night, Paulie fried up pork chops with Wonder bread on the side, which was their favorite. He set the pink Formica table with two folded pieces of toilet paper and put the small snake plant in the middle of it and two forks and two knives. The snake plant looked good in the middle of the table, its sharp thick spikes pointing upward, dark green with no brown like when she took care of it. All the plants looked good. The big one with the ribbon and the pink foil looked great. Uncle Mitch brought it. Uncles were always bringing stuff. Crap. One day before Christmas she told him Uncle Phil was bringing them both Big Wheels and he told her she could shove Uncle Phil and all the other uncles up her ass, but that's what she did anyway, and that's when she opened his cheek with her hair dryer.

Paulie liked the plants. He got a small box of Vitagrow from Foodland and used it carefully after reading the directions several times. "You don't use too much of this stuff or you burn the roots," he said to Merle. And he watered them regularly, but not too much. "She drowned half of 'em and dried up the rest," he said.

He checked the mail each day before he dropped it in a big shopping bag. There was one tremendous, oversized postcard that came from her the second week. It was a big monkey waving from the side of a skyscraper and it was all bent around the edges. "Hi guys!" it said. "Say hi to Kenny. Be good!" It was surrounded by a frame of X's and another pair of Peg's lips in the center. Kenny, she told Paulie a few years back, was his father. He might have been, too, because she didn't call him Uncle Kenny and she didn't seem to like him very much. He was a pale guy who always looked like he wanted to be somewhere else. Kenny didn't seem to see Paulie when he was around. Merle's father was another guy. His name was Merle and Peg named Merle after him, but it didn't do much good because it turned out the guy hated the name. Somehow Peg must have asked Kenny to keep an eye on them. This made Paulie laugh.

On Fridays Paulie dumped out the shopping bag and sorted the mail. He did this when Peg was there too, because she wasn't too good with mail. He separated what was junk, what was important — like Boston Edison — what bills could be forgotten forever practically, and what could be forgotten for a long time. Rent could wait because Peg paid that more or less on time, so Nudorf wouldn't hassle him for probably a month. The phone was no problem because it was gone. Peg flung it at the guy who came from New England Telephone to take it out. She switched her cigarette to her mouth and actually ripped it off the kitchen wall and flung it at this guy's chest, and she was a small lady. She'd do terrific stuff like that sometimes. Paulie asked Merle in bed one night if he remembered the phone guy, but Merle was asleep.

By the third week in February, there was one twenty left in the jar. Paulie walked around with the Edison bill in his jacket, because he felt somehow if he had it on him, they couldn't use it. He knew this was ridiculous, but he still did it. At night he would wake up and see the long envelope, the one he had torn up, he would see it in front of his eyes, but he couldn't see the phone number written on it. That postcard came from New York anyway, not Texas, so who knew where the hell she was. There were other times when he came home and he was positive she had called. She had called Nudorf upstairs. Once he got back from the deli and Merle was in front of the TV, which was on very loud, the way he liked it when Paulie left him alone, and Paulie asked him.

"Did she call?"

"Who?" Merle's eyes stayed glued on the tube.

"Wonder Woman."

"Yeah."

"She DID! Christ! She DID!"

"What?"

"Did Mr. Nudorf come down?"

"No — I think — no."

"Merle!" Paulie pulled him up from the floor brutally and his head hit the side of the TV and he began to scream. In the night, on the rare occasions when Nudorf's phone rang upstairs, Paulie listened breathlessly to the old man's weight creaking over the floor. He'd wait for him to cross over to the door and start down the stairs. "Paulie!" Nudorf would shout outside their door. "Your mother is on the phone! Hey!" But he didn't.

Merle was the real problem. He wet the bed all the time now, and not just wet. The apartment smelled. Paulie kept him home from school a lot and stayed home too. He bought some post-cards and wrote on them and gave them to Merle. "She sent them," he said. "She's coming back soon."

"You sent them," Merle said in a queer voice.

One night, when he made a particularly disgusting mess of his bed, Paulie hit him. He hit him hard, and Merle was quiet for a long time. He seemed all right, there was no mark, but he just wouldn't talk or anything, so Paulie finally picked him up and put him in his own bed and got in with him. He wrapped his legs around him and they slept like that and Merle was all right and didn't do anything. But when they got up the next morning, he made a mess on the floor. Paulie didn't clean it up. He got a ballpoint and a piece of paper from his loose-leaf and he sat down and began to write. He wrote to "Chatters" at the *Boston Globe*. He read "Chatters" sometimes when Peg got the paper. He read it usually after "Garfield" and the ads for the topless bars. People wrote to "Chatters" with their problems, and other people — regular people — wrote the answers.

"Dear Chatters," he wrote. "I have a small boy who wets the bed all the time and now it's more than just wetting. What do you recommend? I don't want to hit him or anything like that. Is there another mother out there with the same problem who has stopped her child from doing this? If you are the one, please answer." He signed it "Big Boy." People always signed the "Chatters" letters with funny or weird names. He mailed it right away and then he waited two days and checked a *Globe* at Soviero's deli, but "Big Boy" wasn't in yet. "Double Virgo" asked how to clean smudges off burnished copper. "Crazed Mom" asked how to stop spanking her four-year-old daughter. "Lamp Lady" asked if someone had the directions for a doll lamp. No "Big Boy."

He thought of asking Ruiz about Merle because, as crazy as Ruiz was, he sometimes gave strangely good advice. He checked for the narrow back with the black and yellow jacket in social studies, but the seat was empty. This was not unusual, half the time Ruiz never showed up. Just before recess, Sister Bonaventure, the principal, came into the classroom and put her hands together so that the big white sleeves fell back like wings and she waited until everyone was quiet. "I'm sorry, boys and girls," she said, and her big ugly face looked sorry. "We've learned that Angel Ruiz has had a terrible accident. Last night he fell off the roof of his home. He died this morning at Children's Hospital." One or two children giggled softly. "We must pray for his family, for his poor parents." Paulie saw Ruiz pass before him smiling, rotating like a wheel in the darkness, and he could not find air anywhere in the room.

"Where is he now?" Merle asked that night. "In a box," Paulie said tonelessly. "Tomorrow they'll cover the box with flowers. They'll put it in the ground and fifty people will come and eat."

The entire class went to the funeral Mass. Rosita was there with a black hat resting like an elbow over her eyes. She was swaying sideways on a smaller, darker man. "At least you didn't get him," Paulie thought savagely, and at that moment Rosita looked up and he had never seen such a sad face in all his life.

In the night Paulie balled up Ruiz and Merle, Peg and the Edison bill and Rosita, he balled up all of it and he punched it until it was hard like a rock and he flung it to the back of his skull. He decided, wildly, to clean the apartment. On Saturday he shoved Merle into his jacket and hat and gloves and put him in front of the TV and then opened all the windows and the cold air rushed in. He worked hard, scrubbing and cleaning, and when he was finished he closed all the windows and took Merle's stuff off and looked around. The place looked and smelled much better, but there was still something. The stuff on the doorknobs looked the worst. At Our Lady of the Snows they had hooks, a long line of brass hooks for coats which Paulie admired, and also rough plastic mats at the side doors where you could scrape your shoes before going inside.

The hooks were easy. He just slipped them inside his jacket at DeVito's hardware and glided toward the door so they didn't chink together. At the door he picked up a bright green rectangle of sharp plastic grass and walked out. He walked fast, waiting for a heavy weight on his shoulder to spin him around. He was ready for it, his chest filled with air, ready to tell them everything, but nobody stopped him.

Back home he made Merle hold the hooks one by one as he pounded a nail through the hole in each one. Merle winced each time, but his small hand remained steady. After three hooks were up, the door flew open and Nudorf stood with his hands clenched, bouncing over his slippers. "You wanna bring the whole goddamn place down!" he cried. "I got two pictures off the wall already! Cut it out! Where's your mother?"

Merle stared at him, his mouth open wetly. Paulie riveted his eyes on the nail and went on hammering furiously and when he was done he flipped the hammer on the yellow chair.

"Get them coats!" he ordered Merle. He turned his eyes on the old man. "Did you wipe your feet?" he asked contemptuously. "That's what the green mat's for! I shouldn't have to tell you that!"

Nudorf found himself scraping his slippers, and then turned round vacantly and went out the doorway. "Close the door!" Paulie commanded, but he was already shuffling up the stairs in confusion.

Paulie worried after he left. The old guy would go upstairs and think about it, he knew, think about just the two of them being there in the apartment. He decided to go up right away and tell him about the aunt.

Upstairs Nudorf opened the door and put out his hand and pulled Paulie in by his shirt. This had never happened before and Paulie was afraid. Inside, the old man let go of him and sank into a chair. Except for the light over a table and the chair, the room was dark. It was cramped with huge furniture and the air smelled like Nudorf, only stronger.

"Paulie." The watery eyes blinked up. "She's gone, ain't she?"

"I've got to go," Paulie said. "My aunt's coming. She doesn't like me to leave Merle alone."

"How long have you been doing this?" The watery eyes swelled open. "HOW have you been doing this?" Paulie slipped back out of the light, and Nudorf was silent. For a moment the old man seemed to forget him. He picked up a spoon that had been buried in some mush and then slowly let it go. Paulie walked around touching things lightly. In the little kitchen there were a lot of large soda bottles lined up behind the sink. Lemon soda.

"What do you do with all the lemon soda?"

Nudorf jerked up, shifting toward the voice. "It goes down easy. I got problems here." He pointed to his stomach. Paulie lifted the dank curtain over the sink and looked out. The bottle of rum looked different from up here. You could see the four spotlights that went on at night and the huge dry flakes peeling off the top. He dropped the curtain and continued walking around, running his hand over the heavy furniture, keeping out of Nudorf's range.

"It's okay," Nudorf said suddenly. "I was a man at twelve! I was an old man at seventeen! Now," he pushed away the mush, "I'm a baby. You'll be all right. Better off in fact!"

Paulie fingered things while Nudorf talked. Nothing in the whole place was worth two cents. He pulled out a drawer and Nudorf stopped talking, his eyes bright with panic. "What's that! What've you got!" Paulie withdrew his hand silently. Inside the drawer he could see loose toothpicks and a photo. It was of a tan boy about his own age in a too small jacket with his arms stiffly at his sides.

"This your kid?"

"Yes. No. It's me, I think." Nudorf started to get up and Paulie slipped out the door. The air in the rancid hallway was like a breath of spring.

"You and your brother," Nudorf cried, sticking his head out the door. "I saw you crossing the tracks. Don't do that! In the snow you can't hear so good. Snow does something funny to the sound!" But Paulie had slipped down the stairs.

Inside Merle was asleep on the floor in front of the TV. Paulie took his blanket off the bed and tucked it around him and sat down and looked at the tube. A lady and two kids were smiling at a very shiny floor. It was extremely shiny, like a mirror. He looked down at the pitted linoleum between his sneakers and rolled away into the couch. He curved his arms and legs around one of the stiff pillows, kicking off his sneakers, and clung softly to what he knew was a spinning ball, with the water not falling off, with fishes hanging in it, bright sunlight on the other side, revolving fast, nothing falling off ever, he clung with his curled toes, clung to the vast cheek, the red hair lifted behind, the cigarette cupped away somewhere out in the universe.

In the morning it was abnormally quiet. It was Sunday, but that wasn't it. The room was filled with a soft luminescence. Paulie got up and shut off the TV and the lamp, but the soft brightness remained. Merle was still asleep on the floor, soaking in the sweet smell of urine. Paulie covered him with the damp blanket and got his own sneakers on quietly and then his jacket and opened the back door. The dazzling whiteness made him wince. He stood there blind in the fiery dazzle, cracking his eyes now and then until the back stairs materialized in a sparkling spiral. He made a first step, plucking his foot back out and inspecting the perfect blue imprint. Below the cars extended in softly glistening humps all the way to the end of the street. It made him suddenly happy. He threw a snowball at her once, she was standing where he was now, looking down, and he threw a fistful of snow and her eyelashes were suddenly full of snow. "Wonderland!" she said, laughing.

At the bottom of the stairs he began to walk slowly through the quiet brilliance. It was too early for traffic on the side streets. Nothing moved. In a short time he reached the overpass where the sidewalk ducked into a tunnel and the world turned abruptly black. Cars reverberated overhead and when he emerged in front of Soviero's deli, the snow was already grey and used.

The Sunday *Globe* was big and he couldn't thumb through it fast enough to check "Chatters" without Soviero bitching at him, so he bought it. Outside he cradled the heavy *Globe* and a box of doughnut holes in both arms and the change stuck inside his glove. There was a dollar thirty-four left. "In a dollar thirty-four," he thought with a strange twist to his lips, "she would be back. Or a dollar thirty-three. She said before it was gone." He jerked the glove off with his teeth and flung the money away. After walking a few yards he stopped, his eyes burning, and went back. He sunk to his knees and began poking through the small, circular tunnels made by the change, then kicked the slush violently from side to side.

There was traffic on their street when he turned the corner, several black rectangles appeared where cars had been removed, and something else. His eyes narrowed, scanning back and forth over the street for what he had seen, over the buildings and the line of parked cars, and there it was, the fender of the deep red Camaro. It sat in front of the snow-filled vacant lot. Mitch's car. He walked up and put his hand tentatively on the windshield, tracing the screaming eagle decal beneath the glass. On the bumper it said, "Cowboys make better lovers." Inside there were several packs of cigarettes on the front seat, her cigarettes. He shifted the *Globe* and the doughnut holes and looked up at the house and the blank second-story porch, still like the others, but not like the others because behind it she was kissing and rocking Merle, and Mitch had his filthy head in the fridge searching for a beer. He sat down on the stoop by the car and leaned back. The blueness beyond the roofs seemed to fall away from his eyes, as if gravity reversed and he could fall up, up, as soon as he let go. He ached to see her, to collapse against her. He knew, in a moment, he would. He would get up and walk the hundred yards and climb the stairs and throw open the door and that would be that. But he just sat there.

A green truck idled a few doors down, the driver leaning on his horn for a car sliding sideways out of a parking space and the sound reverberating cruelly in the wet air. Across the street a boy in a big parka was playing with a little girl of about three. It looked like they were playing hide and seek in front of the stoop. Paulie watched the boy hold both the little girl's hands and spin around. Her eyes were closed and then she would continue to spin around alone, smiling with her arms out, and the boy would dart fast behind a car or the stoop and the little girl would look round and round and not see him and call him and then begin to cry. He would wait until she looked afraid and started to cry desperately, and then he would pop out and she would stop crying and look happy almost immediately and they would start to play again. After a while he would sneak quickly behind another car and she'd call him and start to cry again. Paulie watched as both were repeated again and again, the little girl's joy, desolation, joy, as she continued to play, having too short a memory for despair, or too long for joy. He continued to watch, amazed.

LUCY HONIG

No Friends, All Strangers

FROM THE AGNI REVIEW

I DON'T KNOW. Sometimes I wish they'd all shut up. At work Ronnie has the radio on every minute, and the customers are always yapping, the radio doesn't even drown them out.

When I say customers, Ronnie tells me to say clients. You'd think he was a lawyer or a shrink or something.

A lot of the clients act as if he *was* a shrink, sometimes as if I was, too. I give shampoos and sweep up, they don't know me from Adam, they don't tip me, most of them probably could never tell you what I look like. Still: yap, yap, yap. Life stories. Cheating husbands, lousy investments, condo prices going out of sight.

Ronnie's pretty nice to me. He shares the tips. A lot of times I open up my mouth when all those hotsy-totsy people get on my nerves. "When's the last time *she* had to notice the price of tomatoes?" I say when some woman with a dozen face-lifts gets under the dryer.

Ronnie laughs. He turns the radio up higher. "Shut up and sweep," he says. He says it to be funny.

Sometimes Ronnie *is* funny, sometimes he just thinks he is. He calls the shop Hair and Now. Once he had a luggage shop with his brother next to Penn Station. They called it The Terminal Case.

"That's not funny," I told Ronnie.

"Shut up and sweep," he said. Then he started dancing around the empty chair, dancing to the music. It's nonstop rock-and-roll. Ronnie's nearly bald, he wears wire-rimmed glasses and pin-striped suits and looks like he could be a stockbroker. Only he's always dancing in circles around the chair, even when the fat cat businessmen are sitting there — and he's got a reputation all the way down to Wall Street, let me tell you. But there he is jiving to the rock-and-roll.

The kids play ball in the street, they're yelling and screaming when I get home from work. Mrs. Ryan, the big fat woman next door, she holds court on the sidewalk, standing with her hands on her gigantic hips and giving everyone the once-over; she doesn't miss a thing. And when she wants her kid who's hanging out at the other end of the block, she hauls off and hollers, "Hey Mikey, c'mon in for supper! For SUPPER, I said!" Her voice is like a big, heavy mirror shattering down the street.

The mousy woman on the fourth floor with the baby comes down with the stroller hitting hard on every step, *co-lomp,co-lomp, co-lomp.* The baby cries. The woman stands outside my door yelling at the kid to calm down, but he screams louder, then she screams, they may as well be standing in my kitchen. If I *had* a kitchen. I live in the smallest apartment in Brooklyn, ground floor front. I hear everything from here — garbage trucks whining at five in the morning, car alarms going off. I hear dogs pissing on the hydrants. I hear kids writing their graffiti. KILL TO SURVIVE, says the mailbox on the corner.

Next to my apartment lives a guy who thinks he's a singer, a *folk* singer. He howls for hours on end, like a wolf baying at the moon. And his voice never gives out: if he's not howling then he's humming through his nose. Just to put the garbage out he hums. When he walks past my door humming, I cover my ears.

In a city so big, people live under each other's skin. They have to. Like you have to breathe the air.

I get my quiet on the subway. Some people wear ear plugs because of the screeching and the clanging, but that's the kind of noise I don't even bother to hear. I like that people almost never talk. Sometimes the lights go out, we're stuck in a tunnel, people are packed in tight, standing and sitting, it's like we have this agreement not to touch or kill each other in the dark. It's hush quiet. You hear books and newspapers closing, or somebody sighing because he's late for work again. You feel some stranger's quiet breath on your own neck.

On the train if I concentrate on a person I can feel what he feels. Not that I read his mind, just that I get in somewhere on the wavelength of what's got him in its grip. Like a guy who's reading the racing pages, his whole self is in it, I can feel his gambling greed like it was in my own bones. Or if there's a woman nervous about the sick kid sprawled in her lap, I get her knot in my own stomach. The loneliness of some little old men grabs me in my throat. And the muddle for foreigners, like some Asian refugees, they get so confused when they first land, it's like a big noise in their heads that I can hear. After a while I have to look away.

Once Ronnie bandaged up my finger when I sliced it on the shears. He said, "My parents always wanted me to be a doctor." He made the bandage neat and tight. Then he went right back dancing along to Springsteen.

"Did *you* ever want to?" I asked him.

"Want to what?" Ronnie doesn't have a great attention span.

"Want to be a doctor."

"Naah." He shrugged. "I liked luggage. I like hair. Who needs all the troubles doctors have?" Then he did a fancy little step around the fat cat on the chair.

Ronnie's running a class act, he's got old wood antiques for cabinets, a fancy Oriental carpet up on the wall, he wears these three-piece suits. But Ronnie doesn't want more than he's got. The suits, they're like a joke. These guys come up from Wall Street, they dig it that their hairdresser looks just like they do. Ronnie's not into the rat race. He could hire a couple more cutters, squeeze in more chairs, make a lot more money. But he doesn't want to run a lot of other people. He's satisfied with what he's got, and so am I. We're probably the only two around.

Miguel sells umbrellas from a folding table on the sidewalk in front. Umbrellas, sunglasses, and Duracell batteries, something for all seasons. Every day he's out there, freezing in winter or roasting in summer. But every six weeks to the day he comes in for a cut.

"Hey man, I got my image to keep!" he shouts to Ronnie when Ronnie makes some joke about giving him a new style. Miguel gets real serious. "Bad for business, man," he says, adjusting a couple of hairs to show Ronnie what he wants. "You change me too much around, it's bad for business." Ronnie gives him the same old cut, a little punk but not too crazy, that's how Miguel describes it. "My image, man," he says. Ronnie cuts it for him free, won't take a cent. We've got umbrellas here to last a flood.

The day goes pretty fast. Sometimes it feels like I spend more of it on the train than at the shop. When I get on the train, first I case the car to see if there are any real crazies. Then I look for a person I could talk to in case we got stuck for a long time. Actually I've gotten stuck plenty but I've never talked to anyone. It's not easy for me to start up a conversation with a stranger, and even a track fire only takes an hour or two. I don't know what I'm waiting for, maybe for the end of the world, a nuclear attack, another great big blackout, I don't know, maybe then I'd talk to the person I'd picked out. Still, I get these fantasies. If we were good and stuck, waiting for the end, I dream that I'd arrange the people. I'd get the ones who had seats to change with the ones who were standing, I'd get them to rotate and clear spaces on the floor. I'd get everyone to pool their food and cigarettes and divvy it all up. Maybe I'd get us all to sing for a little while, "Home on the Range" or "I've Been Working on the Railroad" or something else easy that everybody knows. That's what I dream of doing if we were stuck forever. But I don't know.

One day last week, a big handsome powerful-looking black guy got on with a crowd at DeKalb Avenue. If you caught a glimpse of him out of the corner of your eye you would think he was someone important, that's the way he carried himself, erect and strong, but he was lugging shopping bags filled with rags and crumbled papers, and he was dressed like a bum. Then a young white guy got on behind him, an art student carrying a big leather portfolio. He had curly blond hair and a look on his face like he was on a beach on Mars and counting all the grains of sand. He was a billion miles away. The bagman sat on a seat at the end of the car. The kid stood against the door kitty-corner from him. The bagman took out a cigarette, which you're not supposed to smoke on the subway. He was just about to strike a match when he looked over at the kid. I watched the bagman.

He got such a mean and persecuted look on him. I saw it happen. The bagman was spooked by the kid. The kid must have been his boogeyman.

The bagman kept bringing his match to the matchbook to strike it, and every time it was as if some big invisible hand reached out and stopped him, and he glared at the kid, who was off on the beach on Mars. I saw this happen again and again, all through the slow crawl across the bridge.

The bagman got madder and madder.

The lady sitting across from the bagman got off at Grand Street and the kid from Mars went to sit in her seat. And the bagman was furious. His cheeks puffed up with the fury, his eyes got wide and glassy. He couldn't sit across from his boogeyman. It was a personal insult, the kid sitting there. It was evil. The bagman got up, hoisted his bags in both big hands, stood directly over the kid, swaying, and let loose with a stream of obscenities. You could see his spit fly. The kid came back to earth just enough to hear the bagman cursing him and be shocked. *Hurt,* even. He didn't see the spooking going on. A few people smiled sympathetically at the kid. Most of them pretended they didn't hear or see a thing.

I felt bad for the bagman. He went swinging his bags down the car, muttering nasty curses to himself.

Once, in a car that wasn't very full, I realized a guy kept looking at me, but not like someone would look you over to attack or rob you. This guy was stealing looks, as if he didn't really want to but had to keep an eye on me. And then it hit me like a brick: I was his boogeyman. At the next stop, I changed cars. This boogeyman business is the worst.

The opposite of boogeyman, that's the woman, the beautiful black woman I see sometimes, mainly on the ride home, and when I say beautiful I mean the beautiful you can't stop looking at, it's in her eyes and her skin and her clothes and her soul. I don't know where she gets on or gets off, but every so often she's just *there,* making me feel in my bones that nothing bad could ever happen on this train. There's something deep and knowing about her, she's sad and happy at the same time, like she has seen the world from top to bottom, she's been face to face with the worst there is and still come back looking like a million bucks. She's got round eyes that shine and never hide, set in a face with the most perfect, smooth, dark brown skin. In a million years a white woman could never be this beautiful. This woman wears red — sometimes a whole red dress, sometimes red shoes, a red bag, or just red lipstick, but the red is vivid. She's a vivid woman, she stands out. She wears a little bit of very good make-up, maybe some exotic scarf draped over her shoulder, or a hat at an angle no one else would ever think of. Little children in the car can't take their eyes off her, men neither, of course, but women love her too. At the end of a deathly hard day of work you rest your eyes on her and you rest. Angry people stop being angry, the crazy ones stop being crazy when they see this woman. If you're cold you warm up and if you're hot you cool down. This woman turns the subway car into a state of grace.

Once she had long, perfectly painted red fingernails on her long, slender fingers, which all through the trip from Manhattan to Brooklyn went in and out of a red handbag picking pieces of candy from a box in there, and these fingers slid pieces of red candy into a full, broad red mouth, slowly, one by one, I never saw such delicate motions before. It was like the whole car was hypnotized by those hands for a couple of minutes, even the old guy in the yarmulke next to her watched her hands, the two Puerto Rican kids whose earphones were on so loud you could hear them half a car away, they stopped shuffling around for a minute, watching her, two fussy little gray ladies stopped reading, the little Chinese twins who were itching for mischief stood at her knees. The only person who didn't seem to notice was a little black boy who sat right next to her. His eyes were half closed and he looked so tired. Whose was he? You couldn't tell. Maybe a parent of his had a seat somewhere else, or maybe he was with the woman next to him on the other side, a big-breasted woman in sturdy gray-laced walking shoes, she could have been a social worker taking him somewhere. I mean, she didn't touch him or talk to him, but they could have been together. He looked so sad, this boy, he was only about nine or ten, but he watched the manic little Chinese twins as if kids' games were some real far back memory, and then when the beautiful woman offered candy to the twins, he stared blankly in front of him. He paid no attention to the baby who was sitting and screaming on his father's shoulders, or to all the grown-ups oohing and aahing about the other kids. The beautiful woman tapped him on the shoulder and offered him a red candy. He shook his head to say no. And then the two of them looked so separate and so sad, the boy and the beautiful woman, you couldn't believe there could be so much sadness even in the same *world* as the giggling Chinese twins, let alone the same subway car. And then when the train stopped at Prospect Park, the sad little boy got up and left the train all by himself, he just stood up and went out the door. There was no parent, no social worker. The beautiful woman stopped chewing candy, her fingers stopped, the red nails froze beside the red handbag, and her bright wide eyes followed the boy out the door and down the platform until the doors closed and then oh! Her eyes came back inside. And her fingers lay beside the bag, perfectly still, right up until I got off at my stop.

There are days when a big arrow in the sky must be pointing down at me. Yesterday it happened. On the way to the subway there was a woman with a chain of four tiny pale children nearly all the same size holding hands, like old-fashioned cut-out paper dolls. A man was jabbering away at her in some weird language. She stopped me and said in the highest-pitched voice in the world, like a mouse shrieking in a foreign accent, "But where IS the bus stop?" She said it like we'd started the conversation a long time ago, like I already knew exactly why her life had happened to her the way it had and why it made her so frantic. She stood by a sign with the parking hours, and the sign for the bus stop was more than a block away. The husband growled at her with the low-throated grunty noises, and she turned to him and squeaked, *"Nyet! Nyet!"* The bus came down the street. I grabbed two of the kids and she grabbed the others. The husband growled along behind us. *"Nyet! Nyet!"* she screeched. She had one foot on the bus and just before she hoisted herself up she clasped her jaws in both her hands, shook her head, and shrieked to me, "My husband, I am sick and tired for him." She touched my arm and disappeared onto the bus.

On the subway I found a seat and the next stop the most

pregnant woman in New York got on at the other end of the car, walked the whole way down dodging all the standing people, like she knew just where she was going, and stopped right in front of me. What could I do? There went my seat. When I changed for the local, two different men asked me the time and another one asked me directions when I got out on the street. A Japanese couple stopped me to take a picture of them with their camera, in just a particular way so you could see a skyscraper in the background, and when I had it and snapped it, the guy moved. I had to do it again. I got to the shop fifteen minutes late. The day hadn't started but I felt all used up. Miguel with the umbrellas yelled to me, "Hey! You gotta see the new shades!" I waved to him and ran inside.

Ronnie had three women waiting and one guy in the chair almost finished. Gloria, the girl who cuts on Tuesdays and Fridays, hadn't shown up. Stevie Wonder was on the radio. I started to tell Ronnie why I was late; he said, "Shut up and shampoo," and pointed to Roberta. She works at Bloomingdale's. I put the towel around her shoulders and she leaned back into the sink. "Careful near my ears," she snapped, "I just got rid of an infection." Her hair was dyed red, I knew Ronnie didn't do it, the roots were never right from day one.

"Julia Child came and did a demonstration," she said. "And last week I met Pierre Cardin. I got his *autograph.* Like on my jeans. But do you think Andrew even *cares* who I see at work? Do you think he even *listens?* Do you think he'd even notice if I *left* him?"

Nyet, nyet, I said to myself.

After Roberta I swept up from the guy Ronnie cut, then I washed an old woman who went on and on about how the First Lady didn't know enough not to wear orange with red. Tina Turner was screaming out her lungs and Ronnie danced around to turn it up. I heard him talk to Roberta. Now he had to shout so even she could hear him. "You mean you haven't dumped that guy *yet?*" He cut off some of that brassy hair of hers. "So he makes a lot of money. Big deal. So do a million others."

Roberta sniffled just a bit.

"And that yellow blouse she wore to the Philharmonic!" said

the old woman whose temples were in my hand. Sometimes I think I could just squeeze hard on the temples and make them all shut up.

I swept, then shampooed a guy who sang his own song, never mind that Ronnie was singing a duet with Michael Jackson. I got the guy out of the chair. I put him next to the old lady. I put Roberta underneath the dryer.

At one-thirty Ronnie still had four people sitting there waiting, but he told me, "Go get lunch."

"Naah," I said. "I can wait till things slow down."

He stopped cutting and stopped dancing and said, "Shut up and get outta here. The law says you have to have a rest."

So I went out and had a hot dog on the street. Trucks barreled past, Con Ed had a machine coughing up smoke from big underground tubes on the corner, a jackhammer started up across the street. Miguel was wearing one of the new pairs of sunglasses. They were like a wide black strap going across his face. "What do you think?" he asked me. "They make me look like somebody, no?"

"They make you look like Miguel, only blind."

He pointed at a white-haired guy coming down the street who was looking at the numbers on the buildings like he had an address to find. "*There's* somebody," said Miguel. "Man, look at those shoes. Look at that tan. That guy's from California. And what a jacket! This guy makes bucks!"

I said, "Miguel, I see an old guy in jeans."

He shook his head like I was hopeless. I watched the guy go into Ronnie's shop. He had to be the two-o'clock.

"See you later, Miguel," I said, and I went back to work.

The two-o'clock was tall and broad-shouldered, an old guy who didn't look the least bit old and probably never felt it, either. He had beautiful soft white wavy hair. Glasses. A great tan, Miguel was right. And eyes that looked like he was thinking over a hundred different things but never told anybody any of them. Ronnie was still backed up four people. I told this man.

"Well, what the hell!" he said in a big, deep voice, and then he laughed with such deep sound it was like every laugh I'd ever heard before was just pretending, and this was the real thing. He hung the leather jacket on the coat rack. "I'm supposed to meet with a guy at three o'clock. He's been sitting on a script of mine for a year. A year!" He lowered himself into the chair and seemed to take up more of it than most people. "Shit, let *him* wait."

"You write for the movies?" I asked. He nodded. "*Big* movies?"

"Uh-huh. Hollywood movies."

"Did you write *Shampoo?* That's one of my favorites."

He laughed again with that bigger-than-life laugh, I wanted to jump into the sound of it and stay there. "That's funny. I didn't write *Shampoo.* But Warren Beatty's the guy I'm supposed to see at three."

"Huh," I said. "Now that's a coincidence."

He looked right into my eyes which was like right into my soul. I couldn't look away. He had me hypnotized.

"I wrote *Bounder's Dream,*" he said.

"That was a good one," I said. "I saw it a long time ago."

He smiled. "I wrote *The Last Man in Aberdeen,* too."

"Huh," I said. "That one was awful." I put the towel around his big shoulders, but I wasn't in such a hurry to start the shampoo because I didn't want him to dry out before Ronnie could get to him.

"You didn't *like* it?" He sounded hurt.

"It wasn't my type of film, I guess. It was too sappy."

"No!" he exclaimed. He could pack so much electricity in just one word, I thought he'd spring up from the chair. "Really? *Sappy?* No! Why?"

"Either I like a movie or I don't. I don't ask why," I said.

"But *sappy!*" He shook his head, like he was in a real shock.

"But that was a long time ago," I said. "What've you done since then?"

He blushed. Red like a kid's rose up through the tan. I could see his Adam's apple moving in a swallow.

"Here," I said, taking his glasses off gently. "Let me put these aside." Without the glasses his eyes had more little lines all around them; I could see them wrinkle up as he was thinking. But oh what a deep blue they were, deep and full of secrets.

I lowered the chair all the way down and pushed lightly at his head so he'd lean back. His waves of hair glistened on the edge of the basin. I touched them. They made me think of silk. He looked up at me sort of distrusting and resigned at the same time, like he was used to lying back and having women drown him in a basin just like this one.

"So," I said. "Those movies, they were a while back. What've you been doing?"

He glanced up at me just as I started running the water, and his look was that he'd already drowned. A big famous handsome guy like him — what was he drowning for?

"It's okay," I said.

He closed his eyes. "Almost eight years, yeah, since *The Last Man.* What've I done since?" He laughed, squeezing his eyes closed tighter. "I did a lot of cocaine. My wife left me. I started to see a shrink three days a week. I stopped coke. Wrote a script for Di Vallo. He didn't use it."

I worked the suds into his hair. The wet strands foamed up, white on white. I loved the way they felt in my fingers. I kept squeezing suds through slowly.

"So," he said, starting up again. "Then I saw the shrink four days a week. Met a great woman, but she was a nut." He paused for a few seconds. "Then I started seeing the shrink five times a week. So did she. It took me a year to find out that she and the shrink were fooling around." He opened his eyes, gave me one of those down-to-the-soul looks, then he went back to his own soul. "Hell," he said.

I spritzed water onto his hair to rinse off the shampoo. He could tell I was doing it pretty hard. He squeezed his eyes shut tight. I sprayed water on his forehead, on his ears.

"So then you didn't have a shrink and you didn't have a girlfriend," I said.

"Hell," he repeated. "Take it easy with that thing, will you?" He reached up and wiped water from his nose.

And then when he didn't answer me so fast, it was like I knew what really happened. "No, you *didn't* lose the shrink and the woman," I said. I started to feel angry. I don't know what got into me. "You're still seeing the nutty woman. You still go to this shrink five times a week, as if he were actually *helping* you." I saw the color rising up into his face again. "If you want to know the honest truth," I said, "I think that's stupid." I squeezed conditioner and worked it in with my fingers. I massaged his scalp. "And all this stupid stuff, it took you the whole eight years?"

He opened his eyes and looked up at me, and suddenly he seemed ancient, and what I saw for a split fraction of a second was a big old man sitting helpless in the chair with a hole in the middle of his life.

"I told you," he said. "I wrote this other script. Beatty's been trying to decide if he'll do it or not."

I rinsed out the conditioner with a hard blast of water. His hair was so fine and silky. Before I dried it in the towel I put my fingers through once more, all around, just to feel it again. Angel hair, I thought. When I looked back at his face, his eyes were all crinkled and thinking again.

I said, "You talk to me about Warren Beatty. So maybe I like his movies. But in real life, who is he to me? I wash hair. I live next door to a guy who howls like a wolf at the moon."

He smiled and sat up. I wrapped the towel around his head. Gently, I rubbed his scalp. I took away the towel. He looked straight into my soul. This time I looked away. He groped for his glasses. I handed them to him. He put them on. I pumped the chair up.

"Do you want to come with me this afternoon?" he asked me. With the glasses on, his eyes weren't thinking so hard now. "You could tell your friends you met Beatty."

"No thanks," I said. I felt angry again. I don't know why I let this guy get to me so much. "I gotta work. Anyway, I have no friends."

He squinted at me, thinking stuff he'd never tell.

"No friends, just lots of strangers," I said.

He laughed his big laugh, and it seemed as if he didn't believe what I said. So I said, "I fill up on people I don't know, before I ever get to friends."

Suddenly he looked very serious. "Huh," he said. "Like on cheese and crackers before you get to dinner?"

"Sort of," I said.

"Wow," he said.

Ronnie danced over and nodded to the guy. "I'll be there in a second."

"Hurry up," I told Ronnie. "Warren Beatty's waiting for him."

The guy blushed again and closed his eyes. I went and rescued a kid who was burning up underneath the dryer. I gave three more shampoos. I ducked outside and lit a cigarette. Usually I only smoke one a day, but this time I smoked three. The sun was bright. Buds were just starting to come out on the trees. Miguel was doing a big business with the new sunglasses. He wore a different pair now, the frames were fluorescent blue and in the shape of wings. Just as I crushed the third cigarette the Hollywood guy came out. I was glad to see Ronnie didn't chop off too much hair. The guy took my hand and held it. It felt wonderful. His hands were warm and big, my little fingers were lost in his. He looked like he had something important to say, but instead he said, "You sure you won't come?"

I laughed. He squeezed my hand. What a touch he had, I mean it, it gave me shivers down my spine.

"Good luck," I said.

"Yeah," he said. "You too."

He let go of my hand slowly, one finger at a time. I watched him turn and go down the block. He had a real firm, confident stride.

People. They walk into your life, they walk out.

I went inside and got the broom. Ronnie was working on a young blond woman with a split in her skirt up to her thighs. He was singing along with an old Beatles number. I went to the other chair and started sweeping up the little bits of white hair scattered around. I still had the feeling of that man's touch on my hand when I saw those dry white clippings on the floor. I reached down for a small clump. I thought maybe I'd keep it, but it fell apart, the ends of the soft strands were already all dried out and brittle. That's the way cut hair always is, but, I don't know, I felt sad enough to cry.

That night on the train everyone was there. A black woman reading a dog-eared Bible sat next to an orthodox Jew with a long white beard who pored over a Hebrew prayer book. Standing above him was a young guy in a green polyester suit reading *The Watchtower* in Spanish, and across from them all sat a Muslim woman draped in pale yellow gauze from head to toe. It was a real religious bunch in my corner. Sitting just below me was a gum-snapping young woman with purple spike heels and jeans who was reading the *Enquirer.* Upside down I could make out the headlines. "Shark Grabs Ex–Beauty Queen!" "New Tragedy Strikes Kennedys!" "Pony Gives Birth to Panda!" Next to the *Enquirer* was a twisted little old guy who kept muttering to himself. If anyone was going to be crazy it was him, or else the kid who pushed his way through the crowd from one end of the car to the other. He had to be high on something. I tried not to look him in the face. Just down from the jerky little twisted guy sat a frumpy middle-aged woman reading a magazine about chocolate. Two guys in Con Ed shirts were fast asleep next to her. At Grand Street a Chinese family got on and crammed in next to me, with a baby who must have been about three months old and two bigger kids and a mother and father and a set of grandparents. They were loaded with plastic bags filled with groceries, the scallions and the cabbages stuck right out, and the grandfather had a sack of big green shrubs for planting, hoisted on his shoulder. The kids were perfectly behaved. When the train crawled across the bridge, stopping every three inches, they never got impatient, and when it squealed to a complete stop in the tunnel somewhere between the bridge and DeKalb Avenue, these kids were quiet as mice, even the baby with the wide-open brown eyes.

We were stuck.

The woman reading chocolate sighed. The twisted little guy muttered to himself. The orthodox Jew moved his wrinkled finger slowly down the lines of Hebrew. One of the Con Ed men woke up. "What else is new?" he said, and fell back to sleep. The girl with the *Enquirer* looked up at nobody in particular. "Oh for Cripes sake, not again!" she said. The second Con Ed man wriggled his bushy eyebrows at her. "Gimme a break," she groaned, and turned to the next page: "Two-Headed Baby Rejected by Tribe."

We just kept being stuck there.

The Chinese parents spoke to each other in the melody of their language. The black woman started underlining a section of the Bible. I heard a sigh and saw a fat businessman near the

Con Eds stuff a *Wall Street Journal* into his briefcase. The Muslim woman sat still as stone. The jazzed-up kid pushed his way down the car again, looking like he might start to need a fix pretty soon. I read the *Enquirer* upside down. "Star's Daughter Vows No More Drugs!" "Rare Cancer from Kissing!"

The woman reading chocolate turned to mousse cakes. The Chinese baby finally gave a little whimper. "Sssh," said the brother who looked about four. The man with the Spanish *Watchtower* grinned down to the kids.

At last over the loudspeaker came a crackling of static. We all waited for the announcement to tell us what was wrong. The static got raspier and louder so it made me want to hold my ears. Then it stopped, and it sounded like somebody was blowing on the microphone. Then *that* stopped. We waited for the explanation, but nothing came. You could hear a lot of people sighing.

Down the aisle there was a hubbub of motion and voices. "Thank you, *gracias,*" I heard a woman say. I craned my neck around the Chinese shrubs and saw a pregnant woman lowering herself into a seat, a teenage kid who must have just gotten up moving around his shoulders in a stretch. The pregnant woman looked about ready to give birth. I hoped somebody here knew how to do it.

"Sometimes you think you'll be standing here all night," said the woman with the Bible to the Muslim. The Muslim closed her eyes. The *Watchtower* man looked very cheerful. "Oh, they fix it soon," he said.

"Yeah," said Con Ed. "Like tomorrow."

Then it was really quiet, so quiet that it seemed as if there would never be a noise inside this car again, but suddenly the train itself gave a sigh, a little *chuff-chuff-chuff* from near the wheels, and when the train finished sighing there was a silence even deeper and more final than the one three seconds just before. It was eerie, so absolutely quiet that I started to get scared. Me! And then two things happened very quickly.

First, while my neck was still craned around the shrubs, I caught a glimpse of red. A red hat, then red fingernails. Oh, my heart jumped in my throat! A slender black hand with long red nails moved slowly into a paper bag, came out with a small red candy, and moved to the bright red mouth I couldn't see. Her face was hidden by all the people in the way, but I knew those delicate movements. It was her! The beautiful woman who had seen the worst and still come back. She was in my car again — stuck forever, maybe, but she was there! My heart felt so full I could burst.

The other thing that happened, about a second after this, was that the lights in the train went out, every single one. You couldn't see a thing. The tunnel lights went out, too. About a hundred people groaned at once. You could hear everyone shifting around in their places. There was a rustle of papers and a few more groans. "Wouldn't you know it," said a voice. And then silence settled over us again. And it was dark.

You know how when the lights go out you sometimes have the image of the light bulbs in your head. Well, I didn't have that. But what I had was the clearest picture of the red fingernails and the red candies. And I had a picture of the dead dry pieces of white hair stuck in my mind, too. It was like those pictures were stamped inside me. And I had a heart full right to bursting. So I didn't even know it was coming from me when I first heard it, the tune that broke the silence.

I've been working on the railroad
All the livelong day.
I've been working on the railroad
Just to pass the time away.

Those lines were finished and it was silent again in the train and then I knew it *was* me when a little gasp came out of *my* windpipe just before some more little pieces of the tune.

Can't you hear the whistle blowing,
Rise up so early in the morn . . .

And as I started the next line, a voice from down the aisle joined in, a woman's strong contralto. It rose up into the air and filled the car, rounding out my shaky barc tones with a softness and grace.

Can't you hear the captain shouting?
Dinah blow your horn!

We sang the chorus, somebody else started in to hum it, too, followed by a couple more while *her* voice kept up the lead. Then I knew that nothing bad would ever happen in this train, and together we were all so brave!

TOBIAS WOLFF

Smorgasbord

FROM ESQUIRE

"A PREP SCHOOL in March is like a ship in the doldrums." Our history master said this, as if to himself, while we were waiting for the bell to ring after class. He stood by the window and tapped the glass with his ring in a dreamy, abstracted way meant to make us think he'd forgotten we were there. We were supposed to get the impression that when we weren't around he turned into someone interesting, someone witty and profound, who uttered impromptu bons mots and had a poetic vision of life.

The bell rang.

I went to lunch. The dining hall was almost empty, because it was a free weekend and most of the boys in school had gone to New York, or home, or to their friends' homes, as soon as their last class let out. About the only ones left were foreigners and scholarship students like me and a few other untouchables of various stripes. The school had laid on a nice lunch for us, cheese soufflé, but the portions were small and I went back to my room still hungry. I was always hungry.

Snow and rain fell past my window. The snow on the quad looked grimy; it had melted above the underground heating pipes, exposing long brown lines of mud.

I couldn't get to work. On the next floor down someone kept playing "Mack the Knife." That one song incessantly repeating itself made the dorm seem not just empty but abandoned, as if those who had left were never coming back. I cleaned my room. I tried to read. I looked out the window. I sat down at my desk and studied the new picture my girlfriend had sent me, unable to imagine her from it; I had to close my eyes to do that, and then I could see her, see her solemn eyes and the heavy white breasts she would gravely let me hold sometimes, but not kiss . . . not yet, anyway. But I had a promise. That summer, as soon as I got home, we were going to become lovers. "Become lovers." That was how she'd said it, very deliberately, listening to the words as she spoke them. All year I had repeated them to myself to take the edge off my loneliness and the fits of lust that made me want to scream and drive my fists through walls. We were going to become lovers that summer, and we were going to be lovers all through college, true to each other even if we ended up thousands of miles apart again, and after college we were going to marry and join the Peace Corps and then do something together that would help people. This was our plan. Back in September, the night before I left for school, we wrote it all down along with a lot of other specifics concerning our future: number of children (six), their names, the kinds of dogs we would own, a sketch of our perfect house. We sealed the paper in a bottle and buried it in her backyard. On our golden anniversary we were going to dig it up again and show it to our children and grandchildren to prove that dreams can come true.

I was writing her a letter when Crosley came to my room. Crosley was a science whiz. He won the science prize every year and spent his summers working as an intern in different laboratories. He was also a fanatical weight lifter. His arms were so knotty that he had to hold them out from his sides as he walked, as if he were carrying buckets. Even his features seemed muscular. His face was red. Crosley lived down the hall by himself in one of the only singles in the school. He was said to be a thief; that supposedly was the reason he'd ended up without a roommate. I didn't know if it was true, and I tried to avoid forming an opinion on the matter, but whenever we passed each other I felt embarrassed and dropped my eyes.

Crosley leaned in the door and asked me how things were.

I said okay.

He stepped inside and looked around the room, tilting his head to read my roommate's pennants and the titles of our books. I was uneasy. I said, "So what can I do for you," not meaning to sound as cold as I did but not exactly regretting it either.

He caught my tone and smiled. It was the kind of smile you put on when you pass a group of people you suspect are talking about you. It was his usual expression.

He said, "You know Garcia, right?"

"Garcia? Sure. I think so."

"You know him," Crosley said. "He runs around with Hidalgo and those guys. He's the tall one."

"Sure," I said. "I know who Garcia is."

"Well, his stepmother is in New York for a fashion show or something, and she's going to drive up and take him out to dinner tonight. She told him to bring along some friends. You want to come?"

"What about Hidalgo and the rest of them?"

"They're at some kind of polo deal in Maryland. Buying horses. Or ponies, I guess it would be."

The notion of someone my age buying ponies to play a game with was so unexpected that I couldn't quite take it in. "Jesus," I said.

Crosley said, "How about it. You want to come?"

I'd never even spoken to Garcia. He was the nephew of a famous dictator, and all his friends were nephews and cousins of other dictators. They lived as they pleased here. Most of them kept cars a few blocks from the campus, though it was completely against the rules, and I'd heard that some of them kept women as well. They were cocky and prankish and charming. They moved everywhere in a body with sunglasses pushed up on their heads and jackets slung over their shoulders, twittering all at once like birds, *chinga* this and *chinga* that. The headmaster was completely buffaloed. After Christmas vacation a bunch of them came down with gonorrhea, and all he did was call them in and advise them that they should not be in too great a hurry to lose their innocence. It became a school joke. All you had to do was say the word "innocence" and everyone would crack up.

"I don't know," I said.

"Come on," Crosley said.

"But I don't even know the guy."

"So what? I don't either."

"Then why did he ask you?"

"I was sitting next to him at lunch."

"Terrific," I said. "That explains you. What about me? How come he asked me?"

"He didn't. He told me to bring someone else."

"What, just anybody? Just whoever happened to present himself to your attention?"

Crosley shrugged.

I laughed. Crosley gave me a look to make sure I wasn't laughing at him, then he laughed, too. "Sounds great," I said. "Sounds like a recipe for a really memorable evening."

"You got something better to do?" Crosley asked.

"No," I said.

The limousine picked us up under the awning of the headmaster's house. The driver, an old man, got out slowly and then slowly adjusted his cap before opening the door for us. Garcia slid in beside the woman in back. Crosley and I sat across from them on seats that pulled down. I caught her scent immediately. For some years afterward I bought perfume for women, and I was never able to find that one.

Garcia erupted into Spanish as soon as the driver closed the door behind me. He sounded angry, spitting words at the woman and gesticulating violently. She rocked back a little, then let loose a burst of her own. I stared openly at her. Her skin was very white. She wore a black cape over a black dress cut just low enough to show her pale throat and the bones at the base of her throat. Her mouth was red. There was a spot of rouge high on each cheek, not rubbed in to look like real color but left there carelessly, or carefully, to make you think again how white her skin was. Her teeth were small and sharp looking, and she bared them in concert with certain gestures and inflections. As she talked, her little pointed tongue flicked in and out.

She wasn't a lot older than we were. Twenty-five at the most. Maybe younger.

She said something definitive and cut her hand through the air. Garcia began to answer her, but she said "No!" and chopped the air again. Then she turned and smiled at Crosley and me.

It was a completely false smile. She said, "Where would you fellows like to eat?" Her voice sounded lower in English, even a little harsh, though the harshness could have come from her accent. She called us *fallows.*

"Anywhere is fine with me," I said.

"Anywhere," she repeated. She narrowed her big black eyes and pushed her lips together. I could see that my answer disappointed her. She looked at Crosley.

"There's supposed to be a good French restaurant in Newbury," Crosley said. "Also an Italian place. It depends on what you want."

"No," she said. "It depends on what you want. I am not so hungry."

If Garcia had a preference, he kept it to himself. He sulked in the corner, his round shoulders slumped and his hands between his knees. He seemed to be trying to make a point of some kind.

"There's also a smorgasbord," Crosley said. "If you like smorgasbords."

"Smorgasbord," she said. She repeated the word to Garcia. He frowned, then answered her in a sullen monotone.

I couldn't believe Crosley had suggested the smorgasbord. It was an egregiously uncouth suggestion. The smorgasbord was where the local fatties went to binge. Football coaches brought whole teams there to bulk up. The food was good enough, and God knows there was plenty of it, all you could eat, actually, but the atmosphere was brutally matter-of-fact. The food was good, though. Big platters of shrimp on crushed ice. Barons of beef. Smoked turkey. No end of food, really.

She was smiling. Obviously the concept was new to her. "You — do you like smorgasbords?" she asked Crosley.

"Yes," he said.

"And you?" she said to me.

I nodded. Then, not to seem wishy-washy, I said, "You bet."

"Smorgasbord," she said. She laughed and clapped her hands. "Smorgasbord!"

Crosley gave directions to the driver, and we drove slowly away from the school. She said something to Garcia. He nodded at each of us in turn and gave our names, then looked away again, out the window, where the snowy fields were turning dark. His face was long, his eyes sorrowful as a hound's. He had barely talked to us while we were waiting for the limousine. I didn't know why he was mad at his stepmother, or why he wouldn't talk to us, or why he'd even asked us along, but by now I didn't really care. By now my sentiments were, basically, Fuck him.

She studied us and repeated our names skeptically. "No," she said. She pointed at Crosley and said, "El Blanco." She pointed to me and said, "El Negro." Then she pointed at herself and said, "I am Linda."

"Leen-da," Crosley said. He really overdid it, but she showed her sharp little teeth and said, "*Exactamente.*"

Then she settled back against the seat and pulled her cape close around her shoulders. It soon fell open again. She was restless. She sat forward and leaned back, crossed and recrossed her legs, swung her feet impatiently. She had on black high heels fastened by a thin strap; I could see almost her entire foot. I heard the silky rub of her stockings against each other, and breathed in a fresh breath of her perfume every time she moved. That perfume had a certain effect on me. It didn't reach me as just a smell; it was personal, it seemed to issue from her very privacy. It made the hair bristle on my arms. It entered my veins like fine, tingling wires, widening my eyes, tightening my spine, sending faint chills across my shoulders and the backs of my knees. Every time she moved I felt a little tug, and followed her motion with some slight motion of my own.

When we arrived at the smorgasbord — Swenson's, I believe it was, or maybe Hansen's, some such honest Swede of a name — Garcia refused to get out of the limousine. Linda tried to persuade him, but he shrank back into his corner and would not answer or even look at her. She threw up her hands. "Ah!" she said, and turned away. Crosley and I followed her across the parking lot toward the big red barn. Her dress rustled as she walked. Her heels clicked on the cement.

You could say one thing for the smorgasbord; it wasn't pretentious. It was in a real barn, not some quaint fantasy of a barn with butter-churn lamps and little brass ornaments nailed to the walls on strips of leather. At one end of the barn was the kitchen. The rest of it had been left open and filled with picnic tables. Blazing light bulbs hung from the rafters. In the middle of the barn stood what my English master would have called the groaning board — a great table heaped with food, every kind of food you could think of, and more. I had been there several times, and it always gave me a small, pleasant shock to see how much food there was.

Girls wearing dirndls hustled around the barn, cleaning up messes, changing tablecloths, bringing fresh platters of food from the kitchen.

We stood blinking in the sudden light. Linda paid up, then we followed one of the waitresses across the floor. Linda walked slowly, gazing around like a tourist. Several men looked up from their food as she passed. I was behind her, and I looked forbiddingly back at them so they would think she was my wife.

We were lucky; we got a table to ourselves. On crowded nights they usually doubled you up with another party, and that could be an extremely unromantic experience. Linda shrugged off her cape and waved us toward the food. "Go on," she said. She sat down and opened her purse. When I looked back she was lighting a cigarette.

"You're pretty quiet tonight," Crosley said as we filled our plates. "You pissed off about something?"

I shook my head. "Maybe I'm just quiet, Crosley, you know?"

He speared a slice of meat and said, "When she called you El Negro, that didn't mean she thought you were a Negro. She just said that because your hair is dark. Mine is light, that's how come she called me El Blanco."

"I know that, Crosley, Jesus. You think I couldn't figure that out? Give me some credit, okay?" Then, as we moved around the table, I said, "You speak Spanish?"

"*Un poco.* Actually more like *un poquito.*"

"What's Garcia mad about?"

"Money. Something about money."

"Like what?"

He shook his head. "That's all I could get. But it's definitely about money."

I'd meant to start off slow but by the time I reached the end of the table my plate was full. Potato salad, ham, jumbo shrimp, toast, barbecued beef, eggs Benny. Crosley's was full, too. We walked back toward Linda, who was leaning forward on her elbows and looking around the barn. She took a long drag off her cigarette, lifted her chin, and blew a stream of smoke up toward the rafters. I sat down across from her. "Scoot down," Crosley said, and settled in beside me.

She watched us eat for a while.

"So," she said, "El Blanco. Are you from New York?"

Crosley looked up in surprise. "No, ma'am," he said. "I'm from Virginia."

Linda stabbed out her cigarette. She had long fingernails painted the same deep red as the lipstick smears on her cigarette butt. She said, "I just came from New York, and I can tell you that is one crazy place. Just incredible. Listen to this. I am in a taxicab, you know, and we are stopping in this traffic jam for a long time and there is a taxicab next to us with this fellow in it who stares at me. Like this, you know." She made her eyes go round. "Of course I ignore him. So guess what, my door opens and he gets into my cab. 'Excuse me,' he says, 'I want to marry you.' 'That's nice,' I say. 'Ask my husband.' 'I don't care about your husband,' he says. 'Your husband is history. So is my wife.' Of course I had to laugh. 'Okay,' he says. 'You think that's funny? How about this.' Then he says —" Linda looked sharply at each of us. She sniffed and made a face. "He says things you would never believe. Never. He wants to do this and he wants to do that. Well, I act like I am about to scream. I open my mouth like this. 'Hey,' he says, 'okay, okay. Relax.' Then he gets out and goes back to his taxicab. We are still sitting there for a long time again, and you know what he is doing? He is reading the newspaper. With his hat on. Go ahead, eat," she said to us, and nodded toward the food.

A tall, blond girl was carving slices of roast beef onto a platter. She smiled at us. She was hale and bosomy — I could see the laces on her bodice straining. Her cheeks glowed. Her bare arms and shoulders were ruddy with exertion. Crosley raised his eyebrows at me. I raised mine back but my heart wasn't in it. She was a Viking dream, pure gemütlichkeit, but I was drunk on Garcia's stepmother, and in that condition you don't want a glass of milk, you want more of what's making you stumble and fall.

Crosley and I filled our plates again and headed back.

"I'm always hungry," he said.

"I know what you mean," I told him.

Linda smoked another cigarette while we ate. She watched the other tables as if she were at a movie. I tried to eat with a little finesse and so did Crosley, dabbing his lips with a napkin between every bulging mouthful, but some of the people around us had completely slipped their moorings. They ducked their heads low to receive their food, and while they chewed it up they looked around suspiciously and kept their forearms close to their plates. A big family to our left was the worst. There was something competitive and desperate about them; they seemed to be eating their way toward a condition where they would never have to eat again. You would have thought that they were refugees from a great hunger, that outside these walls the land was afflicted with drought and barrenness. I felt a kind of desperation myself; I felt as if I were growing emptier with every bite I took.

There was a din in the air, a steady roar like that of a waterfall.

Linda looked around her with a pleased expression. She bore no likeness to anyone here, but she seemed completely at home. She sent us back for another plate, then dessert and coffee, and while we were finishing up she asked El Blanco if he had a girlfriend.

"No, ma'am," Crosley said. "We broke up," he added, and his red face turned purple. It was clear that he was lying.

"You. How about you?"

I nodded.

"Ha!" she said. "El Negro is the one! So. What's her name?"

"Jane."

"Jaaane," Linda drawled. "Okay, let's hear about Jaaane."

"Jane," I said again.

Linda smiled.

I told her everything. I told her how my girlfriend and I had met and what she looked like and what our plans were. I told her more than everything, because I gave certain coy but definite suggestions about the extremes to which our passion had already driven us. I meant to impress her with my potency, to inflame her, to wipe that smile off her face, but the more I told her the more wolfishly she smiled and the more her eyes laughed at me.

Laughing eyes — now there's a cliché my English master would have eaten me alive for. "How exactly did these eyes laugh?" he would have asked, looking up from my paper while my classmates snorted around me. "Did they titter, or did they merely chortle? Did they give a great guffaw? Did they, perhaps, *scream* with laughter?"

I am here to tell you that eyes can scream with laughter. Linda's did. As I played big hombre for her I could see exactly how complete my failure was, I could hear her saying, *Okay, El Negro, go on, talk about your little gorlfren, how pretty she is and so on, but we know what you want, don't we? — you want to suck on my tongue and slobber on my titties and lick my belly and bury your face in me. That's what you want.*

Crosley interrupted me. "Ma'am . . ." he said, and nodded toward the door. Garcia was leaning there with his arms crossed and an expression of fury on his face. When she looked at him he turned and walked out the door.

Her eyes went flat. She sat there for a moment. She began to take a cigarette from her case, then put it back and stood up. "Let's go," she said.

Garcia was waiting in the car, rigid and silent. He said nothing on the drive back. Linda swung her foot and stared out the window at the passing houses and bright, moonlit fields. Just before we reached the school, Garcia leaned forward and began speaking to her in a low voice. She listened impassively and did not answer. He was still talking when the limousine stopped in front of the headmaster's house. The driver opened the door. Garcia fixed his eyes on her. Still impassive, she took her pocketbook out of her purse. She opened it and looked inside. She meditated over the contents, then withdrew a bill and offered it to Garcia. It was a one-hundred-dollar bill. "Boolshit!" he said, and sat back angrily. With no change of expression she turned and held the bill out to me. I didn't know what else to do but take it. She got another one from her pocket and presented it to Crosley, who hesitated even less than I did. Then she gave us the same false smile she had greeted us with, and said, "Good night, it was a pleasure to meet you. Good night, good night," she said to Garcia.

The three of us got out of the limousine. I went a few steps and then slowed down, and began to look back.

"Keep walking!" Crosley hissed.

Garcia let off a string of words as the driver closed the door. I faced around again and walked with Crosley across the quad. As we approached our dorm he quickened his pace. "I don't believe it," he whispered. "A hundred bucks." When we were inside the door he stopped and shouted, "A hundred bucks! A hundred fucking dollars!"

"Pipe down," someone called.

"All right, all right. Fuck you!" he added.

We went up the stairs to our floor, laughing and banging into each other. "Do you fucking believe it?" he said.

I shook my head. We were standing outside my door.

"No, really now, listen." He put his hands on my shoulders and looked into my eyes. He said, "Do you fucking *believe* it?"

I told him I didn't.

"Well, neither do I. I don't fucking believe it."

There didn't seem to be much to say after that. I would have invited Crosley in, but to tell the truth I still thought of him as a thief. We laughed a few more times and said good night.

My room was cold. I took the bill out of my pocket and looked at it. It was new and stiff, the kind of bill you associate with kidnappings. The picture of Franklin was surprisingly lifelike. I looked at it for a while. A hundred dollars was a lot of money then. I had never had a hundred dollars before, not in one chunk like this. To be on the safe side I taped it to a page in *Profiles in Courage* — page 100, so I wouldn't forget where it was.

I had trouble getting to sleep. The food I had eaten sat like a stone in me, and I was miserable about the things I had said. I understood that I had been a liar and a fool. I kept shifting under the covers, then I sat up and turned on my reading lamp. I picked up the new picture my girlfriend had sent me, and closed my eyes, and when I had some peace of mind I renewed my promises to her.

We broke up a month after I got home. Her parents were away one night, and we seized the opportunity to make love in their canopied bed. This was the fifth time that we had made love. She got up immediately afterward and started putting her clothes on. When I asked her what the problem was, she wouldn't answer me. I thought, *Oh Christ, what now.* "Come on," I said. "What's the problem?"

She was tying her shoes. She looked up and said, "You don't love me."

It surprised me to hear this, not because she said it but because it was true. Before this moment I hadn't known it was true, but it was — I didn't love her.

For a long time afterward I told myself that I had never really loved her, but this was a lie.

We're supposed to smile at the passions of the young, and at what we recall of our own passions, as if they were no more than a series of sweet frauds we had fooled ourselves with and then wised up to. Not only the passion of boys and girls for each other but the others, too — passion for justice, for doing right, for turning the world around — all these come in their time under our wintry smiles. But there was nothing foolish about what we felt. Nothing merely young. I just wasn't up to it. I let the light go out.

Sometime later I heard a soft knock at my door. I was still wide awake. "Yeah," I said.

Crosley stepped inside. He was wearing a blue dressing gown of some silky material that shimmered in the dim light of the hallway. He said, "Have you got any Tums or anything?"

"No. I wish I did."

"You too, huh?" He closed the door and sat on my roommate's bunk. "Do you feel as bad as I do?"

"How bad do you feel?"

"Like I'm dying. I think there was something wrong with the shrimp."

"Come on, Crosley. You ate everything but the barn."

"So did you."

"That's right. That's why I'm not complaining."

He moaned and rocked back and forth on the bed. I could hear real pain in his voice. I sat up. "Crosley, are you okay?"

"I guess," he said.

"You want me to call the nurse?"

"God," he said. "No. That's all right." He kept rocking. Then, in a carefully offhand way, he said. "Look, is it okay if I just stay here for a while?"

I almost said no, then I caught myself. "Sure," I told him. "Make yourself at home."

He must have heard my hesitation. "Forget it," he said bitterly. "Sorry I asked." But he made no move to go.

I felt confused, tender toward Crosley because he was in pain, repelled because of what I had heard about him. But maybe what I had heard about him wasn't true. I wanted to be fair, so I said, "Hey, Crosley, do you mind if I ask you a question?"

"That depends."

I sat up. Crosley was watching me. In the moonlight his dressing gown was iridescent as oil. He had his arms crossed over his stomach. "Is it true that you got caught stealing?"

"You fucker," he said. He looked down at the floor.

I waited.

He said, "You want to hear about it, just ask someone. Everybody knows all about it, right?"

"I don't."

"That's right, you don't." He raised his head. "You don't know shit about it and neither does anyone else." He tried to smile. His teeth appeared almost luminous in the cold silver light. "The really hilarious part is, I didn't actually get caught stealing it, I got caught putting it back. Not to make excuses. I stole the fucker, all right."

"Stole what?"

"The coat," he said. "Robinson's overcoat. Don't tell me you didn't know that."

I shook my head.

"Then you must have been living in a cave or something. You know Robinson, right? Robinson was my roommate. He had this camel's hair overcoat, this really just beautiful overcoat. I kind of got obsessed with it. I thought about it all the time. Whenever he went somewhere without it I would put it on and stand in front of the mirror. Then one day I just took the fucker. I stuck it in my locker over at the gym. Robinson was really upset. He'd go to his closet ten, twenty times a day, like he thought the coat had just gone for a walk or something. So anyway, I brought it back. He came into the room while I was hanging it up." Crosley bent forward suddenly, then leaned back.

"You're lucky they didn't kick you out."

"I wish they had," he said. "The dean wanted to play Jesus. He got all choked up over the fact that I had brought it back." Crosley rubbed his arms. "Man, did I want that coat. It was ridiculous how much I wanted that coat. You know?" He looked right at me. "Do you know what I'm talking about?"

I nodded.

"Really?"

"Yes."

"Good." Crosley lay back against the pillow, then lifted his feet onto the bed. "Say," he said, "I think I figured out how come Garcia invited me."

"Yeah? How come?"

"He was mad at his stepmother, right? He wanted to punish her."

"So?"

"So I'm the punishment. He probably heard I was the biggest asshole in the school, and figured whoever came with me would have to be an asshole, too. That's my theory, anyway."

I started laughing. It hurt my stomach, but I couldn't stop. Crosley said, "Come on, man, don't make me laugh," then he started laughing and moaning at the same time.

We lay without talking for a time. Crosley said, "El Negro."

"Yeah."

"What are you going to do with your C-note?"

"I don't know. What are you going to do?"

"Buy a woman."

"Buy a woman?"

"I haven't gotten laid in a really long time. In fact," he said, "I've never gotten laid."

"Me either."

I thought about his words. *Buy a woman.* He could actually do it. I could do it myself. I didn't have to wait, I didn't have to burn like this for month after month until Jane decided she was ready to give me relief. Three months was a long time to wait. It was an unreasonable time to wait for anything if you had no good reason to wait, if you could just buy what you needed. And to think that you could buy this — buy a mouth for your mouth, and arms and legs to wrap you tight. I had never considered this before. I thought of the money in my book. I could almost feel it there. Pure possibility.

Jane would never know. It wouldn't hurt her at all, and in a certain way it might help, because it was going to be very awkward at first if neither of us had any experience. As a man, I should know what I was doing. It would be a lot better that way.

I told Crosley that I liked his idea. "The time has come to lose our innocence," I said.

"*Exactamente,*" he said.

And so we sat up and took counsel, leaning toward each other from the beds, holding our swollen bellies, whispering back and forth about how this thing might be done, and where, and when.

MARJORIE SANDOR

Still Life

FROM THE GEORGIA REVIEW

CONTRARY to everything my mother has told me, I believe Tante Rose was born in the Midwest on a brilliant afternoon, when the sunlight probed every leaf on the big elm in their parents' front yard. She died on a day like that, in California, where sometimes the sunlight over the desert reaches the darkest parts of the ocean, and you can imagine that if you dared look, everything, all the way to the bottom, would be revealed at once. It's easy to forget about that clarity, for in a kind of homage to Tante Rose, Mother closed the blinds in our guest bedroom, making it so utterly dark that when the ambulance men came to take Tante, I had to squint to see her tiny, childlike form float away from me and up into that violent exposure

It is with this same obstinacy about the dark that, when Mother tries to tell her sister's story, she winds up with only a fragment or two. Beginning or ending, she seems to bend over her words like a gypsy over cards she herself can barely see. Of course I am not being fair; she was twelve years younger than Rose, and raised by parents whose faces, in photographs, bear their own lost childhoods like the shock from a stove burn. And so the pictures containing my mother are like small, safe nets in which she is caught: a rosy, blond, pampered child whose underwear and socks have been allowed, for the day, to lose their elastic. Later, of course, she would conquer all that, but this is who she was when her older sister escaped the lovely, neat house in West Lafayette. Escaped, says Mother, though not before tightly lacing the old-fashioned black boots Grandmother made her wear, when all the other girls had long since begun to wear the slim, handsome pumps of the thirties. Mother remembers this: Rose, on a dark winter morning, tucking a nickel into the finger of one black glove, then bending to whisper in her ear: "This is how working girls keep their carfare safe in the big city."

And she was gone.

Maybe this is why, in my mother's telling, it is always a dark winter morning in a Northern city when Rose gets up and walks to the El, wearing black gloves and a black wool coat, her hair bobbed short in the fashion of the day — though heavy braids had suited her face better, so serious and frowning like one of her mother's generation, eternally clutching a ticket for a further passage. Rose has been lucky enough to find a job in the city, lucky to be able to write a letter home that says how beautifully everything has turned out, how sorry if I frightened you, money forthcoming. She feels her luck at those moments we are told are inconsequential, as when she grips the tram pole with both black-gloved hands, or searches her own eyes in the window as the car goes into a tunnel. On those rides she takes herself in greedily, composing and recomposing the already-sent letter in her mind, while behind it, a secret thought stands with its hands neatly folded, a passenger within the passenger: *Now I am free to live, and to suffer greatly, romantically, as my mother did not.*

But not yet. For the time being she is content to rise each morning and take down her freedom in a series of little notes: the sputter of the radiator, the three-minute egg knocking against the inside of the saucepan in the perfectly square kitchenette. She steps out in the old-fashioned boots she is not quite ready to relinquish, to ride the El into the city where she is a medical stenographer. All day there are more little notes, little barriers she knows she could knock over in an instant if she so chose: headphones, perfect posture, the small lap-typewriter. Her mother would approve if she could see her here, and so Rose has the delicious self-consciousness of the runaway made good, still hiding, breathing in short gasps, locating the smallest, most obscure corners in terminals, rooming houses, cafés.

Of these, her favorite is Sam's Lunch Counter, where Sam

has come to reserve for her the back table, and a chair that does not wobble. She is *Tea with Lemon, White Toast* at ten o'clock, and the daily special at noon, no matter what. For days on end she brings with her the same enormous book — Sam can never see the title, only that it is a heavy book with a rough surface — a book that will not end easily or soon, and that will complicate and complicate until the ending does not matter. What thrills Rose is not so much what's in the book as the bare physical fact of its lying before her in a strange place, a book from her mother's house. Inscribed by someone to someone else, it has managed to reappear in this city that is, for her, a dream wedged between two darknesses. She has tea in the thick white mug Sam brings to her table; she admires the outfits of the other working girls; she eats her sandwich and turns each page of the book with an almost unbearable presence of mind, as if she is not only experiencing it, but is also an old woman looking back on her life, holding it beautifully immobile in her hands.

In such a state she falls in love for the first time. I am expecting it to be Sam, for which Mother eyes me quizzically. Of course not, she says; he is a boy her own age, who works in another department and sees her through the glass between their offices. Rose looks up through the glass, too, and sees the young narrow face, the firm energy of his hands as he lifts parcels, makes notes on a chart. And faintly, too, in the glass, she sees her own reflection as she did in the windows of the El, the dark unsmiling eyes that beg for a fate of cinematic proportions, when everything in her experience has been fixed to run the other way.

My picture of them before their marriage and the war is not of the two linking arms to walk in the snow, but of Rose alone at Sam's Lunch Counter, still reading the same big book and glancing up at the windows, where at any moment he might pass by and see her. She is always alone in my picture of her, always waiting for him to turn the corner and meet her in the terrible suddenness of that kind of love, a pointed flame of anticipation.

Starting to see Rose, I no longer hear my mother's voice telling the story but see Mother, too, as she must have been then, eleven years old, lying on her bed in the white upstairs room of her parents' house, a dappled figure on the coverlet in the afternoon sun, wishing herself into her sister's life. Mother is slimmer, and she, too, has a pair of practical black shoes in her closet. When she lies on that bed, the sound of Grandmother's voice is far enough beneath her that she can imagine herself in the city with Rose and her fiancé, riding the streetcar to the World's Fair, her own nickel tucked cool and silvery into the finger of one glove. She is a little dizzy, so both of them hold her hands and point things out to her, and at one moment, the young man, without any warning at all, puts his hands about her waist and lifts her high into the air above the crowd. For a moment she floats effortlessly above the myriad heads — the chestnut, raven, auburn, all shining, each hair defined as a perfect living strand — and she closes her eyes against any change. Fighting something like gravity, she slows her own descent, finding herself at last on a white bed like her own but wider, more brilliantly white, where the three of them rest, not separate at all, but sister, brother, sister.

Mother is the flower girl at their wedding, and it having been only seven weeks since the courtship began, they are breathless still. Mother is too, seeing not their faces but the way their hands and lips can barely meet during the ceremony, as if the slightest brush of flesh is painful. The next day the young man enlists and is gone to the Pacific. In a month, the family will learn that he is in an infirmary with a minor infection Rose will not name. He will be home soon.

She must have met him at the train station, but neither Mother nor I can imagine it, nor can we imagine him telling her he has been cured, that it won't touch her. We see her alone, awakening before him in the early morning dark, stepping out of bed and out of the house before he stirs, going to Sam's for breakfast now as well as lunch. Now she bends closer to the book she has brought, and the dark print on the white page, the steam rising from her cup, all force themselves upon her to keep her from glancing up. They have made an arrangement that he should not be home in the evening when she arrives from work; he is out at a club with friends home on leave. Then one night she comes home to find him sitting at the kitchen table. One shoulder is slumped and there is a quizzical expression on his face, as if he was expecting a blow. He is twenty-five years old and death leaves no mark, no bruise on his narrow face, only an expression of betrayal she cannot, will not, fathom.

In the boxes of books, papers, and photographs pushed to one side of our guest bedroom, the biggest bundle seems placed there as a false clue, something to throw us off the track. There are too many photographs, all documenting the series of pleasure trips she took after the war. They are elaborately framed, hand-tinted, and Rose's cheeks are in a constant, delicate blush. She is always in a group of men and women, all talking at once, when the shutter clicks. In photograph after photograph, something is wrong; she is too close to center frame for my Tante Rose — too close until I notice the slight outward lean of her body, the only sign that her friends have dragged her into the light against her will. Caught like that, Tante Rose is at a loss. Her bewilderment sets itself in a new slant of the eyes, a small stiff foxy smile that fools the photographer asking her to chat with a girlfriend on the Canadian train, to hold up binoculars and gasp at the great snowy shoulders above Lake Louise. It is not until a new person appears in the photographs that Rose remembers herself, that she lifts her face to the camera and lets her eyes open wide and dark with a child's grievous desire for experience.

He is a big man in a fur coat in one of the Lake Louise pictures, a full-length fur coat and a fedora, with dark eyes set in a sweet, sad, heavy face. On the back of the picture the name *Pincus* is written in light brown ink, and it is easy to see him being introduced to her at a travel-club meeting, swamping her small, dry hand in his, breathing his name to her in puffs of frosty air. *Pincus Rosen,* chants their host, *one of our most celebrated art historians.* Pish, tosh, says Pincus, and Rose lets her hand rest easily in the enormous warmth of his, not considering whether she will ever see him again, let alone marry him.

He appears in more photographs, but never the summer ones. He is always in a fur coat or an overcoat, the fedora slanting down over his bearlike face, his brown eyes gleaming. There is an abundance to him that she might have at first mistaken for wealth, that of an entrepreneur who, taking off one pigskin glove, would sport a diamond ring on his little finger. Gradually there appear photographs of the two of them alone and one, finally, of the two of them on a ship's deck, the whole picture tilting with a larger motion we cannot see. Rose is leaning again, but this time toward Pincus, with a desire so slow and unknown even to her that it is imperceptible as anything more than the magnetism of a larger body for a smaller one. Pincus is inescapable. He is father, brother, lover; a great, heavy man whose wintry breath is kind, and whose own ending sleeps on hidden cushions in his heart.

After their elopement, Pincus's arm is always around Rose's shoulder. She is fragile, getting smaller, losing herself in his generosity as if it is a lullaby. At night they look together at art books larger than the books Rose once carried to Sam's Lunch Counter: self-portraits of Rembrandt in whose glance you can read what you like, great success, great disappointment; in whose dark backgrounds there lies a mystery richer to Rose than the sensual textures of velvet, the points of light on lace, that Pincus lingers over. Pincus draws Rose closer, turning the page to a Venus all scallop-curved from breast to thigh, but she has somehow gone past him. She glances away, then leans toward the book with the impulsiveness of the very young or the very old. This one is better, she whispers, turning the page to Michelangelo's *Creation of Adam,* in which, between the hand of God and the hand of Man, there is a hairline fracture in the solid surface of the chapel ceiling. She looks up at Pincus, laughing, and he bows his head, acknowledging defeat more fully than she can guess, not knowing that he is twenty years her senior and that something is quietly spreading in his body, a tiny crack nobody can see.

It was during this time that Mother met Pincus, at a moment when her life was in danger of holding its adolescent shape forever. She was fifteen, her hair bright and short on a delicate neck, her eyes green and on their way to foxy like Rose's, with the question perennially in them, and perennially denied. She was just defiant enough to have thrown the practical black shoes in the ashcan behind their house and purchased, trembling, a pair of apricot pumps, their slender straps curving around her ankles. Her fingers slipped every time she tried to buckle a strap, and looking down, ready to step out the door, she could hardly believe these were her own feet. That was when the letter arrived inviting her to visit in the city and when, after a fierce argument with her mother, she packed her lightest summer dresses, and was gone.

Why Rose put them together, alone, at the museum, Mother does not say, and purses her lips so that I cannot inquire further. It doesn't matter: now I know who she was, fifteen in her pale pumps and dress, gloves and a low hat, walking through the museum with the great Pincus, whose very overcoat breathes a kind of sleepy power over her, making her sense the faint heat of her skin in the palms of her hands, under the perfect gloves. They move slowly through the rooms, Pincus's face moistening so that he must dab at it gently, though he will not take off the coat. There is something, however, she must see before they go, and they walk through rooms of portraits until they arrive before a painting and he stops, wipes his forehead, and says, *now, there.*

How long does it take for Mother to recognize her future self, to accept the nude's long, languorous thigh and curve of hip, the absolute nakedness of a throat when a single golden collar of jewels lies upon it? The man beside her is motionless, yet a knowledge that is not quite a threat moves between them and the picture like a current of air. How long does it take, and how does Pincus know when to step away from the girl and the painting to appraise her with a look that she knows, in the instant before she blots it out, is not lascivious at all but a cool shaft of wisdom that has somehow, by accident or not, traveled to her through a pair of heavy, sensual lips?

"Don't let them stop you from becoming *this,*" he says, and walks away.

She does not immediately turn ash white and go down, in a heap of pale apricot, on the museum floor, nor does she decide, immediately, never to speak to him again. There is a moment of recognition before the rest, when something gets through to her, before convention, their relations, her sister, her mother, flood her, and she responds in the only way she has been trained: by fainting in a public place.

The next morning Mother will not speak to Rose or Pincus, even when Pincus himself questions her. Her face is stark white, her eyes a snapping green that will not face his for more than a second. She wears a sweater over her dress despite the summer heat. Fiercely, uselessly, she thinks of Grandmother, who will be downstairs dusting the staircase and the sideboard when she arrives. Mother will surprise her, rushing toward her, begging to be enclosed in her house, her arms.

Between Rose and Pincus the incident is never discussed, perhaps because there was some secret, deep collusion between them in the awakening of my mother. In any case it is soon forgotten, for within a month something new has at last gained entrance and is sitting between them on the sofa, waiting to see what they will do with the knowledge of death.

They do what they have always done in the evenings. They look at the great books, at the masters, and now, too, one other thing. Pincus is teaching Rose how to work with pastels. Not oils, not watercolor, but pastels: chalky, delicate, *her* medium, he says, smiling. Rose outlines a pear, a nectarine, a bunch of purple grapes; and for Pincus, lover of light, she allows a silver-gray point to appear on the upper edge of each globe. She rubs a little with the side of her palm, and the salmon, the magenta, and the lavender remain on her wrists for days. She copies still lifes from the big book, and one day, when she is ready, she sketches Pincus. We do not know what season it is, but in it he is wearing his great winter coat and the fedora, and his eyes peer out at us with the ambiguous wisdom of a Rembrandt who cannot decide whether he is ready for death, or whether there is, in fact, something still left to say. If he is looking at Rose, he is trying to tell her something she will need to know after he is gone: that if it is too late to grow up, it is not too late to hold still and let others gather around you, remember you, learn from you.

After Pincus there are no more photographs. There are visits to an apartment in a Southern California town next to ours — an apartment in which there is a kitchenette, a small bedroom, and a stack of art books on the glass coffee table, where I will sit for hours tracing my finger over the hairline crack between the hand of God and the hand of Man. And there will be a day, once a year, when my mother passes me into the hands of Tante Rose. It feels like a conspiracy between the two of them: that day when mother with great ceremony packs my overnight satchel and bends down to me, her creamy skin smelling of *home, home,* and whispers, "Later, you will be glad I sent you."

HILDING JOHNSON

Victoria

FROM STORYQUARTERLY

A CHRISTMAS CARD came today and in it a photograph of Rhoda Spofford. She has gotten quite gray over the past year and still more taut in an unpleasant, spinsterish way, but her smile is intact and resolute. Her feet are set together firmly at the heels, dug in. She is seated in a large, expensive armchair; her husband stands just behind her right shoulder and her two teenaged sons crouch at her feet.

We have nineteen photographs of Rhoda Spofford. Richard saves them, throwing them into the box in the hall closet with the tax receipts and appliance instruction booklets.

"Do you think she's ever forgiven you?" I asked him once. It was the year she had frizzed her hair and it was unbecoming and she knew it and her smile was forced.

"Don't be ridiculous, Victoria. Rhoda is an old and dear friend."

He believes this.

She sends the pictures, of course, as a way of telling him that she has survived without him, but whether this is a profound act of charity on her part or one of spite I do not know.

The first time I saw a photograph of Rhoda Spofford was in Sanjay Station. Behind the infirmary was a patch of rank grass inset with slabs of white stone and called the Marble Garden — all that was left of a great estate planting which had flourished under a Colonel Ritt and his lady during the Raj. It was the sole sport and joy of the workers at Sanjay Hospital to sit there at the end of the day with glasses of rose-flavored water and watch the sun crash gloriously into the plains. And there we sat, Richard and I, long ago.

"My fiancée, Rhoda Spofford." Richard fished the photograph from his shirt pocket; it was slightly warped and damp with sweat.

I held the shiny square between two fingers. "Pretty." And she was. Her hair was neat as a pin and bright as a penny, her nose tilted rakishly, her dimples dear: pert. Rhoda was pert.

Richard tucked the photo back next to his heart. "And she's a wonderful Christian."

"Good. Very good."

He leaned back — his chair creaking loudly, he was too big for it and for everything else here — and on the long, smooth muscles of his thigh the fine golden hairs caught the last light and trembled.

I pulled the pins from my hair and tried to rewind it more tightly about my head but it escaped me and brushed my neck and breasts like fingers.

He said, "We'll be married next year."

The pins were sharp. I pricked my scalp.

Richard had come two weeks before, finding his way alone through the hot afternoon streets of the sun-struck city, bellowing a Punjabi that was struck unintelligible as it collided with his Nebraska twang — and was in any event not what we spoke in that province — he came rising up like the archangel Michael in the door of the hospital, serious, determined, beautiful.

He came to take the place of Doctor Singh, whom I had caused to be transferred to the leper colony at Bhopal to keep us both out of harm's way. There had been a time when Doctor Singh and I and Doctor Sloan, the founder of the hospital, had sat in the Marble Garden at sunset. But Doctor Sloan had died and then it was only Doctor Singh and I who stayed sometimes through sundown, through the rise of the moon and very nearly its set too. His eyes would glisten in the wet dark. My sighs would explode in the night air, heavy with promise, like whiffs of jasmine or frangipani. India dallied in the Marble Garden, doe-eyed and hung with tiny chimes, her belly swollen.

On Saturdays Doctor Singh took to making me incandescent Vindaloo curries on an illegal hot plate in his room. He hung a string bag on the front of his bicycle and fetched me mangoes and sticky buns and bottled orangeade.

The night came — no hotter than any other — when I left the door of my bedroom ajar. But the hours came and slid away, unremarked.

In the morning, early, I went past Doctor Singh's room and his door too was open. We had, it seems, each been willing to be ravished, but not to be the ravisher.

Outside his door was growing that little vine which blooms in the morning, comes to full flower at noon, and whose blossoms by nightfall are little, sticky pools of loathsome corruption: a morality tale on the pleasures of sin for a season.

I called Reverend Soames at Bhopal. I bought a second-class ticket for one on the Greater India and New Delhi, and I had the gardener build a crate for Doctor Singh's bicycle.

I walked him to Sanjay on a bright Monday morning, and there in the dust beside the roadbed he gave way. As the train hooted in the distance he fell to his knees, his upper-class British accent, so suitable for passionless exchanges, deserting him. He wept heavy, perfect tears. He kissed my hands, back and front, with many little kisses. He tried to kiss my feet.

About us stood Sanjay Station — the drivers, the porters, the merchants, the matrons and maids. There near the platform stood Mrs. Voorhees, the wife of the Dutch Reformed minister. Just beyond her was Miss Purdy of the hospital board.

I soothed, I entreated, I implored. I assured Doctor Singh that he could indeed live without me. I gave him a box of peppermints I had brought in my pocket from home and promised to visit Bhopal in the spring. When I handed his valise up after him he was, if not wholly recovered, sounding much like himself again.

Waving, I sent up a brief and totally faithless prayer that everyone who had witnessed this parting be struck deaf and dumb, and went home to write a request for a replacement for Doctor Singh.

*

Richard had come that first day through the door to the infirmary, oversized and blond, with my little nurses already useless — giggling in his wake, jetsam.

He took my hand in a straightforward clasp — not a hearty one, Richard is sincere, not hearty — and said, "Reverend Thornhill said that you are to be my model and teacher. I'd like to think of you as my mother in Christ." Richard says things like that seriously. It is the sort of thing which has made him a magnet for young women in the churches he has pastored, young women who are pale and spiritual and want to discuss celibacy with him, all for the sake of watching such a passion-freighted word emerge from the mouth they would so love to cover with their own.

He held my hand and his eyes were most marvelously blue. "Would you mind if I called you Mother?" he said.

"Yes," I said, "I most certainly would." I am twelve years older than Richard.

"I see."

"You may call me Victoria."

The general first opinion in hospital and town was that Richard was a saint. He made his rounds of the homes of Sanjay's socially elite and his rounds at the hospital with the same degree of slow, sober enthusiasm. He held hands, he probed souls eye-to-eye, he promised with equal fervor to pray for Miss Purdy's arthritis and for the ward sweeper's infected toe.

All of this provoked in me a fierce if unconscionable yearning to catch him out, a yearning I excused on the basis that I had asked for bread and been given a stone — that is, I had needed a physician and had gotten a minister, a distinction my mission board seemed unable to understand.

Whether he was balancing a china cup on one knee in the endless, soporific afternoon of a social tea, or standing across a bed from me over the body of some poor wretch, helping to peel bandages off a suppuration which could have been expected to make stronger men faint, I watched for the cocked eyebrow, the pressed lips, the sigh that would say that the self was at last rebelling.

And, annoyed, I watched virtue prevail.

There was never a word about the heat which oppressed any newcomer very nearly to madness. I heard him pad past my door to the necessary half a dozen times a night those first weeks while he underwent his initiation to our water, but he never talked of this nor of the food, which was new to him and not by any standard good. He even handed away his useless Punjabi — on which he had mistakenly and painfully labored, hunched over his childhood desk in the cold Nebraska nights — and he did it without a whimper. Instead, in the quiet hour after lunch he would sit with cook just outside the kitchen door and repeat "the tree," "the door," or "I am Richard," "This is Sanjay Hospital," with immense patience and steadfast good will in spite of cook's hilarity.

I thought for a short time that I had him. Richard had transported from the plains of the Midwest a wardrobe that was as extensive as it was unsuitable to Sanjay.

Almost on arrival he had found a woman near the depot who would starch his shirts, European style. And early in the day where once there had been only the gentle clank of the water bearers' jars, there was now added the fierce hiss of steam from Richard's charcoal iron. He would stand, sweat dripping onto the board, and press meticulous seams down his light wool trousers. He would touch up the lapels on a flawless blazer.

"Vanity, vanity, Preacher." I could not resist saying it one noon as we set off together for a board meeting, he in his second pristine ensemble of the day. I like to think I would not have been so mean if I had not had a run in my stocking and a spot on my dress.

He blushed slightly. "I'm sorry. I don't think I heard you."

"I said that's a lovely tie."

"Well. Thank you."

"It brings out the blue in your eyes."

He blinked several times, as if noticing for the first time that he possessed those organs. "Oh," he said. "I never thought of that."

And it was clear that he hadn't. And didn't. Not for him the jacket cut to emphasize his broad shoulders, the pants molded hip and thigh. It became obvious that his vanity, unlike his virtue, was only skin deep. He costumed himself as he did out of some atavistic notion that a minister ought always to be dressed up — an evangelical version of falling bands and clerical robes. It had nothing to do with him, but rather his office.

I watched him hold a child's head while she threw up quite grandly down his silk tie, starched shirt, and double-breasted camel's hair jacket, and he never batted an eye.

As Miss Purdy said, "He's Johnny-on-the-spot, good as gold, and pretty as a picture."

That was about the size of it.

At night in my bed, restless and morbidly heated behind the mosquito netting, I composed short petitions to God and Doctor Thornhill. They were of similar nature, although I addressed more of them to the doctor: Dear Sir, Have you taken leave of your senses? Did I summarily dispatch the frying pan only to have you provide the fire? The rains are late this year. We are all under a great strain. Sincerely, Victoria. Or: My dear friend, You have misapprehended the situation.

Actually, I was convinced that word had gotten to Doctor Thornhill, word from staff, from visitors — from those who had stood about in the bright sun at Sanjay Station on that Monday. The word was that I was poised at the very edge of my strength and sensibilities, that I was about to fall over, to — in the most catastrophic and perhaps only real sense of the word — go native, an act that was in those days the one final, unforgivable sin.

Dear Doctor Thornhill! He had thought that Richard, corn fed, would be the perfect antidote to Doctor Singh.

He was.

I became moony and truculent.

I scolded Richard unfairly in front of staff on the ward and simply could not apologize.

I bought him two perfect oranges in the market and put them on his plate when he wasn't looking.

When his laundry was accidentally brought to my room I took

it to his and stood there, stricken, with my nose buried in the soft rumpled cloth, smelling beneath the clean, soapy fragrance his own scent, trembling with outrage at Rhoda Spofford, who would do this a thousand times and never think of it, would handle him casually and without understanding because she was twenty-four years old and pert.

The rains did not come.

The dust settled on our beds, in our food, in the fine lines beside my eyes.

The sunsets were spectacular, and the light in the Marble Garden was rosy and unsettled. In the evenings I would sit on the ground and I would take my hair down and brush the dirt away. Richard would watch me.

We spoke less and less.

On Sunday nights after evening service Arleta Poppy always detains Richard. She is white-haired and small and slow and was a marvelous conversationalist before deafness made her responses somewhat less than to the point. She is lonely and adores Richard and clearly regards this as her special time with him, and he would never disabuse her of the notion.

Only I know the admirable self-control he employs as she pats the pew beside her for him to sit, as her hands clasp the purse and gloves in her lap in pleased anticipation. He leans back and stretches out his legs, every line in him easy; his blue eyes are attentive — no, more: they bore into hers with an intensity that makes them very nearly cross. He is in fact marshaling all that he has in an effort to concentrate.

There is only one place Richard wants to be after Sunday evening service and it is not in a pew in the back of the sanctuary with Arleta Poppy.

I teased him about it once. I said, "I was afraid that in a minute you were going to hold yourself in front, like a little boy." He did not find this amusing.

On Sundays Richard pleads the case of God and man — each to the other — and in the process is tugged by demands celestial and petty, trampled by various and opposing armies, and generally run around the territory once or twice. He is a lightning rod, and by nightfall if he does not discharge he will disintegrate, and that's why I keep the shades drawn in the parsonage parlor on that particular day because we seldom make it to the bedroom. There is a blissful, Pavlovian connection for me in the mingled fragrance of Richard's hair, the slightly acrid smell of his black wool suit, and the dry scent which comes off the old, plush sofa, and Sunday evenings.

Richard likes to think of himself as having a healthy, natural attitude toward sex — one that sees it as tasty, useful, and down to earth, something like bran muffins. He is fond of St. Paul's brisk observation that it is better to marry than burn, feeling that it sums up most of what needs to be said on sexual needs, desires, commitments, workings, and waverings, and that one might just possibly do both has never occurred to him.

Thus Richard sees our Sunday conjunctions as coincidence. He is highly uncomfortable with the idea of the flesh and the spirit being symbiotic: the thought that he was working out any of his spiritual joys or frustrations on the brown plush would be alarming to him, and while God and I do not share this perspective we are fond of Richard and so neither of us mentions it.

In the dim light of Sunday evening, as his breathing slows and he lies, heavy and sated, his mouth at my temple, he likes to play out strands of my hair between his fingers, slowly, to let them fall across the hollow of my throat and the swell of my breasts.

Richard is a highly sensuous man. And he would not admit it — not if you slid little slivers of bamboo beneath his fingernails.

Clouds appeared, low and flirtatious, like a ruffle of sky on the horizon. But they would come no closer.

Flowers stayed tight in the bud, drying in crisp pods and rattling to the ground one by one in the still night.

The bearers brought half as much water, then still less. The children on the wards slid from whining into torpor.

A sacred cow wandered into the hospital courtyard and could go no farther. It was chalky, white, fleshless, its loose dry hide scarred in random constellations, a desiccated wreath of twisted flowers digging into its neck. It stood, eyes closed and head nearly to the ground, for a day and night. Early the next morning I came upon Richard holding a bucket of water beneath the animal's nose.

I said, "We don't have much of that."

"It's what I was allotted for shaving."

I shrugged. "Suit yourself."

In the afternoon the cow knelt, shuddered and died. The sweepers came with great hooks and dragged it out of the courtyard, leaving thin trails of scarlet in the pale dust.

At supper Richard said, "If they think so much of the beasts, how can they let them suffer?"

"To them they're gods. In general, people don't care much about the suffering of a god. You should know that by now."

"That isn't funny."

"It wasn't meant to be."

He came to the door of my room in the dusk, and he looked haggard in the dim light. He said, "I sometimes have the feeling you don't like me."

"What nonsense. I'm very fond of you, Richard." Such understatement did not allow me to meet his eyes.

He went away.

In the night I lay sprawled inside the tent of filmy netting. In town a respectable merchant had tried to poison his mother-in-law. The district's parliamentary representative had openly consorted in the marketplace with a twelve-year-old boy who had languid, kohl-rimmed eyes.

I licked the dust from my lips and thought idly that I might tear up Rhoda Spofford's picture and tell Richard that the monkeys had done it.

I said at lunch, "I'm going down to market this afternoon."

And Richard said, "I'll go with you. I want to post a letter."

The day was sunless, the light diffuse, bright, and tiring. The square was choked with shrill vendors, with lethargic buyers, with farmers' families who had come into town because their livings had failed — they slept, slack-jawed and eyes fluttering, in the shade of the exhausted trees. Dogs licked the trail of drops behind a water bearer.

Richard carried the wicker basket and I put in a melon, cracked, and two pomegranates that rattled like gourds.

A procession came, jostling and clanging, and pressed to pass us. There was a platform carried on men's shoulders with a fierce god upon it — blue, and hung with crepe paper wreaths. There were priests and small, pretty dancers with gold-painted eyelids and tired, worn skirts.

When they had very nearly gone by, something struck me on the wrist.

It was a pellet of water.

"Ah!" A sigh spilled over the square. "Ah!"

Bright drops bounced off the hard ground, squirting up in little fountains, first a few, then many, and then all the drops met in great sheets. Water roared on tin roofs and rattled in gutters. "Ah! It's come."

The blue god teetered on his throne. The crepe paper flowers ran and streams of bright color made rainbow rivers in the dirt. The dancers laughed and began to rock, to sway, to revolve. Their slick brown bodies writhed, their slim hands flickered above their breasts, and finger bells tinkled in erratic, pretty arpeggios.

The basket dropped and the useless melon rolled away into the mud and the pomegranates after it.

The rain sluiced down my face, over my breasts and belly. I pulled off my shoes. I turned and turned again and joined the dance. My feet patted and squeezed the mud. I raised my hands and clapped them over my head. I whirled and my dress thinned to no more than a film — it would have been easy to pull it off altogether, to leave it behind, scrap, like the skin of a sweet fruit.

I spun away from Richard, then back again. He was wavering behind the scrim of water, falling away, drowning perhaps.

I put out my hand to him, laughing. "Dance."

"I can't."

"Dance, Richard." I circled him with a two-step and a flourish. I put my hands around his waist; I tugged and pulled.

"Please don't, Victoria."

I touched the place above his heart with the flat of my hand, and he shuddered and swayed and leaned. "Oh, Victoria!" He very nearly shouted this and it seemed he might be weeping. "You make me so miserable!"

Knowledge came up like joy through my feet. "Me?" I asked. "Me?"

ROBERT STONE

Helping

FROM THE NEW YORKER

ONE GRAY NOVEMBER DAY, Elliot went to Boston for the afternoon. The wet streets seemed cold and lonely. He sensed a broken promise in the city's elegance and verve. Old hopes tormented him like phantom limbs, but he did not drink. He had joined Alcoholics Anonymous fifteen months before.

Christmas came, childless, a festival of regret. His wife went to Mass and cooked a turkey. Sober, Elliot walked in the woods.

In January, blizzards swept down from the Arctic until the weather became too cold for snow. The Shawmut Valley grew quiet and crystalline. In the white silences, Elliot could hear the boards of his house contract and feel a shrinking in his bones. Each dusk, starveling deer came out of the wooded swamp behind the house to graze his orchard for whatever raccoons had uncovered and left behind. At night he lay beside his sleeping wife listening to the baying of dog packs running them down in the deep moon-shadowed snow.

Day in, day out, he was sober. At times it was almost stimulating. But he could not shake off the sensations he had felt in Boston. In his mind's eye he could see dead leaves rattling along brick gutters and savor that day's desperation. The brief outing had undermined him.

Sober, however, he remained, until the day a man named Blankenship came into his office at the state hospital for counseling. Blankenship had red hair, a brutal face, and a sneaking manner. He was a sponger and petty thief whom Elliot had seen a number of times before.

"I been having this dream," Blankenship announced loudly. His voice was not pleasant. His skin was unwholesome. Every time he got arrested the court sent him to the psychiatrists and the psychiatrists, who spoke little English, sent him to Elliot.

Blankenship had joined the Army after his first burglary but had never served east of the Rhine. After a few months in Wiesbaden, he had been discharged for reasons of unsuitability, but he told everyone he was a veteran of the Vietnam War. He went about in a tiger suit. Elliot had had enough of him.

"Dreams are boring," Elliot told him.

Blankenship was outraged. "Whaddaya mean?" he demanded.

During counseling sessions Elliot usually moved his chair into the middle of the room in order to seem accessible to his clients. Now he stayed securely behind his desk. He did not care to seem accessible to Blankenship. "What I said, Mr. Blankenship. Other people's dreams are boring. Didn't you ever hear that?"

"Boring?" Blankenship frowned. He seemed unable to imagine a meaning for the word.

Elliot picked up a pencil and set its point quivering on his desk-top blotter. He gazed into his client's slack-jawed face. The Blankenship family made their way through life as strolling litigants, and young Blankenship's specialty was slipping on ice cubes. Hauled off the pavement, he would hassle the doctors in Emergency for pain pills and hurry to a law clinic. The Blankenships had threatened suit against half the property owners in the southern part of the state. What they could not extort at law they stole. But even the Blankenship family had abandoned Blankenship. His last visit to the hospital had been subsequent to an arrest for lifting a case of hot-dog rolls from Woolworth's. He lived in a Goodwill depository bin in Wyndham.

"Now I suppose you want to tell me your dream? Is that right, Mr. Blankenship?"

Blankenship looked left and right like a dog surrendering eye contact. "Don't you want to hear it?" he asked humbly.

Elliot was unmoved. "Tell me something, Blankenship. Was your dream about Vietnam?"

At the mention of the word "Vietnam," Blankenship customarily broke into a broad smile. Now he looked guilty and guarded. He shrugged. "Ya."

"How come you have dreams about that place, Blankenship? You were never there."

"Whaddaya mean?" Blankenship began to say, but Elliot cut him off.

"You were never there, my man. You never saw the goddamn place. You have no business dreaming about it! You better cut it out!"

He had raised his voice to the extent that the secretary outside his open door paused at her word processor.

"Lemme alone," Blankenship said fearfully. "Some doctor you are."

"It's all right," Elliot assured him. "I'm not a doctor."

"Everybody's on my case," Blankenship said. His moods were volatile. He began to weep.

Elliot watched the tears roll down Blankenship's chapped, pitted cheeks. He cleared his throat. "Look, fella . . ." he began. He felt at a loss. He felt like telling Blankenship that things were tough all over.

Blankenship sniffed and telescoped his neck and after a moment looked at Elliot. His look was disconcertingly trustful; he was used to being counseled.

"Really, you know, it's ridiculous for you to tell me your problems have to do with Nam. You were never over there. It was me over there, Blankenship. Not you."

Blankenship leaned forward and put his forehead on his knees.

"Your troubles have to do with here and now," Elliot told his client. "Fantasies aren't helpful."

His voice sounded overripe and hypocritical in his own ears. What a dreadful business, he thought. What an awful job this is. Anger was driving him crazy.

Blankenship straightened up and spoke through his tears. "This dream . . ." he said. "I'm scared."

Elliot felt ready to endure a great deal in order not to hear Blankenship's dream.

"I'm not the one you see about that," he said. In the end he knew his duty. He sighed. "O.K. All right. Tell me about it."

"Yeah?" Blankenship asked with leaden sarcasm. "Yeah? You think dreams are friggin' boring!"

"No, no," Elliot said. He offered Blankenship a tissue and Blankenship took one. "That was sort of off the top of my head. I didn't really mean it."

Blankenship fixed his eyes on dreaming distance. "There's a feeling that goes with it. With the dream." Then he shook his head in revulsion and looked at Elliot as though he had only just awakened. "So what do you think? You think it's boring?"

"Of course not," Elliot said. "A physical feeling?"

"Ya. It's like I'm floating in rubber."

He watched Elliot stealthily, aware of quickened attention. Elliot had caught dengue in Vietnam and during his weeks of delirium had felt vaguely as though he were floating in rubber.

"What are you seeing in this dream?"

Blankenship only shook his head. Elliot suffered a brief but intense attack of rage.

"Hey, Blankenship," he said equably, "here I am, man. You can see I'm listening."

"What I saw was black," Blankenship said. He spoke in an odd tremolo. His behavior was quite different from anything Elliot had come to expect from him.

"Black? What was it?"

"Smoke. The sky maybe."

"The sky?" Elliot asked.

"It was all black. I was scared."

In a waking dream of his own, Elliot felt the muscles on his neck distend. He was looking up at a sky that was black, filled with smoke-swollen clouds, lit with fires, damped with blood and rain.

"What were you scared of?" he asked Blankenship.

"I don't know," Blankenship said.

Elliot could not drive the black sky from his inward eye. It was as though Blankenship's dream had infected his own mind.

"You don't know? You don't know what you were scared of?"

Blankenship's posture was rigid. Elliot, who knew the aspect of true fear, recognized it there in front of him.

"The Nam," Blankenship said.

"You're not even old enough," Elliot told him.

Blankenship sat trembling with joined palms between his thighs. His face was flushed and not in the least ennobled by pain. He had trouble with alcohol and drugs. He had trouble with everything.

"So wherever your black sky is, it isn't Vietnam."

Things were so unfair, Elliot thought. It was unfair of Blankenship to appropriate the condition of a Vietnam veteran. The trauma inducing his post-traumatic stress had been nothing more serious than his own birth, a routine procedure. Now, in addition to the poverty, anxiety, and confusion that would always be his life's lot, he had been visited with irony. It was all arbitrary and some people simply got elected. Everyone knew that who had been where Blankenship had not.

"Because, I assure you, Mr. Blankenship, you were never there."

"Whaddaya mean?" Blankenship asked.

When Blankenship was gone Elliot leafed through his file and saw that the psychiatrists had passed him upstairs without recording a diagnosis. Disproportionately angry, he went out to the secretary's desk.

"Nobody wrote up that last patient," he said. "I'm not supposed to see people without a diagnosis. The shrinks are just passing the buck."

The secretary was a tall, solemn redhead with prominent front teeth and a slight speech disorder. "Dr. Sayyid will have kittens if he hears you call him a shrink, Chas. He's already complained. He hates being called a shrink."

"Then he came to the wrong country," Elliot said. "He can go back to his own."

The woman giggled. "He *is* the doctor, Chas."

"Hates being called a shrink!" He threw the file on the secretary's table and stormed back toward his office. "That fucking little zip couldn't give you a decent haircut. He's a prescription clerk."

The secretary looked about her guiltily and shook her head. She was used to him.

Elliot succeeded in calming himself down after a while, but

the image of the black sky remained with him. At first he thought he would be able to simply shrug the whole thing off. After a few minutes, he picked up his phone and dialed Blankenship's probation officer.

"The Vietnam thing is all he has," the probation officer explained. "I guess he picked it up around."

"His descriptions are vivid," Elliot said.

"You mean they sound authentic?"

"I mean he had me going today. He was ringing my bells."

"Good for Blanky. Think he believes it himself?"

"Yes," Elliot said. "He believes it himself now."

Elliot told the probation officer about Blankenship's current arrest, which was for showering illegally at midnight in the Wyndham Regional High School. He asked what probation knew about Blankenship's present relationship with his family.

"You kiddin'?" the P.O. asked. "They're all locked down. The whole family's inside. The old man's in Bridgewater. Little Donny's in San Quentin or somewhere. Their dog's in the pound."

Elliot had lunch alone in the hospital staff cafeteria. On the far side of the double-glazed windows, the day was darkening as an expected snowstorm gathered. Along Route 7, ancient elms stood frozen against the gray sky. When he had finished his sandwich and coffee, he sat staring out at the winter afternoon. His anger had given way to an insistent anxiety.

On the way back to his office, he stopped at the hospital gift shop for a copy of *Sports Illustrated* and a candy bar. When he was inside again, he closed the door and put his feet up. It was Friday and he had no appointments for the remainder of the day, nothing to do but write a few letters and read the office mail.

Elliot's cubicle in the social services department was windowless and lined with bookshelves. When he found himself unable to concentrate on the magazine and without any heart for his paperwork, he ran his eye over the row of books beside his chair. There were volumes by Heinrich Muller and Carlos Casteneda, Jones's life of Freud, and *The Golden Bough.* The books aroused a revulsion in Elliot. Their present uselessness repelled him.

Over and over again, detail by detail, he tried to recall his conversation with Blankenship.

"You were never there," he heard himself explaining. He was trying to get the whole incident straightened out after the fact. Something was wrong. Dread crept over him like a paralysis. He ate his candy bar without tasting it. He knew that the craving for sweets was itself a bad sign.

Blankenship had misappropriated someone else's dream and made it his own. It made no difference whether you had been there, after all. The dreams had crossed the ocean. They were in the air.

He took his glasses off and put them on his desk and sat with his arms folded, looking into the well of light from his desk lamp. There seemed to be nothing but whirl inside him. Unwelcome things came and went in his mind's eye. His heart beat faster. He could not control the headlong promiscuity of his thoughts.

It was possible to imagine larval dreams traveling in suspended animation undetectable in a host brain. They could be divided and regenerate like flatworms, hide in seams and bedding, in war stories, laughter, snapshots. They could rot your socks and turn your memory into a black-and-green blister. Green for the hills, black for the sky above. At daybreak they hung themselves up in rows like bats. At dusk they went out to look for dreamers.

Elliot put his jacket on and went into the outer office, where the secretary sat frowning into the measured sound and light of her machine. She must enjoy its sleekness and order, he thought. She was divorced. Four red-headed kids between ten and seventeen lived with her in an unpainted house across from Stop & Shop. Elliot liked her and had come to find her attractive. He managed a smile for her.

"Ethel, I think I'm going to pack it in," he declared. It seemed awkward to be leaving early without a reason.

"Jack wants to talk to you before you go, Chas."

Elliot looked at her blankly.

Then his colleague, Jack Sprague, having heard his voice, called from the adjoining cubicle. "Chas, what about Sunday's games? Shall I call you with the spread?"

"I don't know," Elliot said. "I'll phone you tomorrow."

"This is a big decision for him," Jack Sprague told the secretary. "He might lose twenty-five bucks."

At present, Elliot drew a slightly higher salary than Jack Sprague, although Jack had a Ph.D. and Elliot was simply an M.S.W. Different branches of the state government employed them.

"Twenty-five bucks," said the woman. "If you guys have no better use for twenty-five bucks, give it to me."

"Where are you off to, by the way?" Sprague asked.

Elliot began to answer, but for a moment no reply occurred to him. He shrugged. "I have to get back," he finally stammered. "I promised Grace."

"Was that Blankenship I saw leaving?"

Elliot nodded.

"It's February," Jack said. "How come he's not in Florida?"

"I don't know," Elliot said. He put on his coat and walked to the door. "I'll see you."

"Have a nice weekend," the secretary said. She and Sprague looked after him indulgently as he walked toward the main corridor.

"Are Chas and Grace going out on the town?" she said to Sprague. "What do you think?"

"That would be the day," Sprague said. "Tomorrow he'll come back over here and read all day. He spends every weekend holed up in this goddamn office while she does something or other at the church." He shook his head. "Every night he's at A.A. and she's home alone."

Ethel savored her overbite. "Jack," she said teasingly, "are you thinking what I think you're thinking? Shame on you."

"I'm thinking I'm glad I'm not him, that's what I'm thinking. That's as much as I'll say."

"Yeah, well, I don't care," Ethel said. "Two salaries and no kids, that's the way to go, boy."

Elliot went out through the automatic doors of the emergency bay and the cold closed over him. He walked across the hospital parking lot with his eyes on the pavement, his hands thrust deep in his overcoat pockets, skirting patches of shattered ice. There was no wind, but the motionless air stung; the metal frames of his glasses burned his skin. Curlicues of mud-brown ice coated the soiled snowbanks along the street. Although it was still afternoon, the street lights had come on.

The lock on his car door had frozen and he had to breathe on the keyhole to fit the key. When the engine turned over, Jussi Björling's recording of the Handel Largo filled the car interior. He snapped it off at once.

Halted at the first stoplight, he began to feel the want of a destination. The fear and impulse to flight that had got him out of the office faded, and he had no desire to go home. He was troubled by a peculiar impatience that might have been with time itself. It was as though he were waiting for something. The sensation made him feel anxious; it was unfamiliar but not altogether unpleasant. When the light changed he drove on, past the Gulf station and the firehouse and between the greens of Ilford Common. At the far end of the common he swung into the parking lot of the Packard Conway Library and stopped with the engine running. What he was experiencing, he thought, was the principle of possibility.

He turned off the engine and went out again into the cold. Behind the leaded library windows he could see the librarian pouring coffee in her tiny private office. The librarian was a Quaker of socialist principles named Candace Music, who was Elliot's cousin.

The Conway Library was all dark wood and etched mirrors, a Gothic saloon. Years before, out of work and booze-whipped, Elliot had gone to hide there. Because Candace was a classicist's widow and knew some Greek, she was one of the few people in the valley with whom Elliot had cared to speak in those days. Eventually, it had seemed to him that all their conversations tended toward Vietnam, so he had gone less and less often. Elliot was the only Vietnam veteran Candace knew well enough to chat with, and he had come to suspect that he was being probed for the edification of the East Ilford Friends Meeting. At that time he had still pretended to talk easily about his war and had prepared little discourses and picaresque anecdotes to recite on demand. Earnest seekers like Candace had caused him great secret distress.

Candace came out of her office to find him at the checkout

desk. He watched her brow furrow with concern as she composed a smile. "Chas, what a surprise. You haven't been in for an age."

"Sure I have, Candace. I went to all the Wednesday films last fall. I work just across the road."

"I know, dear," Candace said. "I always seem to miss you."

A cozy fire burned in the hearth, an antique brass clock ticked along on the marble mantel above it. On a couch near the fireplace an old man sat upright, his mouth open, asleep among half a dozen soiled plastic bags. Two teenage girls whispered over their homework at a table under the largest window.

"Now that I'm here," he said, laughing, "I can't remember what I came to get."

"Stay and get warm," Candace told him. "Got a minute? Have a cup of coffee."

Elliot had nothing but time, but he quickly realized that he did not want to stay and pass it with Candace. He had no clear idea of why he had come to the library. Standing at the checkout desk, he accepted coffee. She attended him with an air of benign supervision, as though he were a Chinese peasant and she a medical missionary, like her father. Candace was tall and plain, more handsome in her middle sixties than she had ever been.

"Why don't we sit down?"

He allowed her to gentle him into a chair by the fire. They made a threesome with the sleeping old man.

"Have you given up translating, Chas? I hope not."

"Not at all," he said. Together they had once rendered a few fragments of Sophocles into verse. She was good at clever rhymes.

"You come in so rarely, Chas. Ted's books go to waste."

After her husband's death, Candace had donated his books to the Conway, where they reposed in a reading room inscribed to his memory, untouched among foreign-language volumes, local genealogies, and books in large type for the elderly.

"I have a study in the barn," he told Candace. "I work there. When I have time." The lie was absurd, but he felt the need of it.

"And you're working with Vietnam veterans," Candace declared.

"Supposedly," Elliot said. He was growing impatient with her nodding solicitude.

"Actually," he said, "I came in for the new Oxford *Classical World.* I thought you'd get it for the library and I could have a look before I spent my hard-earned cash."

Candace beamed. "You've come to the right place, Chas, I'm happy to say." He thought she looked disproportionately happy. "I have it."

"Good," Elliot said, standing. "I'll just take it, then. I can't really stay."

Candace took his cup and saucer and stood as he did. When the library telephone rang, she ignored it, reluctant to let him go. "How's Grace?" she asked.

"Fine," Elliot said. "Grace is well."

At the third ring she went to the desk. When her back was turned, he hesitated for a moment and then went outside.

The gray afternoon had softened into night, and it was snowing. The falling snow whirled like a furious mist in the headlight beams on Route 7 and settled implacably on Elliot's cheeks and eyelids. His heart, for no good reason, leaped up in childlike expectation. He had run away from a dream and encountered possibility. He felt in possession of a promise. He began to walk toward the roadside lights.

Only gradually did he begin to understand what had brought him there and what the happy anticipation was that fluttered in his breast. Drinking, he had started his evening from the Conway Library. He would arrive hung over in the early afternoon to browse and read. When the old pain rolled in with dusk, he would walk down to the Midway Tavern for a remedy. Standing in the snow outside the library, he realized that he had contrived to promise himself a drink.

Ahead, through the storm, he could see the beer signs in the Midway's window warm and welcoming. Snowflakes spun around his head like an excitement.

Outside the Midway's package store, he paused with his hand on the doorknob. There was an old man behind the counter whom Elliot remembered from his drinking days. When he was inside, he realized that the old man neither knew nor cared who he was. The package store was thick with dust; it was on the counter, the shelves, the bottles themselves. The old counterman looked dusty. Elliot bought a bottle of King William Scotch and put it in the inside pocket of his overcoat.

Passing the windows of the Midway Tavern, Elliot could see the ranks of bottles aglow behind the bar. The place was crowded with men leaving the afternoon shifts at the shoe and felt factories. No one turned to note him when he passed inside. There was a single stool vacant at the bar and he took it. His heart beat faster. Bruce Springsteen was on the jukebox.

The bartender was a club fighter from Pittsfield called Jackie G., with whom Elliot had often gossiped. Jackie G. greeted him as though he had been in the previous evening. "Say, babe?"

"How do," Elliot said.

A couple of men at the bar eyed his shirt and tie. Confronted with the bartender, he felt impelled to explain his presence. "Just thought I'd stop by," he told Jackie G. "Just thought I'd have one. Saw the light. The snow . . . " He chuckled expansively.

"Good move," the bartender said. "Scotch?"

"Double," Elliot said.

When he shoved two dollars forward along the bar, Jackie G. pushed one of the bills back to him. "Happy hour, babe."

"Ah," Elliot said. He watched Jackie pour the double. "Not a moment too soon."

For five minutes or so, Elliot sat in his car in the barn with the engine running and his Handel tape on full volume. He had driven over from East Ilford in a baroque ecstasy, swinging and swaying and singing along. When the tape ended, he turned off the engine and poured some Scotch into an apple juice container to store providentially beneath the car seat. Then he took the tape and the Scotch into the house with him. He was lying on the sofa in the dark living room, listening to the Largo, when he heard his wife's car in the driveway. By the time Grace had made her way up the icy back-porch steps, he was able to hide the Scotch and rinse his glass clean in the kitchen sink. The drinking life, he thought, was lived moment by moment.

Soon she was in the tiny cloakroom struggling off with her overcoat. In the process she knocked over a cross-country ski, which stood propped against the cloakroom wall. It had been more than a year since Elliot had used the skis.

She came into the kitchen and sat down at the table to take off her boots. Her lean, freckled face was flushed with the cold, but her eyes looked weary. "I wish you'd put those skis down in the barn," she told him. "You never use them."

"I always like to think," Elliot said, "that I'll start the morning off skiing."

"Well, you never do," she said. "How long have you been home?"

"Practically just walked in," he said. Her pointing out that he no longer skied in the morning enraged him. "I stopped at the Conway Library to get the new Oxford *Classical World.* Candace ordered it."

Her look grew troubled. She had caught something in his voice. With dread and bitter satisfaction, Elliot watched his wife detect the smell of whiskey.

"Oh God," she said. "I don't believe it."

Let's get it over with, he thought. Let's have the song and dance.

She sat up straight in her chair and looked at him in fear.

"Oh, Chas," she said, "how could you?"

For a moment he was tempted to try to explain it all.

"The fact is," Elliot told his wife, "I hate people who start the day cross-country skiing."

She shook her head in denial and leaned her forehead on her palm and cried.

He looked into the kitchen window and saw his own distorted image. "The fact is I think I'll start tomorrow morning by stringing head-high razor wire across Anderson's trail."

The Andersons were the Elliots' nearest neighbors. Loyall Anderson was a full professor of government at the state university, thirty miles away. Anderson and his wife were blond and both of them were over six feet tall. They had two blond children, who qualified for the gifted class in the local school but attended regular classes in token of the Andersons' opposition to elitism.

"Sure," Elliot said. "Stringing wire's good exercise. It's life-affirming in its own way."

The Andersons started each and every day with a brisk morning glide along a trail that they partly maintained. They skied well and presented a pleasing, wholesome sight. If, in the course of their adventure, they encountered a snowmobile, Darlene Anderson would affect to choke and cough, indicating her displeasure. If the snowmobile approached them from behind and the trail was narrow, the Andersons would decline to let it pass, asserting their statutory right-of-way.

"I don't want to hear your violent fantasies," Grace said.

Elliot was picturing razor wire, the Army kind. He was picturing the decapitated Andersons, their blood and jaunty ski caps bright on the white trail. He was picturing their severed heads, their earnest blue eyes and large white teeth reflecting the virginal morning snow. Although Elliot hated snowmobiles, he heated the Andersons far more.

He looked at his wife and saw that she had stopped crying. Her long, elegant face was rigid and lipless.

"Know what I mean? One string at Mommy and Daddy level for Loyall and Darlene. And a bitty wee string at kiddie level for Skippy and Samantha, those cunning little whizzes."

"Stop it," she said to him.

"Sorry," Elliot told her.

Stiff with shame, he went and took his bottle out of the cabinet into which he had thrust it and poured a drink. He was aware of her eyes on him. As he drank, a fragment from old Music's translation of *Medea* came into his mind. "Old friend, I have to weep. The gods and I went mad together and made things as they are." It was such a waste; eighteen months of struggle thrown away. But there was no way to get the stuff back in the bottle.

"I'm very sorry," he said. "You know I'm very sorry, don't you, Grace?"

The delectable Handel arias spun on in the next room.

"You must stop," she said. "You must make yourself stop before it takes over."

"It's out of my hands," Elliot said. He showed her his empty hands. "It's beyond me."

"You'll lose your job, Chas." She stood up at the table and leaned on it, staring wide-eyed at him. Drunk as he was, the panic in her voice frightened him. "You'll end up in jail again."

"One engages," Elliot said, "and then one sees."

"How can you have done it?" she demanded. "You promised me."

"First the promises," Elliot said, "and then the rest."

"Last time was supposed to be the last time," she said.

"Yes," he said, "I remember."

"I can't stand it," she said. "You reduce me to hysterics." She wrung her hands for him to see. "See? Here I am, I'm in hysterics."

"What can I say?" Elliot asked. He went to the bottle and refilled his glass. "Maybe you shouldn't watch."

"You want me to be forbearing, Chas? I'm not going to be."

"The last thing I want," Elliot said, "is an argument."

"I'll give you a fucking argument. You didn't have to drink. All you had to do was come home."

"That must have been the problem," he said.

Then he ducked, alert at the last possible second to the missile that came for him at hairline level. Covering up, he heard the shattering of glass, and a fine rain of crystals enveloped him. She had sailed the sugar bowl at him; it had smashed against the wall above his head and there was sugar and glass in his hair.

"You bastard!" she screamed. "You are undermining me!"

"You ought not to throw things at me," Elliot said. "I don't throw things at you."

He left her frozen into her follow-through and went into the living room to turn the music off. When he returned she was leaning back against the wall, rubbing her right elbow with her left hand. Her eyes were bright. She had picked up one of her boots from the middle of the kitchen floor and stood holding it.

"What the hell do you mean, that must have been the problem?"

He set his glass on the edge of the sink with an unsteady hand and turned to her. "What do I mean? I mean that most of the time I'm putting one foot in front of the other like a good soldier and I'm out of it from the neck up. But there are times when I don't think I will ever be dead enough — or dead long enough — to get the taste of this life off my teeth. That's what I mean!"

She looked at him dry-eyed. "Poor fella," she said.

"What you have to understand, Grace, is that this drink I'm having" — he raised the glass toward her in a gesture of salute — "is the only worthwhile thing I've done in the last year and a half. It's the only thing in my life that means jack shit, the closest thing to satisfaction I've had. Now how can you begrudge me that? It's the best I'm capable of."

"You'll go too far," she said to him. "You'll see."

"What's that, Grace? A threat to walk?" He was grinding his teeth. "Don't make me laugh. You, walk? You, the friend of the unfortunate?"

"Don't you hit me," she said when she looked at his face. "Don't you dare."

"You, the Christian Queen of Calvary, walk? Why, I don't believe that for a minute."

She ran a hand through her hair and bit her lip. "No, we stay," she said. Anger and distraction made her look young. Her cheeks blazed rosy against the general pallor of her skin. "In my family we stay until the fella dies. That's the tradition. We stay and pour it for them and they die."

He put his drink down and shook his head.

"I thought we'd come through," Grace said. "I was sure."

"No," Elliot said. "Not altogether."

They stood in silence for a minute. Elliot sat down at the oilcloth-covered table. Grace walked around it and poured herself a whiskey.

"You are undermining me, Chas. You are making things impossible for me and I just don't know." She drank and winced. "I'm not going to stay through another drunk. I'm telling you right now. I haven't got it in me. I'll die."

He did not want to look at her. He watched the flakes settle against the glass of the kitchen door. "Do what you feel the need of," he said.

"I just can't take it," she said. Her voice was not scolding but measured and reasonable. "It's February. And I went to court this morning and lost Vopotik."

Once again, he thought, my troubles are going to be obviated by those of the deserving poor. He said, "Which one was that?"

"Don't you remember them? The three-year-old with the broken fingers?"

He shrugged. Grace sipped her whiskey.

"I told you. I said I had a three-year-old with broken fingers, and you said, 'Maybe he owed somebody money.' "

"Yes," he said, "I remember now."

"You ought to see the Vopotiks, Chas. The woman is young and obese. She's so young that for a while I thought I could get to her as a juvenile. The guy is a biker. They believe the kid came from another planet to control their lives. They believe this literally, both of them."

"You shouldn't get involved that way," Elliot said. "You should leave it to thc caseworkers."

"They scared their first caseworker all the way to California. They were following me to work."

"You didn't tell me."

"Are you kidding?" she asked. "Of course I didn't." To Elliot's surprise, his wife poured herself a second whiskey. "You know how they address the child? As 'dude.' She says to it, 'Hey, dude.' " Grace shuddered with loathing. "You can't imagine! The woman munching Twinkies. The kid smelling of shit. They're high morning, noon, and night, but you can't get anybody for that these days."

"People must really hate it," Elliot said, "when somebody tells them they're not treating their kids right."

"They definitely don't want to hear it," Grace said. "You're right." She sat stirring her drink, frowning into the glass. "The Vopotik child will die, I think."

"Surely not," Elliot said.

"This one I think will die," Grace said. She took a deep breath and puffed out her cheeks and looked at him forlornly. "The situation's extreme. Of course, sometimes you wonder whether it makes any difference. That's the big question, isn't it?"

"I would think," Elliot said, "that would be the one question you didn't ask."

"But you do," she said. "You wonder: Ought they to live at all? To continue the cycle?" She put a hand to her hair and shook her head as if in confusion. "Some of these folks, my God, the poor things cannot put Wednesday on top of Tuesday to save their lives."

"It's a trick," Elliot agreed, "a lot of them can't manage."

"And kids are small, they're handy and underfoot. They make noise. They can't hurt you back."

"I suppose child abuse is something people can do together," Elliot said.

"Some kids are obnoxious. No question about it."

"I wouldn't know," Elliot said.

"Maybe you should stop complaining. Maybe you're better off. Maybe your kids are better off unborn."

"Better off or not," Elliot said, "it looks like they'll stay that way."

"I mean our kids, of course," Grace said. "I'm not blaming you, understand? It's just that here we are with you drunk again and me losing Vopotik, so I thought why not get into the big unaskable questions." She got up and folded her arms and began to pace up and down the kitchen. "Oh," she said when her eye fell upon the bottle, "that's good stuff, Chas. You won't mind if I have another? I'll leave you enough to get loaded on."

Elliot watched her pour. So much pain, he thought; such anger and confusion. He was tired of pain, anger, and confusion; they were what had got him in trouble that very morning.

The liquor seemed to be giving him a perverse lucidity when all he now required was oblivion. His rage, especially, was intact in its salting of alcohol. Its contours were palpable and bleeding at the borders. Booze was good for rage. Booze could keep it burning through the darkest night.

"What happened in court?" he asked his wife.

She was leaning on one arm against the wall, her long, strong body flexed at the hip. Holding her glass, she stared angrily toward the invisible fields outside. "I lost the child," she said.

Elliot thought that a peculiar way of putting it. He said nothing.

"The court convened in an atmosphere of high hilarity. It may be Hate Month around here but it was buddy-buddy over at Ilford Courthouse. The room was full of bikers and bikers' lawyers. A colorful crowd. There was a lot of bonding." She drank and shivered. "They didn't think too well of me. They don't think too well of broads as lawyers. Neither does the judge. The judge has the common touch. He's one of the boys."

"Which judge?" Elliot asked.

"Buckley. A man of about sixty. Know him? Lots of veins on his nose?"

Elliot shrugged.

"I thought I had done my homework," Grace told him. "But suddenly I had nothing but paper. No witnesses. It was Margolis at Valley Hospital who spotted the radiator burns. He called us in the first place. Suddenly he's got to keep his reservation for a campsite in St. John. So Buckley threw his deposition out." She began to chew on a fingernail. "The caseworkers have vanished — one's in L.A., the other's in Nepal. I went in there and got run over. I lost the child."

"It happens all the time," Elliot said. "Doesn't it?"

"This one shouldn't have been lost, Chas. These people aren't simply confused. They're weird. They stink."

"You go messing into anybody's life," Elliot said, "that's what you'll find."

"If the child stays in that house," she said, "he's going to die."

"You did your best," he told his wife. "Forget it."

She pushed the bottle away. She was holding a water glass that was almost a third full of whiskey.

"That's what the commissioner said."

Elliot was thinking of how she must have looked in court to the cherry-faced judge and the bikers and their lawyers. Like the schoolteachers who had tormented their childhoods, earnest and tight-assed, humorless and self-righteous. It was not surprising that things had gone against her.

He walked over to the window and faced his reflection again. "Your optimism always surprises me."

"My optimism? Where I grew up our principal cultural expression was the funeral. Whatever keeps me going, it isn't optimism."

"No?" he asked. "What is it?"

"I forget," she said.

"Maybe it's your religious perspective. Your sense of the divine plan."

She sighed in exasperation. "Look, I don't think I want to fight anymore. I'm sorry I threw the sugar at you. I'm not your keeper. Pick on someone your own size."

"Sometimes," Elliot said, "I try to imagine what it's like to believe that the sky is full of care and concern."

"You want to take everything from me, do you?" She stood leaning against the back of her chair. "That you can't take. It's the only part of my life you can't mess up."

He was thinking that if it had not been for her he might not have survived. There could be no forgiveness for that. "Your life? You've got all this piety strung out between Monadnock and Central America. And look at yourself. Look at your life."

"Yes," she said, "look at it."

"You should have been a nun. You don't know how to live."

"I know that," she said. "That's why I stopped doing counseling. Because I'd rather talk the law than life." She turned to him. "You got everything I had, Chas. What's left I absolutely require."

"I swear I would rather be a drunk," Elliot said, "than force myself to believe such trivial horseshit."

"Well, you're going to have to do it without a straight man," she said, "because this time I'm not going to be here for you. Believe it or not."

"I don't believe it," Elliot said. "Not my Grace."

"You're really good at this," she told him. "You make me feel ashamed of my own name."

"I love your name," he said.

The telephone rang. They let it ring three times, and then Elliot went over and answered it.

"Hey, who's that?" a good-humored voice on the phone demanded.

Elliot recited their phone number.

"Hey, I want to talk to your woman, man. Put her on."

"I'll give her a message," Elliot said.

"You put your woman on, man. Run and get her."

Elliott looked at the receiver. He shook his head. "Mr. Vopotik?"

"Never you fuckin' mind, man. I don't want to talk to you. I want to talk to the skinny bitch."

Elliot hung up.

"Is it him?" she asked.

"I guess so."

They waited for the phone to ring again and it shortly did.

"I'll talk to him," Grace said. But Elliot already had the phone.

"Who are you, asshole?" the voice inquired. "What's your fuckin' name, man?"

"Elliot," Elliot said.

"Hey, don't hang up on me, Elliot. I won't put up with that. I told you go get that skinny bitch, man. You go do it."

There were sounds of festivity in the background on the other end of the line — a stereo and drunken voices.

"Hey," the voice declared. "Hey, don't keep me waiting, man."

"What do you want to say to her?" Elliot asked.

"That's none of your fucking business, fool. Do what I told you."

"My wife is resting," Elliot said. "I'm taking her calls."

He was answered by a shout of rage. He put the phone aside for a moment and finished his glass of whiskey. When he picked it up again the man on the line was screaming at him. "That bitch tried to break up my family, man! She almost got away with it. You know what kind of pain my wife went through?"

"What kind?" Elliot asked.

For a few seconds he heard only the noise of the party. "Hey, you're not drunk, are you, fella?"

"Certainly not," Elliot insisted.

"You tell that skinny bitch she's gonna pay for what she did to my family, man. You tell her she can run but she can't hide. I don't care where you go — California, anywhere — I'll get to you."

"Now that I have you on the phone," Elliot said, "I'd like to ask you a couple of questions. Promise you won't get mad?"

"Stop it!" Grace said to him. She tried to wrench the phone from his grasp, but he clutched it to his chest.

"Do you keep a journal?" Elliot asked the man on the phone. "What's your hat size?"

"Maybe you think I can't get to you," the man said. "But I can get to you, man. I don't care who you are, I'll get to you. The brothers will get to you."

"Well, there's no need to go to California. You know where we live."

"For God's sake," Grace said.

"Fuckin' right," the man on the telephone said. "Fuckin' right I know."

"Come on over," Elliot said.

"How's that?" the man on the phone asked.

"I said come on over. We'll talk about space travel. Comets and stuff. We'll talk astral projection. The moons of Jupiter."

"You're making a mistake, fucker."

"Come on over," Elliot insisted. "Bring your fat wife and your beat-up kid. Don't be embarrassed if your head's a little small."

The telephone was full of music and shouting. Elliot held it away from his ear.

"Good work," Grace said to him when he had replaced the receiver.

"I hope he comes," Elliot said. "I'll pop him."

He went carefully down the cellar stairs, switched on the overhead light, and began searching among the spiderwebbed shadows and fouled fishing line for his shotgun. It took him fifteen minutes to find it and his cleaning case. While he was still downstairs, he heard the telephone ring again and his wife answer it. He came upstairs and spread his shooting gear across the kitchen table. "Was that him?"

She nodded wearily. "He called back to play us the chain saw."

"I've heard that melody before," Elliot said.

He assembled his cleaning rod and swabbed out the shotgun barrel. Grace watched him, a hand to her forehead. "God," she said. "What have I done? I'm so drunk."

"Most of the time," Elliot said, sighting down the barrel, "I'm helpless in the face of human misery. Tonight I'm ready to reach out."

"I'm finished," Grace said. "I'm through, Chas. I mean it."

Elliot rammed three red shells into the shotgun and pumped one forward into the breech with a satisfying report. "Me, I'm ready for some radical problem solving. I'm going to spray that no-neck Slovak all over the yard."

"He isn't a Slovak," Grace said. She stood in the middle of the kitchen with her eyes closed. Her face was chalk white.

"What do you mean?" Elliot demanded. "Certainly he's a Slovak."

"No he's not," Grace said.

"Fuck him anyway. I don't care what he is. I'll grease his ass." He took a handful of deer shells from the box and stuffed them in his jacket pockets.

"I'm not going to stay with you. Chas. Do you understand me?"

Elliot walked to the window and peered out at his driveway. "He won't be alone. They travel in packs."

"For God's sake!" Grace cried, and in the next instant bolted for the downstairs bathroom. Elliot went out, turned off the porch light and switched on a spotlight over the barn door. Back inside, he could hear Grace in the toilet being sick. He turned off the light in the kitchen.

He was still standing by the window when she came up behind him. It seemed strange and fateful to be standing in the dark near her, holding the shotgun. He felt ready for anything.

"I can't leave you alone down here drunk with a loaded shotgun," she said. "How can I?"

"Go upstairs," he said.

"If I went upstairs it would mean I didn't care what happened. Do you understand? If I go it means I don't care anymore. Understand?"

"Stop asking me if I understand," Elliot said. "I understand fine."

"I can't think," she said in a sick voice. "Maybe I don't care. I don't know. I'm going upstairs."

"Good," Elliot said.

When she was upstairs, Elliot took his shotgun and the whiskey into the dark living room and sat down in an armchair beside one of the lace-curtained windows. The powerful barn light illuminated the length of his driveway and the whole of the back yard. From the window at which he sat, he commanded a view of several miles in the direction of East Ilford. The two-lane blacktop road that ran there was the only one along which an enemy could pass.

He drank and watched the snow, toying with the safety of his 12-gauge Remington. He felt neither anxious nor angry now but only impatient to be done with whatever the night would bring. Drunkenness and the silent rhythm of the falling snow combined to make him feel outside of time and syntax.

Sitting in the dark room, he found himself confronting Blankenship's dream. He saw the bunkers and wire of some long-lost perimeter. The rank smell of night came back to him, the dread evening and quick dusk, the mysteries of outer darkness: fear, combat, and death. Enervated by liquor, he began to cry. Elliot was sympathetic with other people's tears but ashamed of his own. He thought of his own tears as childish and excremental. He stifled whatever it was that had started them.

Now his whiskey tasted thin as water. Beyond the lightly frosted glass, illuminated snowflakes spun and settled sleepily on weighted pine boughs. He had found a life beyond the war after all, but in it he was still sitting in darkness, armed, enraged, waiting.

His eyes grew heavy as the snow came down. He felt as though he could be drawn up into the storm and he began to imagine that. He imagined his life with all its artifacts and appetites easing up the spout into white oblivion, everything obviated and foreclosed. He thought maybe he could go for that.

When he awakened, his left hand had gone numb against the trigger guard of his shotgun. The living room was full of pale, delicate light. He looked outside and saw that the storm was done with and the sky radiant and cloudless. The sun was still below the horizon.

Slowly Elliot got to his feet. The throbbing poison in his limbs served to remind him of the state of things. He finished the glass of whiskey on the windowsill beside his easy chair. Then he went to the hall closet to get a ski jacket, shouldered his shotgun, and went outside.

There were two cleared acres behind his house; beyond them a trail descended into a hollow of pine forest and frozen swamp.

Across the hollow, white pastures stretched to the ridge line, lambent under the lightening sky. A line of skeletal elms weighted with snow marked the course of frozen Shawmut Brook.

He found a pair of ski goggles in a jacket pocket and put them on and set out toward the tree line, gripping the shotgun, step by careful step in the knee-deep snow. Two raucous crows wheeled high overhead, their cries exploding the morning's silence. When the sun came over the ridge, he stood where he was and took in a deep breath. The risen sun warmed his face and he closed his eyes. It was windless and very cold.

Only after he had stood there for a while did he realize how tired he had become. The weight of the gun taxed him. It seemed infinitely wearying to contemplate another single step in the snow. He opened his eyes and closed them again. With sunup the world had gone blazing blue and white, and even with his tinted goggles its whiteness dazzled him and made his head ache. Behind his eyes, the hypnagogic patterns formed a monsoon-heavy tropical sky. He yawned. More than anything, he wanted to lie down in the soft, pure snow. If he could do that, he was certain he could go to sleep at once.

He stood in the middle of the field and listened to the crows. Fear, anger, and sleep were the three primary conditions of life. He had learned that over there. Once he had thought fear the worst, but he had learned that the worst was anger. Nothing could fix it; neither alcohol nor medicine. It was a worm. It left him no peace. Sleep was the best.

He opened his eyes and pushed on until he came to the brow that overlooked the swamp. Just below, gliding along among the frozen cattails and bare scrub maple, was a man on skis. Elliot stopped to watch the man approach.

The skier's face was concealed by a red-and-blue ski mask. He wore snow goggles, a blue jumpsuit, and a red woolen Norwegian hat. As he came, he leaned into the turns of the trail, moving silently and gracefully along. At the foot of the slope on which Elliot stood, the man looked up, saw him, and slid to a halt. The man stood staring at him for a moment and then began to herringbone up the slope. In no time at all the skier stood no more than ten feet away, removing his goggles, and inside the woolen mask Elliot recognized the clear blue eyes of his neighbor, Professor Loyall Anderson. The shotgun Elliot was carrying seemed to grow heavier. He yawned and shook his head, trying unsuccessfully to clear it. The sight of Anderson's eyes gave him a little thrill of revulsion.

"What are you after?" the young professor asked him, nodding toward the shotgun Elliot was cradling.

"Whatever there is," Elliot said.

Anderson took a quick look at the distant pasture behind him and then turned back to Elliot. The mouth hole of the professor's mask filled with teeth. Elliot thought that Anderson's teeth were quite as he had imagined them earlier. "Well, Polonski's cows are locked up," the professor said. "So they at least are safe."

Elliot realized that the professor had made a joke and was smiling. "Yes," he agreed.

Professor Anderson and his wife had been the moving force behind an initiative to outlaw the discharge of firearms within the boundaries of East Ilford Township. The initiative had been defeated, because East Ilford was not that kind of town.

"I think I'll go over by the river," Elliot said. He said it only to have something to say, to fill the silence before Anderson spoke again. He was afraid of what Anderson might say to him and of what might happen.

"You know," Anderson said, "that's all bird sanctuary over there now."

"Sure," Elliot agreed.

Outfitted as he was, the professor attracted Elliot's anger in an elemental manner. The mask made him appear a kind of doll, a kachina figure or a marionette. His eyes and mouth, all on their own, were disagreeable.

Elliott began to wonder if Anderson could smell the whiskey on his breath. He pushed the little red bull's-eye safety button on his gun to Off.

"Seriously," Anderson said, "I'm always having to run hunters out of there. Some people don't understand the word 'posted.' "

"I would never do that," Elliot said, "I would be afraid."

Anderson nodded his head. He seemed to be laughing. "Would you?" he asked Elliot merrily.

In imagination, Elliot rested the tip of his shotgun barrel against Anderson's smiling teeth. If he fired a load of deer shot into them, he thought, they might make a noise like broken china. "Yes," Elliot said. "I wouldn't know who they were or where they'd been. They might resent my being alive. Telling them where they could shoot and where not."

Anderson's teeth remained in place. "That's pretty strange," he said. "I mean, to talk about resenting someone for being alive."

"It's all relative," Elliot said. "They might think, 'Why should he be alive when some brother of mine isn't?' Or they might think, 'Why should he be alive when I'm not?' "

"Oh," Anderson said.

"You see?" Elliot said. Facing Anderson, he took a long step backward. "All relative."

"Yes," Anderson said.

"That's so often true, isn't it?" Elliot asked. "Values are often relative."

"Yes," Anderson said. Elliot was relieved to see that he had stopped smiling.

"I've hardly slept, you know," Elliot told Professor Anderson. "Hardly at all. All night. I've been drinking."

"Oh," Anderson said. He licked his lips in the mouth of the mask. "You should get some rest."

"You're right," Elliot said.

"Well," Anderson said, "got to go now."

Elliot thought he sounded a little thick in the tongue. A little slow in the jaw.

"It's a nice day," Elliot said, wanting now to be agreeable.

"It's great," Anderson said, shuffling on his skis.

"Have a nice day," Elliot said.

"Yes," Anderson said, and pushed off.

Elliot rested the shotgun across his shoulders and watched Anderson withdraw through the frozen swamp. It was in fact a nice day, but Elliot took no comfort in the weather. He missed night and the falling snow.

As he walked back toward his house, he realized that now there would be whole days to get through, running before the antic energy of whiskey. The whiskey would drive him until he dropped. He shook his head in regret. "It's a revolution," he said aloud. He imagined himself talking to his wife.

Getting drunk was an insurrection, a revolution — a bad one. There would be outsize bogus emotions. There would be petty moral blackmail and cheap remorse. He had said dreadful things to his wife. He had bullied Anderson with his violence and unhappiness, and Anderson would not forgive him. There would be damn little justice and no mercy.

Nearly to the house, he was startled by the desperate feathered drumming of a pheasant's rush. He froze, and out of instinct brought the gun up in the direction of the sound. When he saw the bird break from its cover and take wing, he tracked it, took a breath, and fired once. The bird was a little flash of opulent color against the bright-blue sky. Elliot felt himself flying for a moment. The shot missed.

Lowering the gun, he remembered the deer shells he had loaded. A hit with the concentrated shot would have pulverized the bird, and he was glad he had missed. He wished no harm to any creature. Then he thought of himself wishing no harm to any creature and began to feel fond and sorry for himself. As soon as he grew aware of the emotion he was indulging, he suppressed it. Pissing and moaning, mourning and weeping, that was the nature of the drug.

The shot echoed from the distant hills. Smoke hung in the air. He turned and looked behind him and saw, far away across the pasture, the tiny blue-and-red figure of Professor Anderson motionless against the snow. Then Elliot turned again toward his house and took a few labored steps and looked up to see his wife at the bedroom window. She stood perfectly still, and the morning sun lit her nakedness. He stopped where he was. She had heard the shot and run to the window. What had she thought to see? Burnt rags and blood on the snow. How relieved was she now? How disappointed?

Elliot thought he could feel his wife trembling at the window. She was hugging herself. Her hands clasped her shoulders. Elliot took his snow goggles off and shaded his eyes with his hand. He stood in the field staring.

The length of the gun was between them, he thought. Somehow she had got out in front of it, to the wrong side of the wire.

If he looked long enough he would find everything out there. He would find himself down the sight.

How beautiful she is, he thought. The effect was striking. The window was so clear because he had washed it himself, with vinegar. At the best of times he was a difficult, fussy man.

Elliot began to hope for forgiveness. He leaned the shotgun on his forearm and raised his left hand and waved to her. Show a hand, he thought. Please just show a hand.

He was cold, but it had got light. He wanted no more than the gesture. It seemed to him that he could build another day on it. Another day was all you needed. He raised his hand higher and waited.

Contributors' Notes

RICK BASS lives in Yaak, Montana. He is the author of two collections of essays, *The Deer Pasture* and *Wild to the Heart.* A third collection of essays, *Oil Notes,* and a first work of fiction, *The Watch,* are to be published in the winter of 1989.

▪ "This story, written eight years ago, was written straight through without pause or punctuation, and it got me through an especially bad week. I'd had two girlfriends leave me within three days, the rainy season had begun in Jackson (my apartment flooded), and though I had just started my new job, I was already getting a lot of ridicule from fellow employees about some of my work habits.

"Everything I did seemed to upset their values. They did not like me running to work and riding up the elevator with them, sweaty and flushed; they did not appreciate the night classes I took at an all-black college, Jackson State; and they scorned my weightlifting, viewing it as the sign of a tiny brain.

"Whenever they began gossiping about possessions, I would get so upset that, as best I can remember, I would sometimes climb up into the pipeworks that ran though the ceiling space above our offices. I told them I was meditating, that it was what a writer did, though all I was really trying to do was escape.

"It even annoyed them that I was a writer, which they did not view as a particularly useful hobby, and that got me to thinking about how so many of the state's writers had left the state recently — Barry Hannah and Richard Ford to Montana, Gloria Norris to New York, and further back, Walker Percy to Louisiana . . .

"I wrote this story after coming back from an especially macabre "business" lunch, during which Piss-Ant talked incessantly about money and Ole Miss football. This was the only story I ever wrote in the six years that I worked for that company — I was never able again to summon and focus that rage, settling instead for a numbing inertia — but in the one year after I got out of that job I was able to write a novel, two collections of essays, three novellas, and twenty-one short stories, and though Piss-Ant is mostly a compilation of characters, and though the pus has drained and the wound healed, I still try to stay as far away from the people I think of collectively as Piss-Ant as is humanly possible."

Richard Bausch is the author of the novels *Real Presence* (1980), *Take Me Back* (1981), and *The Last Good Time* (1984), and the collection *Spirits and Other Stories* (1987). *Take Me Back* was nominated for the PEN/Faulkner Award in 1982; *Spirits and Other Stories* was nominated for the same award in 1988. He has published stories in *The Atlantic, Ploughshares,* and *New Virginia Review,* and he is a recipient of fellowships in fiction writing from the National Endowment for the Arts and the Guggenheim Foundation. He is currently on the faculty of the writing program at George Mason University in Fairfax, Virginia, where he lives with his wife, Karen, and their four children.

▪ "The seed of 'Police Dreams' came to me after one of a series of nightmares I had during the summer of 1985, the worst of which is almost — but not quite — given in the opening paragraph of the story (the actual nightmare was much worse, and much more horribly detailed). I recognized almost immediately that the dream was an anxiety dream having to do with the fear of losing my family in some way beyond my power to stop it, and of course I began to think about it in terms of a fictional character almost right away, not because I intend such vigilance as a writer but because it is a part of my nature to do so. I imagined *someone else* in a situation to which the dream could apply in some nonrandom way: suppose the dreamer I was beginning to make up really *was* in some danger of losing his family. And while I almost never consciously base my characters on any life models, the gentleness and the good nature of a dear friend, Thomas Philion, to whom the story is dedicated, began to inform my character, and as I have learned to do, I followed the impulse. In any case, from there I began to suppose that my fictional dreamer was perceiving something about his situation that his conscious mind had not recognized yet, and though the dreams he has are violent, or suggest violence, the real threat is something not so simple as violence, nor so clear.

"Having said all this, my memory of writing the story is of trying very hard to solve the problems of tense and time in it, problems of structure, pacing, language, all of which I labored over through many, many drafts — with the thematic stuff as a kind of backdrop to the whole struggle, like a coach shouting instructions."

WILL BLYTHE works as a fiction editor at *Esquire.* He's published fiction and reviews in the quarterlies and in *The New York Times Book Review.* He grew up in Chapel Hill, North Carolina.

▪ "Who knows where these things come from? My fiction used to strike me as suspect because it evolved as such a dubious dance of intention and accident. Real writers, I imagined, pulled out of the driveway at Title and drove their stories straight down the Fiction Interstate through the Old West towns of Exposition, Climax, and Falling Action, all the way to Resolution. They drove fast, one hundred miles an hour, with the windows rolled up tight to keep out the dust of coincidence.

"As best as I remember, 'The Taming Power of the Small' began with an image that came to me of two men watching porno movies in a motel room. It was raining heavily in the original scene but I postponed that until another story. Where the image of the men came from, I don't know. The genealogy of origins is as daunting as those epic lists of ancestors in the Old Testament.

"Some things I am certain of.

"As the painters say these days, I appropriated the title, in this case, from the I-Ching. The I-Ching itself floated into the story because my friend and former neighbor, the writer Jack Heffron, used to consult the I-Ching in the days when I was working on this story. He used to throw pennies down on his shag carpet, draw up the hexagram, and interpret those wonderfully enigmatic lines. The I-Ching apparently counseled patience in regard to a screenplay Jack and I were writing in the spring of '85, which was pretty astute, since we haven't finished yet. Somehow, it seemed right and horrible that this same book of divination figure prominently in the journey of the kidnappers. I understand from studying a few interpretative manuals — sort of Cliffs Notes for I-Ching users — that the kind of use I've made of the oracle is dangerous, an abuse of the Way. I hope these manuals are exaggerating.

"While the arrival of the I-Ching was one of those fortunate accidents that I used to question, it is true that Napperstick and Baron didn't exactly run off with the story the way some writers are always claiming. They may have put the ladder of plot up to the window, so to speak, but I had to carry them up and down the ladder, send them on their elopement, and pay for the whole thing as well. Characters don't have free will. And who knows about their authors?

"Finally, when I wrote this story, I was tired of a certain sweetness and light that seemed to emanate from my stories. I wanted to know, in fiction and through fiction, a little more about darkness and foreboding. 'The Taming Power of the Small' is the result."

RAYMOND CARVER published several books of short stories, including *Where I'm Calling From: New and Selected Stories* (Atlantic Monthly Press, 1988). He also published several volumes of poetry, as well as a collection of stories, poems, and essays called *Fires.* He was recently elected a member of the American Academy and Institute of Arts and Letters. Mr. Carver died in August 1988.

▪ "In early 1987 an editor at E. P. Dutton sent me a copy of the newly published Henri Troyat biography, *Chekhov.* Immediately upon the book's arrival, I put aside what I was doing and started reading. I seem to recall reading the book pretty much straight through, able, at the time, to devote entire afternoons and evenings to it.

"On the third or fourth day, nearing the end of the book, I came to the little passage where Chekhov's doctor — a Badenweiler physician by the name of Dr. Schwöhrer, who attended Chekhov during his last days — is summoned by Olga Knipper Chekhov to the dying writer's bedside in the early morning hours of July 2, 1904. It is clear that Chekhov has only a little while to live. Without any comment on the matter, Troyat tells his readers that this Dr. Schwöhrer ordered up a bottle of champagne. Nobody had asked for champagne, of course; he just took it upon himself to do it. But this little piece of human business struck me as an extraordinary action. Before I really knew what I was going to do with it, or how I was going to proceed, I felt I had been launched into a short story of my own then and there. I wrote a few lines and then a page or two more. How did Dr. Schwöhrer go about ordering champagne and at that late hour at this hotel in Germany? How was it delivered to the room and by whom, etc.? What was the protocol involved when the champagne arrived? Then I stopped and went ahead to finish reading the biography.

"But just as soon as I'd finished the book I once again turned my attention back to Dr. Schwöhrer and that business of the champagne. I was seriously interested in what I was doing. But what *was* I doing? The only thing that was clear to me was that I thought I saw an opportunity to pay homage — if I could bring it off, do it rightly and honorably — to Chekhov, the writer who has meant so much to me for such a long time.

"I tried out ten or twelve openings to the piece, first one beginning and then another, but nothing felt right. Gradually I began to move the story away from those final moments back to the occasion of Chekhov's first public hemorrhage from tuberculosis, something that occurred in a restaurant in Moscow in the company of his friend and publisher, Suvorin. Then came the hospitalization and the scene with Tolstoy, the trip with Olga to Badenweiler, the brief period of time there in the hotel together before the end, the young bellman who makes two important appearances in the Chekhov suite and, at the end, the mortician who, like the bellman, isn't to be found in the biographical account.

"The story was a hard one to write, given the factual basis of the material. I couldn't stray from what had happened, nor did I want to. As much as anything, I needed to figure out how to breathe life into actions that were merely suggested or not given moment in the biographical telling. And, finally, I saw that I needed to set my imagination free and simply invent within the confines of the story. I knew as I was writing this story that it was a good deal different from anything I'd ever done before. I'm pleased, and grateful, that it seems to have come together."

Richard Currey lives with his family in New Mexico. He is the author of a novel, *Fatal Light* (E. P. Dutton/Seymour Lawrence), as well as poems and stories that have appeared widely in literary journals.

▪ "My stories usually begin with a single poetic passage that suggests a world beyond it, a world opening outward from a central image. In the case of 'Waiting for Trains,' it is the narrator and his brother, two boys in summer, swimming in a river under a train trestle. That scene seemed haunted to me, both placid and troubled, weighted with its own secrets. From this image the story grew and found its shape. The discovery of a central image is, for me, very much a musical development, and I'm reminded of what the extraordinary musician Van Morrison once said about the process of composition: 'You get this thing coming through — it comes through in different spaces and times — and you don't really know what it is . . . you're receptive to it, you channel it, and you write it down.' "

Louise Erdrich's most recent book, *Tracks,* was published by Henry Holt.

▪ " 'Snares' was written in an effort to explain, in a much later story, the origin of a feud in which the baldness of women was a source of shame and a motive for revenge. About halfway through the story, I got stuck and took a long walk with my husband, Michael Dorris. He had just read a draft of the story and, in an inspired moment, suggested that instead of the piece of cloth I'd used, Margaret's braids be used to tie Nanapush's tongue back and ensure his silence. From then on, imagining the taste of hair in the old man's mouth, the story became for me one of sexuality and vengeance. My mother used to help my grandfather check snares, and set them herself, up on the Turtle Mountain reservation. But they only caught rabbits, never people."

MAVIS GALLANT's most recent book is *Paris Notebooks: Essays and Reviews.*
▪ "All that I can remember is a persistent image of Dédé, outside in the garden of the Paris house, looking in through the French windows to the family in the dining room. I know that there was much more concerning him, some of it taking place in an apartment near Parc Montsouris; but in the end all that seemed to matter was that other house and a fourteen-year-old boy's memory of events."

C. S. GODSHALK has worked as a free-lance journalist. She has lived in Southeast Asia, and is currently working on a novel on Borneo. She is the author of *Anna,* a memoir for the New York State Historical Association.
▪ " 'Wonderland' began with a picture of Paulie sleeping. I 'saw' that skinny child's body in the moonlight, and the immensity of the problem crammed into his skull. The picture was of such clarity that I knew all I had to do was watch him. When my 'head' intervened, momentarily blocking my view, and I wrote something Paulie didn't do, he said, 'I didn't do that.'

"The problem with stories you just have to 'watch' is that while you know what you're seeing, you don't always put all of it on paper. You assume the reader is 'watching' too, and he isn't. He's reading. Dan Menaker at *The New Yorker* helped me with this in the first draft. He said that the character of Peg was not 'specified' enough. This surprised me. I knew her but I did not 'put it down.' It turned out, luckily, that I could do her justice by adding only two sentences. If it had been necessary to do more, it would have seemed too much like major surgery, and I probably would have chucked the story.

"The most difficult part of writing 'Wonderland' was the last paragraph, because two totally new characters suddenly entered my field of vision and would not go away. They were not there casually either; they were there to finish the story. I wrote them in, but my head said, 'This is wrong; this does not flow naturally from what came before. It's an appendage, a third arm.' I took them out. The next morning, I tore down to the room where I write and put them back and felt suddenly on an even keel with the universe."

E. S. GOLDMAN is a full-time writer living in South Orleans on Cape Cod. "Way to the Dump" is his first published story. His first novel, *Big Chocolate Cookies,* will be published in the fall of 1988.

▪ "Essentially, like most writers I sit at the keyboard asking 'What's next?' and the answers come from experience and vocabulary. In that sense, 'Way to the Dump' came to be written sentence by sentence, triggered by what had just been said. Once Elligott thought about Zuerner, the rest was a credible succession: a cup of coffee, the scenery, the people, the events, the options, the motives, the sensations.

"Why that story and not another? Why Elligott and Zuerner? Why the theft?

"I can't honestly say. They are not people I have known and translated deliberately into fiction, and no anecdote I know accounts for the story line. It absolutely is not necessary to have been shot or stolen shrubbery or worked with Elligott or Zuerner or married Daisy to answer the question 'What's next?'

"I can share hints (all I have) of why the story happened:

"All my adult life I have been sensitive to the way people surrender their autonomy in exchange for security, flattery, money — yes, for love — fame, social acceptance; in fear, in need, in mere psychological inclination to be subordinate. I have written other stories on this theme.

"I know also that many years ago my house burned down. Returning to the scene the next morning, I noticed that someone had yanked a rose bush out of the garden. No doubt the rose was now in my neighbor's garden. Which neighbor?

"Finally, the newspapers were full of stories about business takeovers. Usually I wake in the morning with a lingering writing problem solved or a new story idea. That's how the machine works. Perhaps the takeover nerve jogged the autonomy nerve as I slept. Once Elligott got on the road, the theft of a plant recommended itself as a credible answer to 'What's next?'

"There remained to go through the text to see if earlier clues were sufficient for later consequences, to judge if the pace had faltered (remediably), and to see if moments could be more effectively realized. Cleaning up and revising are really 'how' stories come to be written and account for most of the fifteen hundred or so hours of a writing year.

"Conrad might have said all this differently: 'I was sitting at a table in a saloon with Marlow and he told me a story . . .' "

Lucy Honig's first novel, *Picking Up,* was published in 1986 by Dog Ear Press. Her short stories have appeared in magazines such as *The Agni Review, Antaeus, Fiction,* and *Confrontation.* She teaches English to immigrants in New York City.

▪ " 'No Friends, All Strangers' was one of those very rare stories that told itself, nearly whole, on the first try. I wrote it over a period of a few summer weeks in a stifling attic apartment in Flatbush. It seems now to have been a way of making the most of claustrophobia.

"After ten years living in quiet parts of Maine, I'd moved to the tumult of New York. I took the D train from Brooklyn to jobs in Manhattan and the train got stuck all the time. You got stuck more on the lines like this one that went through very poor neighborhoods. The crowding, the breakdowns, the unexplained delays, epitomized for me the punishment New York metes out to those who don't partake in its prosperity or glitz. It seemed a nasty achievement of the civilized world that so many of us spent so much of our lives stuck in dirty metal containers underground.

"But on the D through north Flatbush there was not only hassle: there was spirit. Now, I am not a spiritual person. Spirit has to hit me over the head before I'll notice, and spirit doesn't usually go around hitting. But on this particular train I couldn't help but see: people opened up to one another rather than closing down. Instead of retreating into their Walkmans or their dope, they talked to each other, made room for each other's neuroses, gave seats to each other's tired bones. Different people, every day. And so what could have been the most alienating experience came, little by little, to be the most affirming.

"Many things, many people in the story did exist, like the faces and fingernails on the subway. And the guy who cuts my hair *is* a snazzy dresser; he likes his rock-and-roll. But the combination and sequence of details, the characters, the story itself, were originated and driven by the narrator's voice, which simply started talking to me. I listened to that voice and wrote its story."

Gish Jen lives in Cambridge, Massachusetts. Recent support for her labors has come from the James Michener/Copernicus Society, the Bunting Institute, the Massachusetts Artists' Foundation, the National Endowment for the Arts, and the Massachusetts Bay Transportation Authority. Her work has appeared in assorted magazines, and in *The New Generation,* an anthology.

▪ "As in my story, a zealous Christian couple once really did sublet my apartment for the summer, and they indeed did leave a list of their prayer goals tacked to the back of the broom closet door. I was amazed and a little embarrassed to find it — the most un-Fundamental of undies couldn't have been more revealing — and of course should certainly have put it away immediately. Instead, every inch a grad student, I left it up for my friends to shake their heads at. Straight out of Flannery O'Connor, we agreed. *Wise Blood,* we wisecracked.

"Unfortunately, that same zealous couple also left behind a silver-plated cake server, which they one day returned for, unannounced. I don't know what they made of the fact that the list was still up, but they took it down without asking me about it, quietly. Openly, it was as though the apartment were somehow still theirs; or as if, through some strange time shrink, we had for a moment become roommates.

"They stayed with me, this couple, for several years.

"Meanwhile, I moved from Iowa to California, from California to Boston, leaving behind cake servers and so much else I hardly knew what I missed. My husband and I bought a fixer-upper in which to set down our boxes, then fixed it up. Spackle, mastic, caulk. We fished wires, sanded floors, laid tile, stripped wallpaper. Every week we put out more garbage than the rest of the street combined; the garbage men joked about us. We began to feel somewhat at home. We were at home making trips to the lumber yard, that is — so much so that by the time it came to me that I hadn't written anything in a very long while, I understood it was because my calling in life had to do with trowels.

"A manifest truth. Still, in the cold spring of 1985, I went to the MacDowell Colony to try my hands at a typewriter. In vain and out of vanity, I thought. A middle-aged man's voice whispered from the rafters of my cabin: Nothing is so ordinary as to wish to be extraordinary. Was that why I cared to write? He answered me yes, sometimes in pig Latin. I tried anyway. That couple. That list. It seemed to me they had something to do with a rubber address stamp I'd owned as a child. Once I'd been moved to tell a writing teacher how I'd lost this address stamp down the sewer. 'Vision,' I'd babbled. 'Water faucets.' She had nodded. 'You should write that down.' Now I wrote it down. Although I knew my teacher to be very smart, on the page her idea looked stupid. I thought. Somewhere I had read something to the effect that Updike at times simply stared at unrelated things until they became related. Wasn't that like what I was trying to do? I stared myself cross-eyed, trying to turn a vision involving water faucets and a list I was going to have to make up into an Updike story. This desperate foolishness, to my profound surprise, brought me several pages. Where, though, was the story? Something had to happen.

"Nothing happened.

"I believe that it was out of pure frustration that the father finally threw the mother of the story out the window, and it was a good thing he did, because if something is going to go out a window — and by then, something was bound to — it is best that it be a character. Also it was good because once I heard that burst of glass, I got interested: He threw her out the window? I was shocked. And then what? Did that poor mother die? I wrote on to find out, then wrote some more, and some more; and then suddenly — after so long, too long — I was there again, by the hot hearth of a story.

"Today I'd try many things differently in the piece; often I think of it as one in which I go out on a limb and more or less fall off. Still, though, I have to say: this story saved me. I imagine that without it I would be forever wandering the mazy aisles of some building supply house, looking for something I need; instead, worn out and bewildered, I was, by a miracle, shown a way home."

HILDING JOHNSON has recently finished a collection of short stories and begun work on a novel. She writes, and lives, in Chicago.

▪ "Most of my work is set geographically in northern Minnesota. I write about Swedes and Finns and Frenchmen and, often, the Chippewa. When I had completed this story a friend asked if it was 'another Indian story,' and, startled, I had to say that it was — although of another sort altogether.

"I think now that the plush heat and ripeness of India was simply a little vacation I concocted for myself, a getaway from the snow and ice of my everyday literary turf. For this India is wholly imagined, an India gleefully composed of remembered bits of Kipling, of Halliburton's *Book of Marvels,* and of a thousand missionary slides cast up, bright as day, on the walls of my church's basement.

"It's a nice prerogative we writers enjoy: if we can't find a nice, juicy piece of escapist literature when we want to read it, we write it. May I say that is every bit as much fun as it would seem to be?"

BRIAN KITELEY grew up in Northampton, Massachusetts, and now lives in Cairo, Egypt. He was educated at Carleton College in southern Minnesota and at City College of New York. "Still Life with Insects" is from a collection of linked stories, almost a novel, of the same name. It is his first published fiction.

▪ "I was moving from Seattle to New York in 1982 with a rest stop at my grandparents' in Montreal. My grandfather had a lifelong hobby of collecting beetles, and his locality notebook lay on the workbench by the bed I tried to sleep in on my first night back on the East Coast. I stole four entries from this locality notebook, writing them down in my own journal. They described where he caught batches of beetles and when, with the barest of relevant background information. Nine months later, in a girlfriend's depressing Murray Hill kitchen (bathtub at my elbow), I saw these entries and decided to do an exercise with them. That exercise grew into a very short story, which continued to grow, often without my consent, into something much longer. The entries from this locality notebook reminded me so strongly of my grandfather's tone of voice I had no trouble stepping into his perspective. The laconic description of each place triggered a strong central image, which the scene seemed to freeze around. When I look back on these pieces now, what I still enjoy about them is that they are simply finger exercises, writing without knowing that it is writing."

ROBERT LACY is a native of East Texas who now lives in Medicine Lake, Minnesota, a suburb of Minneapolis. He received a Loft-McKnight Fiction Fellowship in Minnesota in 1984, and in 1985 was a winner of the first Midwest Voices fiction competition, sponsored by Poets and Writers Inc. His stories have appeared in *The Saturday Evening Post, Northern Lit Quarterly, Crazyhorse, Crescent Review,* and elsewhere.

▪ "I began the story about six years ago, and I remember that I had to take it through several drafts before coming up with anything I could even use. In the beginning the story was called 'Navy Relief,' and the whole thing took place in the Navy Relief office over at Camp Hauge, where the company commander has sent the young Marine, Butters, to take out his loan. In the final version all of that has been reduced to a single paragraph of summary narration toward the end. My biggest problem in writing 'The Natural Father' was in coming to like Butters a little bit, or at least in coming to have a little sympathy for him. For a long time I simply wanted to beat up on him, much as all the other 'adults' in the story do."

RALPH LOMBREGLIA has held writing fellowships from Stanford University, the New York Foundation for the Arts, and the National Endowment for the Arts. His story "Men Under Water," also originally published in *The Atlantic,* was included in *The Best American Short Stories 1987*. He lives in Cambridge, Massachusetts, where, having recently completed a first novel, he is finishing a collection of short stories.

▪ "The 'real-life' circumstance that became the seed of 'Inn Essence' — my employment at a restaurant where some members of the staff happened to be college students from Thailand — occurred twenty-one years before I wrote the story. I had just finished the ninth grade, and this was my first summer job. The actual establishment wasn't owned by a Greek philosopher-restaurateur; it was owned by my father's brother. And my job wasn't salad chef and confidant; it was dishwasher — minimum wage, one free meal per day. I labored enveloped in steam — pushing dirty dishes into one end of a large machine, pulling racks of clean ones from the other — while chefs screamed that they had no plates, waitresses screamed that they had no silverware, and my uncle screamed that he could scarcely believe I was his nephew, so tiny was my capacity for honest hard work.

"By itself, what 'really happened' had scant dramatic interest, and I had to bombard it for months with the cosmic rays of imagination before it turned into acceptable fiction. In real life there was no volatile pastry chef, no invisible wife (my dear aunt worked long hours in the restaurant herself), no cabin cruiser named after her, no abandoned railroad tracks. And there were certainly no visits from Immigration — because, of course, the real Thai students were perfectly legal. They *did* live behind the restaurant (without that, I never would have written the story), in a depressing bungalow on an adjacent lot. They couldn't have lived in a 'carriage house' because the real restaurant was never a Colonial inn; when my uncle bought it, it was a glorified hot dog stand on a state highway. He expanded it several times and made it a popular family place; it wasn't called Inn Essence, but that particular morsel I didn't invent — my father thought up the name Inn Essence, and I borrowed it from him.

"So, all right; what happens in the story never happened in life. But what about the other way around? Were there any good bits from life that didn't make it into the story? Many more than I can tell. But among them: my first trip into New York's Chinatown with the real-life Kampy (yes, he had a red Mustang), where, in a much different sort of restaurant and at his insistence, I ate my first chicken foot. My uncle at the big kitchen range stirring his impeccable tomato sauce, seeing me emerge from the dishwasher steam and screaming that he better not ever catch me trying to make something taste 'Italian' by pouring dried oregano into it. And the Thai students' rock 'n' roll band; they had one, I wish I could remember its name, and one day while they were practicing in their little house they taught me to play a staple of their repertoire — '96 Tears' by Question Mark and the Mysterians, still one of the only things I can pick out on the piano."

EDITH MILTON was born in Germany, grew up in England during the Second World War, and came to the United States in 1946. Her story "Coming Over" was collected in *The Best American Short Stories 1982*. In addition to her short fiction, she has written a novel, *Corridors*, and is working on another. She and her husband, an artist, live in New Hampshire.

▪ "I dislike being criticized, so when it comes to fiction I am not very inventive. I run into crises of confidence over trivia: can my hero get from Nairobi to Fez without changing planes? If he decides on a side trip to Algiers will he need a visa? In which case, where does he go to get one? Such considerations can leave one close to paralysis, and drain away the main resource of the fiction writer, a delight in his own fantasy.

"In the past this has kept me tied to a monogamous union with autobiographical fiction, from which I strayed only rarely for wild, desperate, and quite unsuccessful dalliances with total fantasy. Either mode is safely immune from disapproval, but over the years I got more and more tired of both of them, and the sequence of stories of which 'Entrechat' is one is my attempt to escape. When I began it, I had been living in New Hampshire more than fifteen years, long enough to get my characters from Keene to Concord without losing them. I am familiar and comfortable with the landscape and customs that are important elements in these stories and form the background for all of them. I am not likely to make a mistake.

"Still, I am uncomfortable inventing lives I have not lived myself, condemning the unborn to a Dantean eternity of reliving those sins I have imposed on them.

"In 'Entrechat,' the sin is envy. The story started with that. And it evolved around its narrator's painful ambivalence in the face of her unhappy stepsister's charm and vulnerability, and her struggle to distinguish helplessness from deviousness. In earlier versions, the story threatened to be much longer, a novella or even a short novel, and sibling jealousy was a much more explicit theme, involving, among other things, rivalry for the approval and loyalty of John, who has by now become a minor character. In the later drafts, I also deleted the original glimpses of the narrator's romantic yearnings, which, being unacknowledged and unconventional, made the story a bit too Jacobean to control in its present form.

"Now, rereading it, I wonder if it could be extended to something messier, more complicated and more sinister again. And I ask myself — should my narrator really be trusted, after all, to give up the final word?"

MARJORIE SANDOR's stories have appeared in *The Georgia Review, Antaeus, The Yale Review,* and other publications, and in *The Best American Short Stories 1985* and *Twenty Under Thirty.* She teaches creative writing at the University of Florida in Gainesville, and is at work on a novel.

▪ " 'Still Life' got its start twelve years ago when, with terrible earnestness, I set out to write on that classic college freshman theme: A Significant Person in My Life. Having chosen as my subject an aunt who had died the summer before, I proceeded to torture her memory with draft after lugubrious draft, suffocating her with adjectives, adverbs, metaphors, and anything else I could find lying around. When I showed these drafts to my teacher, she sighed. 'Just tell me what happened.'

"Her advice lasted far beyond the terse, exhausted little piece I produced for her, as did my nagging desire to 'get it right.' Over the next decade I made little approaches, and tried on titles like lovely dresses I knew I couldn't afford. And after a while, I forgot all about it.

"Forgot, until a dark January dawn in Boston, when I got on the train to go to work. The subway route from Sullivan Station traverses a desolate landscape, a place of tangled freeway interchanges and a huge sign that reads ACCIDENTS HAVE NO HOLIDAYS, and where, when it's dark outside, the train windows reflect the passengers' images back to themselves. As I stood facing my own figure in its black coat and gloves, I felt, for an instant, a sense of romance in my situation, and a line popped into my head: 'Those moments we think are inconsequential, when we grip a tram pole . . . ' Inexplicably, this line dragged with it the thought that my aunt, when she was my age, must have ridden a trolley into Chicago at dawn, perhaps wearing a black coat herself as a young woman going to work in a city office. This thought was followed by images, one after the other, of the photographs of her that I'd thumbed through as a child, in which the bright, overexposed edges of the frame were much more mysterious than the figures huddled together within them.

"In the drafts written at the office those winter mornings (under the title 'Nature Morte,' which I could not pronounce), only one image from the freshman essay remained: the brilliant summer light over the Pacific on the day my aunt died."

ROBERT STONE, whose most recent novel is *Children of Light,* is the recipient of many awards for his fiction, among them the Houghton Mifflin Literary Fellowship, the National Book Award, the Faulkner Award, the *Los Angeles Times* Book Award, and the Mildred and Harold Strauss Living Award from the National Academy and Institute of Arts and Letters. An earlier short story, "Porque No Tiene, Porque Le Falta," was collected in *The Best American Short Stories 1970,* and his recent essay on cocaine appeared in *The Best American Essays 1987.*

▪ " 'Helping' is about the ways in which people need each other. The question at its center is whether we actually can come through for others when, in a disorderly world, it's sometimes hard for us to see clearly enough to help ourselves. It also addresses the question of whether love is something powerful enough to bridge the gulf that separates one human being from another."

MARY ANN TAYLOR-HALL is a recipient of a National Education Association Fellowship and is the author of a novel, *Places for Dancing.* Her recent work has appeared in *The Kenyon Review, The Paris Review,* and the PEN/Syndicated Fiction Project. She is married to the writer and photographer James Baker Hall and lives on a farm at the northern edge of the Bluegrass Plateau.

▪ "This story came out of grief, as I suppose many stories do. Of course it couldn't stay there. As in life, life takes over, hauls you back to its rambunctious territory. In 1983, I recorded a tiny idea in the margin of a notebook: a woman declines to be saved by her evangelical son. That must have been the seed of this story; at least it's the first note I can find that seems to pertain to it. I'm surprised — I'd thought that exchange between Rosa and her son was an afterthought. Once I took up the burden, the old 'Why?' of that idea, I must already have been in deep. At about the same time — I don't know which came first — a stunned voice was coming to me from time to time, wanting me to write down its story. I forced myself to do it; I yawned the whole time — terror masquerading as boredom. It was all summary. I think I put it away for several months and when I next looked at it, a modest image arose, one with reverberations for me — hands moving through dishwater. Rosa watching her hands moving through dishwater. So the move into her mind began. It wasn't easy. I got her voice wrong. Anger stopped this story's movement, nearly wrecked it. Rosa's anger, and my own, I fear. We had to change our attitude. A partisan can only tell part of a story.

"I worked on this story off and on for a few years. It was a long time before the true, clear action of it occurred to me, and it did so by the usual blind, unreconstructible fumbling and groping. The ending eluded me, as everything else had. A friend suggested I try to see more clearly what Rosa sees when she looks from the hotel window down on the square in Brazil. I thought up the white pony first, then its owner. Later, the little girl appeared; I needed her. The ponykeeper began to swing her around. Then, finally, the next time I had a go at it, the woman came striding along the street with her loaf of bread. I let her stay, out of politeness. One night I lay down with a little too much liquor in me, and the room swung around. The next day I made the connection between the little girl being swung around and Rosa's dizziness. At first this seemed a purely mechanical solution to a complicated problem. I wrote the last sentence over and over. When I wrote it the way it is now I felt, for the first time in the long process of writing this story, good. Thrilled. 'Screaming with joy' was the gift I got; it encompassed both the grief I started with, and the way out of it. I say that phrase to myself often. It means something to me."

Tobias Wolff is the author of a novel, *The Barracks Thief*, and two collections of short stories, *In the Garden of the North American Martyrs* and *Back in the World.* A new book, *This Boy's Life,* will appear in January 1989.

▪ "This story wanted to be written for years before I gave in and wrote it. Part memory, part invention, I can no longer tell where one ends and the other begins. The very act of writing has transformed the original experience into another experience, more 'real' to me than what I started with."

100 Other Distinguished Short Stories of the Year 1987

Selected by Shannon Ravenel

Abbott, Lee K.
Once upon a Time. *The Georgia Review,* Summer.
Revolutionaries. *The Atlantic,* February.
Akins, Ellen
George Bailey Fishing. *Southwest Review,* Winter.
Alvarez, Julia
The Kiss. *The Greensboro Review,* Summer.

Bamber, Linda
The Time-to-Teach-Jane-Eyre-Again Blues. *Ploughshares,* Vol. 13, Nos. 2 & 3.
Barclay, Byrna
Speak Under Covers. *Event: Douglas College Review,* Vol. 16, No. 1.
Barthelme, Donald
January. *The New Yorker,* April 6.
Barthelme, Frederick
Cooker. *The New Yorker,* August 10.
Restraint. *Playboy,* July.
Bass, Rick
Where the Sea Used to Be. *The Paris Review,* No. 102.
Bausch, Richard
The Man Who Knew Belle Starr. *The Atlantic,* April.
Baxter, Charles
Prowlers. *Grand Street,* Winter.
Bell, Madison Smartt
I've Got a Secret. *The Greensboro Review,* Summer.
Bookman, Marc
My Library. *Stories,* No. 17.
Bovey, John
The Calculus. *The Literary Review,* Summer.
Bowles, Paul
In Absentia. *Antaeus,* Spring.
Brown, Larry
Facing the Music. *Mississippi Review,* Fall/Winter.

Cameron, Lindsley
Conversation with Satellites. *Christopher Street,* No. 113.
Canin, Ethan
The Year of Getting to Know Us. *The Atlantic,* March.
Carlson, Ron
Bachelors. *Fiction Network,* Spring/Summer.
Connelly, John
Foreign Objects. *West Branch,* No. 20.
Coover, Robert
Intermission. *Playboy,* February.

DIXON, STEPHEN
Frog Wants Out. *Other Voices,* Fall.
DRISCOLL, JACK
Wanting Only to Be Heard. *The Georgia Review,* Winter.
DUBUS, ANDRE
They Now Live in Texas. *Indiana Review,* Vol. 10, Nos. 1 & 2.
DURBAN, PAM
Belonging. *Indiana Review,* Vol. 10, Nos. 1 & 2.

EISENBERG, DEBORAH
Presents. *The New Yorker,* July 20.

FRANKS, CLAUDIA STILLMAN
Nets. *Zyzzyva,* Fall.
FREEMAN, JUDITH
Family Attractions. *Zyzzyva,* Winter.

GALLANT, MAVIS
Déclassé. *Mademoiselle,* February.
GARDINER, JOHN ROLFE
Game Farm. *The New Yorker,* September 21.
GILDNER, GARY
A Million-Dollar Story. *Western Humanities Review,* Winter.

HALL, DONALD
Argument and Persuasion. *Antaeus,* Spring.
HALL, JIM
Gas. *The Georgia Review,* Summer.
HANLEY, LYNNE
War Stories. *The Massachusetts Review,* Spring.
HAVAZELET, ENUD
The Only Thing You've Got. *The Missouri Review,* Vol. 10, No. 1.
HAVEMANN, ERNST
A Farm at Raraba. *The Atlantic,* January.
HEMPEL, AMY
The Most Girl Part of You. *Vanity Fair,* February.
Rapture of the Deep. *Grand Street,* Spring.
HILL, KATHLEEN
Flood. *The Hudson Review,* Spring.
HOLMES, CHARLOTTE
Metropolitan. *Grand Street,* Summer.
HUDDLE, DAVID
The Gorge. *Denver Quarterly,* Spring.

JONES, BARBARA
Help. *Grand Street,* Autumn.

KAPLAN, DAVID MICHAEL
In the Realm of the Herons. *Crazyhorse,* Spring.
KINCAID, NANCI
Like the Old Wolf in All Those Wolf Stories. *St. Andrews Review,* Spring/Summer.
KINGSOLVER, BARBARA
Rose-Johnny. *The Virginia Quarterly Review,* Winter.
KIRK, KATHLEEN
Impatiens. *Balcones,* Summer.
KRIST, GARY
Ty and Janet. *The Hudson Review,* Winter.

LANDERS, JONATHAN
Nighthawks. *Mississippi Review,* Fall/Winter.
LEFER, DIANE
Quicksand. *The Agni Review,* No. 24/25.
LE GUIN, URSULA
Half Past Four. *The New Yorker,* September 28.
The Ship Ahoy. *The New Yorker,* November 2.
LEITER, SHARON
The Dog. *Descant,* Vol. 29, No. 2.
LEWIS, TRUDY
Half Measures. *Carolina Quarterly,* Spring.
L'HEUREUX, JOHN
Flight. *The Threepenny Review,* Winter.

LIU, M. E.
Enlisting. *Commentary,* July.
LORDAN, BETH
The Widow. *The Atlantic,* August.

MCCAFFERTY, JANET
The Shadders Go Away. *The New England Review/Bread Loaf Quarterly,* Spring.
MCCORKLE, JILL
First Union Blues. *Southern Magazine,* July.
MARTONE, MICHAEL
Parting. *Denver Quarterly,* Spring.
MARVIN, CHARLES
Island of Swine. *Mississippi Review,* Spring/Summer.
MATTISON, ALICE
Bears. *The New Yorker,* March 16.
MAZZA, CHRIS
The Cram-It-In Method. *Mid-America Review,* Vol. 7, No. 1.
MEINKE, PETER
The Deer. *Yankee,* June.
Horses. *New Letters,* Spring.
MILLHAUSER, STEVEN
The Barnum Museum. *Grand Street,* Summer.
MUNRO, ALICE
Oh, What Avails. *The New Yorker,* November 16.

NELSON, ANTONYA
Maggie's Baby. *Playgirl,* November.

OATES, JOYCE CAROL
Sundays in Summer. *Michigan Quarterly Review,* Winter.
Twins. *The Ohio Review,* No. 39.
O'BRIEN, TIM
How to Tell a True War Story. *Esquire,* October.

PENNER, JONATHAN
Rapture. *Grand Street,* Spring.
Smoke. *The Paris Review,* No. 102.
PETERSON, PAULA
I Get an Excuse for Gym. *Carolina Quarterly,* Winter.
PRITCHARD, MELISSA
A Dance with Alison. *The Southern Review,* Autumn.

RAMBACH, PEGGY
Three Summer Houses. *The Indiana Review,* Winter.
RICHARD, MARK
Happiness of the Garden Variety. *Shenandoah,* Vol. 37, No. 2.
The Ice at the Bottom of the World. *The Quarterly,* Winter.
ROBISON, MARY
Seizing Control. *The New Yorker,* May 25.
ROGERS, SUNNY
The Crumb. *The Quarterly,* Fall.
ROSS, JEAN
The Sky Fading Upward to Yellow: A Footnote to Literary History. *Shenandoah,* Vol. 37, No. 2.
RYSSTAD, JEAN
Contiguous. *The University of Windsor Review,* Spring/Summer.

SANFORD, ANNETTE
Limited Access. *The Ohio Review,* No. 38.
SAYLES, JOHN
The Half-way Diner. *The Atlantic,* June.
SCHUMACHER, JULIE
Conversations with Killer. *Four Quarters,* Fall.
SCHWARTZ, LYNNE SHARON
What I Did for Love. *Prairie Schooner,* Summer.
SHAPIRO, JANE
Volpone. *The New Yorker,* November 30.
SHELNUTT, EVE
Voice. *The Chariton Review,* Spring.
SMILEY, JANE
Long Distance. *The Atlantic,* January.

SMITH, PETER J.
Life of Beethoven. *The Hudson Review*, Summer.
STEVENS, EVELYN
The Concession Lady. *Ascent*, Vol. 12, No. 3.
STUART, FLOYD C.
This Is a Delta. *The Georgia Review*, Fall.
SVENDSON, LINDA
Boxing Day. *Northwest Review*, Vol. 25, No 2.

THON, MELANIE RAE
Girls in the Grass. *CutBank*, No. 27/28.

UPDIKE, JOHN
Brother Grasshopper. *The New Yorker*, December 14.

WALLACE, DAVID FOSTER
Here and There. *Fiction*, Vol. 8, Nos. 1 & 2.
WILCOX, BARTON
Ferguson's Wagon. *The Missouri Review*, Vol. 10. No. 2.
WILLIAMS, JOY
Rot. *Grand Street*, Summer.

YOUNGDAHL, KARIE
The Cutting Line. *Fiction*, Vol. 8, Nos. 1 & 2.
YOURGRAU, BARRY
Safari. *The Missouri Review*, Vol. 10, No. 1.

Editorial Addresses of American and Canadian Magazines Publishing Short Stories

When available, the annual subscription rate, the average number of stories published per year, and the name of the editor follow the address.

Agni Review
Creative Writing Department
Boston University
236 Bay State Road
Boston, MA 02115
$10, 15, Askold Melnyczuk

Alfred Hitchcock's Mystery Magazine
Davis Publications
380 Lexington Avenue
New York, NY 10017
$19.50, 130, Cathleen Jordan

Ambergris
P.O. Box 29919
Cincinnati, OH 45229
$4, 4, Mark Kissling

Amelia
329 East Street
Bakersfield, CA 93304
$20, 10, Frederick A. Raborg, Jr.

Analog Science Fiction/Science Fact
380 Lexington Avenue
New York, NY 10017
$19.50, 70, Stanley Schmidt

Antaeus
26 West 17th Street
New York, NY 10011
$20, 15, Daniel Halpern

Antioch Review
P.O. Box 148
Yellow Springs, OH 45387
$18, 20, Robert S. Fogarty

Apalachee Quarterly
P.O. Box 20106
Tallahassee, FL 32304
$12, 10, Allen Woodman, Barbara Hanby, Monica Faeth

Arizona Quarterly
University of Arizona
Tucson, AZ 85721
$5, 12, Albert F. Gegenheimer

Ascent
English Department
University of Illinois
608 South Wright Street
Urbana, IL 61801
$3, 20, Daniel Curley

The Atlantic
8 Arlington Street
Boston, MA 02116
$9.95, 25, C. Michael Curtis

Aura Literary/Arts Review
P.O. Box University Center
University of Alabama
Birmingham, AL 35294
$6, 10, rotating editorship

Balcones
P.O. Box 50247
Austin, TX 78763
$14, 6, Lantz Miller

The Bellowing Ark
P.O. Box 45637
Seattle, WA 98145
$12, 5, Robert R. Ward

Beloit Fiction Journal
P.O. Box 11, Beloit College
Beloit, WI 53511
$9, 10, Clint McCown

Black Ice
6022 Sunnyview Road NE
Salem, OR 97305
20, Dale Shank

Black Warrior Review
P.O. Box 2936
Tuscaloosa, AL 35487-2936
$9, 12, Janet McAdams

Boston Review
33 Harrison Avenue
Boston, MA 02111
$9, 6, Margaret Ann Roth

California Quarterly
100 Sproul Hall
University of California
Davis, CA 95616
$10, 4, Elliott L. Gilbert

Calyx
P.O. Box B
Corvallis, OR 97339
$18, 2, Margarita Donnelly

Canadian Fiction
Box 946
Station F
Toronto, Ontario
M4Y 2N9 Canada
$30, 16, Geoffrey Hancock

Capilano Review
Capilano College
2055 Purcell Way
North Vancouver
British Columbia
V7J 3H5 Canada
$12, 5, Crystal Hurdle

Carolina Quarterly
Greenlaw Hall 066A
University of North Carolina
Chapel Hill, NC 27514
$10, 20, rotating editorship

Chariton Review
Division of Language & Literature
Northeast Missouri State University
Kirksville, MO 63501
$4, 10, Jim Barnes

Chattahoochee Review
DeKalb Community College
2101 Womack Road
Dunwoody, GA 30338
$12.50, 25, Lamar York

Chelsea
P.O. Box 5880
Grand Central Station
New York, NY 10163
$9, 6, Sonia Raiziss

Chicago Review
5801 South Kenwood
University of Chicago
Chicago, IL 60637
$18, 20, Robert Sitko

Christopher Street
P.O. Box 1475
Church Street Station
New York, NY 10008
$27, 20, Charles Ortleb

Cimarron Review
208 Life Sciences East
Oklahoma State University
Stillwater, OK 74078-0237
$10, 15, Mary Rohberger

Colorado Review
360 Eddy Building
Colorado State University
Fort Collins, CO 80523
$5, 10, Steven Schwartz

Commentary
165 East 56th Street
New York, NY 10022
$33, 5, Norman Podhoretz

Concho River Review
English Department
Angelo State University
San Angelo, TX 76909
$14, 7, Terrence A. Dalrymple

Confrontation
English Department
C.W. Post College of Long Island University
Greenvale, NY 11548
$8, 25, Martin Tucker

Cotton Boll/Atlanta Review
P.O. Box 76757
Sandy Springs
Atlanta, GA 30358-0703
$10, 12, Mary Hollingsworth

Crazyhorse
Department of English
University of Arkansas
Little Rock, AR 72204
$8, 10, David Jauss

Crescent Review
P.O. Box 15065
Winston-Salem, NC 27113
$7.50, 24, Bob Shar

Crosscurrents
2200 Glastonbury Road
Westlake Village, CA 91361
$15, 36, Linda Brown Michelson

CutBank
Department of English
University of Montana
Missoula, MT 59812
$9, 10, rotating editorship

Denver Quarterly
University of Denver
Denver, CO 80208
$15, 10, David Milosfky

Descant
P.O. Box 314
Station P
Toronto, Ontario
M5S 2S8 Canada
$18, 20, Karen Mulhallen

descant: The Texas Christian University Literary Journal
English Department
TCU Station
Fort Worth, TX 76129
$8, 5

Epoch
251 Goldwin Smith Hall
Cornell University
Ithaca, NY 14853-3201
$9.50, 15, C. S. Giscombe

Esquire
2 Park Avenue
New York, NY 10016
$17.94, 15, Rust Hills

event
c/o Douglas College
P.O. Box 2503
New Westminster
British Columbia
V3L 5B2 Canada
$8, 15, Maurice Hodgson

Fantasy & Science Fiction
Box 56
Cornwall, CT 06753
$17.50, 75, Edward L. Ferman

Farmer's Market
P.O. Box 1272
Galesburg, IL 61402
$7, 10, John E. Hughes

Fiction
Fiction, Inc.
Department of English
The City College of New York
New York, NY 10031
7, Mark Mirsky

Fiction Network
P.O. Box 5651
San Francisco, CA 94101
$7, 10, Jay Schaefer

Fiction Review
P.O. Box 1508
Tempe, AZ 85281
$15, 25, S. P. Stressman

Fiddlehead
Room 317, Old Arts Building
University of New Brunswick
Fredericton, New Brunswick
E3B 5A3 Canada
$14, 20, Kent Thompsen

Florida Review
Department of English
University of Central Florida
Orlando, FL 32816
$6, 16, Pat Rushin

Formations
P.O. Box 327
Wilmette, IL 60091
$15, 4, Jonathan and Frances Brent

Four Quarters
LaSalle College
20th and Olney Avenues
Philadelphia, PA 19141
$8, 10, John J. Keenan

Frontiers
Women's Studies Program
P.O. Box 325
University of Colorado
Boulder, CO 80309
$16, Katni George

Gargoyle
Paycock Press
P.O. Box 30906
Bethesda, MD 20814
$10, 5, Richard Peabody

Georgia Review
University of Georgia
Athens, GA 30602
$9, 15, Stanley W. Lindberg

Good Housekeeping
959 Eighth Avenue
New York, NY 10019
$14.97, 24, Naomi Lewis

GQ
350 Madison Avenue
New York, NY 10017
$18, 12, Tom Jenks

Grain
Box 3986
Regina, Saskatchewan
S4P 3R9 Canada
$12, 20, Bonnie Burnard

Grand Street
50 Riverside Drive
New York, NY 10024
$20, 20 Ben Sonnenberg

Gray's Sporting Journal
205 Willow Street
South Hamilton, MA 01982
$26.50, 8, Edward E. Gray

Great River Review
211 West 7th
Winona, MN 55987
$9, 6, Orval Lund, Jr.

Greensboro Review
Department of English
University of North Carolina
Greensboro, NC 27412
$5, 16, Jim Clark

Groundswell
The Guild Press
19 Clinton Avenue
Albany, NY 12207
$11, 6, Kristin Murray

Harper's Magazine
666 Broadway
New York, NY 10012
$18, 15, Lewis H. Lapham

Hawaii Review
University of Hawaii
Department of English
1733 Donaghho Road
Honolulu, HI 96822
$6, 12, Holly Yamada

Helicon Nine
P.O. Box 22412
Kansas City, MO 64113
$18, 8, Gloria Vando Hickock

High Plains Literary Review
180 Adams Street, suite 250
Denver, CO 80206
$20, 10, Clarence Major

Hoboken Terminal
P.O. Box 841
Hoboken, NJ 07030
$6, 15, C. H. Trowbridge, Jack Nestor

Hudson Review
684 Park Avenue
New York, NY 10021
$18, 8, Paula Deitz, Frederick Morgan

Indiana Review
316 North Jordan Avenue
Bloomington, IN 47405
$10, 20, Jim Brock

Iowa Review
Department of English
University of Iowa
308 EPB
Iowa City, IA 52242
$12, 10, David Hamilton

Iowa Woman
P.O. Box 680
Iowa City, IA 52244
$10, 12, Carolyn Hardesty

Isaac Asimov's Science Fiction Magazine
380 Lexington Avenue
New York, NY 10017
$19.50, 100, Gardner Dozois

Jewish Monthly
1640 Rhode Island Avenue NW
Washington, DC 20036
$8, 3, Marc Silver

The Journal
Department of English
Ohio State University
164 West 17th Avenue
Columbus, OH 43210
$5, 2, David Citino

Kansas Quarterly
Department of English
Denison Hall
Kansas State University
Manhattan, KS 66506
$15, 20, Ben Nyberg

Karamu
English Department
Eastern Illinois University
Charleston, IL 61920
John Guzlowski

Kenyon Review
Kenyon College
Gambier, OH 43022
$15, 15, Philip D. Church, Galbraith M. Crump

Lilith
The Jewish Women's Magazine
250 West 57th Street
New York, NY 10107
$14, 5, Julia Wolf Mazow

Literary Review
Fairleigh Dickinson University
285 Madison Avenue
Madison, NJ 07940
$12, 25, Walter Cummins

Little Magazine
Dragon Press
P.O. Box 78
Pleasantville, NY 10570
$16,5

McCall's
230 Park Avenue
New York, NY 10169
$11.95, 20, Helen DelMonte

Mademoiselle
350 Madison Avenue
New York, NY 10017
$15, 14, Eileen Schnurr

Malahat Review
University of Victoria
P.O. Box 1700
Victoria, British Columbia
V8W 2Y2 Canada
$15, 25, Constance Rooke

Massachusetts Review
Memorial Hall
University of Massachusetts
Amherst, MA 01003
$12, 15, Mary Heath

Michigan Quarterly Review
3032 Rackham Building
University of Michigan
Ann Arbor, MI 48109
$13, 10, Laurence Goldstein

Mid-American Review
106 Hanna Hall
Department of English
Bowling Green State University
Bowling Green, OH 48109
$6, 10, Robert Early

Minnesota Review
Department of English
State University of New York
Stony Brook, NY 11794-5350
$7, Fred Pfeil

Mississippi Review
Southern Station
Box 5144
Hattiesburg, MS 39406-5144
$10, 25, Frederick Barthelme

Missouri Review
Department of English
231 Art and Sciences
University of Missouri
Columbia, MO 65211
$12, 15, Speer Morgan

MSS
P.O. Box 530
State University of New York
Binghamton, NY 13901
$10, 30, L. M. Rosenberg

Nantucket Review
P.O. Box 1234
Nantucket, MA 02254
$6, 15, Richard Burns, Richard Cumbie

Nebraska Review
Writers' Workshop
ASH 212
University of Nebraska
Omaha, NE 68182-0324
$6, 10, Art Homer, Richard Duggin

Negative Capability
6116 Timberly Road North
Mobile, AL 36609
$12, 15, Sue Walker

New England Review and Bread Loaf Quarterly
Middlebury College
Middlebury, VT 05753
$12, 15, Sydney Lea

New Laurel Review
828 Lesseps Street
New Orleans, LA 70117
$8, 2, Lee Meitzer Grue

New Letters
University of Missouri
5216 Rockhill Road
Kansas City, MO 64110
$15, 10, James McKinley

New Mexico Humanities Review
P.O. Box A
New Mexico Tech
Socorro, NM 87801
$8, 15, John Rothfork

New Orleans Review
P.O. Box 195
Loyola University
New Orleans, LA 70118

New Quarterly
English Language Proficiency Programme
University of Waterloo
Waterloo, Ontario
N2L 3G1 Canada
$12, 15, Peter Hinchcliffe

New Renaissance
9 Heath Road
Arlington, MA 02174
$10.50, 10, Louise T. Reynolds

The New Yorker
25 West 43rd Street
New York, NY 10036
$32, 100

Nimrod
Arts and Humanities Council of Tulsa
2210 South Main Street
Tulsa, OK 74114
$10, 10, Francine Ringold

North American Review
University of Northern Iowa
Cedar Falls, IA 50614
$11, 35, Robley Wilson, Jr.

North Dakota Quarterly
University of North Dakota
P.O. Box 8237
Grand Forks, ND 58202
$10, 10, William Borden

Northwest Review
369 PLC
University of Oregon
Eugene, OR 97403
$11,10, Cecelia Hagen

Ohio Journal
Department of English
Ohio State University
164 West 17th Avenue
Columbus, OH 43210
$5, 4, Don Citino

Ohio Review
Ellis Hall
Ohio University
Athens, OH 45701-2979
$12, 20, Wayne Dodd

Old Hickory Review
P.O. Box 1178
Jackson, TN 38301
$4, 5, Drew Brewer

Omni
1965 Broadway
New York, NY 10023-5965
$24, 20, Ellen Datlow

Ontario Review
9 Honey Brook Drive
Princeton, NJ 08540
$8, 8, Raymond J. Smith

Other Voices
820 Ridge Road
Highland Park, IL 60035
$16, 30, Delores Weinberg

Oxford
Bachelor Hall
Miami University
Oxford, OH 45056
$4, 7, Gail R. Neff

Paris Review
541 East 72nd Street
New York, NY 10021
$16, 15, George Plimpton

Passages North
William Boniface Fine Arts Center
7th Street and 1st Avenue South

Escanaba, MI 49829
$2, 12, Elinor Benedict

Pencil Press Quarterly
2310 East Robinson Street, suite B
Orlando, FL 32803
$10, 5, Charlotte Buak

Plainswoman
P.O. Box 8027
Grand Forks, ND 58202
$10, 10, Emily Johnson

Playboy
Playboy Building
919 North Michigan Avenue
Chicago, IL 60611
$22, 20, Alice K. Turner

Playgirl
801 Second Avenue
New York, NY 10017
$20, 15, Mary Ellen Strote

Ploughshares
P.O. Box 529
Cambridge, MA 02139-0529
$15, 25, DeWitt Henry

Poetry East
Star Route 1
Earlysville, VA 22936
$10, 5, Richard Jones

Prairie Schooner
201 Andrews Hall
University of Nebraska
Lincoln, NE 68588-0334
$11, 20, Hilda Raz

Primavera
1212 East 59th Street
Chicago, IL 60637
$5, 10, Ann Gearen

Prism International
Department of Creative Writing
University of British Columbia
Vancouver, British Columbia
V6T 1W5 Canada
$10, 20, Dianne Maguire

Puerto del Sol
P.O. Box 3E
New Mexico State University
Las Cruces, NM 88003
$7.75, 12, Kevin McIlvoy

Quarry Magazine
P.O. Box 1061
Kingston, Ontario
K7L 4Y5 Canada
$18, 20, Rebecca Vogan

The Quarterly
Vintage Books
201 East 50th Street
New York, NY 10022
$6.95 per issue, 50, Gordon Lish

Quarterly West
317 Olpin Union
University of Utah
Salt Lake City, UT 84112
$8.50, 10, Kevin Cantwell, Jonathan Maney

RE:AL
School of Liberal Arts
Stephen F. Austin State University
Nacogdoches, TX 75962
$4, 5, Neal B. Houston

Redbook
959 Eighth Avenue
New York, NY 10019
$11.97, 35, Kathy Sagan

Richmond Quarterly
P.O. Box 1
Richmond, VA 23173
$10, 10, Welford D. Taylor

River City Review
P.O. Box 34275
Louisville, KY 40232
$5, 10, Richard L. Neumayer

River Styx
Big River Association
14 South Euclid

St. Louis, MO 63108
$14, 10, Carol J. Pierman

A Room of One's Own
P.O. Box 46160
Station G
Vancouver, British Columbia
V6R 4G5 Canada
$10, 12, Robin Bellamy

Rubicon
McGill University
853 rue Sherbrooke Ouest
Montreal, Quebec
H3A 2T6 Canada
$8, 10, T. Peter O'Brien

St. Andrews Review
St. Andrews Presbyterian College
Laurinsburg, NC 28352
$12, 10, Susan Ketchin

Salmagundi
Skidmore College
Saratoga Springs, NY 12866
$12, 2, Robert Boyers

San Jose Studies
San Jose State University
One Washington Square
San Jose, CA 95192
12, 5, Fauneil J. Rinn

Saturday Night
511 King Street West, suite 100
Toronto, Ontario
M5V 2Z4 Canada
Robert Fulford

Seattle Review
Padelford Hall, GN-30
University of Washington
Seattle, WA 98195
$7, 10, Charles Johnson

Seventeen
850 Third Avenue
New York, NY 10022
$13.95, 12, Bonni Price

Sewanee Review
University of the South
Sewanne, TN 37375-4009
$18, 10, George Core

Shenandoah
Washington and Lee University
Box 722
Lexington, VA 24450
$11, 10, James Boatwright

Short Story Review
P.O. Box 882108
San Francisco, CA 94188-2108
$9, 8, Stephen Woodhams

Sinister Wisdom
P.O. Box 1308
Montpelier, VT 05602
$15, 25, Elana Dykewoman

Sonora Review
Department of English
University of Arizona
Tucson, AZ 85721
$5, 10, Antonya Nelson, Scott Wigton

South Carolina Review
Department of English
Clemson University
Clemson, SC 29634-1503
$5, 2, Richard J. Calhoun

South Dakota Review
University of South Dakota
P.O. Box 111 University Exchange
Vermillion, SD 57069
$10, 15, John R. Milton

Southern Humanities Review
9088 Haley Center
Auburn University
Auburn, AL 36849
$12, 5, Dan R. Latimer, Thomas L. Wright

Southern Magazine
P.O. Box 3418
Little Rock, AR 72203
$15, 6, James Morgan

Southern Review
43 Allen Hall
Louisiana State University
Baton Rouge, LA 70893
$12, 20, Lewis P. Simpson, James Olney

Southwest Review
Southern Methodist University
P.O. Box 4374
Dallas, TX 75275
$14, 15, Willard Spiegelman

Sou'wester
Department of English
Southern Illinois University
Edwardsville, IL 62026-1438
$4, 10, William Fennel

Stories
14 Beacon Street
Boston, MA 02108
$16, 12, Amy R. Kaufman

StoryQuarterly
P.O. Box 1416
Northbrook, IL 60065
$12, 20, Anne Brashler, Diane Williams

The Sun
412 Rosemary Street
Chapel Hill, NC 27514
$28, 12, Sy Safransky

The Tampa Review
P.O. Box 135F
University of Tampa
Tampa, FL 33606
Andy Solomon

Threepenny Review
P.O. Box 9131
Berkeley, CA 94709
$8, 10, Wendy Lesser

Tikkun
5100 Leona Street
Oakland, CA 94619
$30, 2

Toronto South Asian Review
P.O. Box 6986
Station A
Toronto, Ontario
M5W 1X7 Canada
$15, 5, M. G. Vassanji

TriQuarterly
1735 Benson Avenue
Northwestern University
Evanston, IL 60201
$16, 30, Reginald Gibbons

University of Windsor Review
Department of English
University of Windsor
Windsor, Ontario
N9B 3P4 Canada
$10, 6, Alistair McLeod

Vanity Fair
350 Madison Avenue
New York, NY 10017
$12, 12, Wayne Lawson

Virginia Quarterly Review
One West Range
Charlottesville, VA 22903
$10, 12, Staige D. Blackford

Wascana Review
English Department
University of Regina
Regina, Saskatchewan
S4S 0A2 Canada
$7, 10

Waves
79 Denham Drive
Richmond Hill, Ontario
L4C 6H9 Canada
$10, 20, Jocen Fern Shaw

Webster Review
Webster University
470 East Lockwood
Webster Groves, MO 63119
$5, 5, Nancy Schapiro

West Branch
Department of English
Bucknell University

Lewisburg, PA 17837
$5, 10, Robert Love Taylor

Western Humanities Review
University of Utah
Salt Lake City, UT 84112
$15, 10, Barry Weller

William and Mary Review
College of William and Mary
Williamsburg, VA 23185
$4, 5, Bruce Hainley

Willow Springs
PUB P.O. Box 1063
Eastern Washington University
Cheney, WA 99004
$8, 8, Elissa Gordon

Wind
RFD Route 1
P.O. Box 809K
Pikeville, KY 41501
$6, 20, Quentin R. Howard

Witness
31000 Northwestern Highway, suite 200
Farmington Hills, MI 48018
$16, 15, Peter Stine

Writers Forum
University of Colorado
P.O. Box 7150
Colorado Springs, CO 80933-7150
$8.95, 15, Alexander Blackburn

Yale Review
1902A Yale Station
New Haven, CT 06520
$14, 12, Mr. Kai Erikson

Yankee
Yankee Publishing, Inc.
Dublin, NH 03444
$22, 10, Edie Clark

Yellow Silk
P.O. Box 6374
Albany, CA 94706
$15, 10, Lily Pond

Z Miscellaneous
P.O. Box 20041
New York, NY 10028
$9, 30, Charles Fabrizio

Zyzzyva
10 Arkansas Street
San Francisco, CA 94104
$20, 12, Howard Junker